MRS. APPLEGATE'S
AFFAIR

MRS. APPLEGATE'S AFFAIR

FREDERIC F. VAN DE WATER

DUELL, SLOAN AND PEARCE

NEW YORK

W
V2867m

A WARTIME BOOK
THIS COMPLETE EDITION IS PRODUCED
IN FULL COMPLIANCE WITH THE GOVERN-
MENT'S REGULATIONS FOR CONSERVING
PAPER AND OTHER ESSENTIAL MATERIALS

PRINTED IN THE UNITED STATES OF AMERICA

To
Virginia Terhune Van de Water,
the author's co-author

MRS. APPLEGATE'S
AFFAIR

CHAPTER I

Mᴏᴍᴇɴᴛs ʟɪᴋᴇ ᴛʜɪs, ʟᴜᴄʏ ᴀᴘᴘʟᴇɢᴀᴛᴇ ᴛʜᴏᴜɢʜᴛ, ᴡᴇʀᴇ ᴀʟᴍᴏsᴛ too beautiful to bear.

The morning sun turned the young grass greener still; changed the flower bed columbines into fiery particles of yellow, white, and scarlet; wrapped even the figure of Cyril Handrow, who languidly pushed the mower, in unlikely glamor.

Trundled blades whirred cheerfully and cast backward a slanting verdant fountain. Cyril, bending above it, seemed less a blue-jeaned hired man than a benevolent magician.

Lucy stood in the doorway of the elderly brick house and felt the dear, half-forgotten miracle return. She had believed such rapture never more would lift her.

Sunlight, smiting the lake's uneasy water, broke into sparkling fragments against the deep blue. It spread on the enclosing hills antipathies of brilliance and shadow. It filled the windows of the Spofford cottage, on the further shore, with fire. Distance was dwarfed, perspective shrank in the cool, clear radiance that accorded the garden wall and the furthest mountain the same sharp outline and made the concrete span at the lake's narrows a gleaming toy, lifted bodily from a Willow Ware plate. The whole prospect, Lucy thought, might have been cunningly and tenderly wrought in miniature. She yearned to lift it from its unapparent frame and hold it to her breast.

Her smile, as she looked down at her half-raised hands, made her face as youthful as her artless blue eyes beneath dark curved brows that seemed forever raised in eager inquiry. She turned her head slowly, as though the tightly bound mass of amber hair were an appreciable weight. The old, intense spell possessed her. She wanted to laugh, to sing, to cry aloud—and something more.

She had no further and fitter tribute to pay the morning's splendor—only this sense of breathlessness and joy, this fluttering of her kneecaps, this great lightness of heart, this sense of inner buoyance, as though all her more important internal organs sang together.

3

Otherwise, she must remain passive and mute. She had no gifts, beyond small routine skills that fourteen years' matrimony had standardized, with which to celebrate and fix forever some echo of this present loveliness. That frustration was a proper part of the ecstasy itself.

She recalled other, earlier moments when this awareness of unearthly beauty had overwhelmed her—sunrise on Mount Mansfield; her first ankle-length frock; the kiss that someone—she rather thought his name had been Spencer—had shared with her in the moonlight; that instant when the nurse had first laid Ashley in the crook of her arm and his warm mouth had closed upon her breast. All these had been of the same texture as the golden, windy morning. Each had shamed her by stressing her impotence.

Lucy stood, maturely tall in her crisp blue gingham, and wished that she might paint a picture or create music or even write a poem for this enchanted moment. Since these were beyond her, she yearned for someone with whom she might share her rapture. Muriel, her nineteen-year-old sister, had driven to the station with Dick Banning. Ashley, Lucy's twelve-year-old son, was supposed to be studying history in his own chamber.

Cyril was the only available comrade, and unpromising—were Lucy to address him, Cyril would talk away at least fifteen cents' worth of his daily wage. She wondered, turning the problem gravely over in her mind, why Yankees were supposed to be reticent folk. Perhaps it was because of the number of words they employed to clothe a single thought.

The wind went through the tall twin pines of the dooryard with endless sighing. It herded white-maned waves shoreward and brought to Lucy's nose the mingled scents of resin, stranded waterweed and newly cut grass. The wind hooted in her ears and rushed on to set the line of white birches along the driveway to dancing. The birches flung their arms about and bent bright bodies in oriental gyrations. Lucy wondered if birches were imports from Asia and decided to ask Harrison.

But she couldn't ask Harrison. There she went, stumbling once more over the obstacle which lay across so many paths of thought. For four months, less thirteen days, she would not see her husband. That had been the compact they had made, soberly, sanely. Lucy felt no grief as she considered it now. It had been parcel of the glee that had enveloped her when she had come out of the house into the brilliant morning.

Harrison's and her agreement had set her free. She was, she considered, freer than the sun that was bound punctually to observe the almanac's timetable; freer than the blue and white waves, all docilely moving in the same direction; free as the wind itself, the gleeful, adventuresome wind.

She paid small heed to the inevitable inner voice that clucked at her elation. She was sure it was habit, not conscience, that spoke. Conscience was something that went "Boo" in the dark and whispered thereafter "Suppose they should find that out!" Conscience or people in general—Lucy was never quite certain which was which—could unearth nothing scandalous concerning her and her husband's current relationship. It was plain and wholly honest.

Harrison had left his war-crippled firm to become a lieutenant colonel in the Ordnance Corps. For the next four months, while he served in Washington, his wife, their son, and Muriel Ashley, the boy's young aunt, intended to occupy the Applegate summer home near Walden. These were the facts, straight, smooth, offering gossip no roost. The conference that had established them had been a confidential interchange between husband and wife, immune to legal intrusion and therefore certainly no province whatever of conscience.

Memory of that long, cool discussion neither troubled nor shamed Lucy. It had been so logical, so direct, so free from emotional pose that she was proud to recall it—proud of herself; proud of Harrison.

Harrison had been sweet. Of course he had lived with her too long to be dismayed by anything she said. Thoughts that dwelt, simple and bright in Lucy's mind, were likely to appear before the world in a startling disarray. Harrison had told her once that her ideas were too direct for the subterfuges and circumlocutions of the English language. Harrison didn't really care how things she said sounded. Usually, he knew what she meant.

"I think," she had told him on the night he had received his commission, "there ought to be trial divorces, as well as trial marriages. I mean, if you ought to be sure going in, you ought to be surer coming out."

Her husband lit his pipe with steady fingers and laid the match down carefully.

"Let's not," he said, "be afraid of words. Divorce; is that what you want?"

"Harrison, I don't know. Do you?"

"Lucy, let's be honest; let's always be honest. There's no other man? And there's no other woman. So what?"

"That's," she told him earnestly, "what I think we ought to find out. I mean, how can you know if you don't care for anything any more if you always have it? I mean, you haven't got just one suit and I just one dress; we don't wear these out and then go and get others just like them. I don't think anything is any fun if you do it all the time, do you?"

"And being married isn't fun any more," he said, half questioning, half agreeing. "Is that what we married for, Lucy? Fun?"

"Didn't we?" she asked. "Doesn't everybody, really? I mean, maybe fun is the wrong word. Maybe happiness is better. That's in the Constitution, isn't it—the pursuit of happiness?"

"The Declaration of Independence."

"Well, anyway, it's what I mean. We haven't got it very much any more, have we, Harrison? I think it's because we have had so much of it that we haven't any."

He waited a moment before he nodded.

"We're stale. Is that it?"

Suspicion returned, unbidden, and he stared at her. Her fair face, with the small, straight nose, the arched brows, the warm, still girlish mouth that the short upper lip forever urged to smile wore its normal look of eager-to-be-pleased inquiry. The blue eyes, wide and frank like a child's, met his own and abashed him.

"Things that used to be very important," she said with her direct gaze unclouded, "just aren't any more. I mean, the nights we spend together are like the meals we eat together and the places we go together and the people we see together. They don't do that even to teachers, do they?"

"Develop that a little more," he begged at last.

"We haven't been apart from each other, Harrison, for more than a week at a time for fourteen years. Don't teachers get a year off every seven? Don't they call it a—a—"

"Sabbatical," he supplied and looked at her with new interest.

"Sabbatical, Harrison—I mean, that's what we need. It's been fourteen years now and, my goodness, no wonder! I mean, I don't think a year is necessary. Four months ought to show us and you have to be in Washington that long, anyway. I'll take Ashley to Walden and Muriel, I know, would love to come. Unless we're ill—or need each other dreadfully, Harrison, let's take a four-months Sabbatical."

"I think," he began, "you have something there—maybe."

Her smile, so approving, so bare of regret, galled him a little. He pursued in a different voice:

"We'll try it, since you like it, but I still don't see why we need to. Other couples who have been married just as long don't."

"Do you want," she asked, "us to be like other couples who have been married just as long?"

"No," he acknowledged after a silence. "No; you're right."

He drew on his pipe and looked at her in gravely friendly fashion through the smoke.

"Thank you," Lucy said, "for being so sweet about it, Harrison."

"Thank you, my dear," he answered in the same tone, "for talking straight—I mean thinking straight, anyway. Most women would have played this right up to the hilt."

"You don't want a doctor or lawyer who dramatizes your problems, do you?" she asked, smiling at him. "I mean, one who flourishes his operating knife or runs around his office pulling his hair."

"No," Harrison said. "No, I think I see what you mean."

So Lucy now stood, elatedly, in the presence of the lyrical sun and water and the singing wind, and Harrison was writing her a weekly letter from Washington, under the compact that they had agreed otherwise would unbind them wholly.

Each was untethered, irresponsible, for the experiment's duration. At its conclusion—that end was still too remote for Lucy to look toward it past the joys about her. She grinned so widely that small wrinkles in her eye corners gave her the look of a contentedly naughty child.

Cyril, still pushing the mower, passed before her. She called to him impulsively, lifting her clear voice over the sound of the blades:

"Isn't it lovely, isn't it beautiful this morning?"

Cyril stopped with overwilling alacrity. He mopped his face with a gesture eloquent of exhaustion and seemed to chew upon the question with an astonishing pursing of his toothless mouth. Ingrained economy, Lucy knew, impelled Cyril to seat his dentures only at mealtime.

"Ehyah," he assented, "now you speak of it, I mistrust it is, Mis' Applegate. Don't pay no heed to such things gen'ly. Maybe havin' 'em around ye all the while blinds ye to 'em, sort of. Still and all, when the wind comes down like that off'n Stratton we'll have fair weather most likely. 'Old Barometer' my Pa used to call her. I mind how he used to git up mornins and look out of the window. 'Wal,

Cyril,' he'd say. 'Old Barometer's hid herself t'day. Means we'll—' "

A shining car rolled up the drive past the birch houris. A length of cloth, bound across its radiator like an ambassador's ribbon, proclaimed: "Walden Defense Council."

"Bailey Ward," Cyril said, in the dry, special voice Yankees reserve for mention of the wealthy. "Huntin' for parachuters, mebby."

Lucy knew he was exhuming an ignominious passage in the history of the Walden council that Ward, its director, and all his subordinates willingly would keep buried. It had to do with a short-sighted air-raid warden, a kite that had broken its tether, and the succeeding involved alarums and excursions. Cyril, unanswered, sighed and resumed his mowing. Lucy raised an arm and cried "Hello."

Bailey Ward, realtor, chief defender of Walden, wealthy widower and purposeful suitor to Muriel Ashley, waved his Panama in reply, but before he approached, circled his car to inspect closely each precious tire. He was not, Lucy told herself firmly in response to a slurring inner voice, so very old—scarcely more than forty and he bent quite easily. He was genial and cannily ardent in his pursuit of Muriel and she was flattered by his open purpose.

So the sister told herself with rigorous openmindedness; yet she wished, as Ward approached, that she could break her habit of theoretically undressing persons, as though the problem they presented could better be solved in their imaginary nudity. In this perverse whim, there was no trace of prurience or the heat with which lustful men in novels pursue such fancies. Hers was only a ruthless and realistic curiosity. It was for her young sister's sake that she now disrobed Bailey Ward.

As the man drew near, Lucy wondered whether Muriel's fondness for her suitor could blind her to the presence of his indubitable if still minor paunch. It was round; it probably was pink and fuzzy and its circumference almost equaled his chest's. Lucy found it difficult to imagine romance and the bare Bailey Ward occupying the same chamber, yet youth's ardor could ignore many masculine defects. Personally, she liked men with flat abdomens. She thought of Harrison's lean waist. The smile she gave her visitor had a satisfaction that properly was not his due.

"Hello," she said again in her clear voice and held out her hand. "Isn't it too lovely for words?"

"Isn't she," Ward asked with a polite leer, pressing her fingers in a warm, soft palm. Tan hair was retreating uphill from a brow whose benignity the canny eyes belied. His face was clever and pleasant yet it had, Lucy thought, a leathery quality, a faint shrunkenness, a too-deep graving of the lines that curbed his mouth, as though the visage's substance remorselessly was being drained downward to his rotund middle.

"Muriel, you mean?" asked Lucy.

"Both of you, Duchess," Ward told her with a little bow, but his voice lacked ardor. It was clear that he saw in Lucy's eager face and ripe body, whose excellence the strait blue gingham could not quite conceal, merely a faded distortion of the younger sister's less emphatic charms.

"I didn't," Lucy said, "mean either of us. I meant all this. It's too beautiful for words."

Bailey Ward, realtor, supplied the words from his own published works.

"It is the loveliest, most glamorous region of a surpassingly lovely and healthy state," he said earnestly. "It's a land that has chosen to remain geared to an older, more stable economy, where beauty means more than booty and character more than cash."

He paused, clearly awaiting approval or irrepressible applause.

"All this, in substance," he resumed, after clearing his throat and according his enthusiasm a self-indulgent smile, "I have been telling the representative of Stryker & Company. Confidentially, Duchess, they are much interested in the old Frost place as the site for a factory. You can imagine what the presence of a firm like Stryker & Company will mean to this region. If they do buy—and I think the chances are excellent—I'll take little credit. The things of which we have been speaking will be the deciding factors. The eternal verities, if I may say so, that you and I esteem."

"Yes, of course, I suppose so," Lucy said uncertainly. "That still isn't exactly what I mean—not that it makes any difference. It's just that a morning like this—well, it does things to me."

She nodded at the narrow lake whose fierce color bleached the sky; the sun-drenched hills that guarded the valley; the gleaming bridge and the smoke of Walden in the further distance and, close at hand, the brilliance and the wind-rocked shade upon the lawn where Cyril seemed wholly infatuated with his mowing yet, Lucy knew, was filing for future reference each single phrase of their conversation.

Her smile begged her visitor's patience with her enthusiasm. She wondered how much of it was due to the bright day's splendor;

how much to the absence of Harrison and the blithe consciousness of freedom.

Ward cleared his throat again. He always, Lucy had discovered, uttered a politely modulated hawking sound, as though dislodging crumbs of pretense when preliminaries were over and he approached his real purpose.

"The Pulchritudinous Person?" he asked with the unconvincing air of raillery that accompanied his every reference to Muriel. "Don't tell me she is still abed."

It wasn't, Lucy told herself, either sex loyalty or family pride that made it easier for her to understand what attracted him to Muriel than to see what the girl found of merit in him, over and above his financial stature. Men were like books, though: You couldn't judge their contents by their covers.

"Abed," she repeated. "No indeed. She drove off in the station wagon before I was dressed." She hesitated and deliberately planted the barb—as reprisal for the archly uttered "Pulchritudinous Person" nickname—where she judged a joint to be in Ward's armor.

"I think she took Dick Banning to the train."

For an instant, the whir of Cyril's mowing, the kindred sighing of wind through pines were the only sounds.

"Dick's a nice boy." Ward's tribute was resolute, but the lines about his mouth were deeper, as though they had pulled hard to extricate the words.

"Simply swell," Lucy agreed. The man, groping for comfort, laid hold upon a fragment.

"Leave's over?" he asked with less difficulty. "Gone back to the marines?"

"He's been transferred. Assigned to Navy Intellect, I think he said."

"Intelligence," Ward corrected with a martial air. "Well, there's this much can be said for war, horrible as it is, Duchess: It brings out things in boys no one thought was there."

He stepped out of the path of the oncoming mower.

"Morning, Cy."

"Hi, Bailey," Mr. Handrow said, apparently aware for the first time of the visitor's presence, and pushed on by. Lucy held open the screen door, acutely conscious of the furtive interest of their perambulating audience.

"Won't you come in?"

"No." Ward glanced at his wrist watch. "No. I better not. There

are some things to iron out with the District Director this noon.
We get little credit, Duchess, and less publicity, but we're doing a
bang-up job, if I do say so. 'They also serve who only stand and
wait,' as Scripture has it."

"It isn't Scrip—" Lucy began and then hushed herself, not being
quite certain whether it was or not. Ward pursued with the hardy
air of a man who follows duty for its own sake.

"Muriel has been interested in our work. There's a place for her
in the organization, if she'd care to have it. That's what I wanted to
see her about."

"She's coming now," Lucy broke in and added, more warmly:
"Oh, my goodness!"

From the wheel of the approaching car, her young sister lifted
a hailing hand. Ward flourished his hat but Lucy only stared. Something incredible occupied the seat behind Muriel; something black,
immense. It certainly was animate. It couldn't be a bear.

The station wagon stopped sharply behind Ward's car. The creature, whatever it was, was flung forward by momentum. It vanished
entirely for an instant between the seats, save for a plumed and
thrashing tail, reappeared and beamed at Lucy, Ward, and even
Cyril, who had halted his mowing. Bared fangs gleamed in the inky
visage. An incredible length of tongue lolled from gaping jaws.

"Hi," Muriel called brightly and hid beneath vehement pride
whatever doubts she might cherish of her passenger's reception.
"See what I have. Isn't he enchanting?"

She pulled up the brake and cut off the engine.

"Bailey," she cried, identifying him as her most likely ally, "isn't
he something special? Isn't he lovely? But lovely!"

She ran an affectionate hand over the monster's domed skull and
pulled one of the dangling plush ears. Its eyes, rolling in ecstasy,
showed a startling amount of white.

"Muriel," Lucy faltered, "what on earth is it?"

"It's a dog," Ward said briefly. Cyril puckered his toothless
mouth and nodded.

"Dog," he confirmed. "Newf'n'land, too. Got him off Dick Banning, didn't ye? Mistrusted so. Dick's mother said she wouldn't keep
him, no more. More grief than the hurricane, to hear her tell it."

Yet even his chronically sour gaze brightened as Muriel sprang
down from the car and came eagerly forward. She walked, Cyril
thought, like a barren doe in October. Held her head the same way.

Good figger, too, when she'd filled out a mite, and even now she was prettier than the girl on the Good Measure Market calendar.

"Lucy," Muriel cried—and at the look on her sister's face jumbled the sequence of the arguments she had rehearsed on the drive home while her new possession had breathed fondly down her neck and occasionally had licked her ear.

"Dick sent you his love and he said he belongs to both of us. He's a thoroughbred Newfoundland and very intelligent and he needs more exercise than Mrs. Banning can give him. You'll simply adore him. His name is Azrael. Isn't that enchanting? Azrael, the dark angel, you know."

At mention of his name, Azrael, who had panted goodwill at his audience from the seat's height, poured himself from the station wagon. An immense length of haphazard body, covered with black, wavy hair, came down from the vehicle. Its fore end reached the ground before its hind had wholly disembarked. Azrael, sketchily reassembling himself, lurched forward and fell heavily on his chin.

Though the grunt caused by the concussion was loud, the puppy did not seem otherwise discommoded. He picked himself up carelessly and ambled onward. His legs seemed independent and strong-minded personages averse to co-operation. Muriel smiled upon Ward, clasped her sister's waist with a warm, compelling arm and spoke hastily.

"He swims beautifully. He's a water dog really, Dick says. He'll walk better, too, when he's had more exercise. Darling"—her squeeze strove to press assent from Lucy—"you do like him, don't you?"

"I think—" Lucy began in a firmly hostile voice. The immense creature had paused before Ward, who stood quite still. Azrael's blunt, deep muzzle ran up one trouser leg with a vacuum cleaner's long inhalation. He looked up into the man's stiff face and finding there neither the welcome nor the affection he sought, turned to Lucy.

"I think—" she began again and paused once more. There was, if you ignored the whimsically assembled membership to which it was party, a dignity about the great head looking up wistfully at her hastily withdrawn hand. There was benevolence there, too, and the sherry-colored eyes with their heavy lids were sorrowfully adoring. She saw in them appeal for love and understanding, so candid, so unassuming that she wondered, irrelevantly, what she could withhold from a man who regarded her with like humility.

"I think he's sweet," Lucy heard herself say. Her hand ventured to smooth the velvet of the benignly curved skull. You couldn't repel a creature so obviously in need of you. Faith and hope were plain upon the black visage. The current world was not oversupplied with either. At her touch, Azrael sat down as though his rapture were too great a burden. A tail like a frayed black hawser beat up the newly shorn grass. His eyes rolled upward as though he were about to swoon.

"He's a darling," Muriel endorsed, heedless of the two men's dissenting expressions. Ward's smile was pinned on firmly, but there was an obduracy in his eyes that indicated he included the great dark beast and Richard Banning, Azrael's late owner, in common detestation. Cyril wore the look of wooden pessimism with which it was his habit to greet each unaccustomed event.

Oblivious to this unuttered dissent, Muriel pursued:

"It'll be a comfort to have him, angel. But definitely! He loves children. He'll be someone besides Barbara Spofford for Ashley to play with. And he'll make a splendid watchdog. He'll protect us from everything, won't you, mother's lamb?"

Cyril uttered a derogatory sound.

"Who," he asked, "is gonna protect us from him?"

No one acclaimed his question, though he marked approval's shadow on Ward's face.

Lucy's gesture surrendered the problem. Muriel's reference to her son suddenly had reminded her that the silence in his room overhead had endured long enough to have become definitely sinister.

"I'll leave him to you," she said and gave the dog a final pat. "Feed him, tie him up—whatever you think best. I must see if Ashley has finished his lesson."

CHAPTER II

As LUCY TURNED THE KNOB OF THE CLOSED DOOR BEHIND WHICH her only child was supposed each morning to do penance for his resolute opacity to American history during the school year, the unexpected murmur of voices within so startled her that she thrust open the portal with abnormal violence.

"Oops!" said Ashley, and then, "Hi, mom, old-timer."

He was sprawled in his chair in so involved a posture that the mere sight of him made Lucy ache. His grin spread the freckles on a face undecidedly emerging from babyhood's chubbiness. Lucy regarded her son with the incongruous mingling of affection and suspicion mothers of twelve-year-old males commonly display. She stared with a simpler emotion at Barbara Spofford. This plump child of their neighbor had an eerie gift for appearing in the most unexpected places, but never before had Lucy encountered her on Ashley's bed.

Barbara lay prone across the counterpane, her posture calling attention to her most startling contour. Lucy considered the outthrust, briar-scored, bare legs and, transferring her regard to the child's further end, marked that Ashley's history book lay open before it. Barbara lifted a round, impassive face in which lovely gray eyes were imbedded and said calmly:

"Hello, Mis' Applegate."

"Where," Lucy asked, striving for equal placidity, "did you come from?"

"I walked around by the bridge," the little girl recited. "My mother said she was too busy to row me over. She sent you her love, though, Mis' Applegate. I couldn't find Ashley, so I thought maybe he was here, and he was an' I've heard his history lesson. He was real good, too. Can he come out now?"

Not for the first time, her complete serenity and the open devotion with which she regarded Ashley baffled Lucy who now tried again, with no more success than heretofore, to recall her own

14

occupations and reactions at the age of ten. The intimacy of her son and this apparently lethargic child bewildered her.

It was true that in this region no other juvenile associates were available for either, but the bond between them seemed forged of something stronger than mere propinquity. None of the strange glamor, so plain to the participants, so painfully invisible to the outsider, with which adolescence adorns its brief unions was present here. Barbara and Ashley spent their entire leisure in common enterprises, cryptic or infinitely dreary to adult minds. In these, he was the leader and she the frequently abused, constantly berated, infinitely loyal follower.

Lucy sighed. It might have been wiser, as Harrison had suggested, if Ashley had been sent to camp. Her son, hearing and misinterpreting the sound, now spoke with a desperate glibness as though by words he might conceal vulnerability:

"Barb has heard it, Mom. And, boy, was I hot! The whole lesson —pfft: like that. Didn't I, Barb? Mom, my little chickadee, how's for my going out now? Eh, Mom?"

Ashley overplayed his part. His volubility quickened the suspicion of an expert in filial subterfuge. Lucy held a hand out to the little girl and received the history book.

"The Jamestown Settlement," she read the chapter heading. "Is that what he recited today, Barbara?"

"Oh, nuts," Ashley muttered.

"No wonder," his mother pursued, "that he was good, then. You heard the same lesson I drilled into him yesterday. Didn't she, Ashley?"

She compressed her lips, lest she smile at the scowl of her hardpressed son. His was a resourceful, not easily subjugated spirit, but Lucy felt that she had cornered him now.

Ashley twisted about in his chair and assumed a more humanly plausible attitude. He spoke with the patience of the deeply misunderstood.

"Well gee-gosh," he mumbled. "You gotta review things sometimes. How'm I gonna remember all this stuff if we don't have reviews?"

The brown eyes that looked up at his mother were filled with honest grievance. Ashley observed no slackening of her forbidding expression and played his last desperate card.

"Besides, even in school"—he spoke of it as a graduate might refer to Alcatraz—"you never had to work on Saturdays."

"Saturday," Lucy exclaimed. "But this isn't—my goodness, is this Saturday?"

She looked at Barbara and missed the glare of poisonous warning her son also bestowed upon the child. The little girl nodded gravely.

"Saturday," she confirmed.

"Oh, well then!" Lucy said, relaxing, "that's different. The days are so alike here I don't keep count and this is a specially lovely one. It shouldn't be wasted indoors. Run along then, you two. Ashley, Muriel has brought something home I think you'd like to see."

"Dick Banning?" her son hazarded with a weary air. "He's no good when she's around. They gawp at each other."

"Not Dick. A dog; a big, black Newfoundland pup."

Ashley jumped up, his face shining. Barbara scrambled from the bed.

"A dog," the boy babbled. "Oh, boy, a dog. Come on, Barb. Hot diggety—a dog."

They stormed, shouting, from the room. Lucy smoothed the rumpled bed and retrieved garments, papers, pencils and other jetsam from the floor. She stared at the sporting page, spread open on Ashley's table.

"Little devil," she said at last. "I was almost certain today was Friday."

Gradually, her frown faded. Her face assumed that look of bland innocence which masked her most earnest thought. She would not pursue her perfidious son and haul him back into duress on so brilliant, so joyously singing a day. Freedom, however earned, was too fair a thing for another mortal to stifle. Perhaps, she thought, looking her most virginal, liberty gained by subterfuge was the sweetest freedom of all. Humorous wrinkles deepened in the corners of her clear eyes. Her wide mouth twitched as she went downstairs.

Rena Handrow, mate to Cyril and approximately twice his size, turned from the back door as a full-rigged ship comes about. Her ample face, as Lucy entered the kitchen, wore its accustomed look of patient resignation, yet there was disapproval in the small voice that issued, mouselike, from the apron-bound mountain. While she spoke, she chewed solemnly on some remnant of breakfast or forerunner of lunch. Meals were only fortissimo passages in Rena's day-long grazing.

"That dog goin' to stay?" she asked.

"We'll see," Lucy evaded. "He's a sort of present."

"Take an awful lot to feed him," Rena said and Lucy suspected there was rivalry in her comment.

Before the elderly, gray-shingled barn that, apart from occasional occupations by Cyril when in particularly high dudgeon, housed no livestock, an intense little group had gathered. Its center was the gigantic puppy, who pulled mildly at the lead Mr. Handrow held while he delivered a lecture to an attentive juvenile audience. Barbara, well beyond the reach of the lurching dog, stood with stout legs spread and hands behind her, as though they were edibles she was determined to withhold. Ashley, slightly more daring, leaned far over, reached his hand to the utmost and patted Azrael's head.

Beyond this group, Bailey Ward leaned against the station wagon and talked to Muriel. His speech was low and earnest but Cyril's homily came clearly to Lucy as she opened the kitchen screen door.

"No, I can't letcha lead him, bub. This here's a big animal. Takes a man to handle him, 'twill he learns manners."

"Isn't he sweet, children?" Lucy called, advancing. "Did you know his name? It's Azrael. That means—"

She caught her breath in what was literally a reversed scream. From afar off, the puppy had recognized her as a friend, too long missing from his circle, and at her mention of his name had plunged forward to greet her. Cyril accompanied his advance with a false show of eagerness. Actually, he had no choice. The brute's leap had amazing power and had jammed Cyril's hand in the loop of the leash.

Azrael bounded toward Lucy, ears flapping, eyes rolling with glee, only slightly deterred by the weight he drew behind him. The momentary glimpse of Cyril's stricken and dissenting face was stamped forever on Lucy's memory. Cyril's eyes were wide, his toothless mouth was pursed into a small dark hole of anguish. The brim of his felt hat, blown back by the wind of his progress, gave him an incongruously western air. His knees pumped with surprising rapidity; his strides were mighty, but he could not keep up with the elated dog.

Still running furiously, Cyril leaned forward and fell. His collapse was complete, yet even prostrate he did not tarry. Gravel rasped as Azrael pulled him over the remaining breadth of driveway. With the grass of the circle beneath him, the unfortunate's passage was smoother and swifter. The puppy, reaching Lucy, leaped upward in a frenzy of greeting and strove to set great forepaws on her shoulders. It was Cyril's still-attached weight that saved her from overthrow.

"Don't," she cried. "Azrael, down; down, I say."

Other voices joined hers. Muriel shrieked; Ward shouted and hastened forward. In the distance, Ashley yammered his delight and Barbara bounced like an over-large ball. The tumult made plain to Azrael that he had obscurely sinned. He sat down before Lucy and looked bewildered but still agreeable.

With the movements of immense decrepitude, the recumbent Cyril raised himself on his elbows. Ward, bending, helped him slip the leash's loop off his wrist.

"Cyril," Lucy faltered. "Are you hurt?"

Cyril sat up and plucked at matted grass upon his chest.

"Some, I mistrust," he said in a hollow voice.

Bailey Ward was gravely denunciatory.

"An animal like that isn't safe with women and children. He's like a—a wild bull."

He addressed them all, but he looked sidewise at Muriel who had joined her sister. Something in her face counseled him to go no further.

Lucy spoke quickly to avert the girl's indignant reply. No special fondness for her sister's mature suitor inspired her, but she shrank from discord as a saint recoils from sin. Life could be fair only when pleasant, contented persons were about her. Often she wondered from what lurid fate her early marriage to Harrison had saved her, since she found it so difficult to meet any appeal with an unqualified "no." Now she said, soothingly:

"He's just a baby still. It's hard to be an infant with a body like that. I think he really was just trying to be pleasant."

Cyril had raised himself from the turf by a series of brief motions. In the intervening pauses he obviously conducted inventory of his person. He stood erect as Lucy ended and looked at her bleakly while he pulled at his raiment.

"Comfortin'," he told her in a bitter voice. From the kitchen Rena piped:

"Cy, when you're through foolin' with that critter I could use more stove wood."

Cyril turned and plodded toward the barn whose gloomy depths were appropriate haven for a darkened spirit. In passage, he paused and over his shoulder addressed his wife.

"No doubt," he said.

"Oh, children," Muriel counseled suddenly. "I'd be a little careful."

Ashley and Barbara had approached Azrael, impelled by the ancient attraction of large dogs for small human beings. Azrael had risen, had beamed upon them both and then had taken them to his unscrupulous heart. Ashley now was tugging at his leash and bawling brisk commands to which the puppy paid no heed. After sniffing Barbara, he was approving her savor by lavishly licking her face.

"You quit," the little girl ordered and when the puppy paid her no heed, slapped the blunt and questing muzzle. Azrael clearly was enraptured. He beamed upon her, unhinged his forelegs and prostrated his head upon the greensward. With roguishly rolling eyes, with elevated rear and violently sweeping tail, he challenged her.

"Nix," Ashley cried, irked by the excess attention lavished on his companion. "You stand up. Hear me?"

When the puppy gave no sign, the boy cast aside the leash, buried his hands wrist-deep in the thick hair of Azrael's ruff, and tugged. He drew up the better part of a yard of hide but the majority of the dog remained semi-prostrate. Even while Ashley hauled, ignoring his mother's appeals for moderation, Azrael's rear end collapsed. He lay on his stomach and chewed in lazy rapture upon the dangling leash. Ashley released his hold and sniffed at his hands through a wrinkled nose.

"He needs a bath," he diagnosed. "He smells awful like a dog."

A joyous thought came to him and lifted his voice higher.

"Mom, how's for taking him for a swim? Down to the lake, Mom. We could teach him to bring in sticks."

"Oh, boy," Barbara said solemnly.

Lucy looked from her grave face to Ashley's appealing one and laughed.

"Go along then, all three of you," she bade, "and don't you get any wetter than absolutely necessary."

They swept, shouting, around a corner of the house, Azrael leaping about them like an elated calf.

Ward had climbed into his car and Muriel stood beside it. They laughed together. The sound was sweet to Lucy's ears. The difficult moment had passed and they still were friends. It was good to be friends with everyone when the sun was warm and the wind cool and white cloud squadrons rode high in the blue. She wondered whether that small glow of anger she had seen on Muriel's face when Ward had disparaged Banning's farewell gift meant that the child had seriously involved herself with Dick.

Lucy hoped her sister had made no binding pledge. She herself had been betrothed when she was Muriel's age, but then, Lucy was sure, she had been much more mature. All women since Eve, considering their juniors, have cherished identical fallacies.

Ward's car came rolling round the circle. He bowed to Lucy as he passed. Whatever his mission had been, Muriel clearly had not rebuffed him. Her sister waited while the girl clambered into the station wagon, drove it into the barn, and reappeared. She walked across the circle as though she moved to music. Perhaps she did—to lilting measures that only the desired and nineteen years old could hear.

She was truly lovely, advancing through sunlight to that inaudible rhythm. The flat curves of the body in the soft green rayon might have been stamped from resilient metal. There were sparklings and streaks of fire in her coppery hair, and thick dark lashes spread shadow below her jade-hued eyes. Something more like pity than envy welled up within the older woman. Her sister was so fair, so young a creature, so sure of herself, so pitiably ignorant.

It would be swell, Lucy thought, if she might enlighten Muriel. Not to the facts of life; her sister had a speaking acquaintance with more and gaudier than Lucy ever had met. Facts were no good, anyway; and knowledge wasn't much better. It was wisdom that counted. Wisdom was finding out for yourself by bumps and bruises that two and two always made four and not five. Maybe that was why the world had always been in so terrible a state. You really couldn't ever give wisdom to anyone else, no matter how much you wanted to; no matter how hard you strove.

Muriel's hard young arm slipped about her sister.

"Never a dull moment," she said. "Having fun, darling? Well, wallow in rural simplicity while you can. Do you know who Bailey has heard may be coming here for the summer? Mrs. Eliphalet Starkweather—Lydia Starkweather in person—complete, with family and servants. Isn't that enchanting?"

She spoke with a determinedly maintained derision that her sister made no effort to match.

"Mrs. Eliphalet Starkweather?"

There was candid awe in Lucy's voice as it uttered the redoubtable name which even the less decorous newspapers had treated with respect for half a century. Clouds of legendary glory already adorned it, though its owner still was aggressively and truculently alive. Daughter of a governor—wife of a senator, mother of an ambassador, wealthy in her own right and thrice so since her husband's demise, austere social arbiter and embattled suffragist of an earlier era, Lydia Starkweather spoke with superiority to Cabots and, probably with less than that family's reverence, to God.

"Bailey says it'll mean a boom in local real estate if she does come," Muriel said, still in a resolutely amused voice.

"Isn't he sure?"

"No, darling. It's just a rumor, but he's much interested. He thinks it might even affect the Stryker & Company deal."

"I don't believe it's true," Lucy said, stoutly trying to ignore a dozen glowing tableaux in which she and Muriel and Mrs. Eliphalet Starkweather were central figures. She watched Cyril emerge from the barn and come toward them with dignified if halting gait. She called:

"Cyril; just a moment. Have you learned anything about Mrs. Starkweather coming here for the summer?"

Mr. Handrow's mouth, puckered and unbraced by dentures, wandered reflectively over the lower half of his face.

"Not much," he confessed. "Lute Hathaway's got the contract to repaint and repaper the big house the Senator built up to Blue Mountain. She won't be here 'fore the middle of the month, way I hear it. Ain't openin' her camp in New Brunswick this year on account of she thinks it's too dangerous now, near the ocean. Mistrust she's 'feared some German submarine might scuttle her and spile our chances of winnin' the war. Goin' to live here real quiet for a spell, with nobody but mebby a half-dozen help an' a handful of relatives—Mis' Moncure, that's her granddatter, an' Larry Moncure, him what lost a foot fightin' in Spain, and their little girl and mebby a few more."

He paused. Muriel said:

"If you ever do find out anything, Cyril, let us know, won't you?"

"Mr. Handrow's small, bitter eyes flickered.

"Ehyah," he said, and as he hobbled away, added: "Be pretty nice when we're all in s'ciety, won't it?"

"Come out of it, darling," the girl told Lucy, linking an arm in hers. "Don't start to look dewy-eyed and aspiring. Lydia Starkweather could live next door to us for the rest of time and never be aware of us."

"I wasn't aspiring," Lucy denied. "I was just surprised."

"Of course you were," Muriel assured her. "But definitely!"

Yet, when they entered the long, calm livingroom, so faithful to New England's traditions that only an outlander possibly could have contrived it, Lucy surveyed the pale green walls, the crisp buff hangings, the honey-colored maple furniture with rapt eyes.

"Wondering where you'll put La Starkweather when she comes to tea, angel?" Muriel asked so penetratingly that her sister flinched.

"You know," she retorted, "she might; she really might."

"Who cares?"

"I do and so do you. Don't pretend you wouldn't like Mrs. Eliphalet Starkweather to be fond of you—and she couldn't help it, darling, if she ever met you."

"I'm doing all right, thank you. I don't need any Colonial Dames in my life. I'm not a snob, angel."

Lucy wandered about the bright chamber, pulling the hangings into place as though the arrival of Mrs. Starkweather were imminent.

"You know," she said thoughtfully, "there are just two sorts of people. There are those who say they aren't snobs and really are and those who don't say they aren't."

Muriel gave the small throaty chuckle her sister adored, perched on the sofa, crossed lovely legs and lit a cigarette.

"Right now," she accused, "you're getting this room ready for my ever-so-splendid marriage to some ever-so-important Starkweather scion. Well, he'll have to wait, darling. There are orders ahead of his."

She squinted at her sister through the cigarette smoke. Lucy spoke carefully, knowing that Muriel confided most when pressed least.

"You got Dick to his train all right?"

The other nodded.

"You know," she said after a pause, "I wish he'd be more serious about the war. You'd think he was going to a—a clambake or something. He hasn't Bailey's sense of responsibility, but he was sweet to give me Azrael, wasn't he?"

"That's what I think, too," Lucy returned, guarding her voice carefully lest it sound too heartily approving. Muriel was likely to mistake enthusiasm for persuasion and thereafter to set her face against its object. Lucy liked Dick Banning. She could serve his cause best by never praising him.

She lingered by a window, after she had regulated its drapery, to look out at the sun, the wind-troubled shade and the nodding heads of the columbines. She was troubled by an odd mixture of tenderness and resentment. Nature or God or whatever, she thought, might have managed things better. By grace of youth's transcendant glow that redoubled her loveliness, Muriel was a greatly privileged being. She didn't know it because no one ever knew how lucky she was until she was no longer so lucky.

Ten years hence, Lucy's sister would have a greater need for sympathy, tolerance, admiration than now, but she then would have to work ten times as hard to win one-tenth as much. Lucy found herself slightly out of patience, not with youth, but with the prejudiced fashion in which life conducted itself.

While one portion of her mind considered resentfully the lop-sided pattern of existence, the rest of it was aware that Muriel, perversely thawed by her sister's apparent indifference, was confiding in her.

The girl, sprawled on the sofa, talked of Bailey Ward with a warmth that roused in Lucy the least, vigilant twinge of dismay.

Ward, it appeared from Muriel's disjointed speech, cherished Alexandrine ambitions. Already the chieftain of civilian defense had organized Walden with terrific thoroughness against not-imme-diately-probable air raids. There were watchers for every roof, captains for each block, wardens, firemen, and rescue squads in lush profusion.

Bond committees, housing committees, canteen committees col-lided with each other on their rounds. The complicated mechanism set up by the state council, which had read innumerable British pamphlets on civilian defense and had digested none of them, had been further embellished by Muriel's suitor, yet this still was not enough for his patriotic aspiration.

Ward's intention now was to form a Women's Auxiliary Corps to deal with whatever unlikely problems the current organization was unequipped to handle. Muriel was vague on the duties of this new band, but on one item she was specific and voluble.

"It'll be only a small group—a very special group," she explained. "Just a dozen of the younger, more energetic women of Walden who are willing to spend sixty dollars apiece for the cause. We're to wear uniforms. We'll be the first unit in Walden to have them. And—"

She paused and lit another cigarette. When she spoke it was with the light, the careless air that Lucy knew concealed excitement.

"Bailey," Muriel went on, blowing smoke ceilingward with a world-weary gesture, "wants me to organize the group and be their leader. Not that I care about that, angel. It's really just a diplomatic move on Bailey's part. If he gave the post to one of the four local women who think they should have it, the others would be furious at her. And of course my training in college does count for something."

"I think," Lucy said, policing her voice with care, "that that's very interesting, darling."

Muriel arched one eyebrow higher than the other and regarded her sister quizzically while Lucy wandered uneasily about the room.

Bailey Ward was using his eminence in civilian defense for other than national purposes. The post he was offering Muriel was really a forward move in his courtship. Lucy found herself disliking the bland, resourceful man and sympathizing with the recently departed Dick Banning.

Of course, Ward's intentions were what the world called "wholly honorable." She was startled by the realization that she would find him more interesting if she could distrust him. Bailey Ward, the prosperous realtor, had himself for sale and there was a prospect in view. He was turning the heat on his client as cannily as though she were Stryker & Company.

CHAPTER III

LUCY STARED DOWN INTO A VASE OF YELLOW IRIS UPON THE LIVING-room table. While her hands unnecessarily rearranged them, her mind ran on. Ward was old enough to be Muriel's father, granting him considerable precocity. She told herself firmly that she could not imagine her sister falling in love with a man so much her senior.

But then, she considered drearily, it had been extremely difficult to imagine what most girls of her acquaintance had seen of allure in the men they had taken for husbands. Disparity in age, in tastes, in background had not seemed to be important.

Desire, passion, romance apparently weren't essential, either. Sometimes, Lucy thought while her hands moved among the iris, love actually was a hazard. Marrying for love was like building a house about a fire already kindled. If you were greatly fortunate, you got the structure completed and a safe, sure hearth beneath the blaze. Sometimes, the dwelling burned down before the roof was on. Sometimes, you paid so much attention to the surrounding building that when you sought the finally enclosed fire, only its ashes remained.

"That's a rather nice idea, Mrs. Applegate," she said beneath her breath. It was her habit to address herself formally when she felt she particularly deserved approval.

She was truly startled by the poetic flavor of her thought. Concepts so ornate seldom came to her. For an instant she was urged to share this with her sister and then refrained. Muriel, crammed with the intolerant self-confidence of youth, would only jeer. She found herself wishing for Harrison. He would listen to her and would not laugh.

She firmly thrust the thought of Harrison away, stood back from her rearrangement and dried her fingers on her handkerchief. She wished that there were some final authority on marriage—some matrimonial Bible from which one might expound the eternal law to lovely, headstrong children like Muriel. But there wasn't. People

25

who were happily married never seemed quite sure why, and few of the mismated ever admitted that any part of the discord had been their own fault. As for Scripture itself, its dictates on matrimony were confused and frequently scandalous.

She sighed as she turned away from the vase. She had ended precisely where her thought had begun. She still wished that Bailey Ward had gone to war and that Richard Banning had tarried as the director of Walden's civilian defense. Inadvertently, she met her sister's acute eyes and felt her own face and neck grow warm.

Muriel chuckled and clasped slim hands over the copper helmet of her hair.

"Wondering," she asked with mockery, "how to warn innocent little sister against Bailey? Honeychile, don't you trouble your pretty head. Sister can take care of herself. But definitely! And besides, if Bailey Ward is a wolf, his sheep's clothing is practically perfect and he's never taken off a stitch in my presence."

"Whatever in the world are you talking about?" Lucy demanded and Muriel chuckled again.

"Angel, when you get that dead-pan look, I know perfectly well that you are thinking of my future and are wishing you dared lecture me."

"Aren't you smart?" Lucy asked in weak derision. She turned toward the door and the blazing world without. "Let's go and see whether the children and Azrael have drowned each other completely."

She led the way. Muriel, following, laid her haste to sudden maternal anxiety. She did not know that her sister actually fled from a vision, a horrid picture that Muriel's metaphor suddenly and starkly had evolved. Lucy tried, as she walked across the lawn and through the coarser grass beyond, to rid her afflicted mind of a portrait in full color of Bailey Ward's paunch—round, pink, fuzzily abhorrent.

The wind finally blew it away. The wind, with the sun, had turned the lake a still more fiery blue. Cloud shadows slid down the western hills, sailed across the water to climb eastern slopes. Whitecaps hurried shoreward and, far down the lake toward the gleaming bridge, a red canoe was making heavy weather. Lucy could see it swing and check. Sunlight flashed from the hard-plied paddle.

On the narrow, pebbly beach, where small waves prostrated themselves and withdrew, Ashley and Barbara sat damply together.

Before them, at the water's edge, the sleek, shockingly reduced shape of Azrael waited in sodden expectancy. His hair, wetly plastered down, revealed a loosely hung, gaunt frame whose emaciation none, in the puppy's drier moments, possibly could have suspected. Water dripped from pointed tufts beneath Azrael's belly and draggled the plumed tail. His head seemed disproportionately large. His ears were lifted, his face was eager. Incongruously, he panted and also shivered.

"Hi, Mom," Ashley called. He jumped up and ran toward her, shouting.

"Boy, can that pup take it! Honest, we thought once he'd drown, but he didn't. Mom, my little plum, we've thrown him sticks, and we've thrown him stones, too. Haven't we, Barb? Most of the stones he can't get but he dives for them. I think he's part seal. He's got us all worn out, haven't you, Azrael? Come on, Azrael."

The dog, after a final appealing look at Barbara, who showed no inclination to cast more missiles for his pleasure, lurched up, dripping and beaming.

"I think he's tired," Lucy said. "I think you've all had enough for today." She ended her hazard in an unpremeditated squeal. "Azrael. Good gracious. Don't."

The puppy had ranged alongside her. Momentarily he disappeared in a silvery haze as he shook himself. Thereafter, he looked from Lucy to Muriel with such honest goodwill that their reproaches, as they mopped themselves, were only technical.

"He did that to me," Barbara reported. "Three times. It's kind of like a shower bath."

"Barbs," Ashley shouted, shrill with importance, "where's a stick? Mom, you take a stick and throw it. See how good he is."

"Azrael hides them all," Barbara said, limply arising, "in the bushes somewhere. I guess he's making a collection. Here's one. It's pretty big, though."

She tugged and finally drew a half-embedded snag from the gravel. Azrael at once cast aside his water-logged languor and bounded about her with hoarse exhalations.

"You quit," Barbara bade. "You let Mis' Applegate throw it."

She bore her trove, keeping her plump person between it and the eager dog, to Lucy.

"Throw it, Mom," Ashley directed shrilly. "Just as far as you can."

Azrael was bounding about Lucy now. With all her energy and

a feminine sketchiness of direction, she drew back the misshapen bludgeon. It slipped in her grasp, as she tried to fling it, and did not fly but smote the expectant puppy on the head. Azrael squealed, shrank, and then leapt heartily upon her.

The shock of her fall left within Lucy only a dim sense of ill usage. She heard Muriel's scream and vaguely was aware that she sat upon the beach and suffered the attentions of a whimpering, urgent creature whose body was wet and cold, whose ardent tongue was wet and warm.

Muriel, uttering inarticulate sounds of fright, laid hands upon the puppy's neck and strove futilely to pull him away. Still whimpering, he thrust himself against Lucy's deterring hands, nuzzled the bosom into which breath only gradually was returning, and once more thoroughly licked her face.

"Oh, God!" Muriel cried, routed by fright from her normal indifference. She gripped a larger fold of resilient skin. "Angel, are you hurt? Did he bite you, Lucy?"

Azrael, conscious of the mounting excitement, diminished his attentions and gave way a little. Damp and dazed, Lucy looked about her. The other spectators seemed not to share her sister's alarm. Ashley was doubled over in a posture of unfilial mirth. Amusement actually had changed Barbara's usually impassive face.

"He does that," the little girl interpreted, "if you hit him. I did, with a stone. I didn't mean to. He knocked me down, too. He's trying to say he's sorry it happened, I guess."

Her diagnosis, Lucy admitted as she sat up and pulled the drenched gingham away from her breast, seemed correct. There was neither anger nor resentment upon the great black muzzle that still yearned toward her and reluctantly withdrew under Muriel's continued traction. Azrael sniffed appealingly. The eyes beneath the benevolent brow were filled with humble worship.

The puppy's intention grew clear to Lucy. She had hurt him. Azrael was sure it had been accidental and had striven to make her understand there were no hard feelings. Lucy fumbled vaguely with her hair. Still shaken and slightly out of breath, she felt compassion for the gentle, forgiving, infantile spirit so incongruously enclosed in a giant, haphazard body.

"Angel," Muriel begged, still clinging to Azrael, "are you all right?"

"It was my fault," Lucy said, gathering herself together. "I hit him. He thought he'd done something wrong and did his best to apologize. You know, he's really sweet."

The hand with which she sought to pat the puppy's head remained half outstretched. She stared past Muriel with so odd an expression that the girl turned.

"Sorry," the man said. "I'm afraid I'm trespassing. I'm a castaway," he added and his smile was boyish yet wholly composed.

"Oh," Lucy gasped, reaching for any available words. "Of course."

He had come so silently that he might have dropped from the windy sky. Not even Azrael had heard him. The puppy growled faintly now and looked at his associates for further directions. Barbara, globular and solemn, offered no clue. Neither did Ashley's inane gaping, nor Muriel's rigid pose. Azrael considered Lucy's face and, turning again toward the intruder, ventured an experimental "Whuff."

"Stop it," Muriel said, sharply. The man smiled again.

"He's quite right," he said. "I would too. You see, I got blown ashore. In a canoe. The wind was stronger than I thought. I'm Larry Moncure."

He spoke his name as though it were complete explanation and endorsement. No trace of Lucy's embarrassment was visible on the blunt, young face beneath its shock of pale wind-blown hair. For all his look of youth, he was, Lucy thought, older than he appeared. He was quite calmly amused and his keen gray eyes were bold. The brilliant tartan shirt he wore, the worn khaki trousers, dropping straight from narrow hips, gave him an alien air, yet his almost insolent features were not foreign and Lucy had found a southern slur in his speech. Already, while she rummaged through her mind to trace the name that seemed unaccountably familiar, the silence had grown awkwardly long.

"I'm Lucy Applegate," she told him, abandoning the futile search. "This is my sister, Muriel Ashley."

He bowed at her mention of each name with grace that made her question his nationality again, and considered Muriel deliberately before he turned and explained to Lucy:

"I had to beach the canoe in the cove, yonder. There was too much wind for a single paddler. I'd be mighty grateful if you'd let me use your telephone."

"We could drive you," Lucy offered. His teeth flashed again as he smiled and shook his head.

"That's right sweet of you, Mrs. Applegate, but I reckon it'll be simpler all around if I phone."

His unabashed regard obviously approved of her face and dropped to admire the mature body in the wet disordered dress. The scrutiny was like physical contact. Lucy tingled. Suddenly, she was conscious that her hair was tousled and that the blue gingham, shabby at best, was a sodden ruin. There was a pleasantly uncertain feeling about her knees.

Moncure's easy speech had paused only a second. Now it continued, smoothly:

"I'll have them send down the truck. It can take me and the canoe home together."

He grinned in friendly fashion at Ashley and Barbara, who were watching him with a candid interest like his own. Azrael sniffed at his spray-spattered trousers and expressed approval by limber sweeps of his tail. Moncure patted the dog's head and said:

"Let's go, then."

He stepped forward unevenly. Awkwardness seemed foreign to the long body. The limping gait shocked, then enlightened Lucy.

"Oh," she said so sharply that both Muriel and Moncure turned and stared. "Sorry," she pursued. "It's just that— I've just placed you. You're Mrs. Starkweather's—"

She paused, groping for the relationship.

"Grandson-in-law," he supplied. "A sort of John the Baptist preparing the way for the Coming."

"Angel," Muriel cried. "Of course. Who else?"

"I'm very stupid," Lucy said and felt her face grow warm.

"That's not any of a dozen words I've been tryin' not to say," he replied. Muriel told him with the implicit rivalry the most devoted women feel in a strange male's presence:

"This isn't one of her bright days. She's really quite intelligent."

"Sheer lily-gilding," he said and Lucy, looking straight ahead, felt his eyes upon her again.

At the house, she bade Muriel lead Moncure to the telephone and ran upstairs to strip off her soiled dress. Her hands, she found, were uncertain. One part of herself grew sorely out of patience with the insurgent remainder and called it ignominious names while she hesitated before her open closet door. She reached toward the yellow linen frock in which she knew she looked well, withdrew her hand with Puritan resolution and selected instead the shepherd's plaid mate to the blue gingham. When she came down the stairs with her hair freshly done, she heard Muriel's eager voice, Moncure's drawl in the livingroom.

Lingering exasperation with herself sent her into the kitchen, where she bewildered Rena with unnecessary questions about lunch. She had been forced to transfer her queries to dinner before a truck rolled into the yard. Even then, she felt she had not been disciplined enough and tarried until she heard the roar of the engine, the bellowings of Azrael, that signaled the vehicle's departure.

Lucy, returning from the kitchen, met Muriel in the hall.

"He's gone, darling," the girl told her with a trace of sisterly malice. "Too bad all the primping was wasted."

"Don't be a goop," the other bade. "The primping was for propriety, not him."

"I doubt whether they are the same thing," Muriel said, thoughtfully. "Anyway, he left you ever-so-courteous farewell messages in a most attractive way-down-South voice."

"He is attractive," Lucy admitted.

"He is," her sister agreed. Azrael scratched at the door's screening and uttered high, canary-like twitters of appeal.

"No, you can't come in," Muriel told him, "and I suppose I better get Cyril to tie you up before you get into more trouble."

She left for the barn. The puppy capered along beside her. Lucy watched them thoughtfully out of sight. She wondered, with a pang which she assured herself was only sisterly concern, whether Muriel was as indifferent as she seemed. It was hard to imagine how anyone could look with favor upon Bailey Ward yet be blind to the newcomer.

Lucy's wandering mind stumbled over a fact and she said, "Why, of course!" aloud. Moncure was married. She had ignored that till now. Ward was single and Muriel's professed disregard for the stranger was easy to understand.

Her feet carried her into the livingroom, but her thoughts bore her further, if less surely. Muriel would deny it with heat; Muriel, clinging desperately to the illusion of independence and equality which were her shield, would become furiously angry if the accusation were pressed, but the truth of the matter was that Muriel, poor child, needed to get married. All of her sex and age did. Sometimes they wanted to so very much that their yearning turned in upon itself and they got queer.

Nature, Lucy thought, was playing its horrid joke on Muriel.

Each girl advertised herself, exactly as Bailey Ward publicized his properties. Muriel's beauty, her accomplishments, her very clothes were her cash on hand and with these she would buy herself at length the very best husband she could afford. Wasn't courtship really a marketing transaction, after all? Moncure wasn't for sale, so Muriel simply wasn't interested.

Lucy sat on the livingroom sofa and smoked a cigarette. Her clear eyes were more than normally guileless; her face, wholly innocent. She was thinking: "Women are the guardians of morality. That's what people say but all it means is that women work to keep up a market for themselves."

That was why women were so much harder than men on ladies of light, if any, virtue. These cut prices; they sold cheap. If they weren't suppressed, there'd be a crash like 1929's, only more widespread and disastrous—to women.

"I do think," she found herself saying aloud, "that virtue might be just a little more elevating."

"What?" Muriel asked. Lucy jumped.

"What on earth are you talking to yourself about, you silly old thing?" the girl asked again and leaned over the sofa's back to puff down her sister's neck.

"Stop it," Lucy gasped, through laughter. Muriel came to sit beside her.

"Angel," she said fondly, "whatever were you arguing with yourself about?"

"Virtue," Lucy told her.

"Darling, how enchanting! Have you lost any?"

"That's what I mean," Lucy explained. "That's the one thing everyone thinks about if you mention virtue."

"Well?"

"I mean it might have some more elegant symbol. There are all sorts of virtues, aren't there?"

"Including Mr. Lawrence Moncure's?"

"I wasn't thinking of him."

"Don't," her sister advised. "He's going back to Boston this evening."

"I wonder what his business is," Lucy said, vaguely.

"You mean," Muriel corrected, "what is his avocation. Don't look so determinedly innocent, darling. Don't try to tell me you don't recognize a wolf, even in wolf's clothing."

"You know," Lucy told her, fondly regarding the lovely intemperate face, "it was amazing how much I knew, too, when I was nineteen."

"It's astonishing, angel, how much knowledge a married woman can forget in fourteen years. I suppose that's because she doesn't always have to keep her chin tucked in and protect herself in the clinches."

"Well, anyway," Lucy evaded, "he's gone. Probably we'll never see him again."

"Don't tell me," Muriel begged in mock astonishment, "that you've given up the tea you were planning for Mrs. Eliphalet Stark-weather?"

Azrael sat in shade cast by the barn; for the present an entirely willing captive. The rope that ran from his collar to a ringbolt in the wall might well have kept an elephant in duress. Its dimensions were a tribute to the puppy's strength yet it was not the implicit flattery that soothed Azrael's simple spirit.

Close at hand, though well out of reach of his eager, ablutionary tongue, Ashley and Barbara sat and talked. Azrael's still brief vocabulary enabled him to understand only a little of what they said, but their presence supplied the human companionship that a Newfoundland needs as urgently as meat and drink.

Still damp, still somewhat spent by his aquatic morning, the puppy squatted on widespread, loose-jointed haunches. His eyes were half closed, his tongue lolled. Occasionally he chewed vaguely on the rope, but for the most part he was satisfied to sit and be lulled by the rise and fall of childish voices. The fact that their tone was generally acrimonious did not disturb Azrael's unscrupulous mind.

Ashley's chin was on his knees. His thin hands were locked about his shins. Barbara, restrained by amplitude from a like pose, sat with stout legs thrust out before her and leaned backward on her arms. To an adult eavesdropper, their communion would have seemed quarrelsome. Politeness does not exist normally between a boy of twelve and a girl of ten, even on first acquaintance, and Ashley and Barbara had been in association now for a full fortnight.

Their union was as nearly platonic as any the world affords, yet it was still imperfectly sexless. Ashley seemed, thus far, immune to nature's sardonic jest and regarded his companion as though she were another occasionally obstinate but generally co-operative small boy. To his whims and crotchets, his impatiences and downright defamations, Barbara presented an impassive tolerance that bore a prophetic similarity to the pose of a tried and resolutely patient wife.

Even in the very young, the direly circular pattern of life can be perceived. Here were the plain bones of human intimacy. Ten years hence, for each in its own fashion, romance would cover and adorn the skeleton. Romance, under the attrition of the years, eventually would wear away, revealing the original structure once more. Its final pattern would match that which, now, Ashley and Barbara unwittingly followed.

The freckled boy chewed upon a grass stem and considered the puppy's ungainly bulk with wistful eyes.

"Gosh," he said. "He's big. Muriel says he's gonna grow a lot more. Maybe he'll get so big I could ride him, like a pony. Boy, would that be somethin'."

"I bet," the portly little girl offered, "we could now, pretty near."

"You couldn't." Ashley surveyed her outline and snorted. "You'd bust him."

"I'm gonna be thinner some day," Barbara replied calmly. "My mother says so."

"Nuts. I bet you'll be the—the fat lady in Barnum'n Bailey's."

"I don't care. I'll bet that would be fun."

Considering the prospect from all angles, Ashley was forced to concede, secretly, that it probably would be fun. He glowered and spat out the grass stem. Azrael panted loudly. Barbara sat straighter. Boredom, which only their elders in time learn to endure patiently, pressed upon both children.

"Look," the little girl said at last. "We gonna sit here all day? Let's do somep'n."

"'Let's do somep'n,'" Ashley mimicked in falsetto. "What, for gossakes?"

"I dunno. Just—somep'n."

"We could play commandos," her companion offered with a flicker of interest. Barbara's hands went to her unapparent waistline at the final word. She shook her head.

"No," she said with decision. "I got blue marks all over my stomach already where you bayoneted me. Anyhow, there's too much wind. We'd blow away if we went out, like that Mr. Moncure."

"You're full of ants," Ashley scoffed. "A boat isn't a canoe. I'll bet he can't paddle for sour apples, anyway."

"I'll bet he can, too," Barbara insisted. "I think he's nice. He looks like Gary Cooper or Tyrone Power or somebody—sort of, that is; only different."

"He does not. He can't even walk right."

"That's on account of he got a foot shot off in the war. I heard Cyril say so."

"No kiddin'?" Ashley sat straighter. There was genuine interest in his question. "How? In this war?"

"Maybe," she replied with a pardonable uncertainty. "I don't know. It was some war."

"Gosh," said Ashley and they lapsed into pessimism. "Well, if he hangs around here, I know what'll happen. He'll start lookin' at Muriel like—like Azrael does right now an' he'll get to followin' her around like Dick Banning and that old Bailey Ward. She's —awful."

The uncomplimentary sound he uttered was his own tribute to Muriel's charms.

"He will not either," Barbara insisted. "He's married already."

"Well!" said Ashley in the blighting voice of one who finds further dismissal unnecessary. Azrael sighed and lay down. The process perceptibly shook the ground on which they sat, for the puppy achieved prostration by lowering himself a small portion of the way, then relaxing completely and falling the remainder.

Something in the creature's recumbent posture quickened Ashley's lively imagination.

"He's like a lion, sort of," he said, ignoring a host of radical dissimilarities. "Look: I know what."

"Well," Barbara prodded at length, when his calculating silence grew unendurable.

"How's for playing exploring? We could row Azrael over to Martin's Island an' leave him there. Then we could go back an' sort of explore and he could be wild animals."

The little girl considered the proposal with solemn approval into which doubt gradually crept.

"Your mother'll be awful mad if we go out in that boat again," she demurred, "and anyways, he's tied up. Cyril tied him up awful tight."

She indicated the uneven rosette of knotted rope adorning Azrael's collar, just below one ear. Ashley sprang up and approached the puppy, who rose as eagerly to meet him.

"Here now," said a voice so rasping that he jumped.

There still were grass stains on Cyril Handrow's shirt, and his worn look indicated that equally unsightly blemishes remained upon his spirit.

"You," he commanded, "leave that critter be, bub. 'Tie him up,' Miss Ashley said, and tied he stays. You children go somewheres else. If that dog gets loose, I ain't a gonna ketch him again."

Ashley backed away from Cyril's sour regard and Mr. Handrow turned upon Barbara, who regarded him blankly.

"It's most dinner time," he prompted. "You best be gittin' home."

"I don't know," the little girl answered.

"Don't know what?"

"Whether Mis' Applegate's gonna ask me to stay," Barbara said with grave simplicity and further disturbed Cyril's mind by adding in explanation:

"I asked my mother if I could if she did and she said I could and I will if she does but she hasn't yet."

CHAPTER IV

THE DEPARTURE OF LUCY AND MURIEL, A FEW SATURDAYS LATER, ON one of their infrequent journeys to Walden was attended by more than its normal babble and confusion. Such expeditions, limited by gas rationing, always were delayed at their outset by enough last-minute additions to the project, final instructions, reminders and warnings to equip an army embarkation.

Two of the chosen voyagers sat in the station wagon waiting with diverse expressions for Lucy to embark. Muriel's brightly painted fingernails tapped on the steering wheel. Twice she had begged, "Oh, do come on, angel!" to her apparently deaf sister and her face now wore a look of patient despair. On the rear seat, Azrael craned his neck to sniff her ear and withdrew hastily as the girl raised her hand. She forebore to slap him, having learned by now how thoroughly he would overwhelm her with disheveling apologies.

Azrael sat up straight with a deceptively austere expression. Actually, his simple heart overflowed with satisfaction and pride. Motoring was his dearest joy. He strove by frontal assault or canny stowing away of himself in the station wagon's rear to be included in all expeditions. His motor trips usually were limited to a brief, ecstatic passage between barn and house. Today, if his mild canine mind could fathom human conduct at all, he was to be included in a longer drive.

Lucy had nominated him. It had seemed to her, after considerable trial and error, the wiser course to take him along. If she bore away Ashley and Barbara—who had become almost as constant an associate of the small boy as his trousers—Azrael, left to his own devices, dug holes in the lawn, chewed the porch mats, or excavated in the flowerbed bathtub-like depressions where in coolness he might take his ease.

If the puppy were tied up during the family's absence, he mourned. His lugubrious, deep-chested moans sent ominous shiverings along Rena Handrow's spine, for they presaged, she professed to believe, imminent death in the household. The long-drawn organ notes pushed Cyril gradually toward the brink of a canicidal frenzy that would have justified his wife's dread.

Finally, as Lucy had explained to her sister who had been uncordial toward Azrael's inclusion in the shopping trip, you simply couldn't leave the children and the dog together. That combination had been tried, disastrously.

"Goodness knows," the older woman had said, "Ashley and Barbara—I wish she'd stay home; I really think she leads Ashley into mischief—well, I mean they get into enough trouble by themselves. If they play with Azrael, too, almost anything can happen. He's gentle, I know, and very obliging, but they make believe he's an elephant, or a rhinoceros, or a German army or heaven only knows what. Yesterday, they pretended he was a submarine and all three of them almost drowned. I mean, it will be safer to take him along, Muriel; it really will."

Now, Azrael sat with what assumption of arrogance so light a spirit could portray and beat upon the station wagon's seat with his tail and beamed over a dangling tongue at the group beside the car. Cyril suddenly had materialized with an order for grass seed that he had almost forgotten. Rena had come under full sail from the kitchen with a last-minute appeal that rice and table salt be included on the list. Lucy had now turned to address final admonitions to the attendant children.

Ashley and Barbara lingered, side by side, and each wore that wooden opacity of countenance which always disturbed Lucy. She strove desperately to block by firm mandate whatever fell intention their impassivity concealed.

"Now play together, chicks," she said, "and have a good morning. But listen to me, Ashley Applegate: Stay out of the barn, and don't tramp through the vegetable garden, and leave Cyril's wheelbarrow alone. Don't light a fire anywhere and don't touch the ax. If Rena tells me you've been in the kitchen again, I'll have to punish you, Ashley. Don't paddle in the lake and get yourselves soaked and don't—"

"Aw, Mom," Ashley broke in, "gee-gosh, we're not babies. We won't. I promise. Is that enough?"

His earnestness touched his mother. She was unaware that it was born, not of duty, but of Ashley's knowledge that her prohibitions were creeping nearer his and Barbara's secretly cherished purpose of evading Cyril, abducting the flat-bottomed boat, and rowing over to Martin's Island, there to become two dauntless fugitives from

Bataan. The boat was a permanent prohibition and he knew it, but if he were not warned afresh, he might possibly blame subsequent use of it on forgetfulness.

"Oh, do come on, Lucy," her sister begged. "You know we promised Bailey, and we're late now."

"Oh, goodness," Lucy exclaimed contritely and climbed in. She had forgotten, in the turmoil of departure, that their trip today had a double purpose. They were to purchase supplies, but first at Defense Director Ward's express invitation, they were to visit the new control center, only recently equipped and not to be open to public inspection until this evening.

Just the smallest handful, Ward had explained with the air of one who burnishes a precious gift, would attend this preview. He had chosen his list with care and had urged them, since local jealousies were always an affliction to even a statesmanlike defense director, not to mention their invitation to anyone.

Muriel muttered and jammed the gears in her haste. The car bucked as it moved away and Azrael lurched perilously on his seat. Lucy settled herself in hers and gave a sigh. It was a relaxed sound, yet her mind was not wholly at peace. She wondered how much of her sister's impatience was due to the protracted delay, how much to growing interest in Bailey Ward. She would see enough of him in the future, heaven knew. The uniform which would call the attention of Walden to the high, if vaguely purposed, post to which Ward had appointed her, had been tried on thrice and was to be delivered next week. Thereafter, Lucy supposed, Muriel would be a duly qualified subordinate, subject to the director's every call.

She clasped her hands firmly in her lap. It was none of her business. Muriel was old enough to know her mind—granting that any-one of nineteen, or thirty-four, or even seventy, ever did. Besides, there was no use in trying to influence Muriel. Lucy wondered now, as the line of white birches whirled past and the car went uphill toward the highway, whether she would dare sway her sister, even if she could.

Lucy had found nothing in her further acquaintance with Ward to warrant condemnation or even disapproval. Barring an over-heavy sense of his own importance, a playful pomposity of manner, he appeared to be an estimable person. "Estimable!" Lucy wondered why this and kindred adjectives—"worthy," "respectable," "re-ligious," "virtuous"—could be applied to no one without damaging his character.

The station wagon drew up beside the metal postbox at the driveway's end and Muriel, leaning out, extracted the mail. She shuffled through the letters and handed all of them to Lucy, save one whose unstamped corner bore the signature of Lieutenant Richard Banning. This she thrust into her jacket pocket and drove on.

Was it indifference that had made the girl conceal the letter unopened? Or did she wait for some more private moment when she might read it? Lucy dared voice neither question and bent over her own mail. Harrison's weekly letter was there, punctual as usual. He could not yet have had her answer to his last.

Reading its pleasant, tempered sentences—even in courtship Harrison had not been imaginative—Lucy could see her husband, unmilitary even in a lieutenant colonel's uniform, writing late at night in his hotel room. She firmly suppressed the sense of pathos the picture inspired, finished the letter and dropped it into her handbag.

"Harrison sends you his love," she told her sister.

"Regular as clockwork, isn't he?" Muriel smiled. "Does he say when he's coming up?"

Lucy wondered whether it was wholly her imagination that made the girl's brief glance seem narrow and searching.

"No," she answered lightly. "He doesn't. They're all very busy."

She debated whether Muriel's suspicions had been roused. Lucy hoped she had not betrayed Harrison's stipulation that their separation—"Sabbatical" was a word she found she still liked better—was to be considered due to the war, not to their own sober choice.

Muriel, after youth's immemorial fashion, was at once ingenuous and canny, inquisitive and hotly intolerant of curiosity about her own affairs. Well, if Lucy managed to mind her own business about Bailey Ward, the least her sister could do would be to keep her conjectures about Harrison to herself.

"We're fifteen minutes late," Muriel said. "Get your apologies ready, darling."

They jounced across the railroad track where Main Street began, in grimed shabbiness plastered by soft drink signs, and followed its waxing respectability to the common. Elms rose like immobilized green fountains and upon his pedestal a cast-iron Civil War soldier leaned gloomily on his musket, shamed, Lucy imagined, by his flagrantly unpressed trousers.

Buildings walled the verdant rectangle. The barrier was adorned by the tarnished gilt signs of local enterprises and the gaudier façades of chain stores. Muriel found a vacant space between two

white lines and inserted the station wagon deftly. She made certain
Azrael's leash was firmly tethered.

"Step on it, darling," she urged.

Lucy followed her along the crowded sidewalk where natives and
summer people mingled, yet preserved their identities as strictly
as oil and water. Bizarrely dressed men and practically undressed
women passed overalled farmers and their straitly garbed mates
who considered the outlanders with an admirable blankness beyond
Lucy's utmost effort.

It was queer, she thought as Muriel hurried her toward a large
brick block, that males expressed their holiday mood nowadays by
putting on strange raiment, while females took off as much as possible. Noontide's glare did not lend glamor to seminakedness. That
obviously demanded tolerant dusk or, in most instances, complete
darkness, to be alluring. People who saw evil in a scant but strate-
gic costume of halter, shorts, and sneakers were all mixed up in
their minds. They thought such exposures offended morality.
What they really meant was that they wrecked illusions. Nakedness wasn't indecent, it was just depressing.

Muriel and Lucy entered the brick building and climbed by brass-
bound steps to a dim hall. Men and women descended, exchanging
sounds of approval. The office door that had closed behind them
bore a freshly painted legend on its glass panel:

CONTROL CENTER
Walden Civilian Defense Council
Bailey Ward, Director

Lucy followed Muriel into a high-ceilinged chamber and its sole
occupant advanced. On Bailey Ward's brown, precociously wrinkled face, relief and welcome warred with disapproval. He glanced
at his watch before he held a soft hand out to each of them. The
door, thrust shut by its spring, uttered a cluck of reproof in his
stead.

"Sorry, Superior," Muriel said. "It's my sister's fault."

"You're here at last," Ward told her with a beaming smile in
which he belatedly included Lucy. "That's the main thing. Well"—
he turned and his gesture included the entire office—"what do you
think of it?"

"Wonderful," the sisters said together but Lucy did not know
what actually to think. The chamber with its wall map and tele-

phones, its chair-attended table and its colored electric bulbs seemed to her the implausible offspring of a board of directors' room and the Christmas spirit.

"Let me explain the whole set-up," Ward begged and did not wait for their assent. The table, Lucy gathered as the important voice ran on, was where Walden's defense chieftains would assemble at the least hint of peril, with Ward in the seat of honor. Each chair, she saw, bore across its back in large letters the title of its occupant-to-be—the Chief Air-Raid Warden, the Chiefs of the Housing Committee, the Police, the Motor Corps, the Medical Corps, the Fire Department and at the far end—she found herself hoping that its distance from Ward's chair was symbolic—the place assigned to the Chief of the Women's Auxiliary Corps.

Before each post was a telephone and pad of paper, and beside Ward's seat stood a typewriter, complete with desk and chair. The table's sole decoration, a bizarre centerpiece, fascinated Lucy. It was a vertical oblong pile and on each of its four sides, like carefully spaced barnacles, bulbs yellow, blue, red, and white adhered.

"Imagine for the sake of clarity," their preceptor was saying, "that Walden at this moment is subjected to air attack. What happens? I'll show you."

He assumed his place with a hardy air and fiddled with a panel of push buttons on the table beside him.

"We have received from the district warning center the preliminary alarms: 'Air-Raid Warning Yellow' and 'Air-Raid Warning Blue.'"

At mention of each color, he pressed a button and the corresponding lights glowed on the center column, giving the table, Lucy thought, an increasingly festive air.

"My staff," Ward pursued with drama creeping into his voice, "has assembled. Each as he enters and takes his place can see by the colored lights the exact intensity of the alarm. My adjutant, sitting here at my elbow, receives the signal 'District Warning Center: Air-Raid Warning Red.' That means that in five minutes enemy planes will be overhead. I—"

He stopped suddenly. Awe and disbelief were so plain upon his face that Lucy in a spasm of fright fancied that she herself could hear the roar of approaching Heinkels. Ward was staring at the door. He scrambled up with a scuffle of feet and a scrape of chair legs. The spectacle that had smitten him speechless did not seem at first glance noteworthy to her.

More visitors were entering the post of control, led by a raw-boned woman in black. Three females attended her and behind them limped a man, tall, blond, and plainly bored. Lucy had no time to debate whether sight of Larry Moncure had made her heart leap. Full and sudden consciousness of who led the invasion supplied her with a number of distracting symptoms which included breathlessness and a touch of vertigo.

Ward was advancing with haste toward the group at the door. Lucy turned to Muriel who stood at the table's far side. Each at the instant spoke voicelessly the same august name for the other's unnecessary enlightenment.

"Mrs. Starkweather," their lips formed in unison. Thereafter, with an effort at indifference, Muriel slightly wrinkled her nose; but it was plain to see that she too was shaken.

"Mrs. Starkweather," Ward was saying, like an amplification of their own utterance. "This is a great honor and a privilege and—and a pleasure. I didn't dare to hope when I sent you the invitation that you'd—well, honor us. It means a great deal to our civilian effort. Please come on in."

The invitation seemed belated for Mrs. Starkweather already was advancing. Ward stepped out of her determined path, mopped his face and looked toward Lucy and Muriel. In this intense moment it was clear that he regarded them as life preservers.

"May I present," he babbled, "Mrs. Applegate and Miss Ashley, summer residents here like yourself."

"How do you do?" Mrs. Starkweather asked in a startling baritone. Her regard was gray and bright and sharp as a needle's jab, pricking Muriel and Lucy briefly before it returned to Ward.

"Summer residents like myself?" she asked. "Damn it, young man, I lived here for years before you were born."

"I know, of course. Pardon me; a slip of the tongue," Ward said, sweating. Over his shoulder, Moncure's eyes sought for and held Lucy's for an instant. Before they moved on to Muriel, the wrinkles at the corners deepened. He limped forward, not to Lucy's side but to Muriel's, and addressed both of them beneath his breath.

"Don't take the royal visitation too seriously, I beg of you, or be shocked by the ancestress's profanity. It's her only dissipation," he begged and added in a louder voice, "Mehitabel, honey, these are the nice folks on whose shore I was canoe-wrecked. Remember?"

One of the figures about Mrs. Starkweather—who had appeared hitherto as only a general environment—approached.

"My wife," said Moncure. "Mrs. Applegate, Miss Ashley."

"Hello," said Mehitabel Starkweather Moncure and offered a thin, hard hand. She was blond and flat of hip and breast and her faded boyish face bore a streamlined version of her grandmother's beaky nose. Her eyes surveyed the chamber's furnishings with candid interest.

"You know," she told them, "this all looks as though it would be rather fun."

"If my wife," Moncure explained gravely, "had been called to a more useful station in life, she'd have been a blessing to the automobile trade. She loves gadgets." ·

"It's a harmless vice," Mrs. Moncure said in an expressionless voice and turning, bridged the gap between the sisters and the other newcomers with introductions. The exhausted-looking woman with the twisted stockings was, it appeared, Miss Pinch, Mrs. Starkweather's companion. Mrs. Throckmorton, with three chins, gold-rimmed glasses magnifying perpetually startled eyes, and a figure so well rounded fore and aft that it seemed reversible, was cousin to Mrs. Starkweather who, after conversing with Ward, now looked about the chamber and said to them all in a louder voice:

"Well, this is very interesting, I'm sure, though I don't understand what it's all about."

Her face, where a rapacious nose contended with piercing eyes and a grim mouth under a perceptible mustache for dominion over the sallow, folded flesh, was startlingly vital. Her personality had none of the neutrality age imposes. Lucy wondered whether Mrs. Starkweather had not been spiritually male all her days and whether now at last masculinity was not triumphing over the dwindling influence of glands and all that.

"Very interesting," Miss Pinch was saying.

"Very interesting *and* important," Mrs. Throckmorton supplied, playing a trump.

Both regarded their patron with identical expressions. These were so closely kin to the look Azrael assumed at tea-time when he hoped without any real expectation that he might be fed, that Lucy grinned though she knew Mrs. Starkweather was watching her. She saw the keen eyes widen.

"Oh, goodness!" she thought, "now I've done it." But the bleak regard impaled her briefly and withdrew.

Ward, in a halting style that bore scant evidence of sundry previous repetitions, was launched upon his explanation of the control center's mechanics. Moncure's wife listened intently, her grandmother with forbearance, while the elderly ladies-in-waiting watched Mrs. Starkweather intently to see what their attitude should be. Moncure himself lounged by Muriel's side, occasionally bending to whisper in her ear.

"I see," Mrs. Starkweather said at length in a tone that made Lucy doubtful whether she understood at all. "And then, after all these lights—this Christmas tree effect—what happens? How do you alarm Walden? You haven't told us that."

"As best we can," Ward replied and mopped his glistening face. "By church bell, factory whistle, telephone. It isn't wholly effective. We need an alarm siren, badly."

"Get it then, for God's sake."

The defense director looked unhappy. He confessed:

"Unfortunately, it costs more money than our little organization can afford."

"Nonsense," Mrs. Starkweather informed him briskly. "Buy anything you can, my dear man, while money has any purchasing power left. Well, I think you have done very well indeed. I am glad to have seen all this."

"Well, Mrs. Starkweather," Ward said, as though the words had precious flavor, "we'll all do our best in this time of danger."

"Hell, man, why shouldn't you?" the old woman asked. "Do or die, isn't it? Let me tell you one thing, though: None of this would have happened if the Senator had lived."

The Senator, Lucy calculated, would be a hundred if he still existed. She was made aware by his widow's scrutiny that she had grinned again. There was incongruous humor in the old woman's rugged speech. Moncure muttered something to Muriel and they both laughed. Lucy tried to look as though she had merely shared their amusement. Mehitabel Moncure had strolled across the room and was inspecting the wall map of Walden and the rack of vari-colored pins beneath it. Ward said, in a manner which combined the worst features of a ringmaster and a small boy on the verge of recitation:

"If you can spare the time, I'd be glad to explain—"

"I can't," Mrs. Starkweather interrupted. "I want a hat."

Her brusque demand dazed the defense director, who seemed not certain whether it had been aimed at him personally. Muriel whispered to Moncure who said:

"Go get your hat then, Ancestress. Mehitabel and I'll stay and learn about this. We're interested."

"I'll go with you, Cousin Lydia," said Mrs. Throckmorton.

"So shall I, of course," said Miss Pinch.

"Will you?" Mrs. Starkweather inquired. "Where?"

"Why, to—to a milliner's," Miss Pinch faltered.

"I didn't ask 'To What?'; I asked 'Where?' " her employer corrected. Miss Pinch colored a murky orange. The old woman turned from her satellites to Lucy.

"Do you know where one may buy a hat in Walden?"

"Horton's is the best place," Lucy told her.

"At last," Mrs. Starkweather acclaimed. "Some helpful information. Where is it? Or would it be too much trouble to you to take us there? Walden has changed since I last was here."

"I'll be very glad," Lucy told her.

She glanced at Ward, whom Mehitabel now was questioning and at Muriel and Moncure, still talking mirthfully. She would have liked to have pulled a derisive snoot at her sister, but the girl seemed oblivious to the fact that Lucy actually was about to help Mrs. Eliphalet Starkweather buy a hat.

Mrs. Throckmorton, breathing hard yet triumphantly, helped her distinguished kinswoman down the stair. Miss Pinch had the outer door open before Lucy reached it. When Mrs. Starkweather had passed through, Miss Pinch, with the most nearly defiant glance so dim a person could produce, attached herself to her employer's free arm. Three abreast, they moved slowly along the narrow sidewalk, while their guide followed, occasionally calling directions.

Lucy, ignominiously trailing, told herself that she pitied the two poor old things, so obviously dependent, so pathetically jealous of that dependency, but found herself doubting her own broadminded reassurance. The picture that she had immediately hung up in her mind when Mrs. Starkweather had asked her to accompany them had been bright. Its removal woke a sense of outrage.

She had seen herself walking arm in arm for all of Walden's common to mark and envy with the daughter of the Governor, the widow of the Senator, the Ambassador's mother, who was the region's most celebrated, if temporary, resident. Lucy had imagined the gay sallies she would offer. She had fancied Mrs. Starkweather's manner thawing from interest into approval. And now, none of this was happening.

She strode, alone and ignored save when she offered instructions, like a plowman behind three imperceptibly hitched, infirm horses. She tried to be amused but only found herself increasingly indignant. All right; then she was a snob. Muriel had said so. Muriel, if she had been equally disregarded, probably would not have submitted at all to such disparagement.

There was one comfort. She cherished it vindictively. No one seemed aware that the gaunt woman, with her unalluring supporters, was a Personage. Walden's policeman shouted when the trio ignored traffic lights. He had no least idea that he was chiding Mrs. Eliphalet Starkweather.

"Here we are," Lucy called at last. "Here we are," and when her charges plodded on, unheeding, ran in front of them and turned them by word and gesture toward the entrance to the millinery store. Miss Pinch, Mrs. Throckmorton looked affronted. Lucy hoped they were.

"This is Horton's," she said, ignoring them and speaking only to their convoy. "I hope you find what you want. Good-by. It's been so pleasant."

"Good-by," Mrs. Throckmorton and Miss Pinch said at once.

"Good-by?" Mrs. Starkweather repeated, apparently unaccustomed to so willing a departure. "But you're coming with us. Of course you are; I insist. I want your advice. I'm never sure of my hats."

If her companions had looked a shade less repellent, Lucy might have refused. Her spirit still simmered as she followed them into the shop.

She lingered in the background while Mrs. Starkweather's cousin and companion seated her before the triple mirror and then fell back a pace to stand like ancient acolytes on either hand. Mrs. Starkweather removed her own hat and set it before her. A bored girl brought several more and placed one upon the thin, white hair.

"Now this," she began, "is a Lucille model. We have—"
Strong old hands pulled hers away.

"Young woman," the baritone voice bade, "just bring me hats and let me try them myself. I'm quite capable of putting them on."

The attendant met Lucy's glance and, sensing sympathetic amusement, gave her a small despairing grimace. It altered Lucy's forming intention to leave as soon as possible. She wanted to see the girl's expression when she discovered her customer's identity. Most of the world's important persons should be labeled, after all. There really was no other way to identify them.

Mrs. Starkweather had pulled and twisted the hat about to her satisfaction. She turned her head, consulting each of the triple mirrors.

"That," she proclaimed, "is the way it should be worn. Do you like it?"

"Very much," Mrs. Throckmorton said promptly.

"Oh, very, very much," Miss Pinch endorsed.

Their automatic enthusiasm galled Lucy. In their eyes she saw once more the ignominious counterpart of Azrael's tea-time hopefulness. With mingled pride and alarm, she heard her own voice proclaiming:

"It isn't at all becoming, Mrs. Starkweather."

She had done it now and yet, though she saw the originally shocked expressions on Miss Pinch's and Mrs. Throckmorton's faces grow gleeful, Lucy wasn't sorry. She felt that her speech had made her more respectable. She didn't care what happened now. She had told the truth. That was a minor comfort; the fact that she had been braver than she had had any idea she could be was her chief support. Mrs. Starkweather was speaking in a voice that might be balefully muted but certainly was not explosive:

"Indeed, Mrs. Applegate? And why?"

This was no time for shuffling or retreat. Lucy had chosen her own position and would hold it to the end.

"It hasn't dignity," she said clearly. "It's a very ordinary little number and besides, it's a whole size too small for you."

The acolytes waited in silence like that which intervenes between the lightning's flash and thunder. Miss Pinch bit her lip; Mrs. Throckmorton elevated her high shoulders a trifle further. Both stared expectantly at Mrs. Starkweather.

"You know," she said at last in a startlingly thoughtful voice, "I think you're right. It doesn't become me and it is too small."

She chose another hat and raised it to her head. Pity, the easily bestowed pity of the victor, warmed Lucy as she observed her rivals' collapse. Miss Pinch, Mrs. Throckmorton were regarding her with astonishment in which there was no trace of understanding.

The poor old things! They were more than dazed; they were completely stunned—a couple of yes-women who had emptied themselves of everything personal so that there might be more room for the assent and acclaim they deemed their principal's constant need.

"And this?" Mrs. Starkweather asked, after having wrestled extensively with the hat.

Mrs. Throckmorton looked wretched; Miss Pinch as though in another moment she might cry. Neither offered comment. Incredibly, they were looking to Lucy for guidance. She hoped they realized that she gave them a sympathetic, not a gloating, smile.

"I don't like it," she said briskly. "In the first place, it's too tall for your face and, in the second, you've pulled it all out of shape. Let me help you."

Supremely confident now, she removed the offending headpiece and chose another from the selection on the table and set it on the thin hair, so carefully brushed to hide the skull's brown baldness. Mrs. Starkweather made no protest.

"That's better," Lucy told her cheerfully. "That's really quite attractive. I think it would be improved still further, if that feather were removed. It spoils the lines, doesn't it? A little velvet bow, for instance."

Daniel, she thought, must have felt equally blithe toward the lions.

"Quite," said Mrs. Starkweather briskly. She removed the hat herself but immediately supplanted it with another.

"Oh, no," Lucy cried. "That won't do at all. It's all wrong."

She was puzzled by the expression on the mirror's reflection of Mrs. Starkweather's face.

"Goddamit, Mrs. Applegate," the baritone proclaimed. "This is my own hat, the one I wore in here."

"I can't help it," Lucy said at last in a dull voice. She could not bring herself to look at Miss Pinch and Mrs. Throckmorton.

CHAPTER V

IN THE WALDEN CONTROL CENTER, BAILEY WARD HAD EXPOUNDED ALL the technicalities of spreading an air-raid alarm for an audience of three that compensated by its quality for its lack of size. It was sweet to lecture in Muriel's presence and with a proper air of authority to two accredited members of the Starkweather family. Besides, Mrs. Moncure's attention had been flatteringly intense and her questions intelligent.

Her husband, Ward thought, had been less impressed. He was not at all sure that he could grow fond of Moncure, who kept muttering things to Muriel that made her giggle. After all this wasn't theory; this was war.

Whatever irritation Moncure supplied was mild in the light of advantages and privileges so miraculously gained. Hereafter in Ward's presence the name "Starkweather" would not be merely a regional legend, but instead an invitation to personal reminiscence.

"Mrs. Eliphalet Starkweather? I know her quite well. Magnificent character. Said to me in the control center the other day—"

Ward thought with a thrill of anticipation that he would spend an hour or so at the Elks Club that afternoon.

Muriel giggled again and felt her chief's eyes rest on her in brief reproof. She said to Moncure in a low voice:

"Quiet, please. You're not being polite."

"Gal, I can be so polite it'll surprise you—fine, old, sugar-cured, hickory-smoked Virginia politeness, if you'll promise."

"Promise what?"

His eyes were bland. He deliberately broadened his faint accent:

"Honey, you're mighty vigilant, ain't you? Just promise you'll come up and see me—us, I mean."

"To look at your etchings?"

He shook his head.

"I keep them elsewhere, infant. It's your place to call on newcomers. Ain't you had no rearin', chile?"

"None whatever," Muriel told him solemnly.

"That's what I was hopin'."

Mehitabel had turned from Ward and was looking at Muriel so wholly calmly that the girl wondered with dismay if she were resentful in a bloodless, aristocratic fashion.

"Larry," his wife said, "we better go. Gram will be waiting."

"Beautiful," he objected, "she won't be nowhere near through. She couldn't buy hats like hers just offhand. Besides, I've almost persuaded this uninstructed child that it's her folks' duty to call on our folks, first."

"Don't make it a duty," Mehitabel advised. Her voice seemed as barren of warmth or animus as her straight, tweed-clad body of sex. "Come on, Larry."

"Yes, ma'am," he acknowledged in a travesty of meekness.

The wife's cool voice woke in Muriel uneasy consciousness of offense and formed a purpose that the disapproval in Ward's eyes solidified.

"I must be going, too," she said. "I'll have to find Lucy."

They found her beside a parked Rolls Royce, so ancient that only the wealthiest patrician willingly would use it. Lucy looked startlingly pretty, Muriel thought, as she, Mrs. Throckmorton, Miss Pinch and the chauffeur labored to get Mrs. Starkweather comfortably deposited on the rear seat.

"Mehitabel," the dowager addressed her granddaughter. "Mrs. Applegate has a son just little Lydia's age. We must have them all to lunch one day."

"That will be nice," the young woman replied. Moncure squinted at the astounded Muriel.

"A well-bred leer," he said in explanation.

The immense old car backed out like a liner from its pier. Lucy waved and then caught her sister's arm. Her eyes were bright, her color high. Laughter rocked her as she strove to speak.

"Whatever on earth—?" Muriel began.

"Darling," Lucy quavered. "Tea at our house later, maybe, but lunch at hers first. You heard her."

"Angel, how did you do it?"

"Do you know who I am?" Lucy asked, her mouth tremulous with mirth. "I'm the person who fell down a manhole and came up with her handbag filled with pearls. Muriel, I insulted her taste in hats and she loved it. And little Lydia likes to play with boys, darling."

"You don't make sense," her sister told her.

"Most things that actually happen don't," Lucy answered blithely, but a shadow crossed her face.

"The little girl," she said more thoughtfully, "is lonely with no one of her own age to play with. I hope Ashley will be nice with her."

"We'll make him," Muriel promised grimly. If either of them at that moment could have been transported to Martin's Island, they might have laughed at the vanity of their worry.

Disregard for heavy odds, which is the common possession of American fighting men, and guile learned in weeks of bitter jungle warfare had enabled two theoretical fugitives from a hypothetical Bataan to accomplish half their purpose. Ashley and Barbara had evaded the chronically suspicious regard of Cyril Handrow, now magnified into an entire Japanese army, and had embarked in the lean, fleet motor torpedo boat that to unenchanted eyes might have seemed nothing but the flat-bottomed, unwieldy scow usually beached in the Applegate cove.

Freedom already was half attained. With Ashley at the helm and Barbara in the double role of engineer and engine—a post she had accepted after some vehement objection—the craft stood out to sea. Its captain gave his orders only in a whisper and remained as oblivious as possible to the loud splashings of the heavy oars, wielded by a fat little girl.

To the imagination of the very young, which is a bright, magically transforming and pitifully brief possession, the mild stretch of water was perilous tropic sea and the willow-crowned acre of land that actually was Martin's Island, a lowering haunt of peril.

Barbara splashed and strained and splashed again. Ripples slobbered against the boat's blunt nose and were resolutely ignored. From the bow where he stood to the further detriment of accurate rowing, Ashley scanned the horizon and rasped huskily into the cupped hand that for the moment served as speaking tube:

"More speed, Bill: there's smoke beyond that headland."

The engine's effort quickened, unrhythmically.

"For Pete's sake," the commander begged, dropping out of character for an instant, "look where you're goin', will ya?"

"How," the hard-pressed engineer demanded in brief gusts of speech, "can I row—and look where—I'm goin', too?"

There was unanswerable logic in this query that drove Ashley back into character.

"Quiet, Bill," he warned in hushed savagery. "Want those Japs to hear us?"

His exhortations to silence, though vain, grew more vehement as the island drew near. Reeds and arrowheads' pointed leaves rasped as the boat poked its square prow through shallows. The craft grounded and the engineer shut off the overtaxed engines. She sat and wheezed while Ashley dramatically peered for signs of danger in the pleasant prospect before them.

Willow leaves glittered in the gentle breeze and beyond the fern-clad ridge of Martin's Island, the lake was a darker blue. A turtle with a black rubber shell who had been basking on a half-submerged snag seemed to find Ashley's wariness contagious and dropped into the clear water with a "plop" shockingly loud.

The commander gave the familiar scene—the trees, the islet's gray rock spine—a final, vigilant stare and turned to his partly recovered comrade.

"Don't like the looks of things, Bill," he muttered, "but we'll go ashore. Have your machine gun ready."

"Okay, Bill," Barbara responded, loyally.

Their sharing of a single name that seemed to each, for no clear reason, the essence of virility, was not sheer accident. At the outset of their association, each had laid claim to it. There had followed much corrosive argument by Ashley, monumental obstinacy by Barbara, before it had been agreed that it should be their common possession.

The expedition crept ashore, pushed through the thronging willows and advanced toward the ridge.

"Take cover, Bill," Ashley shouted suddenly and flung himself down.

"Tacka-tacka-tacka-tacka," he exclaimed, spraying bullets upon an advancing yellow horde. Presently Barbara, who had driven forth most of her recently recovered breath by the realism of her own fall, began unsteadily to echo the sound.

Under the deadly hail, the Japanese broke and fled.

"Cease firing, Bill," Ashley ordered. "Come on."

He led the way through windrows of slain and at the island's inconsiderable crest, paused. At the foot of the further slope, rock ledges went down into the water, each more duskily green than the last. A small and rickety jetty, where picnickers moored their boats, reached out from shore. Barbara said suddenly:

"Someone's comin'."

Ashley considered her with bleak disapproval. By implicit agreement, all the better lines in their melodramas belonged to him.

"Hey, nix," he protested; "lemme do this."

Her mild face did not alter at the reproof.

"Someone's comin'."

She pointed with a plump, brown hand. A red canoe, already quite close to shore, was pointed in their direction.

"Oh, nuts," said Ashley. "Hide!"

His voice echoed the pang of alarm that had skewered him. There was panic in his haste. Intrusion by strangers on childhood's more intimate pastimes is always indecent outrage. Ashley scuttled behind a ridge of rock and flung himself prone.

"Come on," he whispered acridly to Barbara who, of stouter fiber, stood staring at the approaching craft.

"It's nobody," she said calmly. "It's just a little girl."

The tidings did not soothe him.

"Come on," he bade again with such urgency that she complied.

They lay on their stomachs behind the island's crest and peered warily over. It was as Barbara had reported. The canoe's occupant was a child. Her uncertain paddling proclaimed her inexpert, in the bargain, but she was wholly a stranger to Ashley and he shrank.

The voyager's hair was black and bound in a heavy braid that glistened iridescently in the sun. She was thin and sallow with the sharp movements of a bird and even Ashley's unskilled eyes were aware that the scarlet dress she wore was not designed for canoeing. The craft yawed. He breathed more easily as it pointed away from the island, then grunted as another awkward stroke turned it definitely toward the crumbling pier.

"Hey," he whispered to Barbara in rising panic. "Let's get outa here."

He half rose, cast a craven look behind him and saw with a leaden sinking of his heart the familiar obdurate look solidify his comrade's face. She seemed immune to the spasm that had afflicted him and he found himself wholly unable to justify it.

"Whatcha wanna go for?" Barbara asked in honest inquiry. "We were here first. We got just as much right here as she has."

Her clear regard shamed him. He mumbled to himself and then muttered, more clearly: "Maybe she won't stop," as he settled himself again in his hiding place. Thereafter, he gave a muffled groan, for the canoe drew in against the pier and its occupant, stretching forth an arm and squealing briefly as she nearly capsized, managed to grip the structure and thrust the craft ashore.

She advanced with little, mincing steps. The socks above her dainty shoes were the same bright hue as her dress and the length of lean leg between them and the inconsiderable skirt, cut with French brevity, was spectacular.

She walked with a self-conscious grace, almost as though she were dancing, a brilliant, exotic figure against this rural serenity, fragile and yet, in some obscure fashion, hardy. None of this was Ashley able to fix in words. He only knew that she was fascinating and therefore doubly terrifying. He saw the thin, dark face turn toward him and ducked his head.

"Get down," he muttered to Barbara, who still was peering over the ridge with a visage as roundly grave as the rising moon's.

He could hear the intruder's voice humming a tuneless song as she moved about. The sound drew closer. He cowered and, suddenly lifting his head, looked up into the thin, dark face.

"E-e-e-e-e!" It was a shrill sound and it pierced him. He scrambled up and stared with an inane grin at the stranger who had withdrawn a space to stand with thin hands clasped upon her chest in an elegant gesture. Her gray eyes were wide. She was scared, Ashley thought with a pang of guilt, almost to death.

Barbara sat up deliberately. Voicelessly, the three stared at each other a long instant while into the clear mind of the fat small girl crept that smarting sense of inferiority that is jealousy's meat and drink.

The intruder dropped her hands and looked from one child to the other with haughty reproof.

"You scared me frightfully," she said and added, "What are you children doing here?"

Her superiority was still another item on Barbara's rapidly growing list of detestations. She doubted the authenticity of the other's fright. You didn't squeal like a whistle, sort of, if you really were scared; you hollered, loud.

She glanced at Ashley, expecting his endorsement, and was daunted by what she saw. Her comrade on a dozen theoretically stricken fields, her leader in many an imaginary foray, never had regarded her with a like expression. Something seemed to have rendered him temporarily speechless. It was Barbara who asked the newcomer:

"What are *you* doing here?"

The other answered lightly, as though her name were warrant for any intrusion and she spoke to Ashley, not to her faintly glowering questioner.

"I'm Lydia Moncure," she said with eloquent simplicity. "Do you own this island?"

Her smile dazzled him. She wasn't pretty exactly but the way she looked at him made him feel important. Maybe she was pretty, at that.

"Sure," he said with no regard for veracity, "but you can come here, if you want to."

The glib mendacity stung Barbara.

"Oh, he does not, either," she said and the faint trace of a scowl bore witness to her indignation. "His mother doesn't own it, even. We just came over to play."

Ashley's glower did nothing to quiet the unwonted emotions that seethed within her. The elegant Lydia's scrutiny was scarcely to be borne.

"How quaint!" she said with cosmopolitan amusement. "Playing what?"

Ashley's glare actually choked Barbara. He answered with ill-fitting carelessness:

"Oh, nothin'; just playin'."

Lydia smiled upon him again and did something radical to his respiratory passages. She looked about her with an air of bland condescension which her audience could not know was a copy of Mrs. Eliphalet Starkweather's state manner.

"It's rather pretty," she condescended, "in a quaint sort of way. Do you live here?"

"Nope," Ashley gulped. "Just summers."

"It's pleasant in Walden, but rather boring, don't you think?"

"Sure," he said. The way Barbara was looking at him made him nervous. "Sort of, that is," he amended.

Miss Moncure sought for a handkerchief in the region where someday a bosom might be; extracting it, she delicately passed it back and forth beneath her impressive nose.

"That's why I took the canoe," she said with languor. "I was frightfully bored. Greatgram and the others had gone into the funny little town and Mamselle was so tiresome. There's nothing like a good paddle, I find."

Barbara, unable to harbor all the assorted emotions compressed within her, offered: "You don't paddle very good," but neither of her companions seemed to hear her.

"Where are you prepping?" Lydia asked Ashley. It was a question that no one just barely in the sixth grade could hear without magnified importance.

"Oakes-Hallam," he said. She had reduced him to a state in which he found it difficult to utter more than a few syllables at a time. He sweated. Miss Moncure passed her handkerchief over his forehead. The perfume, pilfered from her mother's toilet table, dizzied him.

"It's a nice little school," she said. "Most of the men I know go to St. Lucian's. Are you in the Knickerbocker Grays?"

"Nope," Ashley said warily, having no idea what they were.

"It's very quaint," Lydia told him with an acquisitive look in the eyes she had inherited from her father. "I'm sure I've seen you somewhere."

Ashley grinned, then shot an instinctively wary glance at Barbara and, such is male opacity, was heartened by her indifference. She sat, still and expressionless as the rock ridge beneath her, and stared out across the lake. Bewilderment, not apathy, had immobilized her. She suddenly had found herself a cage for violent impulses and emotions so wholly unfamiliar to her hitherto placid nature that she could not even label them.

Lydia fanned herself with her redolent handkerchief, paced to and fro, twirled on one toe. She was one of the wiry children whose mood is never passive.

"Oops," Ashley exclaimed, "Lookut," and ran for the pier. A gust of wind had caught the canoe, drawn aground beside it, and was swinging its stern about. Lydia squealed and followed. Barbara continued to sit, fat legs crossed before her, like a miniature Buddha in khaki.

No flicker of expression stirred her face as Ashley caught the canoe and pulled it further inshore. She watched Lydia trip out along the jetty and look down from its far end, so carelessly that for a moment hope rose within her.

"Watch it," Ashley warned in his longest speech so far. "It's deep out there."

She smiled at him. It was plain she considered his warning quaint. "Pooh!" she said. "My dear boy, you needn't worry; I'm a superb swimmer."

A newborn hope died in Barbara at the other's calm assurance.

Lydia gave Ashley a brilliant smile and, skipping back along the shaky structure, grasped his arm.

"Let's walk about a little. Let's explore."

He stumbled now and then as they strolled along the island's shoreline. He was so numb that he was not even aware of Barbara's intense regard. For the moment, he had forgotten that she even existed.

His erstwhile comrade still squatted on the island's rocky spine, overlooking in her general wretchedness the fact that her perch grew increasingly hard. Physical discomfort was an insignificant matter to Barbara, whose spirit now was one with Andromeda's, Circe's, and innumerable subsequent and undeservedly abandoned.

Her pose was overstuffed, faintly comic. Compassion might have lingered beside her but Romance would have passed her by. There was little of poetry's substance in her grievously roiled spirit. Barbara watched Ashley and Lydia. She listened to the girl's brittle speech and the boy's clumsy replies with a face as blank as a kettle bottom, but presently a tear rolled down her cheek to linger on a flange of her snub nose. The gesture with which she brushed it away was deliberate. Her thoughts were not soft and self-pitying. They dealt with assault and a variety of mayhems hitherto unfamiliar to her childish soul.

Outcry, crossing the breadth of water from the Applegate home, roused her at length and, listening, she sat straighter. The tone of the summons was doomful but it brought her relief. She lifted her own voice and relayed the signal to the apparently deaf small boy.

"Ashley, Ashley, your mother's hollerin' for you."

He turned and his scowl gradually was replaced by a look of genuine alarm as reality smote him. It had been far from his intention to have authority trap him so flagrantly, so indefensibly out of bounds.

"Oh, aw right," he mumbled ungraciously. Lucy called again and her offspring, hearing her for the first time, flinched.

"I guess maybe I better go," he said hastily to Lydia. "G'by."

He hurried toward Barbara. Dread was plain on his freckled face. Once more, his mother called. The summons was frantic, piercing. He shouted in reply:

"I'm co-o-oming!"

Behind him, Lydia fluted:

"Good-by, Ashley. Don't forget what you promised."

"Yeh," he said vaguely. "Oh, yeh, sure." To Barbara, who was rising stiffly, he snarled: "Hey, step on it, willya?"

So great was his agitation that he took the oars and let her settle herself in the stern without the customary dispute. They moved jerkily toward the further shore with a deal of frantic splashing which grew in violence when Ashley, casting a guiding look over his shoulder, marked his mother and aunt waiting for him ominously on the distant shore.

Even while he made haste, his agile mind sought for some alley of subterfuge or downright falsehood that might lead out of his predicament. Usually, it was not too difficult to abate his fond mother's displeasure but this time, he knew, his offense had been grave. He had been caught in the commission of a disobedience particularly defiant and he had known by the peculiar note in his parent's summons that she had been frightened and now would be angry.

Twice in their shoreward progress, as a possible loophole presented itself, he said to Barbara: "Hey, look—" and got no further.

What had seemed for an instant a way out each time proved futile on further inspection. In addition, there was something in the very blankness of his associate's countenance that made him doubt whether, at present, she would prove a reliable accomplice. He got the impression that she had become solidly unco-operative, though in all verity he could not tell why. Ashley plied the oars more explosively, stressing each heave with small, groaning sounds.

These at first gratified Barbara. Newly-roused femininity proclaimed it only just that he should suffer, yet their repetition and the candid look of apprehension that twisted Ashley's freckled face woke pity and gradually restored her loyalty. She forgot grievance in genuine concern over her associate's plight. She guessed Mrs. Applegate would be awful mad. She might even say they couldn't play together any more. So lively grew her dread that she presented to Lucy and Muriel, when the boat at last ground through the shallows and came to rest before them, a specially lumpish and immobile spectacle.

Ashley had no such shield. He quailed as he rose from the rower's seat and faced his mother and aunt. They plainly were inflamed by the wrath that is the aftermath of lively and unwarranted fright.

"You've scared us almost to death," Muriel told him violently. "We couldn't find you and then we saw the boat was gone. If you were mine, Ashley Applegate—"

"How many times," Lucy broke in, "have I told you never to go out in the boat and, particularly, never over to the island unless there was a grown person with you?"

She chose to consider his glowering silence an effort at computation and, after a pause, supplied her own answer.

"A dozen times, at least. Isn't that so?"

"Guess so," he granted, huskily.

His mother's face wore an expression that was memorable, though rare.

"Go right on up to the house," she bade him with boding quiet. "And for a whole week, Harrison Ashley Applegate—"

Barbara, who had endured the storm with a boulder-like calm, now spoke.

"Mis' Applegate, it wasn't his fault. We just thought we hadda go, kinda. On account of we were worried about her, sort of."

Lucy was in no mood to reassemble this disordered statement. Neither was she aware that inspiration had smitten Barbara at the moment of her comrade's direst need. No one, observing her chubby, dull face and oversize eyes could possibly have deemed her inspired.

"I haven't the least idea," Ashley's mother said crisply, "what you're talking about, Barbara, and it can't possibly excuse him, anyway."

"Yes'm," Barbara assented. She felt pleasantly warm within for Ashley was staring at her with an astonishment that was admiration's first cousin.

"Only," she persisted in the face of Lucy's obvious disregard, "she was having trouble with her canoe, sort of, and we thought she needed help so that's why we took the boat because she was on the island."

"She? Who?" Muriel inquired on the heels of Lucy's gesture of despair.

"This girl. She had a red dress on," Barbara vouchsafed so implausibly that both women regarded her with scorn.

"I don't suppose," Lucy said with icy politeness, "that this girl in the red dress possibly had a name."

Irony did not mar even the surface of the fat little girl's composure.

"Yes, she did. It was a funny name. Ashley helped her with the canoe."

Ashley, whose face bore the look of one who beholds a miracle, cleared his throat with difficulty and offered:

"Lydia was her name. Lydia Moncure. I guess she stays round here, somewheres."

There was an instant of utter silence. At its end, Lucy said in a solemn voice:

"Ashley, don't you lie to me."

Such accusation, leveled against the speaker of the sole chemically pure verity so far offered by the defendants, was hard to bear.

"Mom," he replied in the tone of one who suffers for righteousness' sake, "she said that was her name. Maybe," he cried, stimulated by a sudden thought, "she's related to that Mr. Moncure with one leg. It looked like the same canoe."

"Lydia Moncure," Muriel repeated in an entirely changed voice. "Are you sure that was her name?"

"Course I'm sure," he snapped and Barbara nodded her head solemnly.

"And how," Lucy asked, her own speech miraculously smoother, "did you help her?"

Ashley cleared his throat again and stirred up the gravel with one foot while he strove to embroider accurately Barbara's original version.

"Well, she was out there on the lake and she couldn't paddle awful well."

"She stinks," his associate supplied without expression. It gave him time to rally breath and imagination.

"And she was trying to get to the island and the wind kept blowing the canoe around, so we thought we'd better go help her and—well, we did."

"How?" Lucy asked, and for the instant he was hard pressed.

"Look," Muriel cried suddenly. "There she is."

Beyond the green mound that was Martin's Island, a red craft, small in the distance, moved up the lake. A tiny figure in red plied a sparkling paddle. This and the following wind hurried the canoe along. Lucy watched its passage for a long moment and no one spoke until she said at last, in a new voice:

"Well, I think that was really very, very nice of you, Ashley."

She smiled down upon the two dazed faces, one puckered with amazement, the other inscrutably calm.

"Come, darlings," she said fondly. "It's time for lunch."

CHAPTER VI

Harrison wrote in his calm, good-humored way of Washington's heat. Lucy reread his letter on the shaded porch and felt how the small sense of guilt, quickened by her husband's complaint, was overwhelmed by the pleasant contrast between her lot and his. She wondered as she slipped the pages back into their envelope whether contentment did not really spring from the knowledge that you had something pleasant someone else was without.

Lucy turned the thought over idly. Surely Harrison's account of his discomfort had made her own surroundings lovelier still. It was warm even here. The sun's heat had driven Ashley and Barbara into the shade of a pine where they pursued with muted voices the bickering that was the chief apparent product of their association. At Lucy's feet, the puppy Azrael lay in a contorted posture of utter ease. He puffed apoplectically in his slumber but he was a constitutionally overheated creature and the mild gusts that blew in from the flaw-haunted lake were truly cooling.

It was good, Lucy thought with a sudden upsurging of glee, to be alive. No matter how reprehensible it might be, it was good to know that other folk were less blessed than she. It added luster to a morning already dazzling.

To others, the day might have appeared standard equipment for late June. There was dust on the leaves of the birches beside the driveway, and in the garden the iris had passed their prime. Roses were in bloom. Lucy fancied she could smell their faint perfume through the strong pine scent the sun distilled. Her eyes assured her that the morning was faintly sultry and dull of hue: her mind found in it dazzling radiance. This was a day to be forever memorable.

In two hours now—Lucy glanced at her wrist watch and made certain it had not stopped—she and Muriel and Ashley would lunch at the ancient, the lately revived and rehallowed mansion of the Starkweathers. Her heart squeezed in response to the thought, as already it had a hundred times since Larry Moncure had brought the invitation, set down at Mrs. Starkweather's dictation in Miss Pinch's copperplate hand.

It was, Lucy thought—and consulted her watch again—almost time that Ashley went upstairs to bathe and array himself in ceremonial attire. She was glad her son was to be exposed to association with a contemporary more suitable than his persistent, lumpish playmate. She let her mind run pleasantly on advantages that might accrue through intimacy between Ashley and little Lydia Moncure and thought, with a shade less ease, of the inordinate amount of time it was taking Muriel to dress.

Something lately had muted Muriel's gaiety the barest trifle; had turned her more than usually absentminded; had swung her back and forth between periods of intolerant scoffing and of a quietness almost wistful. Lucy wondered, not for the first time, whether Muriel was falling in love.

If this were so, it surely was not Bailey Ward who disturbed her. Despite the arrival of the tan and silver uniform of the Women's Auxiliary Corps and the sundry drills and meetings to which the girl had worn it, Muriel treated the director of Walden's defenses a shade more carelessly than heretofore.

Lucy hoped her sister was missing Dick Banning more than she would admit. With a recurring twinge that was the mental replica of a tooth's foreboding stir, she wondered if Muriel were in the process of losing her head about Larry Moncure.

They had seen him twice since their meeting in Walden's control center—once when he had beached his canoe on their shore and had limped up to ask himself to tea; again when he had brought them Mrs. Starkweather's invitation. Lucy remembered both visits with an almost daunting clarity. There was a boyish eagerness about the man that warmed her, yet he was wholly at ease and he laughed, perhaps over-much, with Muriel and paid her impudent compliments. Each time, the girl's color had been higher, her eyes brighter, her manner more distracted after his departure.

Lucy sighed. You couldn't warn Muriel. And besides, what was there to warn her against? Nothing, the older woman admitted with an empty feeling; nothing for which there were other than dusty old words, ancient, half-comic copybook maxims.

She found herself wishing suddenly that Harrison were here. She needed to talk to someone about Muriel, and Harrison was the sole person of her acquaintance who would understand and would not laugh at her. For an instant, she actually missed him and was so startled by this sharp fact that she sat up straighter in the cane rocker. It creaked and Azrael, rousing, whacked the porch dreamily with his tail.

Lucy looked at her watch again and called to her son:

"Ashley, it's time you were getting dressed. You'll have to excuse him now, Barbara. He's going out to lunch."

Her son rose with that look of sorely-tried patience mothers learn to expect. Barbara got up more slowly and rubbed herself with untempered candor.

"I know," she said. "He's goin' to that Lydia Moncure's."

"To Mrs. Starkweather's," Lucy corrected and hoped that Barbara would be accurate in relaying the tidings to her mother. "Hurry, Ashley. I've laid everything out on your bed, darling."

"Well, g'by," the plump child said. Her comrade only grunted. Lucy told her:

"Perhaps we'll have little Lydia over here some day soon and you can all play together. That'll be nice, won't it?"

"No'm, it won't," Barbara said without expression and trudged away. Her air was not desolate, she waddled slightly as she walked and her round face was wholly calm, yet Lucy found pathos in her progress.

The expedition, by dint of a final furore, managed to depart on time. Though a full hour had been allowed Ashley in which to dress, Lucy found him toward its close only half clad and was obliged to thrust him into the remaining garments. Then, when all three had embarked, it was discovered that Azrael, by deft stealth of which so haphazard a creature seemed incapable, had stowed himself away in the station wagon's rear. He refused with genial obstinacy to be evicted until Lucy, Muriel, and Cyril pulled together and drew him forth like a cork from a bottle.

Azrael and Mr. Handrow, wrapped in a common air of disillusionment, shambled off to the barn, where amid wry objurgations the puppy was tethered on the shady side. Azrael lay and chewed with moody relish upon the imprisoning rope, and in the subsequent hours made appreciable progress. The station wagon started, halted while Ashley, who it was belatedly discovered lacked a clean handkerchief, went back under protest to find one, moved off once more and did not pause again.

Ashley, seated between his mother and aunt and considerably cramped on either hand, wriggled and mumbled to himself, yet was more nearly at ease than either of his companions. By the standards of childhood where democracy most nearly takes brief root, this was just another grown-up party to which he was being hauled and not even the thought of Lydia's presence could wholly dispel its prospective dreariness. For him, it had no deep significances, no overtones of splendor. He expected, not too meekly, to be bored.

Neither of his seatmates shared his resolute gloom. Lucy, in white sharkskin jacket and skirt and a blue silk blouse, sat stiffly erect, hands folded in her lap. Her costume, she felt, might be prim yet its severity should recommend her to Mrs. Starkweather. In any event, it furnished a foil for Muriel's brilliant loveliness. The girl's green rayon frock deepened the hue of her eyes and stressed fiery glintings in her hair.

She was, Lucy thought with a throb half pride, half pity, beautiful. The long, fair curves of her body ran upward sweetly to hold aloft the eager head and meet in the tender molding of her breasts. She seemed wrapped in a radiance, a dusky intense glow that Lucy wished Dick Banning might see. She was not so sure that she wanted Moncure to observe it.

They talked in brief, brittle sentences. Muriel drove a shade more jerkily than usual. It wasn't, Lucy thought with a surge of tender indignation, fair. It wasn't just or merciful that life, everlastingly, should play such unpleasant jokes upon the young, giving them intense, alluring bodies and withholding maturity of mind to steer them clear of anguish. Most people were more intelligent and kind than the Providence they praised so highly.

The trees whirled past on either hand; the road ran back beneath the engine's hood. Gradually, as they neared their goal, Lucy's and Muriel's inconsequent speech slackened. It died as the car rolled between vine-draped gateposts onto a lately repaired driveway, past an empty lodge, past an immense and now deserted stable, through shade cast by a gloomily austere file of Norway spruces. These moved back to reveal the Starkweather dwelling to which the Senator had brought his bride, in which the Ambassador himself had been born.

"Here we are," said Lucy, unnecessarily, but triteness seemed better than the increasingly taut stillness.

The house lay, ungainly as a couchant giraffe, upon its knoll, and looked uncomfortable in its suit of fresh buff paint. A tower, adorned with windows of stained glass, rose above the structure's awkward mass. Gables shouldered each other and the wens that were bow windows looked as though they had reached an operable stage. It was queer, Lucy thought, that people of a time when all things were plain and sure should have made such jumbled intricacies of their dwellings, with iron balconies and arched doorways and each clean line of ridgepole or eaves broken and tangled by scrollwork. The same impulse, she supposed, had been responsible for the lace ruffles women of that day wore, to their considerable discomfort, upon their drawers. She giggled nervously and felt Muriel look at her.

The station wagon halted beside the granite horseblock, beneath the porte-cochere. Wide steps ascended to a vine-shaded veranda with startling wooden columns.

"We should have come," Lucy thought, "in a barouche. We should have bustle-augmented rears for all beholders to admire as we get out."

Muriel switched off the engine, opened the door beside her and jumped down, moving so calmly that Lucy knew she too was frightened. She could generally tell how Muriel felt by looking at her and believing the opposite.

"Come, Ashley," his mother prompted and added in a hushed voice for the twentieth time that morning, "And you will remember your manners, won't you, darling?"

Ashley only stared about him with an enviably calm interest. A man whom Lucy recognized as chauffeur of the Starkweather heirloom appeared from nowhere at Muriel's elbow. He touched his cap.

"Keys, Miss?" he asked. Muriel gave them to him. He drove the station wagon away as though it were a blight to be abolished as swiftly as possible. A maid in uniform had appeared in the doorway and waited there for them to climb the steps. Lucy wondered, ascending, how it would be possible for her to eat when her stomach already was packed with lead. Her knees were quaking.

She paused an instant on the porch and looked back over the shorn but still uneven lawn to the lake, shining between tall elms, and at the ornate boathouse on its edge. Larry Moncure's amused voice asked:

"If you're lookin' for the iron deer, he's gone. He'd rusted so badly Grandmother gave him to the scrap drive. Doesn't seem quite right without him, does it?"

He stood at Muriel's side and smiled into her startled face. His white suit harmonized with his deliberately broadened drawl—the gray, bold eyes sent a prickling disturbance along her spine.

"Come in," he bade. "I've built a special cocktail in your honor, over Grandmother's protest. The Senator never drank anything stronger than sherry until afternoon, but he generally managed to be thoroughly cooked by bedtime, I understand. Grandmother's in the parlor."

Moncure held open the screen door and grinned at the small boy who trailed in.

"Hi, Ashley," he said. "Oh, listen:"

He dropped his voice and spoke more rapidly.

"Lydia's told me about running away in the canoe. Don't say anything to her mother about it. I promised we wouldn't. You know how mothers are."

He squeezed the boy's shoulder and guided him through a dim hall, marble-tiled, with looming dark furniture, into a high-ceiled room. Sunlight streamed through the tall windows but, entering unannounced, ventured no further into a chamber where gloom had dwelt too long ever to be routed.

Lucy got a confused impression of overstuffed chairs, of tables with edges fretted and legs bulbous in the most unlikely places, of wall portraits regarding her with kindred expressions of disparagement. A vast and gilded clock surmounted a funereal marble mantelpiece and a monstrous crystal chandelier, an inverted, dully gleaming fountain, promised at any minute to give way and immerse Mrs. Eliphalet Starkweather who sat beneath it. In the event of such downfall, Lucy thought, it would be the prisms, not the grim old woman, that would break.

"You're scared," Lucy's mind informed her. "You're frightened stiff, Mrs. Applegate. You don't belong in this—this mausoleum. If you had the sense God gave to chipmunks, you wouldn't have come."

She wished that her legs were as stiff and firmly fixed as her smile. She wished that the portraits wouldn't glare at her so and that the three elders who sat together in this gloomy chamber reminded her less of a fragment of Macbeth. It was silly, Lucy told herself severely, to be scared of a mustachioed dowager in a black dress. She tried to regain confidence by a desperate, imaginary disrobing of Mrs. Starkweather. That, she found, didn't help. Her mind would advance only so far as a picture of the matriarch in corset cover and underwear—probably lace-trimmed, too—and this was even more daunting than the actuality.

Miss Pinch, who had been seated at her employer's side, sprang up and stowed away pen and notebook with a wan smile. On the dowager's other hand, Mrs. Throckmorton, gray and vague and limp as the knitting she held in plump hands, beamed mildly at no one in particular. It was Mehitabel Moncure, slim, preposterously modern in white, who advanced from the shadows. One hand was held out in greeting, the other towed a thin, long-legged child.

"I'm so glad," she said, clasping Lucy's and then Muriel's palm with cool, firm fingers. "Grandmother," she prompted, turning. "You remember Mrs. Applegate and Miss Ashley?"

"Remember," Mrs. Starkweather echoed in her startling voice. "Don't be an idiot, Mehitabel. Good God, who asked them? Come here, my dear. Miss Ashley, how do you do? And this is your son, Mrs. Applegate? Excellent. My son, the Ambassador, used to be a homely little boy with freckles."

Doubt as to the actual sex of the deep-toned, mustached enigma before him so thoroughly confused Ashley that he missed disparagement in the utterance. His blank bewilderment momentarily lent him a spurious air of self-possession that filled his mother's heart with pride.

"This," Mehitabel said, "is my daughter, Lydia."

There was an uncommon note in her voice as she presented the child to Lucy and Muriel in turn. Lydia's long legs bent in a creditable curtsy. She held out her hand, on introduction to Ashley, with a precociously dazzling smile.

"Hi," he mumbled and ducked his head.

"I'm so glad," said Lydia. "I miss people of my own age."

Mehitabel smoothed the child's dark ringlets with a tender gesture that warmed Lucy. However remote and numb the young woman might be, it was plain that she was a devoted parent.

"Suppose," Mehitabel suggested, "you and Ashley stroll about the grounds until luncheon time."

Her eyes fondly followed the children from the room.

"Do sit down," she begged the remaining guests. "Larry will bring cocktails in a minute."

"Unless," Mrs. Starkweather amended, "either of you prefers sherry. The Senator always said, 'Cocktails are drinks for twenty-five cents and imbeciles.'"

"Miss Pinch has gone for the sherry, Grandmother," Mehitabel assured her, and turning to Muriel and Lucy added, "You'll disappoint Larry if you don't like his brew. It's a drink he learned to make in Spain."

Mrs. Starkweather patted the chair Miss Pinch had deserted and said to Lucy:

"Come and sit here. My better ear is on this side. Tell me something more about this Walden defense effort. Bailey Ward seems an industrious young man."

Lucy hesitated an instant and was about to say that her sister was a better authority on Ward and local war activities than she, but Muriel had seated herself already on a small, ornately carved sofa and Mrs. Starkweather's eyes were compelling.

The old woman's questions were so brisk, her interest in the other's replies so apparently candid, that Larry was holding out an amber-filled glass to Lucy before she was aware that he had returned.

"A hellish thing," Mrs. Starkweather announced, looking upon it with disfavor. "You're sure you wouldn't prefer sherry? Whatever has become of Pinch?"

"Here, Mrs. Starkweather," her companion's breathless voice replied. She circled Larry with her laden salver exactly, Lucy thought, as though she feared he might profanely tweak her.

"Pay no heed to Grandmother," the man advised. His eyes met hers so earnestly that Lucy found herself momentarily breathless.

"I've made these special," he pursued. "They're my best public accomplishment."

Lucy took the glass a shade unsteadily. His regard was as physical as an intrusive hand. He moved away, bearing his tray.

Mrs. Starkweather lifted her sherry glass with a stiff-elbowed gesture that Lucy wondered if she had learned from the Senator and, emptying the contents into her mouth, rolled them about with a calculating frown before she swallowed.

"Better," she announced at last, "than that swill they sent from Boston. It's as difficult to get decent sherry these days as it is to elect a person of breeding to office."

Larry Moncure stood before Muriel, glass in hand, and looked at her so steadily that she felt her face grow warm.

"Honey pie," he reproved, "was I twins, I could squeeze in on both sides of you at once. Move over, just a mite. Not too much."

Ashley and Lydia strolled along the gravel walk that led toward the boathouse. Gruffness, compounded of his mother's admonitions to politeness, unfamiliarity with his surroundings, and a waxing admiration for his companion marked the boy's responses to her vivacious chatter. A man in blue jeans who hacked with shears at a line of rankly overgrown shrubs looked up and touched his cap as Lydia passed.

"Good morning, Wilkins," she said in so oddly condescending a voice that Ashley stared.

"He's our gard'ner," Lydia explained as they moved on. "We've had him for ever so long."

"Gosh," Ashley conceded, "you keep a lot of help."

She lifted her slight shoulders.

"My dear, don't be quaint," she protested. "We're practically servantless. Just four in the house, if you don't count old Pinch, and Wilkins for the outside work and Roberts. He's chauffeur. Of course," she added defiantly, "there was Mamselle too. Only she's gone."

"Yeah?" he asked. "Who was she?"

Lydia took a dancing step forward before she answered. She wasn't so bad, Ashley thought, when you got used to her. She was sort of homely at first and then she looked nice, kind of. Her eyes made you feel all prickly when she looked at you hard. Emotions that six years hence would be as routine with him as breathing were invading Ashley's hitherto unromantic ego for the first time.

Lydia whirled about, stood for no clear reason on tiptoe and wriggled attractively before she asked:

"Did Daddy speak to you about the canoe?"

Ashley nodded.

"Uh-huh. He said not to say anything."

She came and stood quite close to him.

"That's because," she confided with her gray eyes hard at work, "there was an awful row and Mamselle got fired. She called me a liar."

Her awe at the magnitude of this offense roused Ashley's curiosity. He blurted:

"Why?"

"Oh, because," Lydia replied lightly, "I said I hadn't been out in the canoe."

"Huh?" he asked, bewildered. "You had."

"I know," she admitted with no trace of humility, "but she had absolutely no right to call me a liar. Daddy said so. I told him all about it, finally, and Daddy said we wouldn't tell Mother. She gets upset so easily. She's high strung, Daddy says."

Ashley stared at the possessor of so sympathetic and co-operative a father. His open and flattering envy pleased Lydia. She gave a small gesture, so Gallic that it must originally have been a possession of the routed Mamselle.

"The whole thing," she told her companion, "was very tiresome. I'm a born canoer. Daddy thinks so, too. And anyway, if I did tip over, what difference would it make? I could swim back and forth across the whole lake a couple of times without getting tired."

Male pride impelled Ashley, whose watery prowess was limited to a few strokes while a reassuring toe dragged on the bottom, to say:

"Sure; who couldn't?"

Lydia broke a twig from a shrub and smelled it, but her large eyes remained fixed on him.

"How," she asked suddenly, "is that quaint, fat little girl?"

"Barbara? Okay, I guess."

"She's your sweetheart, isn't she?"

The idea was so preposterous that he gaped before he found his voice.

"Her? No!"

"I'll bet you have a dozen, though. Boys are all alike," Lydia told him in plagiarized tone.

Her eyes, once more, were doing something radical to his interior. She sidled closer and he shared without knowing it the fascinated apathy of the snake-charmed bird.

"No," he insisted, like an over-eager applicant for a job. "I have not, either. Honest, Lydia."

His companion drew closer still. He could see his own face, reflected small and clear in her compelling eyes. Lydia said softly:

"I like you, Ashley. I think you're nice."

He wondered what would happen if he kissed her. He wondered, groping and fumbling among urgent and wholly unaccustomed emotions, where he had got the growing impression that she wanted him to. Her face was close to his. Her mother's voice shattered the spell.

"Darling," it called from the porch, "Lydia, precious. Lunch is ready. Come along."

"Oh, damn," Lydia snapped in exasperation. He followed her up the gravel walk, too wholly bereft of wind to say anything.

Yet a glow enwrapped him as he sat beside his mother at the table laid on a screened end of the veranda. The white shine of the cloth, the glitter of silver and glass were dull compared to the radiant, if blurred, visions that swam in and out of his overstimulated mind. He was too preoccupied with these to pay any special heed to what went on about him. He could not have been aware, even in a more observant moment, that his mother shared several of his phenomenal sensations. Lucy had drunk, under Larry's persuasion, three of his cocktails. She was grateful now that she had withstood his attempt to pour her a fourth.

Anything could have happened if she had not refused the last, she thought while giving apparent heed to Mrs. Starkweather's blow-by-blow account of the ancient battle for suffrage. Larry's creation had abolished her earlier taut vigilance. She was relaxed and pleasantly at ease. Inner warmth that neither the chilled melon nor the cold, bland Madrilene dispelled mellowed her. Her senses seemed augmented, too. She could hear, despite her hostess's virile voice, what Larry, at the table's far end, was saying to Muriel and Lydia on his either hand.

"Governor Deal said to me, 'Mrs. Starkweather, you're letting enthusiasm run away with you and I cannot follow.' He might have been president if he had not ignored my counsel."

"How extremely interesting," Lucy said. She wondered whether it was the cocktails or what Larry now was whispering to her that made Muriel's face so brilliant. She was worth any man's admiration, yet Lucy debated whether the man's indifference to his grandmother-in-law's brief glances was born of innocence or defiance.

The glass beside her plate had been filled with straw-colored wine. It was cool and sweetly sour.

"Delicious," Lucy told her hostess, yet she regarded the glass warily. It might be best not to tinker with the lovely balance she had achieved. She did not wish to blur the clear, warm satisfaction that was hers now.

"Johannisberger, '29, Gram," Mehitabel was saying.

"Excellent," Mrs. Starkweather pronounced. "Good still comes out of Nazareth."

Her alert gray eyes strayed from the wine before her to the table's far end. Larry gave a comic gesture and he and Muriel laughed together. The child, Lydia, was lolling in her chair with a sullen look, but Miss Pinch, who sat between her and Ashley, uttered a mild titter.

"It's all right," Lucy reassured herself, disturbed for an instant by the intensity of the old woman's regard, "or that poor parched creature wouldn't think it was funny. I do wish though that he would stop entertaining Muriel quite so much. Maybe his wife doesn't mind but I'm positive Mrs. Starkweather doesn't like it."

She had the feeling that the lid had been removed from the matriarch, revealing, briefly, normally hidden significances. The disclosure made Lucy uneasy but the tingling sense of well-being repossessed her and made her serenely philosophic.

Everything had its lid, after all—a covering beneath which it wasn't decent for people to pry. Houses covered the not-always-agreeable intimacies of their inmates; enamel's and tile's and chromium's glittering purity was used to conceal the unsanitary occupations to which bathrooms were dedicated. Clothes probably were first worn not as protection from cold but to keep mankind from being dismally reminded of what it looked like.

Life, Lucy reflected, with a feeling inside her as though the morning stars sang there together, was really an onion—layer after layer of protection overlying not very much. Mrs. Starkweather's cover was back in place, anyway. She was speaking calmly to Mrs. Throckmorton who had suspended her bovine attention to food.

Lucy thrust her recent mild distress away. This was no time to worry about anything. This was really a lovely old house, inhabited by extremely delightful people. Even Miss Pinch and Mrs. Throckmorton were agreeable, after you got to know them—or after the third drink.

What had Larry Moncure put into those cocktails to give one so sweet a sense of ease, so glowing a self-confidence, so happy a conviction that all present were her dear and charming friends? Everything was too lovely for words.

There was, however, something wrong with the tablecloth. As Lucy stared, it actually rippled, rolling in small slow waves in her direction. She blinked. The white billows subsided.

"Get hold of yourself, Mrs. Applegate," she bade with a pang of alarm. "Why, you're tight as a hoot owl."

She looked about her cautiously but no one else seemed aware of her condition. Lucy smiled with new confidence. She realized that the waitress stood at her elbow, offering a jellied oblong, intricately adorned.

"I hope," Mrs. Starkweather supplied a footnote, "that you like eggs in aspic. We had them specially today because I know children are fond of them. They are my great granddaughter's delight."

Lucy transferred a quivering segment from dish to plate. Moncure and Muriel were talking more earnestly now and Lydia was slumped still further in her chair. Children had not yet acquired plausible coverings. That was what made them so delightful—part of the time.

Mehitabel was looking fondly toward her daughter. Lydia sat up straighter and stared at the dish the waitress offered for a long instant before she shook her head.

"No, thank you," she proclaimed, "I don't care for any."

Out of the brief silence, her mother spoke:

"Don't you care for any? But, darling, they're eggs aspic."

Lydia shook her head. Lucy felt the child had created this scene because, heretofore, she had not been receiving the attention she considered her due. Now she said firmly in response to Mehitabel's protest:

"I know. I just don't want any."

"Aren't you well, precious?" Mrs. Starkweather inquired, but her great granddaughter ignored her. Mehitabel's remote expression had crumbled into a look of genuine concern that echoed in her voice.

"Is anything the matter, darling?"

Larry regarded the child more narrowly.

"What is it, Lyd?" his lazy voice inquired. "An ache or an act?"

His daughter, now the center of the entire table's regard, told her mother languidly:

"I'm perfectly all right. I just don't care for eggs aspic any more."

"Something else then?" Mehitabel urged. "A little cold chicken? A nice slice of ham?"

Lydia shook her head at each suggestion. She said at last:

"I might be able to eat a little omelet."

"Delia," Mehitabel told the waitress, quickly, "tell Mary to cook a plain omelet for Miss Lydia."

So easy a solution of the problem did not satisfy Miss Lydia.

"A Spanish omelet," she persisted. "The way you do it, Mummy." Mehitabel pushed back her chair.

"Excuse me just a few moments," she said. There was apology in her voice but relief shone in her eyes. One could be, Lucy reflected, too devoted a mother. Lydia's triumph irked her. It did not wholly gratify Mrs. Starkweather who confided in a husky mutter:

"The child is whimsical. She is with older people all the while and we indulge her too much. She needs association with children her own age. She's a dear little thing, though; remarkably clever."

Pride broke through her disapproval. She smiled upon her name-sake and Lydia, triumphant, beamed in return and sat straighter in her chair.

Lucy considered Ashley, perched mute and sleek beside her, with an unusual commingling of satisfaction and savagery. She found herself half wishing that he might commit some insurgency. Unable to offer Lydia the chastisement she felt the child deserved she would have welcomed the opportunity of punishing her own son in indirect reprisal.

The outrageous yearning faded. The mellow sense of well-being possessed her again. His wife's absence seemed to have thrust responsibility upon Larry, who talked no longer solely to Muriel but addressed the entire company in his amusing drawl. Even Mrs. Throckmorton, whose sole interest in the gathering had been, here-tofore, alimentary, smiled at the obviously fantastic anecdotes he related of Lydia's babyhood and the problems it had presented. Mrs. Starkweather grinned.

"She likes him," Lucy told herself. "She's really very fond of him, and yet I don't think she trusts him."

He might not be trustworthy. Anyone of his probable age whose blunt features were still so preposterously boyish, must be instinctively adept in subterfuge. Anyone who could make the lethargic Mrs. Throckmorton quake like the aspic and wring an unpremeditated titter from the wan Miss Pinch surely could charm whomsoever he chose.

The warmth of her feeling for Larry startled Lucy, yet he truly was appealing. His bland impudence of a naughty youngster; the air of verity with which he recited obvious extravagances, glazed and half hid the underlying baffling derision.

Mehitabel, flushed of face, returned to her seat while they were still laughing over her husband's burlesqued reminiscence of the Spanish Civil War. It would be exciting, Lucy thought involuntarily, to live intimately with such a man. It would be perilous and painful, too, but certainly it could never be dull.

The waitress set the omelet before the recently torpid Lydia who ate with vigor. In the ease and relaxation that Larry Moncure bestowed, Ashley made his first public utterance since the meal had begun.

"Were you a general, sir?" he asked and reddened at the sound of his own voice and the grin the man gave him. He floundered on. "I mean, you were a leader of some kind, I'll bet. Weren't you?"

"I was," Moncure said with extreme gravity. "I was indeed, and the Duke of Plaza Toro was my inspiration. When there was any fighting, my place was in the rear; if the line broke, I assumed command and led the retreat—well out in front at the start and gaining every jump. When I lost my foot, I lost my job."

"How?" the boy demanded, eagerly.

"Ashley Applegate!" His mother pounced upon him. "You mustn't ask personal questions."

"Nonsense," Moncure said. "No other sort is ever worth asking, Ashley. The foot? I lost it in a taxi accident, son. In Madrid. Very, very savage to strangers, those Madrid taxicabs."

"Oh, Daddy, you did not, either," Lydia squealed over a mouthful of omelet. "That is, not exactly."

"Oh, positively," Moncure said gravely. His eyes narrowed a trifle as his wife spoke. She said crisply, as though she were abolishing objectionable pretense:

"He drove a cab-load of ammunition up to the lines at the University under fire—and got it there, too."

Larry grinned at her explanation. He seemed to have recognized reproof.

"Since then," he told Ashley, "I've been a very peaceful man, cringing at the least harsh word and jumping as far as I can if a firecracker goes off within earshot. By the way, Lyd-honey; no crackers for you this Fourth of July. Everyone's fresh out of 'em. No more for duration."

"Aw, gee," the child said and looked annoyed.

"Never mind," her father assured her. "We'll cook up some way of celebrating Independence Day."

"A celebration?" Mrs. Starkweather's baritone inquired. "A requiem would be more fitting."

"Oh," Lucy said, smitten by a sudden purpose. She marked the faces turned toward her and felt her own grow hot.

"I mean," she explained, "I just had an idea. We have a picnic on the Fourth. On Martin's Island. It's very simple but lots of fun, we think. We'd love to have Lydia go with us—and, of course, anyone else who is easily amused."

"Why, how very delightful that sounds, doesn't it, Lydia, darling?" Mehitabel said after slight hesitation. Her husband added, and Lucy fancied there was latent mockery in his voice:

"July Fourth, at noon? Magnificent. Can we reserve places for three, close to the lunch basket?"

Muriel's blank regard, which might be public substitute for warn-ing or dismay and most certainly was not wholehearted approval, made Lucy aware of the dimensions of the project she had under-taken so lightly. She herself felt momentary awe, but the warm tide of well-being swept in again and abolished it. These all were charming, simple people. They would be fun to have at a picnic, whether Muriel approved or not.

"That will be simply swell," she said, yet added, "If you're sure it won't bore you."

"Preposterous," Larry assured her. Lucy wished he wouldn't al-ways speak with mockery or extravagance. Didn't he ever have an unpremeditated moment? Anyway, her current plight was largely his fault. His cocktails had been responsible for her rash invitation. All right, then; let him and his wife be bored, or con-descendingly amused. Lucy told herself stoutly that she didn't give a whoop. Nevertheless, for a panicky instant, she wished words were not such inevitable things. Life would be simpler if they were like checks that could be torn up or stopped from payment, if you changed your mind at the last moment. She faltered:

"They're rather modest affairs, our Fourth of July picnics, but Ashley always enjoys them and I hope Lydia will. Martin's Island is really pretty, anyway."

"Martin's Island," Mrs. Starkweather repeated thoughtfully. "I haven't been there in more than forty years."

"I wish you might come, too," Lucy said. Here was one invita-tion at least that she could press without alarming consequences.

"I shall be delighted," the old woman said resonantly. Lucy choked, found her wine glass and gulped half its contents.

"Grandmother!" Mehitabel protested. "It's a picnic."

"I'm aware of that," Mrs. Starkweather replied, ruffling herself like an aged but indomitable hawk. "We used to have picnics on Martin's Island when the Ambassador was no older than Lydia is now. I should like very much to go again."

"Splendid," Lucy said and wondered whether the word sounded as faint as she felt.

"But how, Grandmother?" Mehitabel persisted. "Martin's Island is out in the middle of the lake."

"It always was," her ancestress returned. "The Senator's boat in which he used to fish is still in the boathouse. Larry, tell Wilkins to launch it and, if it leaks, as it probably does, to calk it."

"It shall be done," Larry assured her gravely, but he glanced at Lucy with mirth in his eyes. "Furthermore, I shall row you in state, personally, to the revel. Lyd and Hit can take the canoe."

"Thank you," Mrs. Starkweather said, "for not thinking up any more objections. I shall probably die, eventually, of something much less agreeable than a picnic. I accept with pleasure, Mrs. Applegate."

"Attagirl, Greatgram," Lydia shrilled. The old woman beamed upon her, then turned to Lucy. Her eyes were vital, her voice strong.

"Pay no attention to these children, my dear. I'm not made of wet tissue paper, and I have no intention of dying for at least another ten years. I'm determined to see the outcome of this catastrophe into which the Democrats have plunged us. I think its conclusion is bound to be a pleasant surprise. Certainly it can't be as frightful as I have every reason to believe it will be."

CHAPTER VII

Larry Moncure stood beside the station wagon. he gave an extravagantly Spanish gesture.

"Until July Fourth," he said. *"Hasta la vista."*

He dropped his voice and added in Lucy's ear:

"If you find you don't want us, you can always be ill."

He gave her a peculiar smile, at once boyish and adroitly mocking.

Muriel paid disproportionate attention to her driving until the station wagon had passed through the vine-clad gateway. She glanced at her sister with a hard little grin.

"Well, darling, I didn't know even you could stick your neck out so far."

"I know," Lucy admitted with nervous laughter. "Neither did I. Whatever made me do it, I wonder? Isn't it awful?"

"Won't it be awful," Muriel correctly grimly. "Angel, those people have been everywhere, done everything. Can you picture them enjoying themselves with Barbara's mother—"

"Martha Spofford is a thoroughly nice person," Lucy defended, partly from conviction, partly because Ashley was listening.

"She is," her sister agreed. "And that's all. And there'll be Ben Spofford, too. He'll be even harder to take and he's bound to be here for the weekend. Won't he and Larry have fun together?"

Lucy's compressed lips checked the instinctive question. She was glad it had not been uttered. First names were easy handles for girls of Muriel's age. Her use of Moncure's probably did not mean a thing. Lucy glanced at her sister, so young and bright, so flagrantly sure of herself, and for an instant seemed actually to feel the warm, purblind forces that struggled beneath sophistication's enamel shell. For a breath's space, insight endured and then was blurred by an unlikely mingling of suspicion and tenderness that welled up about the older woman's heart.

They drove out of sunlight into shadow cast by pines' thick stand. Lucy said:

"Well, I've done it, anyway. Maybe it will be good for them to find out how the other nineteen-twentieths live and maybe they'll all have fun, too."

Muriel said in a softer voice:

"Larry Moncure really is the most amusing person and yet, somehow, I get the feeling that he isn't happy."

"I'm practically certain his wife isn't," Lucy answered and her sister laughed.

"Darling," she said, in the difficult tone Lucy long ago had labeled her Voice of Experience, "don't be so stuffy. You needn't remind me he's married. He— Oooh!"

A man had stepped out of a path into the road, directly before them. They saw fright twist his face at the brakes' squeal, but he did not draw back. A frantic leap bore him past the locked and sliding car. He scrambled, dingy, furtive, up the bank and with a single backward glance, dodged like a fleeing rabbit between the pines until their boles, massing in the distance, hid him entirely.

Over the head of the aggrieved Ashley, who nearly had been pitched into the windshield by the violence of the station wagon's halt, Lucy and Muriel stared at each other. The man had appeared and vanished with laughable haste but there had been something in his flight that checked mirth.

"What was that for?" Muriel asked at length. "Why, he went like—like a wild animal; as though someone were chasing him."

"Or he was chasing someone," Lucy added. Her sister chuckled.

"Men so often are, eh, angel?"

Nothing followed the fugitive. For a long minute, cowering behind the trees' barrier, he sought only for breath. Thereafter he wiped his dripping face with a shaky hand. Fright still twitched at his china-blue eyes.

Presently, the man spoke in a low, flustered voice. He cursed himself thoroughly while he squinted down the brief, ill-defined aisles beneath the pines' dark ceiling.

He could have kicked the whole thing over by acting like a maniac because he met a car. There was sour, yet comforting amusement in remembering the blank faces of the station wagon's occupants. They had been scared as he; scareder maybe.

Panicky flight had done his legs no good. They would not hurry enough, yet they bore him at last out of the pines into a cut-over waste of swamp and slash and scrub. He found himself moving through the open with shoulders hunched and breath warily drawn.

He had come a long way and, on the whole, fortunately. If his luck only held for a little longer, if the shack only was still there, he would find safety at last—shelter and security in which he could dwell all summer if necessary until the hunt died down.

The path ran, at last, into a dim lumber road. He followed this for a space and then halted. He looked warily about him. Things had changed since he was here last, but now he was certain. His weary legs pulled him up out of the road and into the gloom of a tall hemlock grove. Through this he hurried as well as he might, pausing as weariness overcame him, pushed on again by waxing anxiety.

He crossed a ridge, went down more quickly over the further slope and thrust his way at length out through clogging under-brush into an ancient clearing studded with moldering stumps, stippled between them by the young green of new growth. The gasp he uttered was fatigue and triumph combined. In the center of the open space stood a crumbling cabin, relic of an ancient lumbering job.

Only black scabs of tarpaper remained on its roof and the stove-pipe slanting up from its side was sagging and rusted, but the structure was fair to the fugitive's tired eyes. No one possibly could come here purposefully. No one, since his uncle, aunt, and cousins all seemed to have left the region, would even remember that this disreputable but heartening haven was here.

Brush rattled about his legs as he lurched toward the cabin. Rusted hinges squealed as he pushed the sagging door open. The stove, redder, more scaled by rust, still was there. Here were all the comforts of home, if you didn't mind sleeping on warped floorboards, if you could manage to live chiefly on air and brook water.

Hunger caught up with him, now that the first and most dire necessity was accomplished. He drew from his coat pocket a pack-age and unwrapping it, considered two sandwiches. Their warped bread slices indicated they already were past their prime. He hesi-tated, rewrapped one and thrust it back into his pocket before he attacked its mate.

Bailey Ward's car was parked in the Applegates' turning circle. Bailey himself came down from the porch to help Lucy, Ashley, and Muriel disembark, with hearty sounds and ponderous raillery aimed chiefly at the Pulchritudinous Person. His costume proclaimed that this was not a mere social or business call but an Occasion.

Ward wore the piebald shoes, white flannels and chocolate brown sports coat that were his festive attire. He was sleek, radiant, determinedly youthful and his geniality was as wilting as a blast from an overheated stove.

Whatever his mission, Lucy thought while Bailey jested ponderously with Muriel whose retorts grew faintly snappish, he had chosen the worst possible time to accomplish it. He would have fared better in his concealed yet doubtless amorous purpose if he had waited until recollection of the merry grace of Larry Moncure had grown a trifle dimmer.

"Duchess," said Ward, beaming upon her, "you looks absolutely tops. You and this little number might be twins."

Lucy pulled her stiff mouth into a smile. It must have been satisfactory, for the glow on the leathery face did not abate. She was ashamed of her acid irritation. Bailey was good and kind and honestly devoted. These were qualities far more to be esteemed than charm or wit. Bailey was virtuous, yet she found herself wishing that he would reveal his still hidden errand and go away.

"So you had a good time, eh," Ward boomed. "Well, that's fine. And I'll bet it was give and take, too. You gave the nobility just as much as you got yourselves."

"It was very pleasant," Muriel told him coolly.

Ward cleared his throat. He seemed immune to chill.

"I've something to tell you," he said in a suddenly awed voice. "Mrs. Starkweather"—if Bailey were High Church, Lucy thought, he would have genuflected at mention of the name—"Mrs. Starkweather has given Walden an air-raid siren."

"How nice," Lucy said. Her sister was startled out of her resolute hauteur by the tidings.

"Not really, Bailey," she cried. "Not the big one?"

"The big one," Ward confirmed solemnly. "We can alarm the whole town without picking up a telephone."

"How enchanting," the girl said. "Isn't she a nice old thing, really?"

Ward said in a husky, reproving voice:

"Mrs. Eliphalet Starkweather is a magnificent character." He cleared his throat again. The sound was a vocal gavel blow, demanding attention.

"There is something more"—pride drove reverence from his voice—"that I hope will interest you. I've sold the Frost property to Stryker & Company."

"Who?" Lucy asked. Walden's leading realtor looked at her reproachfully.

"Stryker & Company," he repeated. "The Frost property."

"Oh, yes," she said dimly. Ward looked unconvincingly modest.

"It will mean much to Walden; that is my first thought. The biggest small arms concern in the East has bought a factory site here for a—a considerable amount, shall we say? Construction begins at once. The payroll will be tremendous."

He contemplated its unrevealed immensity with awe and then discarded dignity.

"In cash involved, it is the biggest transaction ever closed in this part of the state, and I think it warrants a celebration tonight. I hope you both, and the scion too, will make wassail with me at the Old Tyme Tavern. I've already engaged a table."

This, Lucy thought, was the most important thing that had ever happened to him; this was the great achievement of Bailey Ward's career. It was dismaying to see what men really deemed life's chief significances. It would be cruel to mar his perfect elation too. He looked exactly as Ashley had when he got his hockey skates.

She considered the confidently expectant man with genuine sympathy, yet the thought of an evening spent in his version of revelry was daunting.

"Why—" she began, still uncertain of what she should say, but Muriel's crisp voice cut through hers. The girl had been regarding her mature suitor with a singular expression.

"Of course we'll come, Bailey," she told him. "All of us."

"Well, say, now," Ward babbled. "That'll be something."

He beamed on Muriel in what it was clear he believed to be an ardent and compelling manner, glanced at his watch and regarded her again while he mumbled something about getting along soon. He did not stir. It was Lucy, sensitive to atmospheric tension, who rose and hastily excused herself.

Growing exasperation accompanied her upstairs and into her pleasant bedroom where windows looked through pine branches to the distant lake and the silver toilet set that Harrison had given her shone coolly on her dressing table. Lucy wondered how much of her ill temper was due to dislike of Ward, how much to the bleak sense of exclusion that oppressed her. This was one of the times when a man and a woman formed a small, inviolable world of their own where no other might pardonably trespass.

By all visible signs and further portents that only her instinct discerned, Ward was about to propose to Muriel. That, Lucy thought spitefully, was just like him. No overpowering surge of passion, no irresistible urgence had swayed him. His damned siren and his double-damned real estate triumph had convinced him that this was his lucky day. He would, therefore, press his fortune further.

And suppose Muriel accepted him? Lucy's spirit sank at the thought. Suppose she refused him? That didn't seem to hold much comfort either, for it might mean that the girl had been truly fascinated by Larry Moncure's shameless attentions. Either way, Lucy could not see how she was to get much comfort from the outcome of the downstairs conference from which she implicitly had been banished.

She wished for an insurgent instant that she had not invited her sister to spend the summer here. She was growing a little weary of worrying over Muriel. She might as well be a vizier or eunuch or whatever he was.

It might be interesting—even entertaining—to have problems like these to solve for herself. She had rather hoped that they might intrude upon her Sabbatical but all she had done was to struggle helplessly with her sister's affairs. Well, she was an old married woman. What else had she expected?

There was scant satisfaction in being dismissed and sent upstairs so that a man considerably older than herself could prosecute his wooing undeterred. There wasn't much fun in solitary fuming, either. She wished that Harrison were here. It would be a real satisfaction to sputter over her grievances to someone who understood her.

Lucy's mind came to a sudden halt. That was the second time in a few hours that she had wished for Harrison. What had come over her? Did she really and honestly miss him?

Only, she admitted as she undid her skirt and blouse and hung them in her closet, in moments of distress like this.

Harrison was good, she told herself quickly, really and truly good. He was a wise father, a faithful and tolerant husband. Harrison, his wife thought with a faint dismay, had all Bailey Ward's virtues; of course with several additions. Was that why she had felt this trial separation necessary? Had she just grown tired of living with a considerate gentleman?

She heard a prim portion of her mind protest as though it were an independent entity: "Tired of him? Why, my dear, he gives you everything!"

"Phooey!" said Lucy in so loud a voice that she startled herself. That was the trouble. Harrison gave her everything that he could afford, which in many departments was considerably more than she craved. Harrison was reliable and kind and his responses were as unromantically certain as the gush of water when you turned on the faucet.

Why didn't someone, Lucy wondered bitterly as she wrapped herself in a dressing gown, proclaim the resolutely ignored fact that women—even almost elderly wedded women of thirty-four— still craved adventure; still longed for uncertainty and pursuit to break and illumine the routine into which matrimony after fourteen years so inevitably fell?

She pulled her dressing gown more tightly about her and stood before the long mirror bolted to her bedroom door to consider the rounded slope of her shoulders, the ripe yet still firm outline of her breasts, the reciprocal curves of waist and hips, with mixed pride and exasperation. Biologically, she was in her prime; in the full flowering of her body's purposes and their attendant emotions. If she were a horse or a cow everyone would say so. But she was only a married woman and her life, each year for fourteen, had become more serene. Or maybe the right word was routine. The care and the effort that she had spent to keep herself clean-limbed and supple had been just so much wastage. She was one of the comfortably wedded middle-aged. She might as well relax and let herself spread.

Well, she wouldn't. She glared at the gracious reflection as though it actually had proposed surrender. Other wives could alter their values—and their outlines—if they wished, magnifying domesticity, exalting insignificances, exchanging the last remaining vestiges of wild yearning for a stout, if needless, adherence to continence. They surrendered to routine; they settled back into a comfortable matrimonial niche—and then pretty soon someone had to enlarge the niche.

Lucy thought again of Muriel and felt her mind snap back to the remote beginning of its resentful straying. Muriel's youthful valor would wilt; her nymph's body and her gay spirit would coarsen if she became Bailey Ward's wife. Either that, or else she would revolt and kick things over and create resounding scandal.

"Don't be a goop, Mrs. Applegate," Lucy told the figure in the mirror and smiled at the extravagance of her worries. She grew interested in the smile, turning her head about to judge at what angle it seemed most attractive. It fled and a look of alarm replaced it as a car door slammed loudly below and Bailey Ward drove away.

Lucy forced herself to wait. Questions would only drive Muriel into one of her touch-me-not silences. The screen door closed and, after a pause, feet were upon the stair. Their progress sounded ominous.

If Muriel went directly to her room, Lucy wondered whether she herself would have the fortitude not to follow her. The footsteps faltered in the hall and came laggingly toward Lucy's door.

"Come in," she called, at the hesitant knock.

Muriel's air was hardy and she held her head high but her eyes looked larger and her mouth was glaring red against her pallor. The lips, Lucy saw with relief, still were clearly outlined. Bailey hadn't kissed her, or if he had, his salute had been chaste.

"Well?" said Muriel. The words were a challenge.

"Hi, darling," Lucy answered. She turned, opened a bureau drawer and bent above it. "What time is the party?"

The girl lit a cigarette and shook the flame from the match with unnecessary violence. She said, squinting at the smoke:

"There won't be any."

"Postponed?" asked Lucy composedly, selecting a fresh pair of stockings. "I'm not really sorry. We've had enough party for one day."

"Canceled," Muriel reported. She swallowed and pursued in a dry tone:

"It would be rather cockeyed to give a party for a woman who had just refused to marry you, wouldn't it?"

"Yes, my dear," Lucy said quietly, "I suppose it would."

She saw with a pang of sympathy how the girl's brilliant mouth twitched. Suddenly, incredibly, Muriel's grim expression broke up into a grotesque grimace of woe.

"Oh, baby," Lucy said and took her in her arms. Muriel clung to her, shaking her sister's body with the violence of her weeping.

"Darling," Lucy begged, "what is it? Don't cry so, sweet. Are you sorry you sent him away?"

The girl shook her head, spilling warm tears on Lucy's shoulder.

"It isn't that," Muriel sobbed. "I hated to hurt him, but—"

She gasped, tried to get hold of herself and wept again.

"I wish," Muriel wailed, "women weren't so damned female."

CHAPTER VIII

ASHLEY SLEPT LATE ON FOURTH OF JULY MORNING, LULLED BY the fact that there were no firecrackers with which to make dawn hideous, but Lucy woke at daybreak and lay, dreamily listening to the self-righteous announcements of an early robin before recollection of the date roused her completely.

This was not only the anniversary of Independence's birth; it was the, to Lucy, more important day on which the Martin's Island picnic was to be immortalized by the presence of Mrs. Starkweather, her descendants and her grandson-in-law. Other attendants, Lucy recalled with an appreciable diminishment of glee, would be Mr. and Mrs. Spofford and daughter. Neither she nor Muriel had been able to evolve even the most remotely plausible method of recalling their invitation.

Contemplation of the things that must be done before the materials for the festival were in order urged Lucy to be about them at once. She rose and stood for a long moment at the window.

The sky was a pale blue and the beginning of the sunrise a satisfactory yellow, though no dew sparkled on the lawn. Coolness crept beneath her nightgown to touch her breasts and calves. In the woods at the drive's far end, where dusk reluctantly gave way, a hermit thrush wound his penny horn.

Lucy drew in the soft, sweet air. Reluctantly she turned toward bed again. It would be, she told herself as she drew up the sheet, an undignified admission of infantile excitement if she were to go downstairs before the rest of the house was astir. Further sleep, she knew, was beyond her. Her mind leaped with agility from the need of warning Rena to slice the ham thin, to Ashley's costume for the day; from stuffed eggs, to Bailey Ward's still persistent pursuit of Muriel—he had brought her home from a defense meeting only last night.

Lucy wondered whether the watermelon would be sufficiently chilled and inconsequently recalled Larry Moncure's farewell coun-

88

sel that she could always plead illness in time of stress. She smiled. Never had she felt more thoroughly, exhilaratingly alive.

She heard, at last, a stir in the kitchen where Rena and Cyril breakfasted early and more volubly than usual. The shower's chill downpour set Lucy's body to tingling in harmony with her spirit. For the first time, she understood why Harrison sang in the bathroom.

Though she compelled herself to dress slowly, she was downstairs early. Sunlight came through the screen door to lay a crooked rug on the living room floor and the outside world smelled new. Azrael, who was set free at night as a theoretical deterrent to marauders, came ambling from nowhere, panted at her through the screen panel in hope of admission and, rebuffed, let himself fall heavily upon the doormat. Almost instantly, he slept—an occupation to which, Lucy suspected, he had devoted the previous ten hours. Azrael, she reflected, would be a successful burglar alarm only if the criminal actually were to fall over him.

The kitchen door slammed. Cyril came along the drive. He obviously had left the breakfast table recently and hurriedly, for his dentures, still in battery, gave his profile an abnormal protuberant outline. Azrael raised a drowsy head and lazily beat the porch floor with his tail. His geniality did not soften the altered visage of Mr. Handrow who had come to regard the dog an extra affliction in a world already oversupplied. He addressed the puppy with more than his usual bitterness and some inadvertent teeth-clickings.

"Wish ye was mine, by Godfrey. I'd tend to ye quick, ye, ye—"

While he sought for a sufficiently searing epithet, Lucy spoke.

"Good morning, Cyril," she said brightly. "Isn't it a lovely day?"

"Rain 'fore night," her servitor reported promptly. "Mis' Applegate, Rena's wonderin' if ye took the ham."

"The ham?" Lucy repeated. "The ham for the picnic? Good gracious, no."

"Figgered ye hadn't," the other answered with grim relish. "All the same it's gone."

"Gone? You mean Rena can't remember where she put it?"

"No, ma'am." Ill tidings were balm to Cyril's corroded spirit. "She biled it an' baked it an' sot it on the table last night to cool. Plate's thar; ham's gone."

"But," Lucy objected, "who on earth—?"

"Who?" Cyril echoed vehemently and leveled an accusing finger at Azrael who acknowledged the attention with more violent flop-pings of his tail. "Him; that's who! That dam scavenging critter."

"Azrael? A whole ham? Oh, Cyril, what nonsense!"

"Mebby," Mr Handrow acknowledged, yet the glare he bestowed on the puppy was accusation's distillate. "It ain't my ham, Mis' Applegate. It ain't yours no more, for that matter."

"I'll talk to Rena," Lucy promised, and hurried through the house to the kitchen. She and Cyril entered it simultaneously by opposite doors.

Breakfast was ready and Mrs. Handrow was girding herself with a white apron that lay upon her bulk like a mountain-borne glacier. There was uneasiness on Rena's large, commonly bland face and a quaver in her piping voice. She was subject to that excessive feminine timidity which usually afflicts those women who need it least.

"Mis' Applegate," she said, "it's gone." She indicated a greasy platter and added hopefully, "It must have been that dog."

Recognition of the difficulties that would have handicapped Azrael in this felony rather than any simple faith in his integrity upheld Lucy's skepticism.

"The door wa'n't locked," Cyril confirmed. "He tuck it all right."

"My goodness," his employer cried. "A great, clumsy thing like Azrael couldn't turn a knob and open a door. It's ridiculous."

"It could of been unlatched," Cyril persisted, the unaccustomed thrust of his false teeth giving him the look of an ill-disposed horse. "He could of pushed it open."

"Was it open when you came down this morning?" Lucy asked and Rena shook her head. At a new thought, her eyes showed white. She clasped as much of her bosom as her hands could compass.

"Do either of you believe," Lucy inquired coldly, "that that puppy, if he had stolen a ham, would stop to shut the door after him? Rena, think; are you sure you haven't put it away somewhere?"

Her question was ignored. Mrs. Handrow's mind now dealt with a new and terrifying theory.

"It was burglars," she said, coming as close to twittering as her dimensions allowed. "If it wa'n't that dog, Mis' Applegate, it was burglars."

Suddenly the fate of the picnic hung in the balance. Rena's normal and monumental calm was on the verge of collapse into a chaos of earthquake proportions and Lucy, reading with alarm the signs of disintegration, shelved her own bewilderment.

"It probably was the dog," she agreed. "Whatever happened, it's over and there's no use fussing about it now. There's canned ham in the cold room, Rena. We'll use that for the sandwiches and remember to slice it thin. Cyril, take Azrael and tie him up, tight. I don't want him to cause any more trouble today. Rena, I think the others have come down. We'll have breakfast as soon as it's ready."

She was relieved to see that the imminent tumult was subsiding. Cyril departed with sour relish to haul the puppy into duress. His spouse's bosom heaved perceptibly less as she turned to the stove. There was nothing in moments of crisis, Lucy told herself, as she went back toward the dining room, like giving everyone in sight something to do.

Argument with Ashley, who in preparation for the festival had plastered down his hair with water but had used little on either face or hands: admiration of Muriel's new green crepe frock and the subsequent appearance of Rena with breakfast materials, postponed further consideration by Lucy of the Mystery of the Vanished Ham. The meal was almost over before she mentioned it to her sister.

"Huh," said Ashley, wide-eyed. "I'll bet it was Azrael, too. He eats awful. He'll eat anything, Mom, and then if he doesn't like it he'll just throw it up. Maybe all that ham'll make him—"

"Never mind, eat your breakfast," Lucy bade, thankful that she had already finished hers. Muriel asked in bewilderment:

"But suppose it was an intruder, a burglar, why on earth should he take just a ham?"

"If he did," Lucy told her, "he must have been starving and I'm rather glad he got it. We'll lock the doors at night, hereafter."

She smiled at her sister, bright and fair as a newly minted coin, and thought of the unabashed admiration sight of her would quicken in Larry Moncure's eyes. She did not analyze why she wished for an instant that Muriel were not quite so pretty.

"We've ten dozen things to do between now and eleven," Lucy said. "Azrael's been tied up, Ashley. I don't want you to go near him."

Azrael amiably suffered himself to be towed by Cyril to the back of the barn. When in an obliging mood, one place was as good as another to the great puppy and this seemed, as his jailer tied him with vindictive mutterings, to have the merit of coolness. The Newfoundland collapsed in the shade and instantly slept. Later, he entertained himself for ten minutes by biting the atmosphere vigorously before his clashing jaws succeeded in enclosing the fly who had had the temerity to wake him. He swallowed his annoyance and in lieu of other provender, chewed, more from habit than enterprise, upon his tether. He did not mark what Cyril, too, had overlooked. Repeated mastication had worn the rope precariously thin.

The great black dog looked up at last and hauled himself to his feet. A procession headed by the basket-laden Cyril and including all Azrael's most cherished associates marched through the middle distance toward the lake. The puppy wagged his tail, pricked his ears and looked unjustifiably expectant. The parade plodded down the bank toward the cove and vanished. Azrael barked promptingly and then essayed an organ-toned howl of woe.

"Hah," Cyril told him, reappearing empty-handed, "yell your head off. Rena and me's goin' home and they won't be no one to hear ye, ye dinged air-raid alarm."

He strutted triumphantly from view. Reflections on the still lake were agitated by ripples now. They shook, stretched and shrank while across their disturbance Azrael saw the blunt-bowed boat move slowly out to sea. Muriel plied the oars, Ashley sat in the bow and Lucy, with a monument of provender before her, occupied the rear seat.

Alarm and bereavement beyond any howl's encompassing overwhelmed the puppy. Those whom he loved were departing, accompanied by an inordinate amount of food whose farflung scent tormented a keen nose and Azrael, through some mistake, had been forgotten. Further outcry would be vain. With a great earnestness, the Newfoundland strove to atone for his intimates' carelessness by purposeful lunging against his tether. Occasionally he paused to wheeze but as soon as his throat had eased, he flung himself forward again. He weighed a great deal and the rope was frayed.

Ashley's nomination of himself as rower had been resolutely quashed by his mother and aunt.

"Darling," Lucy had soothed when it had appeared that mutiny would break out before the craft was launched, "you can row us home. We must hurry now. They're coming already."

She pointed over the shining water to where a distant scarlet particle moved almost imperceptibly. A darker oblong that Lucy knew must be the lamented Senator's fishing boat followed.

Muriel, tugging at the oars, said in short bursts of speech:

"Wouldn't it be frightful—if they were to meet the Spoffords—without our being there as interpreters?"

"You needn't hurry so," Lucy soothed. "We've really plenty of time."

The boat labored about the willow-clad point of Martin's Island. A man balanced himself on the rickety jetty's end.

"Hi," cried Ashley and pointed. "There's Mr. Spofford. He's all dressed up, too," he added in mingled surprise and scorn.

Barbara's father made binoculars of his closed hands.

"Yo-ho," he called with excessive cheer. "What ship is that?"

Lucy waved in response. Muriel, tugging more vindictively at the oars, said through clenched teeth, "He means 'Ahoy,'" and glared at her sister as though the mingling of Spoffords and Stark-weathers at a picnic were Lucy's brand new offense.

Benedict Spofford, whose weekend sojourns in Walden had been distinguished heretofore by an enthusiasm for disreputable raiment, now proclaimed by his costume, even before he spoke again, his awareness of the looming event. White flannel trousers, evidently new, a blue serge coat and a yachting cap gave him a nautical air not quite in keeping, Lucy thought, with a rural picnic, yet she did not disparage them even to herself. She was thankful Spofford had not appeared in the mud-stained slacks and sweatshirt that wholly justified its name, in which she most frequently had seen him.

"Greetings, my friends and well wishers," Spofford said, leaning gingerly down from the pier to pull the boat's prow shoreward. "Glad to see you is no word for it. We were afraid royalty would arrive first and we shouldn't know how many salaams it rated. As far as that goes, I think I've seen everything now. Muriel, you look like a million dollars, and as for you, Mrs. Applegate, you're a sight for sore eyes, to coin a striking phrase."

Lucy smiled resolutely at the face whose clipped mustache and haggardly brisk look always reminded her of a hungry terrier's. Barbara, a squat cylinder in her starched blue dress, appeared beside her father and said "Hello" gravely. She alone seemed wholly immune to the feverish liveliness, the anticipation slightly spiced with dread, that made her associates display abnormal gaiety. Barbara rubbed herself—she evidently had been sitting down for a considerable length of time—and watched with solemn eyes while her father and Ashley unloaded the craft of its packages and baskets, its case of ginger ale, its watermelon, blackened coffeepot and folding chair for Mrs. Starkweather.

Mrs. Spofford, who had been kindling a blaze in the stone fireplace, came forward as her husband with voluble gallantry handed Muriel and her sister ashore; and Lucy, though she smiled and uttered blithe words of greeting, felt her heart sink. Mrs. Spofford, with all the permutations and combinations of costume at woman's command, had elected to attend the picnic in a playsuit.

It was, Lucy realized, covering dismay with light laughter and even more brittle talk while they bore the picnic's substance up to the table, a new playsuit and a very pretty shade of pink. Martha Spofford was a good neighbor and a sterling character but at the moment these seemed inconsequent reasons why she should not be quietly murdered and submerged in deep water at the jetty's end before the Starkweathers' arrival.

Though the garments still retained their original form; though they hung upon their wearer in approximately their designed fashion, no playsuit contrived by man could wholly drape or muffle the redundancies of Martha Spofford's figure. Her daughter's amplitude was a maternal inheritance but implacable life had not yet begun its fell work on Barbara's chunky figure. Hers still was a single compact piece, unafflicted by curves, innocent of the excessive protuberances and startling eminences that an optimistic cliché termed "feminine charms."

With these Martha Spofford was overequipped. They were apparent now. Presently, when exertion and warmth had molded her pink costume more closely to her body, Martha, Lucy knew, would appear at first glance practically nude. She wore sunglasses, possibly the better to endure the radiance that would flare from the distinguished guests. That was something, Lucy thought grimly. If she didn't take them off, one small precinct of her extensive person would appear fully clad.

"There," said Mrs. Spofford heartily, setting the heavy basket she bore upon the table. "I've started the fire, dears, and we've brought charcoal. We won't have to be smoke-cured while we cook, Lucy."

She laid a large, soft arm across her hostess's shoulders.

"I think it was wonderful of you to ask us," she said with warm candor. "I was saying to Ben only this morning that you're a real friend. When I think of the important people who would give their eyeteeth to be here today—well, I think you're wonderful."

"My dear, don't be fantastic," Lucy begged and now felt ashamed of herself. "I'm sure we'll all have fun together."

They would, too, she thought, with an upsurge of sympathy and loyalty that half routed consternation. If Mrs. Starkweather didn't like the picnic, that would be just too bad. She'd practically asked herself, anyway. Thus fortified, she endured the covert look of despair Muriel gave her and accorded it no response.

"I can buttle magnificently," Spofford offered over-heartily. "Waited on table all the way through college. I'll be Meadows, the old family retainer, if you think that'll add distinction to the repast. Might stand on the pier and announce them as they arrive."

He threw out his chest, angled his elbows and intoned:

"Her royal grace, Mrs. Eliphalet—"

"Sh-h-h," his wife bade with panicky sibilance. "Here they come."

The scarlet canoe slid into a breadth of water revealed by a gap in the willows, turned and headed shoreward. In its stern Mehitabel Moncure, slim and competent in gray slacks and a blue shirt open at the throat, wielded a silently deft paddle. Lydia, in the bow, swung hers with a hardy air. She smiled at Ashley who stood beside Barbara on the pier and he responded with an awkward wave.

"She paddles lousy," Barbara told him.

"Shut up," he bade. He did not identify the look she gave him, though women had worn it repeatedly since Lilith's day, yet it vaguely abashed him.

"Take it easy, willya?" he begged. "Alla time they been tellin' me I gotta be nice to her."

Barbara found in this the substance of apology. She did not look relieved. She appeared only the more completely calm while the canoe came on and her elders, headed by Lucy and Muriel, hurried to the shore.

"Hi," Mehitabel called in her boyish voice. "Did you order this day on purpose? Careful, darling."

The curved bow grated on the sand and Lydia, who had half risen, sat down again to address her parent.

"Mother," she cried, "I know perfectly well what I'm doing."

Lucy bent and held the canoe. Mehitabel's appearance in slacks soothed her apprehension. If Mrs. Starkweather approved her granddaughter's costume, she would not be over-shocked by Martha's. Mehitabel had removed the problem of trousers for women from the realm of morals into the comparatively safe province of cut and contents.

Lydia, ignoring her mother's repeated warning, thrust a spidery leg overside and strode ashore. She scrambled up on the pier beside the children.

"Hello, Ashley," she said with a smile that dazzled him anew. She considered his companion with elaborate uncertainty. "Let me see," she pursued, lifting her eyebrows, "your name is Barbara, isn't it?"

"Yup," the other replied. Her complete absence of facial response disconcerted the new arrival, who turned again to the boy.

"Such a morning," she exclaimed and fanned herself with her handkerchief. "Mother was so worried about Greatgram that she could hardly paddle at all."

"She sick?" Ashley blurted. Lydia's eyes again were doing unprecedented things to his interior.

"Oh, my dear, not at all," the child explained with a manner ten years too large for her. "But she simply insisted on coming and Mother was afraid it would overtire her. The heat and all. Poor Mother."

She glanced with elaborate sympathy toward her parent who was now the center of the group that looked intently along the island's shore. A broad-beamed boat, ancient but freshly painted, moved deliberately into view around the point and a murmur rose from the gathering on the beach. Larry Moncure suspended his lazy plying of the oars to smile and wave. He spoke to his passenger and laughed.

"You are such a damned fool, Larry," Mrs. Starkweather's indulgent voice came, startlingly resonant and clear, across the water. Beneath the shadow of the parasol, held firmly in one hand, she sat erect and with an air of weathered antiquity in the boat's stern. Not even the day's sultriness had induced her to change from the black raiment that was her uniform. Heat had not softened the harsh vitality of the high-nosed old face.

"Isn't she wonderful?" Martha Spofford whispered as the craft turned sluggishly and came along the shore. "And at ninety. Imagine it!"

Moncure threw a calculating glance over his shoulder as the boat nosed toward the beach and Lucy felt for a second his bright, amused eyes upon her.

"The natives," he said loudly to his passenger, "seem well disposed. Shall we go ashore, Commodore?"

Mrs. Starkweather's grin was removed from sight, for her oarsman, with a single thrust and pull, whirled the heavy boat about. He was, Lucy thought, for all his laziness, tremendously strong. He thrust the craft, stern foremost, toward shore and rammed it solidly upon the gravelly beach. He rose and, holding out his hands for his passenger's, drew her to her feet.

Lucy caught one sharp old elbow, Muriel laid hold on the other. While Mehitabel uttered warnings and the Spoffords exclaimed together, the disembarkation was accomplished. Mrs. Starkweather stood in her strait raiment among the brightly garbed folk who were so much her juniors, lean, warped, yet indomitable, like one mysteriously projected from an earlier, firmer world. If Lucy found pathos in the spectacle, no trace of that soft emotion blurred her guest's uncompromising visage.

"There," she said. The single word was weighted with triumph over objections and difficulties that had been advanced by her descendants. Here she was, despite them all. Mrs. Starkweather peered about her.

"The trees," she said at last in a voice of remote complaint, as though some exterior decorator had taken liberties with Martin's Island. "There were no such trees when the Senator used to bring me here."

"That was forty years ago, Grandmother," Mehitabel reminded her.

"Forty-seven, this very summer," the old woman amended. "Your father was eleven years old."

"I want my friends to meet you," Lucy said gently and introduced the Spoffords. Contemplation of the pink playsuit wrought no change in Mrs. Starkweather's expression.

"How do you do, I'm sure," its wearer faltered and her husband said more briskly: "I've read so much of your work, Mrs. Starkweather; that is, I mean, of your accomplishments."

"You're absolutely sure it didn't tire you too much?" Mehitabel begged. Her husband, bringing cushion and parasol from the boat, smiled widely.

"Why, she loved it," he jeered, "didn't you, Ancestress? She lectured on morals every foot of the way. I don't know what her discourse did for me but I'm sure she's a better woman for it."

He shared his look of mockery with Mrs. Starkweather and Lucy as though the three were parties to some exclusive jest.

"You devil," the old woman told him fondly. "Don't make me scold you again going back, Larry."

"Why not?" he retorted. "It's good for both of us."

"There's a chair for you in the shade yonder," Lucy said a trifle hastily for she fancied that beneath the raillery she heard the rasping of crossed blades. "We brought it especially."

She took one arm. Spofford sprang forward and grasped the other. With Mehitabel leading, Larry bearing the cushion, Muriel the parasol, and Martha Spofford walking alertly behind Mrs. Starkweather, plainly ready to supply additional motive power, the party moved deliberately toward the island's plateau where the fireplace spouted smoke and the table was piled with provisions and the folding chair had been established below the largest willow.

"Oops-a-daisy and here we are," Spofford exclaimed, as he and Lucy lowered their burden into the seat. "Monarchess of all she surveys, to coin a striking phrase."

"You are very kind," Mrs. Starkweather said austerely.

"To all and sundry," he assured her while Lucy quailed, "I'm known as kind Ben Spofford, the old Boy Scout."

Careless of his new white flannels, he sat down on the grass at the dowager's feet. Lucy's haste as she moved toward the table where Martha opened bundles resembled outright flight.

"No, you don't," said Mrs. Spofford, heartily. "You've brought the picnic and we're going to serve it, aren't we, Mrs. Moncure? You rest yourself a little, Lucy."

Mehitabel, not perceptibly thawed by the woman's warmth, opened a basket.

"Yes, indeed," she said without expression, but Lucy fancied she was not pleased.

CHAPTER IX

On the island's stone backbone Larry and Muriel stood together. Lucy, not quite certain whether Mehitabel had been irked by being drafted for menial service, strolled toward them in time to hear the man say lightly:

"It's a right pretty dress, sugar. Makes you look like a dryad, sort of."

Muriel answered, "So good of you," got up and walked away to join Mehitabel and Martha at the table.

The girl wore a look that successively quickened in Lucy surprise, relief and, finally, a small and dreary dismay. Something that heretofore had worried her was missing now from the man's and girl's voices. Warmth that Lucy uncomfortably had sensed in their earlier meetings seemed absent.

For a moment, she was glad. Then, an unhappy sense that the picnic was turning out, not as she had planned but as she had feared, oppressed her. Moncure sat down upon the rock without a single glance toward the retiring Muriel. He lit his pipe and stared through a rift in the trees at the foliage-framed fragment of lake and, far beyond, a gable of the Applegate house. Lucy, uneasy and irresolute, looked about her.

She did not believe the three women at the table were enjoying themselves—she was certain that Mehitabel was offended in her bloodless, patrician fashion—but at least they were thoroughly occupied. Spofford still sat beside Mrs. Starkweather. Lucy had the impulse to intervene and rescue her guest from Ben's dismayingly high spirits. Then she saw that he actually was not talking but was audience. A fragment of Mrs. Starkweather's homily came to her.

"The family, as you say, Mr. Spofford, has done much for America, but there is one thing you haven't mentioned that is its chief pride. It is clean, sound stock on both sides, reputable, upright. No breath of scandal ever has sullied it and, by God, Mr. Spofford, none ever shall while I live."

"It doesn't sound gay," Lucy thought, "but since she's doing the talking, she's probably enjoying herself."

She glanced toward the small beach where the children lingered. Their inactivity might be due to boredom, yet Lucy envied the distant trio. If she had been able to penetrate the obdurate façade of Barbara Spofford and observe the alarming state of her spirit, she would not have yearned to change places with plump, outwardly calm child.

Barbara sat on the landward end of the pier, almost completely mute audience to conversation between Ashley, her cherished comrade, and Lydia, a young woman of the world. Barbara's face was chubbily bland. The eyes that observed Miss Moncure's postures and vaporings betrayed only close attention, but the brain behind them dealt wistfully with a number of grisly projects, varying from assault to manslaughter.

Among the things that Barbara didn't like about Lydia was the way she couldn't stand still but had to go dancing around all the while just like she was trying to get Ashley to chase her. She abhorred her voice, too, and the way she batted her eyes and called Ashley "oh, my dear," but most specially, most intensely Barbara did not relish the fashion in which the airy small girl made fun of her. Of all mortals, dogs and women at any age are most deeply lacerated by mirth at their expense.

Lydia drew a curve in the gravel with one pointed toe.

"Oh, my dear," she said to Ashley, "swimming is my favorite sport. I adore tennis and golf, of course, and Daddy says I'm the best rider he ever knew, for my age, but I'm practically at my best in the water."

She smiled upon Ashley as though her prowess established an intimate bond between them, then turned to the child who sat, squat and immobile as a boulder, on the pier's shoreward end.

"You swim of course, don't you, Barbara?" Lydia asked as an indulgent teacher might address a specially dull pupil.

Barbara shook her head.

"Nope."

"How quaint," the other cooed, with a sly look at Ashley. "I don't see how anyone so fat could simply help floating."

Lucy turned away from contemplation of the distant children and gave a wistful sigh. She did not know how unjustified envy could be.

Moncure looked over his shoulder and saw her standing irresolute.

"I was thinking about you," he told her with a suspicious gravity and rose. "And there you are. Come and share my rock. I'll let you have the softer half."

They stood together, looking out over the shining breadth of still water. Lucy found, and was shamed by the discovery, that she had grown short of breath. There was something about the man, a provocatively disorganizing quality, that was at once a spell and a danger. His grave, gray eyes, where she knew mirth lay ambushed, again reminded her of intrusive hands.

"I'm glad I came," he said with specious solemnity.

She said lightly: "I—we wondered whether you would—" and because to her own ears the speech sounded too humble, went on a shade hastily: "It's such a warm day and a simple little picnic isn't much inducement. Mrs. Starkweather—"

"The picnic wasn't the chief inducement," he interrupted. "I—we"—he mimicked the stumble in her own speech—"should have come if I—we had had to swim. No foolin'," he added as Lucy smiled.

She wasn't a child. Why should she be awkward and tongue-tied under his bold regard? She wasn't Muriel, impelled and bewildered by forces she had not yet wholly fathomed. It was ridiculous that any mere acquaintance could make her feel this way.

"It would have been a long swim," she told him, and her smile was candid, "for really very little."

His eyes moved from her face and peered out over the water. There was relief in having him look elsewhere. She found herself admiring, against her will, the way his blond head was set upon his shoulders.

"Very little?" Moncure repeated. "I'm not so sure. I think it might have been worth the swim."

The soft quality left his voice. He squinted and said more briskly:

"Someone shares my opinion, anyway. Here comes Leander, Hero."

He pointed and laughed. The lake's still surface bore a wide arrowhead of ripple and in its apex moved a dark particle.

"A muskrat?" Lucy faltered. "A duck? Oh, no, it isn't."

She turned and cried to her sister in consternation:

"Muriel, come and look. It can't be. I told Cyril to tie him tightly."

The three who were serving the picnic hurried toward her. Spofford leaped up to stare.

"It's a bird; it's a plane; it's Superman," he shouted, while Mrs. Starkweather winced.

"Oh, my goodness," Muriel wailed at her sister's side, "it's Azrael."

"Azrael?" Mrs. Starkweather's stalwart voice repeated. She sat up straight.

"Muriel's dog," Lucy explained. "A Newfoundland puppy. He's swimming to the picnic."

She lifted her voice, as the dowager leaned back again, reassured. "Ashley, darling, see who's coming."

From the island's ridge, the company watched the approach of the unbidden guest. The blunt black wedge that was Azrael's head drew deliberately nearer. It seemed lower in the water than when Lucy first had marked it.

"You don't suppose, do you," she asked nervously, "that he'll sink? It's an awfully long swim."

"We can launch a lifeboat," Larry offered.

"It won't be necessary," Muriel told him in a crisp voice. "He won't sink, but," she added bitterly, "he'll certainly scuttle the picnic. Why couldn't Cyril do as he's told, for once?"

Proof that Mr. Handrow had obeyed directions completely, if unobservantly, was concealed from her. A two-foot fragment of a severed rope trailed submerged over Azrael's laboring back. Though the weary puppy was bringing to the party a portion of the tether that had snapped at last under his furious lunging, no consciousness of sin accompanied him. Azrael truly believed that he had been omitted from the festivity through oversight. His swim, ten times as long as any he had heretofore attempted, was a gracious effort to make amends for someone's carelessness.

The puppy found himself, while still far from the island, increasingly tired. His legs grew heavy and their weight seemed to pull him down so that occasionally he drew in water with his difficult breathing. A small distressed whimper crept into each puff Azrael uttered. He was almost spent, but no trace of fear curdled his shining spirit. His blurred eyes already had marked dear intimates and other, undoubtedly delightful, people waiting for him on the island. With so large a reception committee at hand, Azrael was completely certain no harm could befall him.

Yet he was dizzy and half blinded by fatigue when his toenails at last scraped the island's shallows. He lifted his water-logged body and lurched to shore, a suddenly sleek, wearily drooping creature who appeared in his water-logged state to be only four-fifths his normal size.

Azrael coughed heavily, blinked drops from his eyes and advanced. He wabbled and wavered as he came but his head was lifted and on his artless countenance was a haggard joy.

His reception, as he drew near, was mixed. Lucy cried: "Oh, look. He's broken his rope. He would." And Muriel, smitten by her possession's expression of sure delight, murmured: "Poor baby; mother's lamb."

"Hey," Spofford demanded, staring. "Is all that just one dog?"

They swarmed about the dripping monster. Attention seemed to restore a meed of Azrael's vigor. When the company was wholly within range, he shook himself, vanishing for an instant in a haze, amid loud outcries from his neighbors.

The victims wiped water away with determined mirth. Martha Spofford's playsuit was horridly adorned now with darker, ensanguined blotches. Her husband cried in resolute gaiety:

"Old Faithful, the reliable geyser, to coin a phrase!" and looked down ruefully at his yachtsman's costume, now realistically besprayed.

"Or, 'As welcome as a wet Newfoundland,' if you'll permit trespass on your special province," Moncure supplied, lazily.

Azrael was unabashed by human consternation. He panted and beamed upon them all with such unsullied happiness that Muriel impulsively patted the great, damp head. She spoke to the dog but Lucy felt, with a qualm, that she aimed her words elsewhere.

"You are welcome; aren't you, sweety-pie? You weren't invited but you at least did want to come. That's something."

"Ouch!" Lucy thought. "Why did she have to do that?" and glanced in alarm at Moncure. Her sister's shaft seemed to have missed its target. The man was looking blandly out over the lake.

A leaden despair possessed Lucy. This was going to be worse than she had feared. Mehitabel had not been pleased by her enlistment in the culinary department. Moncure, for some perverse reason, had deliberately angered Muriel. The Spoffords were ill at ease under the other guests' polite austerity and Mrs. Starkweather, sitting bleak and mummy-like in her chair, obviously was bored.

Lucy wished Azrael had not appeared. For that matter, she wished heartily that she herself had stayed at home. The picnic was dead, even now at its outset, and hours must elapse before it could be decently interred. She laid hold of the soggy fragment of rope and towed the Newfoundland into the middle distance.

"Lie down," she bade, pointing to earth, "and stay there. You're a curse and a scourge, Azrael, and I don't know why I endure you."

She had no need to repeat her command. Azrael collapsed. He was content to lie still for a little. Within ear- eye- and nose-shot were the folk whom he loved best and others whom he was eager to know better. Nothing, save possibly some food when he got his breath back entire, was lacking in Azrael's cup of contentment. He lay in a disjointed attitude and worshiped those who, at the summons of the dampened Martha Spofford, moved toward the picnic table. Love for them all warmed his weary body. Even for a dog, Azrael had a singularly simple heart.

Moncure and Spofford helped Mrs. Starkweather from her chair, drew it to one end of the table and seated her there. With Muriel and Mehitabel on her either hand, she considered the laden board before her with aristocratic dismay.

"I believe," she told Lucy who had sat down facing her, "that I haven't seen so much food in a year."

"Look at it while you can," Spofford advised jovially, preparing to place himself between Lucy and Martha at the table's far end. "What a feed, Lucy; what a feed. A Lucullan repast, to coin a striking phrase."

There was an empty space between Muriel and Barbara. Moncure turned toward it, hesitated the barest instant and then limped around the table to stand behind Spofford.

"Mister," he drawled, "where I come from, there's a law that imposes a heavy fine on a man who sits at a picnic beside his own wife. I mention that now as delicately as possible, sir, because I want your place."

"Okay, chum," Spofford cried, springing up. "Anything to oblige. Especially," he added, hustling about the table and settling himself, "when it places me where I am now."

He grinned at Muriel and at the little girl who already chewed upon a sandwich with a ruminative air. Lucy marked with concern the trite smile her sister had pinned on. Beneath it she fancied Muriel's face had grown paler. Larry sat down at Lucy's left hand and grinned like a small boy, proud of his own cleverness.

She wondered whether her responsive smile were as trite as Muriel's and again she was oppressed by the dull feeling of despair. Strife actually was proceeding between her sister and the man who now sat at her own elbow and whose hushed drawl already was making Martha Spofford shake with laughter.

Lucy thrust the problem away. You couldn't, after all, enter into all the doubts and distresses and crises of even your sister's life. It was hard enough to be hostess at a moribund picnic, without assuming Muriel's grievances.

She passed the salad bowl to Moncure and was pleased to see how attractively Martha had arranged its contents. A sense of respite suddenly possessed her. All the assembly were profitably employed for a while, at least. In the willows' shade, Azrael slumbered in a contorted posture of utter ease. Now, while her guests were occupied for a space, a worried hostess might relax. The respite was brief. Lydia looked at the salad bowl that her mother held before her and said loudly:

"No, thank you."

"Oh, my good Lord," an unbidden voice spoke clearly within Lucy. "Here we go again."

"I said," the child insisted, in response to Mehitabel's murmured persuasion, "that I don't care for any. I'm really not in the least hungry."

"Oh, precious," her mother protested and Lucy, glancing at Moncure, wondered again whether Mehitabel reserved that warm tone for her child alone. "Do try just a little. Everything is delicious."

"No, thank you," Lydia replied wanly.

Lucy said, carefully disciplining her speech, yet regretting it immediately she had spoken:

"I'm afraid we haven't any materials for an omelet."

She saw Mehitabel's sexless face color and then stiffen.

The attention which the child had drawn upon herself was shattered by Moncure's voice.

"If she doesn't want it, leave her alone, Hit. It'll be good for her to skip a meal."

He grinned at the outrage upon his daughter's face.

"You eat too much, anyway, Lyd," he told her. "You're actually getting fat."

He did not mark how suddenly and firmly Barbara's eyes were fixed upon him, nor could he have read in their calm regard the intense adoration his mockery had quickened.

"Oh," Lydia shrilled. "Daddy, that isn't so. I'm ever so much underweight."

He shook his head with a sorrowful air.

"Fatter every day," he deplored. "Do you good, honey, just to live on your hump for a while."

"Larry," Mehitabel said and the way she spoke his name increased the unpleasant tension. "Please!"

He shrugged and turned to speak to Mrs. Spofford again. Lydia's mother said:

"Her appetite is so very whimsical. Darling," she urged, bending over her daughter once more, "just a little piece of chicken."

Lucy hoped that her face betrayed only polite anxiety. If she had known the parallel yearnings filling Barbara's spirit, their scope and their bloodthirstiness, she would have regarded the stout and solid child with comradeship.

Lydia picked languidly at the breast of chicken Mehitabel had placed upon her plate and then, as attention gradually withdrew from her, ate more briskly. Surface serenity returned to the picnic table.

The tense look on Mehitabel's face faded as she observed her child's magically recovered appetite. Spofford, while Lucy held her breath and squirmed, told a story that proved to be almost as funny as he deemed it. Moncure devoted himself to Martha, muttering things that turned her pleased face a brighter hue than her playsuit. Ashley, at his mother's elbow, comported himself with decorum and through the babble and laughter, Barbara ate on with solemn relish and a corroding hatred in her soul.

Spofford leaned back at last and looked with regret at his half uneaten slice of watermelon.

"The table," he announced, "fairly groaned with delicacies and so did Benedict Appetite Spofford, the demon eater. Oops!"

Something snuffed close to his ear and blew a warm gust upon his neck. The man twisted about and gazed at close range upon the still damp but humbly eager countenance of Azrael, for whom at last the smell of food had dissipated exhaustion's slumber.

"It's all right," Muriel assured him. "He's just hungry, aren't you, angel?"

"Generous Ben Spofford would share his last slice of melon with you," the man offered, "but you wouldn't care for any."

He spoke without knowledge. Azrael eagerly accepted the pink and green semicircle, lay down, absorbed it with gusto and, rising, asked hopefully for more.

"Ye Gods," asked Spofford of his wife and Lucy who had set

about cleaning the table, "why burn up anything when you've got this around?"

"We're saving him plenty," Lucy replied and, at the sound of her voice, Azrael ambled about the table to sit before her. In his eyes was adoration, shot with anguish as each apparently edible item was consigned to the flames.

The apathy to which all picnics are subject when their principal purpose has been achieved now laid its dire spell on the company. Mrs. Starkweather spoke no more. She wore increasingly that look of brooding wisdom into which the faces of the old relax when their owners are sleepy. Larry and his wife languidly stowed the luncheon's furniture away in baskets while Muriel folded the table-cloth with the ostentatiously puffing Spofford's aid.

Mrs. Starkweather's head inclined forward. She uttered a sound that, if its author had been of less distinguished lineage, might have been recognized as a snore. Her granddaughter said in a low, half apology:

"She likes to take a nap after lunch."

Mehitabel advanced and, as the matriarch jerked up her head at the younger woman's touch, said:

"Time for a little shut-eye, Grandmother. Let me fix the cushion; now, lean back. All right?"

"Excellent," Mrs. Starkweather proclaimed and slumbered straightway in earnest. Spofford regarded her wistfully.

Barbara had removed herself from the table and now sat upon a nearby rock. Lydia had come dancing to grasp Ashley by the hand and draw him away from his plump companion's side. They stood together in the background now, whispering. Barbara stared at the mountainously heaped platter of odds and ends which Lucy set before Azrael, yet did not consciously see either the meal or the ravenous dog. Lydia advanced upon her mother as Mehitabel returned from Mrs. Starkweather's chair, pulled her aside and muttered urgently.

"The canoe?" Mehitabel said aloud. "Oh, no, darling, I don't think so."

"Mummy, please," the child implored, wriggling violently. "Just a little way, Mummy. I promised Ashley we would. You can watch us every minute, Mummy."

Her voice rose into a pent squeal.

"Sh-h-h, darling," her mother warned. "Greatgram is taking her nap."

"Mummy, Ashley and I want to go out in the canoe."

"Darling, Mummy said no."

"But I say yes," Lydia returned with agitation. "Yes—yes—yes." She gulped and checked a waxing tantrum as Moncure limped to his wife's side.

"What's all this?" Larry asked. "The canoe? I say no—no—no, honey. For why? Because your old man wants it himself."

"Daddy," Lydia cried, stamping her foot, "you do not. You—" The easy drawl pursued.

"Lyd, I'm going to take Mrs. Applegate out on the lake for a little while. I've already made her promise to go. I can't let her down, can I? Well, then, you think up something else you shouldn't do, sugar."

He met Lucy's surprised regard with wide-eyed innocence. Her impulse to deny his calm falsehood faltered and died. At least he had succeeded in abating his vehement small daughter.

"Oh," said Lydia blankly, recovered and skipped back to the small boy.

"We'll explore the island, then, or something," she proclaimed. "Come along, Ashley."

He suffered himself sheepishly to be towed away. Barbara, upon her stone, observed the abduction with no more expression than her perch displayed. Lucy asked:

"Don't you want to go, too, dear?"

"No'm." Barbara shook her head. "I don't feel so good inside, sort of."

"And no wonder, considering what you've put there," her mother told her with light confidence. All previous interior disturbances of her daughter had been strictly alimentary.

Azrael, having polished the last trace of flavor from the platter, lurched toward the desolate little girl and flung himself down with a hearty grunt at her feet. She mistook plethora for sympathy and patted his domed head with a briar-scored hand. Tears welled into her eyes, but they did not fall.

Muriel was saying to Spofford in a clear, gay voice:

"You know, it wouldn't be a bad idea if we all were to go out on the water for a little. It might be cooler there."

"Count me in," he announced. "If Mrs. Moncure and Martha will come along as chaperons."

"I'll stay here with Grandmother, thanks," Mehitabel said precisely.

"I'd be glad to—" Martha began, considered the quiet, faintly scornful young face, gulped and added, "Why, of course."

"I shall row if no one else wants to," Spofford announced loudly and, when his claim went uncontested, added: "That's what I was afraid of. Well, no doubt it will be good for me."

"I'm certain it will," Muriel told him and led the way. Her stride, the carriage of her head reminded Lucy of a hurt and defiant small child, striving by activity to pretend complete indifference.

Moncure spoke from close beside her:

"Reporting for duty, hostess. I'll always be just as prompt in keeping my dates with you."

His candidly gleeful face made it hard for Lucy to cherish irritation that sympathy for Muriel had quickened.

"You know perfectly well," she told him as severely as she could, "that we haven't any engagement. Do you always lie so glibly?"

"Mostly," Moncure replied, "I do better. Generally my lies sound more truthful than verity itself. It's a gift—and a recommendation. Please, ma'am, let's go canoeing."

Lucy hesitated, lured by the eagerness behind his pose of mockery, alarmed by excitement within her.

"You'll be quite safe," Moncure assured her solemnly. "We'll have company"—he jerked his head toward where the others were launching the Spofford boat with much splashing—"and a canoe is a woman's safest refuge. You can't make passes in a canoe, honey."

"You are an idiot," Lucy laughed despite herself. Her impulse to go was so strong that she felt obliged to resist it, at least a little. That was foolish, too. Why shouldn't she go and for no other reason than that she was eager to be with him? The opposition she instinctively had summoned belonged in the serried ranks of duties and taboos that were supposed to attend a Wife and Mother.

"I'm on my Sabbatical," Lucy thought insurgently, "and phooey to all of them."

"If madness be a sign of idiocy—" Moncure had begun, when she interrupted him. Her questing eyes had marked the inert and portly child, still seated on the rock with the great dog slumbering at her feet. It was something less admirable than the forsaken Barbara's pathos—actually she appeared no more pathetic than a sack of meal—that moved Lucy to ask:

"Darling, wouldn't you like to go canoeing for a little with Mr. Moncure and me?"

She regretted her invitation as soon as she uttered it and was relieved when the child shook her head.

"No'm, I guess not. I guess I'd rather just sort of sit here with Azrael."

Moncure laid a firm hand on Lucy's arm and turned her toward the lake. The pressure ran up to prickle on her breasts.

"One of the things I like about you," he said, guiding her downhill, "one of the many things, is that you're so female."

The canoe slid from shore. Lucy half closed her eyes against the glare of sun on water and momentarily was grateful that the heat could be blamed for her heightened color.

Ripples set reflections of the willows flapping like languid banners and the deep water at the pier's end was dusky green. Spofford hallooed to them from off the distant point, before he turned his boat toward the shade of the island's further side.

Lucy waved. Moncure swung the canoe with a single paddle stroke. A sense of his easy strength ran through the fragile craft and thrilled its passenger. They followed deliberately in the course the others had taken. The man's bold eyes caught Lucy's and clung.

"Alone at last," he said, with a grin. "Machiavelli rides again."

She marked the undertone of excitement in his voice. It echoed her own unwilling elation. His gaze went downward from her face and instinctively Lucy pulled her skirt more closely about her. There were amusement and a new, dismaying tenderness in his laughter.

"Either way, my dear, you look ravishing. That is a good beginning, isn't it? How's for conjugating the whole verb?"

He had again that blithe juvenile audacity. That was no reason, Lucy told herself with what firmness she could muster, that under his openly ardent regard her cheeks should feel numb and tumult should rise within her.

"When I look at you," Moncure said solemnly, "I feel like I'd swallowed a live pigeon."

His eyes were appealing. Lucy caught hold of herself as well as she might and told him severely:

"You're being very ridiculous."

He laid his paddle across the gunwales and leaned forward upon it, earnestly.

"But faintly plausible?" he begged. "At least that?"

She did not answer. For an instant, while weathered and supposedly eternal standards toppled, she wished with something like panic that she were ashore once more. Why was he able to set her pulses pounding in her ears like conga drums? How could a single look from him make her senses start to run away with her?

"I'm quite mad about you, Lucy," Larry Moncure said in a quiet voice, "and if you pretend that's news, you're less honest than I think."

She tried righteously but with small zest to rally the already dispersing rectitude, loyalty, self-respect that should have been her staunch allies. Lucy lifted her head and looked with fraudulent absorption at the island's shore, slipping so smoothly past.

"You're talking complete nonsense," she began.

"Please put me ashore at once?" he completed in a tone of inquiry and laughed. "You don't dare look at me and say it."

"You're talking nonsense," Lucy repeated and felt her face grow red beneath his amused regard. He laughed again, a tender, cherishing sound.

"Excellent, darling, and extremely unconvincing."

His voice grew grave; his face for the first time wholly earnest. The Southern cadences lengthened his speech.

"We've a deal to give each other, you and I—exaltation and delight and a great fulfillment. I think we've both known that, Lucy, since I first came up out of the water like old man Ulysses himself. Something important cried for you then. It's been hollering louder ever since."

She watched her hands clasp and unclasp as though they were independent, alien entities. A warmly urgent tide tried to sweep her mind clear of its last remnants of common sense. He was only playing with her, she told herself. He knew in some unholy fashion that he would reach within her and jerk from obscurity the old and buried yearnings mature women store away with memory books and a handful of letters and ancient dance programs—all the dear useless relics of youth.

She had said no word and yet he answered her, still with that heart-shaking, gentle reverence, but he laid above it now a veneer of mockery.

"If you knew how I've worked for this handful of minutes, you'd believe me a mite more easily. Why do you suppose I conducted my heavy-footed but apparently convincing pursuit of your pretty little sister? Good God, woman: I'm adult whatever else you think of me. I don't want green fruit that'll need at least another ten years to ripen. Children of her age play for keeps, my dear."

A faint breeze swung the canoe's bow. He corrected its course and pursued, slowly plying the paddle:

"It was strategy, darling, for both our sakes. Your little sister ran interference for us, that's all. Discretion, my dear, covers a multitude of sins. It hides them so thoroughly that no one sees them but the fortunate sinners. I'm extremely discreet. That, honey, is why we're here."

He gave a shameless chuckle.

"It was tough going. Unless you knew me much better, you wouldn't have an idea. But now we have our reward—or its first, small installment."

He pursued with solemn amusement:

"The Ancestress took me to task this morning. I knew it was coming, but I didn't think she'd wait so long. She lectured me for two nautical miles on the iniquity of turning a young girl's head. She bade me reform. I think she's pleased by my promptitude. So here we are, you and I, alone, with Starkweather approval heavy upon us. You can trust me, Lucy, and"—she heard him swallow dryly before he added with simplicity—"Lucy, I need you very badly."

They had rounded the island's far end and slipped now into shade that reached out from its eastern shore. It was cooler here and water-weeds smelled rankly sweet. Far ahead, Spofford labored at the oars. Flecks of sunlight, piercing the willows' foliage, slid over Moncure's thick, pale hair. He paddled on deliberately, waiting for her to speak.

Things like this didn't happen to middle-aged married women. Men did not pursue; fires that had waned beneath routine's ashes did not suddenly flare into daunting brilliance. Dire needs that had been the adornment and the affliction of youth did not come surging, strengthened and doubly compelling from the tomb, at the summons of a gently drawling voice.

Surprise was part of Lucy's silence. You couldn't deal at once and deftly with a glowing, imperative emotion that had no business by all the standards of morality, poesy and fiction to exist at all. Romance, once over, was not supposed to return in flame to women of mature years. Dr. Faustus had no female counterpart.

She found, with a shock, that she was clinging stoutly but automatically to the dogmas and statutes she believed she had discarded —and wondered why she held to them when it would obviously be so sweet, so shot with ecstasy, simply to let go. She looked half appealingly upon the earnest face that bent toward her.

"Oh," she cried, inadequately, "stop it."

He shook his head.

"My dear," he told her gently, "neither of us possibly can stop it."

CHAPTER X

LUCY WAS SO DAZED BY STRIFE WITHIN HER THAT FOR AN INSTANT she actually believed the uproar were a part of it. The startled look on Moncure's face cleared her own mind. The tumult's source was the island's far shore: its substance, shrill, childish yelling, splashings, Azrael's deep-throated barking and, piercing all these sounds and binding them together in associated ghastliness, an edged and terrifying screeching. This ceased in mid-utterance, to rise again with a new, horridly gurgling accent.

Fear blew through Lucy's mind and left it bleakly empty.

"Good God," Moncure muttered and, at his paddle's thrust, the canoe reeled and drove shoreward.

"Hey," Spofford called in the distance, "what goes on?" and splashed wildly as he swung his unwieldy craft.

The canoe lanced through the shallows and tilted. Moncure stabbed his paddle into the mud.

"Get out," he bade. "I'll hold it."

Lucy floundered ashore. She did not wait for him but plunged through the malevolently clinging strands of the willows, the weeds that tried to throw her, uphill toward the island's crest and the profusely announced yet still unidentified disaster. Her knees wabbled; her mouth was dry and salt with terror. Above the roaring in her ears, she heard a crashing through distant undergrowth and caught a brief glimpse of Spofford's ungainly, stumbling figure, and Martha who followed him.

The same terror roweled all of them. The hope that the source of that desperate screaming was another's child clung, Lucy thought miserably, to each parent.

The tumult had ceased when the island's stony ridge rose before her. She paused an instant, holding fast to a sapling, and found a vestige of breath before she could go on. The dire thing had taken place. Silence proclaimed it. She was, the thought swam dimly through her spent mind, too late for whatever help or rescue she might have supplied. . . .

The stone on which Barbara had sat so long at last had grown too hard for even one of her extreme self-possession longer to endure. She stood up, inadvertently stepping on Azrael, and looked about her. She and the awakened puppy were the only conscious creatures in view.

Mrs. Starkweather, reclining in her chair, still slept loudly, and beside her the long body of her granddaughter lay slumbering on a rug. They offered scant prospect of sympathetic companionship to one whose mind had been so thoroughly roiled.

Barbara restored circulation to a numbed area by earnest rubbing and watched the Newfoundland, now thoroughly awake, move like a vacuum cleaner beneath the table in unrewarding search for anything edible that might have been overlooked. Her father's distant voice came to her from the lake and she heard her mother's responsive laughter. Barbara, in her present state of banked rage, earnestly resented the sound of merriment. Lydia and Ashley had been gone a long while.

Instinct, which later she would learn to label "pride," whispered that it would be unfitting for abductress and abductee to find her, on returning, approximately where they had left her. She must not appear deserted. She went down the slope, past the slumbering women, to the lake's shore and Azrael, finding no better occupation, followed her.

She sat down on the rickety pier—not at the extreme end whither her mother had forbidden her to venture, but as close to it as was legally possible, and swung fat legs over the dusky water. Azrael came and lay behind her with precipitancy that shook the structure. She patted him but there was no purpose or spirit in her caress. Barbara was discovering that other things, less genial than the Newfoundland, had accompanied her to the pier.

The reflection of her swinging legs, foreshortened and supernormally rotund, went back and forth upon the water's surface. To the unintuitive eye, the grave little girl with the great dog beside her was an engagingly placid picture of carefree childhood. In reality, Barbara was a squat container for seething, ensanguined thoughts that would have made a Mohawk envious. Like a dormant volcano, to which in her sedentary posture her outline bore rough resemblance, pent forces wrestled terribly within her.

So guileless had been her past, so childishly unfamiliar was she with her own emotional content that she could not identify the elements—jealousy, bereavement, hatred—that were ingredients of her still frenzy. Fifteen years hence, she might employ such forces to compose literature, music, or alienation of affection suits. Now, all she could do was endure; all she knew was that her eyes smarted; that there was a knotted feeling in her abdomen; that, in her mind, seethed a mighty desire to abolish Lydia Moncure as deliberately as possible.

Azrael raised his head, lifted saddlebag ears perceptibly, made a scraping lurch preparatory to getting to his feet, thought better of it and relapsed. Barbara, following the direction of his mournful gaze, saw Ashley and Lydia coming toward her along the shore. They swung linked hands as they advanced. Reliable instinct told the fat child that this had been Lydia's idea and by the louder tone and frequent laughter her rival employed, she knew too that Lydia had seen her. Retirement now would be defeat's equivalent. Barbara's spirit, which also was stout, rebelled against it. She continued to sit, intent on the reflection of her swinging legs, while the others drew near.

"Why," Lydia shrilled dramatically, "there she is now! We were just talking about you, Barbara. Whatever are you doing?"

"Nothing," the other replied. The sheepish look on Ashley's face was a new grievance on a portentous list. This ill-at-ease, feebly grinning creature was all the enchantress's fell wiles had left of a forthright, valiant, and domineering comrade in unnumbered scenes of hypothetical carnage.

"You're a funny child," Lydia told Barbara with more amused condescension than fourteen months' seniority warranted. "We've had a delightful time. It was fun, wasn't it, Ashley?"

"Yup," her escort gulped. His abductress released his hand and started to climb up on the pier.

"Ooo!" she squealed as Azrael rose to tower above her.

"Whatcha scared of?" Ashley asked with male eagerness to display superiority in at least one department. "Go ahead; he wouldn't hurt a flea, wouldja, Azrael ole boy?"

The Newfoundland's eagerly waving tail beat upon the back of Barbara's neck. Her satisfaction at her enemy's elaborate portrayal of fear was short lived. Lydia recovered at once.

"My dear," she begged with an air, "you don't have to tell me not to be afraid of dogs. I've yet to see one I couldn't handle. I was just surprised, that is all."

She pulled herself up to Azrael's level and got her face enthusiastically licked in transit.

"Goodness," she exclaimed, "isn't he slobbery!"

She pushed the dog's head away and, standing erect upon the pier, scrubbed her cheek with a handkerchief.

"A regular bath," she protested. "Wouldn't it be nice to swim right now?"

She sidled past Azrael and tiptoed out to the pier's end to stare with an appearance of immense wistfulness down into the smoky green depths.

"Ouch; don't; you tickle," she told the Newfoundland who had followed and now stood, with his rear close to Barbara and his muzzle industriously sniffing her rival's legs.

"Wouldn't it be wonderful," Lydia persisted, still peering into the water with a veteran air, "if we had our bathing suits, Ashley? My dear, wouldn't it be divine?"

"Sure," he lied, thankful that he would not be obliged to reveal his lamentable lack of skill before so expert a practitioner.

"Barbara could come, too," Lydia told her infatuate as though the stolid child were not present. "Even if she can't swim, we could use her as a life preserver or something. I'm perfectly positive she'd float."

The titter with which she greeted her own wit, the nasty skill with which she placed the dart, was more than even flesh and fortitude as obdurate as Barbara's could bear impassively.

Lydia's victim twisted about to stare at her tormentor and Ashley gasped. Never had he seen her usually mild face look so pink or so stonily solid. The brilliance of the normally calm eyes frightened him. They seemed to search the surroundings for a weapon or missile and fell at last with inspiration on what promised to be a combination, fortunately presented.

Heedless of the dire portents behind her, Lydia remained bending above the water, while Azrael still sniffed at her with a connoisseur's attention and brushed Barbara's baleful face with a waving tail.

"I'd dive in just as I am," Lydia announced hardily, "if this dress I'm wearing wasn't an import and Mother weren't so tiresome about it. She'd simply be furious if I ruined it. Barbara, why don't you go in? It certainly wouldn't hurt your clothes."

Her lacerating giggle changed to a squeal of fright. With the palsied terror of a nightmare's victim, Ashley saw Barbara get to her knees. He opened his mouth to cry warning before the grimly infuriated fat child threw herself upon her persecutor, but the assailant's purpose was too swift and complex.

Barbara gave Azrael's rear a shove so savage that, despite the puppy's instinctive resistance and accordion-like compression, a large part of the original impetus was forwarded to Lydia by the butt he involuntarily dealt her. The victim's squeal swelled into a strident screech of terror, suddenly hushed. Azrael, pushed forward against his will, now stood alone on the pier's end and stared down with intense interest at the turbulent waters that had swallowed Lydia entire.

"You darned fool," Ashley said to Barbara in a voice of awe. The rage that momentarily had transformed her had left no visible trace. The little girl stood, solid and composed, upon the pier and seemed to accept the boy's comment as a tribute.

"I guess," she said composedly, "her mother will be pretty mad at her now. I guess—"

Her voice faltered and was still. She stared with growing doubt at the empty water beyond the pier's end where Azrael crouched and whined. For a swimmer so expert as she, Lydia was taking an inordinate amount of time in reappearing.

Azrael uttered deep, ear-troubling barks. Confusion regathered at the spot where the jettisoned child had vanished. A clutching hand, an arm, groped upward and from the center of foam and clashing water, the wide-mouthed mask that had been Lydia Moncure's face emerged. Even before her scream tore the silence, the aspect of that wet white visage with strands of sodden hair plastered across its features replaced the doubt in Ashley's and Barbara's minds with stark horror.

It was plain to them both; it was becoming apparent even to Azrael who whimpered, stood irresolutely erect and crouched again, that Lydia's vaunted prowess as a swimmer had been vastly exaggerated. This revelation brought no triumph whatever to Barbara. She found herself not only witness to but also the probable author of a murder by drowning. Her honest intent had been only to ruin Lydia's dress, but already the deed had gone far beyond its simple purpose. Terror and woe were blended in Barbara's wail.

Ashley's screeches were articulate. He yelled for help, but the sound his associate uttered was the wordless, ascending whoop of a siren gone mad. Their combined cries furnished brisk competition to Lydia's.

Barbara's victim flailed her arms about and succeeded only in removing herself a little further from the pier. The sleek soaked head, the ghastly face deliberately were sinking again into the foaming turmoil. Water garbled the screaming. Mehitabel, roused from deep slumber and wondering whether she still were not in the midst of some evil dream, called:

"Children? Lydia? Whatever is the matter?" and received only the vague enlightenment supplied by uproar.

"Hey? I beg pardon?" Mrs. Starkweather asked, reviving. "The matter? Yes, yes; I hear it. Someone's drowning; it's perfectly plain."

The sound of a great splash confirmed her diagnosis.

Mehitabel ran toward the shore. When she reached it, the tumult had died away.

As Lydia's head sank through the froth, Azrael's agitation climbed higher. He barked no more. He only wept in brief, minor trillings. By the taut lines of his crouching body, by the intent pose of his head, it seemed that the great dog listened to a voiceless command.

It came more clearly now, not in the speech of men but in the simpler, compelling tone that addressed his heart. It was his ancestry that exhorted him. Azrael's forefathers were calling his infantile spirit to the present duty that had been his race's ancient standard.

The dog watched the darkly glistening head go still lower and wept no more. He raised his own head high, assembled his ungainly body. A deep bark proclaimed complete and joyous enlightenment as Azrael launched himself from the pier's end.

Spray, flung high, fell upon the dog and drowning child but before he recovered the breath concussion had expelled, Azrael was swimming powerfully.

Hooked fingers grazed his nose, slipped away and lodged fast upon his collar. Lydia's free arm sought avidly to clasp her rescuer's neck. Azrael snorted and backed away, but the strangling hold clamped fast. The child, strong with the fear of death, strove to lift herself above the dog's body.

Azrael's head went down into bubbling green. He fought his way to the surface and got a blurred glimpse of the shore. Toward this he swam, burdened by Lydia's weight, hampered by her feeble struggling.

Progress was agony. The torments of slow suffocation; of water drawn in with each whistling breath; of legs that labored immensely merely to keep a handicapped body afloat, dazed a simple mind, yet despite these manifold distresses Azrael felt no fear.

The cryptic wisdom that men label "instinct" had inspired the puppy's leap. Its inaudible guidance still mastered him. While he obeyed, he could not be afraid though each breath was a greater achievement, though eyes grew dim and strength alarmingly was waning. After his fashion, Azrael was fulfilling his destiny.

Yet he himself had advanced far toward drowning when still another hand found his collar, raised his flagging body and pulled it forward. Lydia's weight suddenly was removed and Mehitabel, waist deep in the water, gathered up her sodden and strangling child and bore her to shore.

There was clamor and human movement that Azrael did not even seek to understand. With solidity once more beneath his quaking legs, with abundance of breathable air about him, the puppy stood, shoulder deep in the shallows and cleared his swamped lungs with retching coughs.

No one heeded him for the moment. Azrael was willing to be ignored. He had accomplished what the power had bidden him perform and he had no glimmer of an idea whether his conduct in men's eyes had been good or ill. So much that a puppy deemed logical and proper was sinful to human mortals.

Azrael had not been overwelcomed when first he had joined the picnic. Now, something in his dim mind whispered, his reception might be even more hostile. When at last he drew himself up out of the water, he moved with stealth that was dread's half-brother.

The sodden wreck of the import clung like fresh paint to Lydia's angular body, still clasped in the arms of her mother who had sat down at the water's edge.

"Darling," Mehitabel babbled, "are you all right? Lydia, precious, can't you answer Mother? Baby, do you feel better?"

Her face was haggard; her low voice more tragic than outcry. Lydia stirred in the wet embrace but whatever utterance she intended issued only as a viscid gurgling. Lucy, quaking with emotion and recent violent exercise, gasped:

"Let me take her. You're simply soaking, yourself." But the woman clung to her child with elemental ardor and asked again:

"Lydia, can't you speak? It's all right, darling; Mother's here."

The child struggled feebly and gave a rattling cough. Lucy looked from the gradually reviving Lydia to Barbara and Ashley who stood in the apathy of consternation on the pier's landward end. She was heartened to see that her own child not only was intact but wholly dry, though plainly dazed.

"Ashley," she demanded breathlessly, "whatever happened?"

Her son gulped. It was Barbara who answered. Hers was the pinched, wan speech of the nauseated.

"She most drowned, I guess."

Her heart was sick with guilt and the contagion had spread to her stomach.

Moncure stood beside his wife and, behind him, Muriel and the Spoffords helped Mrs. Starkweather toward the shore. Lydia uttered a series of gargles and a faint wail. Her father told Mehitabel in a quiet voice:

"She's completely swamped, Hit. Let me drain the water out of her."

His wife shook her head with violence.

"No," she said in a passionate voice. "She's mine. I want to hold her. Go away, Larry."

Moncure hesitated, then raised his shoulders an eloquent trifle. Mrs. Starkweather's masculine voice bade her granddaughter:

"Don't be an idiot, Mehitabel. Give him the child."

Moncure stooped and lifted the slight, drenched figure from his wife's no longer avid arms. He turned Lydia over and decanted her lavishly. Lucy looked away and approached the stunned children. She asked in the low confiding voice she hoped would bring explanation:

"How did it happen, Ashley?"

Her son endured her regard for a long instant, then glanced at Barbara. Her face was calm but there was something in her eyes— a helplessness, a resignation that bothered him. Ashley answered, gruffly:

"I guess she just sort of fell."

The victim, who stood unsteadily and clung to her father, heard the report. She squalled weakly:

"I didn't fall; I didn't. Somebody pushed me."

The recent infatuate looked upon his late enchantress with obvious distaste. He was revolted by the alien quality that clings for a space to those who have been close to death and found now in the draggled and colorless child no trace of earlier charm. Lydia's water-logged condition may have kept her from sensing his revulsion, yet she stamped her foot feebly and wheezed:

"You did, yourself. I felt you."

Honest outrage heated Ashley's reply.

"Me? Gee-gosh, I wasn't even on the pier, let alone near you."

"I—" Barbara began in a faint yet resolute voice that no one heeded as Ashley pursued, addressing his mother now:

"An' Barbs was sittin' down. She couldn't of reached her unless her arm was eight feet long."

"Did she fall or was she pushed?" Spofford asked in a loud voice and laughed with determination.

"Probably," said Mrs. Starkweather who sat on the rug that Muriel had spread for her, "it was retribution, Lydia. Anyone who can't swim a stroke has no business near deep water."

Opposition such as this was more than an over-indulged child in so disorganized a state could, or chose to, endure. Lydia's utterance of woe was strident but encouragingly hearty. Mehitabel, with a swooping gesture, pulled the child away from Moncure and held her close.

"There, there, darling," she soothed and pushed back the sodden mass of Lydia's hair. "Mother knows. It's all right. The only important thing is that you're safe."

"Is there a towel on the premises?" Moncure asked Lucy. "She could do with a little drying."

His look of intimate appeal unsettled her voice.

"There's nothing," she faltered, "but the tablecloth. You could wrap her in that, perhaps."

"Excellent," he told her with a deepening of the wrinkles at his eyes' corners. "I'll get it."

Muriel strode by the children and advanced upon Azrael who lingered with damp uncertainty in the background. Moncure went to seek the lately packed tablecloth. Ashley and Barbara sat in silence, side by side on the pier. Neither of them spoke, yet they felt oddly cleansed and at peace. Nothing can bind friends together more firmly than falsehoods valiantly told in each other's behalf.

All this Azrael beheld from his warily chosen observation post with no comprehension and distinct traces of worry. So elemental was his puppy mind that he had no idea that he was a hero—or even what one was. He did possess a lurking, uncomfortable suspicion that he might be, once again, an involuntary criminal.

Life, heretofore, had been a series of enterprises, undertaken with the best possible intentions yet accorded by his human associates no higher tribute than reproof or punishment. He observed his owner's approach now with warranted suspicion and, as she drew near, attempted an air of innocence that combined ineptly a cringe and a swagger.

The girl laid a hand upon the sodden, beetling brow. Despite the puppy's deliquescent state, she bent and put an arm about his neck and drew him close to her.

"Darling," Muriel whispered in a dripping ear, "you were simply swell. You're a good dog, Azrael. No one notices you but Mother, but she's proud of you."

Mrs. Starkweather's sharp old eyes dwelt upon them. The baritone voice addressed Mehitabel and the child, who sniveled in her arms.

"It occurs to me that instead of sympathizing with Lydia, it might be well to thank in some way—how, I haven't the least idea—that magnificent dog who saved her life."

"Yes," Mehitabel said, lifting her head and emerging from intense maternal solicitude. "That is so. I'd forgotten him. He was"—an unwilling quaver came into her voice—"he was trying to drag Lydia ashore when I reached her."

"I'm not," her grandmother told Lucy, as Deity might have discussed His creations of the Fifth Day, "particularly fond of dogs, but I—we would like to do something for yours. What would he like? A new collar? A—a—what do dogs usually like?"

"He hasn't many wants," Lucy laughed a trifle unsteadily. She too now recognized the valorous achievement of the calamity-haunted puppy. "Food seems to be his chief enthusiasm."

"If there's a beefsteak left in the land, it belongs to him," Moncure announced.

"I'll raise it two pork chops," Spofford added. "That's a dog worth feeding."

Sentiment warmed and relaxed them all. Lucy called to Muriel who still lingered beside the newly acclaimed hero.

"Bring him here, darling. We want to tell him what a good dog he's been."

His owner tugged Azrael forward by the severed rope. He advanced in spurts, urged on by the kindliness of the human faces, deterred by doubt whether he was being presented at court or haled to a courtroom.

The Newfoundland's relief, once he was sure that the general cordiality hid no reprisal, was almost more than he could bear. He understood few of the words lavished upon him but their tone was unmistakably flattering. Azrael beamed as Mrs. Starkweather patted his damp cranium with the gesture of one bestowing knighthood. He wriggled, pulling his pliable body into the most unlikely pos-

tures, while the rest of the gathering offered him caresses and untempered approval.

Urged by her mother, Lydia dismally patted the ecstatic head
and a lowing sound of acclaim rose from his audience as the great,
damp beast licked her puckered face.

From the pier, where they still stood in isolation that more suspicious folk might have identified as the product of guilt, Ashley
and Barbara observed the acclaim and their unwilling accomplice's
rapture. It had always been Azrael's dearest wish to be considered
the life of the party. Now his cup was overflowing.

Lucy set before the slightly dizzy dog tribute more substantial
than praise—a handful of sandwiches, a half bag of potato chips,
and the breast of a broiled chicken.

The lavishness of the puppy's reward, the applause which his
parched spirit so eagerly absorbed, were stamping a pattern on his
mind. Newfoundland nature is immensely tolerant of punishment.
Approval is the truly educative influence and Azrael was, even
now, linking cause with effect in simple sequence. All this un-
imaginable popularity, this lavish delight, was the consequence of
his recent achievement. He filed the fact away in his memory.

The excessive attention he was receiving irked the comparatively
ignored child the dog had rescued. Lydia stirred impatiently in
Mehitabel's embrace.

"Mummy," she whined, "I'm cold. I want to go home."

She managed a convincing shiver.

"Yes," said Mehitabel with quick compunction. "We must go;
at once, darling."

She held out a hand for the tablecloth. Wrapped in its folds with
only her angular, weary face protruding, Lydia resembled, Lucy
thought, a miniature and dissipation-worn Eskimo.

Moncure and his wife guided their offspring to the canoe and
settled her against the backrest. After brief, hushed discussion, the
man surrendered the paddle. Mehitabel thrust the craft from shore.

"Good-by," she called with a dutiful smile.

Moncure, with help from Spofford and Muriel, drew his grandmother-in-law to her feet.

"It's been a very exciting afternoon," Mrs. Starkweather proclaimed to Lucy. "And you've given us a delightful time."

It hadn't really be a delightful time at all, and Lucy knew it.
She was aware that all her guests shared her own opinion. Save
for its violent climax, it had been a boresome and stodgy picnic.

Mrs. Starkweather and her kin had endured with breeding a festival that had ended in nothing more exhilarating than a near-drowning. Only one brief passage of the whole affair had been worth while, she reflected impenitently yet uncertainly as she watched Spofford and Moncure help the woman down to the boat, and Mrs. Starkweather certainly had not included that in her trite acclaim. Memory of a drawling voice and an ardent face dispelled some of the flat misery hostesses endure when dismal parties are ending.

It would be better not to think of Moncure now, or to remember what he had said. Lucy knew her face was never inscrutable and there were observers about her. Besides, he was a southerner and therefore, no doubt, was faithful to the code which decreed that men must make dutifully impassioned passes at all womankind. It was over now; finished. Larry could have been assailing her with softly ardent words merely as an antidote to complete boredom.

Lucy, Muriel, and the Spoffords from the shore; Barbara and Ashley from the pier, watched the embarkation. Mrs. Starkweather's cushion was properly placed. Her grandson-in-law lowered her upon it and opened her parasol. As he seated himself and picked up the oars, he spoke to Lucy. His voice was careless but his eyes for an instant looked deep into hers.

"I'll bring back the tablecloth," he promised, and pushed the craft away from shore. At Lucy's heels, Azrael whimpered but she did not heed him.

The Newfoundland was genuinely bewildered. All those who so lately had paid him admiring tribute now stood with their backs to him. Men and women who had accorded him praise for which his insatiable soul still thirsted had, for no reason that Azrael could discern, forgotten him now. He was too young to know that it is a hero's fate to be ignored as soon as conveniently possible. He was too wholly a dog to realize that the acclaim of men is the most volatile of tributes.

Something had happened, past Azrael's ken but not beyond his spiritual hurt. Those who a few minutes earlier had been eager to bestow on him praise, caresses and delicious, if something less than adequate, food, seemed unaware now that he existed. He was the same dog who had been admired by all; he had done nothing to tarnish the deed that had won him such lavish reward, yet he was completely ignored.

Azrael's owner, her sister, and the Spoffords stood with their backs to him and stared at the lake. On the pier, the children watched the progress of the boat and Barbara rose and moved to the structure's end the better to observe its passage.

"Honey, be careful," her mother warned, nervously.

Mrs. Starkweather's craft moved sedately out to sea. The puppy whined promptingly. No one even glanced at him.

Azrael's reasoning was sound. He had performed what was evidently a praiseworthy feat which had been accorded unexpected and precious acclaim. That dear reward, equally evidently, was strictly rationed. He had received its total and the transaction, quite clearly, now was closed. Until further performance, no more pay would be forthcoming. Inspiration shed a bright and animating light on Azrael's mind. He lumbered toward the pier.

The canoe was now a toy craft far out on the quiet water. Barbara, posed in a faintly Napoleonic attitude, watched the rowboat's progress. Mrs. Starkweather looked back once more, then turned and spoke to Larry. When a faintly reminiscent tumult drew her attention again, it was too late for her to witness Azrael's encore. Even those close at hand had no time to intervene.

Beaming and brisk, the Newfoundland scrambled up on the pier. The structure quaked as he passed Ashley purposefully and ambled out toward the end where Barbara stood. The actual instigator of Lydia's immersion looked toward the approaching black monster but did not identify him as poetic justice incarnate.

Azrael's blunt muzzle prodded Barbara forcefully in the stomach. She had taught him the technique. He was an apt pupil. The spectators' wail was blotted out by an immense splash. Azrael lingered on the pier's end for a second's space, surveying with conscious pride his palsied and incredulous audience. Already, he had acquired a stage presence. As Barbara bobbed to the surface, the Newfoundland flung himself, elated, heroic, intent on the rescue beyond which, his simple mind was sure, lay the tribute of human approval and still more food.

Yet it seemed, even as he oriented himself in the flying spray and struck out promptly for the victim, that the outcry on the beach voiced something other than applause. He was daunted when the bow of a hastily launched boat intruded between him and Barbara. He was genuinely confused when her father retrieved his daughter by hauling her over the gunwale.

Azrael was completely bewildered. Spofford uncordially fended him off with an oar when he showed a willingness to follow Barbara into the boat, and the prodding hurt. His reception as he swam ashore fell so short of his expectations that he slunk away. At a discreet distance he shook himself sadly and sat down to ponder on the enigmatic ways of man. He knew that in some mysterious fashion he had thoroughly depopularized himself again, but he had no least glimmer of an idea why or how.

He did not understand the speech that passed between the Spoffords in the boat and the two remaining women on the shore but Azrael knew it concerned him and he could tell by its tone that it was denunciatory.

Barbara sat in the craft's bow and wiped her face ineffectually on the soaking sleeve of her dress. Immersion had emphasized her redundance but otherwise had not appreciably altered her. Hers was too stout a substance for water easily to affect. Spofford, his gala raiment piebald with patches of wet, said to Lucy:

"Would you mind very much if we went home now, before that little pet of yours thinks he should rescue someone else?"

Laughter did nothing toward clarifying Azrael's mind. He sighed and lay prone. Almost instantly, he slept. His was an enviably philosophic nature.

CHAPTER XI

WHEN THE APPLEGATE BOAT WAS LADEN, MURIEL ROUSED AZRAEL and hauled him to his feet. Still holding him tightly, she urged him aboard.

"Lie down," she bade, striving with incomplete success to keep mirth from her voice, "and don't you dare move until I tell you."

Azrael meekly obeyed. With Ashley at the oars, the boat pursued a whimsical course toward shore. The ripples were languid and leaves on the trees hung without movement. Sunlight stung Lucy's shoulder-blades through her sheer dress and completed the wilting process which, when she had entered the boat, already was well advanced. Her low spirits, she reflected, were the result of injudicious association with too many varieties of people and foods.

"Well, anyway," she said aloud, half defiantly, "Mrs. Starkweather had a good long nap."

Muriel, seated in the bow, looked up sharply. More vigor was in her reply than Lucy's idle remark had warranted.

"You know, angel, I'm rather tired of Mrs. Starkweather and all her tribe. But tired! I could use a change of diet, really. Mrs. Starkweather this; Mrs. Starkweather that; Mrs. Starkweather at a picnic; Mrs. Starkweather along the Amazon with gun and camera. And who the hell is Mrs. Starkweather?"

"A rather important person, I've always understood," Lucy replied a little stiffly. "Why be so stuffy, darling?"

"A once important person," the girl corrected. "Now living on her momentum, and that goes for all her relatives, too. They certainly turned a picnic into a shambles. But certainly!"

"It was my fault," Lucy confessed, "for asking the wrong people."

"It was your fault, angel, for asking the Starkweathers. I hope you're not deploring the Spoffords."

"I'm doing no such thing," Lucy replied with heat. "Really, Muriel, I don't think it's very wise in Ashley's presence—"

"Because," the girl broke in without heeding, "I can tell you that Ben Spofford, at whom all our patrician guests looked down their noses, has more warmth and humanity in a single breath than Larry Moncure could produce if he were to blow forever."

"My dear, I'm not arguing; let's skip it," Lucy begged. Muriel's violence was revealing. Her sister tried to avoid further contact with the girl's sore ego.

"It'll be nice to get home," Lucy sighed, "and just relax on the porch. Later, if we're hungry I'll get a cold supper. Rena and Cyril won't be back till late."

But Muriel's grievance still smarted, though pride forbade her actually voicing it.

"Not for me," she said firmly. "There's a meeting of the Defense Council tonight and Bailey asked me to have dinner beforehand. I said I couldn't, but now I shall. Somehow I need the antidote of real people after an overdose of aristocracy."

She had been hurt, Lucy realized with a twinge of wretchedness. The self-esteem of lovely young women, thanks to the practically universal acclaim men accorded them, was inflated and unduly sensitive. Muriel's humiliation really served her right. It would be good for her to have her ears pinned back now and then—if it weren't for Bailey Ward.

Alarm pricked Lucy. She wanted to beg her sister:

"Oh, please don't be an utter idiot; don't tell Bailey that you'll marry him, after all, just because you're angry. That won't hurt anyone but you, darling."

But she said nothing. Appeal would only harden Muriel's purpose, if she really intended now to encourage her mature devotee. Moncure's indifference was Ward's opportunity. Lucy prayed, as the boat after its devious travels at last ground upon the cove's beach, that the alert realtor might neither see nor grasp it.

Lucy sat on the porch with Azrael slumbering at her feet and Ashley asleep in the room above her.

"Don't wait up for me, angel," Muriel had bidden her briskly. "I may be late and I know you're tired."

Lucy was tired, she supposed, and yet her mind was alert and restless. It wasn't the sort of night that is designed for slumber.

Over the garden, fireflies formed and erased their brief constellations. Imperceptibly moving air brought the scent of flowers. Stars were dim in a low sky and the hushed darkness enveloped Lucy with a warm persuasive ardor. Heat lightning pulsed, dimly revealing the outline of hills and once, Lucy thought, she felt rather than heard far-away thunder.

The humid stillness did not soothe her. If she listened purposefully, the silence was not absolute. Beneath its cloak blood was singing in her ears while on the hushed lawn, the misty fields beyond, in looming trees, small voices cried.

The night was softly tremulous with trills and thin chirpings, faint rattles and stridulences of the lesser folk. These, docilely obedient to warmth and darkness, sang each after his fashion of love.

Lucy thought of Muriel, yet somehow, here in the quiet and the intimate shadows, her sister's welfare had become a vague and trivial question. It was easy to ignore it; it was easier still to remember an earnest face that bent toward hers; a quiet voice that spoke words no righteous married woman willingly would hear.

The little clamorous voices dinned in Lucy's ears. They harmonized with thoughts that, with a pleasant sense of yielding, she no longer strove to discipline. She lay back and did not try to minimize what Moncure had said to her. His voice and the night sounds were of identical substance. She should have been shocked by Moncure's naked speech, yet wasn't it true that men who clothed desire in muffling raiment were secretly ashamed of it?

Lucy wondered how he did it. What enabled Larry Moncure, neither by word nor gesture but by his simple presence, to stir and lift and leave her breathless? What did he have which others lacked that made an alluring brilliance of things mature married women were supposed not to think about—but only to perform in dutiful routine? How was he able to transfigure an enterprise sorely needing fair adornment, until it shone with luster past even adolescence's imaginings?

She had felt, under his adulterous spell—Lucy recoiled from the word but then decided to accept it since she could think of no substitute—not tarnished or soiled, as a proper wife should, but, in a disconcerting fashion, virginal.

Perhaps—interest in the thought made Lucy sit up straighter—she had something there. Maybe she had stumbled upon the actual source of the restlessness that had brought about her and Harrison's experiment. Wasn't this illusion of virginity, this feeling that she stood on the brink of strange wonder, the clearest possible justification for her Sabbatical? Maybe she had found, at last, something she had sought and sorely lacked all her days.

It wasn't, she protested with reflex loyalty, that she no longer loved Harrison; or that she really loved Moncure. Love was one matter, Lucy told herself firmly; other things were—other things. You didn't actually love champagne yet when you were dry and dull, you yearned for it.

Or you had when you were young. In that bright time, champagne had been a festive rarity. Champagne now—she was pleased with the parallel she had found—was stored, case upon case, in Harrison's cellar. It was always there if you felt the least wish for it and, because it continually lay at hand, the excitement and romance had vanished and you didn't crave it any more.

The trouble with what everyone, except possibly the participants, smugly pronounced a happy marriage was that such unions supplied too much. Abundance smothered the dear striving, the difficult triumph. The fortunately wedded fed too fully appetite's small beginnings, supplied drink before one thirsted, attended with equal blighting promptitude the rites that the most explicit novels customarily dismissed with three stars—* * *.

Lucy wondered if these originally could have been ratings, like those in moving picture guides or Harrison's investors' manuals.

She sighed and lay back again. She had found no remedy for anything, but she thought that, perhaps, she had done some unusually acute thinking—for her.

Too much of anything was never exciting or exalting. Not enough was the substance of poetry, of music, of what was keeping her awake.

It wasn't quite as impersonal as that. It wasn't just philosophical moralizing that had driven slumber away; it was a man, another woman's husband. The sense of him saturated Lucy. His voice, tenderly caressing, struck fire from her. His hands were long and strong, yet she knew they would be deftly gentle and she felt her body tingle at the thought. There was a glow about him that, she was certain, could become flame to consume compunction's last vestige. He was graceful and mirthfully insolent; he was openly predatory and enthralling. He was—

Propriety's voice spoke without her least conscious wish. It bade Lucy, in the tone she had first heard her mother employ to discuss bees and flowers and obscurely related topics, to cleanse her mind of indecency. She heard the prim mandate, but it roused in her no zest for compliance. How could you feel penitent while a chorus of amorous voices endured in the humid darkness?

The myriad beasts or bugs or whatever they were who so shamelessly proclaimed their need, obeyed no carking standards contrived by their elders. They plainly had had no mothers to guide them. Lucy wondered how much of the rigid instruction her seniors had spent on her had been the reflection of their own stark rectitude; how much had been hypocrisy of the identical brand she herself already had used on Ashley.

She thought of her anxiety and disapproval when Muriel had been fascinated by Larry. Lucy had no such moral concern now about herself. Sin, it appeared, was committed by other people. Your own insurgencies, contemplated or actual, seemed at worst only justifiable irregularities.

In any event it was too late—or too early—for the uninfluential portion of her mind where her elders' preachings had lodged to summon her to repent. She hadn't done anything; she had merely been thinking and if the quality of her thoughts had been unpuritanical, so had Solomon's on the same general subject and he had managed to get a number of his into The Bible.

It wasn't any good appealing to conscience. Conscience, she had learned, was only a lively dread of what other people would think.

Azrael lifted his head and growled. Lucy saw the driveway birches spring into radiant being as a car's headlights brushed across them. She gripped the Newfoundland, lest one of his hare-brained impulses move him to charge. This must be Muriel returning. Lucy was surprised to appreciate how thoroughly for a little while she had forgotten her sister and Bailey Ward. Azrael struggled conscientiously and relaxed. The car's loose-jointed tumult proclaimed that it bore, not Muriel, but Cyril and Rena.

They halted beside the porch and she went out to speak to them. "Wal," Cyril's rancid voice proclaimed, "I mistrusted ye all was abed. I says to Rena, 'They been clean tuckered out by that picnic of theirs an' they—'"

"No," Lucy replied, lightly, "it's so warm I've just been sitting out. Did you have a good time?"

"Good as you do mostly to a family gatherin'," her servitor reported. "Mis' Applegate, m'sister's lost two dozen eggs—her as married Henry Howell that runs the gas pump over to—"

"Lost them, Cyril?"

"Tuck off the kitchen table last night, just like our ham," Rena said in hollow satisfaction before her husband could reknit the severed thread of his disclosure.

"Well, Azrael certainly didn't steal them," Lucy pointed out and ran her hand over the dark head close beside her.

"Jes' mebby he didn't take the ham neither," Cyril granted, overlooking old hostilities in the zest of spreading fresh tidings of calamity. "They's burglars abroad, Mis' Applegate, sure's you're a foot high. I says to Rena—"

"Burglars," Lucy broke in, "with a liking for ham and eggs. Be sure and lock the kitchen door tonight, Rena."

"That's one thing you don't have to tell me," Mrs. Handrow said fervently and in the headlights reflected glow her eyes rolled whitely.

The car creaked as Rena twisted about on the seat. Lucy blamed her agitation on the crime wave until Cyril prompted acidly:

"Wal, ask her. It's your niece."

"Mis' Applegate," his wife said in a burst of determination, "could me and Cyril take off tomorrow afternoon? I'd be back to git supper. My niece, Rena Washer—she's my namesake, too—is gittin' married, sudden-like. 'Tain't what you might think; Rena's a good girl, but her boy-friend, Will Norton, he's got called in the draft an' he wants they should git married 'fore he goes."

"S'if a war wa'n't enough," Cyril commented. "Won't be till after dinner, anyways, Mis' Applegate, an' I'll start in on the barn roof tomorra mornin'. I got the shingle stain. Seen Mort Twitchell down street and he opened his store special so I could. Knowed Mort ever since he was knee-high to a puddle duck. He—"

"Why, yes," Lucy returned a deferred answer to Rena's question by thrusting her way through the spate of Cyril's reminiscence. "Of course you can go."

She said good night and went into the house before Cyril could relaunch himself. While she got the blankets that served Azrael for a bed and spread them before the door, she yawned until her eyes swam. The thoughts that had repelled slumber had withdrawn now. She felt each bone she owned had its individual weariness.

Lucy was already half asleep when she heard Muriel return. She made a mild attempt to rouse herself but decided her sister's problems would keep until the morrow and was dozing, once more, when Muriel spoke hesitantly:

"Asleep, angel?"

"No," Lucy answered, resolutely dragging herself back to consciousness and blinking at the silhouette, spruce and trim in uniform, against the lighted hall. "Did you have fun, darling?"

"The usual set-up," her sister answered with a carelessness that heartened Lucy. "A two-hour meeting over problems that could have been settled in ten minutes."

Her voice quickened, though its owner strove for indifference. "Dick Banning's back. I saw him in the Olde Tyme Tavern."

"Dick? Why I thought he'd gone for duration!"

"So did I," Muriel said briefly.

"Is he back for long?" Lucy was wholly roused now and heartened. With Banning here, the persistent, honorable intentions of Bailey Ward should be less dangerous.

"He didn't say," Muriel reported in the dry voice she used when emotion was near the surface. "I think he's out of the service. He wasn't even in uniform."

The Olde Tyme Tavern, Walden's leading restaurant, had atmosphere that citizens believed was metropolitan and the less scrupulous summer residents called "quaint." Recently blackened timbers of no structural intent criss-crossed walls of rough plaster and by dim light from imitation horn lanterns waitresses in peasant costumes that seemed to represent the consequences of incredible miscegenations served patrons who sat in shoulder-high booths on red leatherette benches, with provender more scenic than savory. A slot machine phonograph furnished excessive noise per nickel and, adjoining the fumed oak bar, lay a rug-sized dance floor.

"Mr. Ward's table; reserved," Bailey told the head waitress with a worldly air and followed her toward the dim chamber's further wall with his uniformed subordinate bringing up the small procession's rear. He pulled the table aside for Muriel to seat herself.

"Happy Fourth of July to you," a voice said close to her ear. She stared and Dick Banning grinned, standing as nearly erect as his table's edge would permit.

"Thanks," Muriel replied. "And to you and all your folks. I thought—"

She saw that Banning's companion, a hulking person with muscles too big for his clothes and a long, red face, was regarding her with extreme admiration and she omitted what she thought.

"Miss Ashley," Banning said in a formal voice, "may I present my friend—Mr. Dade?"

Muriel wondered why he hesitated over the name. The other man tried to rise, surging vainly against the table's edge. The girl begged:

"Sit down, both of you. Mr. Dade, this is Mr. Ward."

She glanced over her shoulder. Bailey, lingering reprovingly by his own table, said "Pleased" in an unconvincing voice. Indignation, now that surprise was evaporating, seeped into Muriel's mind. She was finding in Dick's unheralded presence here sound cause for grievance.

His eyelids crinkled under her closer regard. He was paler and he looked tired. The sharper edges of his facial bones accented his homeliness and his civilian raiment made him look shabby. There were shadows of weariness about the irreverent eyes.

"When did you get back?" Muriel asked with abruptness that was close to suspicion. She thought it was not ease but careful pretense that made Dick's grin serene.

"Last night," he replied and, in vague apology, added, "Even Mother didn't know I was coming. I ran into Mr. Dade at the Eagle House. He's looking for timber land."

The explanation was glib but the girl found herself questioning it. In the awkward pause, Ward cleared his throat promptingly.

"Are you—?" Muriel began and hesitated, unable to ask bluntly in Dade's presence why Banning wore civilian clothes. He understood her silence and grinned again. She got the irritating idea that he deliberately was tormenting her.

"It's a long, sad story. I'll tell you about it some time. You're in uniform"—he considered her tan and silver costume with heavy admiration that she did not find wholly flattering—"and I'm out. That's the gist of it."

She wondered how he could smile so broadly at his own misfortune—whatever it was. She had the uncomfortable feeling that he was amused by her disapproval.

"Nice to have seen you," she told him as she turned away. His question checked her.

"How's Azrael?" he inquired lightly.

"Bigger and better," she answered, rationed a trite smile to Dade, and moved on. Banning twisted about to follow her with his eyes.

He and his companion were leaning toward each other and talking earnestly by the time Muriel seated herself. Anxiety and thwarted curiosity wrung speech from her:

"I think," she told Ward, "that Dick's been dropped from the marines. It must be that—but what for?"

"Any of a number of things," her chief told her. She was too irked by her own unwilling distress to resent his slur.

A little later when their own meal had just begun and Ward was starting to outline his plans for reorganization of the Volunteer Office, Muriel saw the men in the adjoining booth rise and leave. She found something sinister in their purposeful haste.

"And that," she told Lucy the following morning, while they tarried over breakfast, "is that, angel."

"But," her sister hesitated, "I don't quite—understand. He'd just got his commission, hadn't he? Why should the marines—?"

"Exactly," Muriel replied, with a shrug. "Why should they? You tell."

Lucy was so dismayed that she allowed herself a double ration of sugar in her coffee. Dick's worth as an ally in her own undercover campaign to thwart the persistent Bailey would be lessened if, as Muriel seemed to think, the marines had discharged Banning, or expelled him, or whatever it was that soldiers did to offenders.

She herself was out of patience with Dick. His strategy was very bad. He should have confided at once to Muriel whatever misfortune had cast him back into civilian life. The girl, for all her sophisticated gloss, had a warm and loyal heart. Dick could have reached it by confession. Instead, he had excluded her from share in his plight and, if Muriel's narrative were unprejudiced, had derided her as well.

"It's all very strange," Lucy said.

"But strange, not to say peculiar," her sister endorsed. "And the man he was with—this Dade if that's really his name! A lug if ever I saw one. Bailey was determined to notify the police. Really, he's a hard-looking baby."

"Hey, lookut," Ashley gulped in his effort to propound a theory and swallow a mouthful simultaneously. "You know what? Maybe he is a crook; I betcha maybe he's the burglar who ate our ham."

"If he did, it wasn't burglary; it was cannibalism," Muriel told him.

"Aw," Ashley objected, dimly disturbed by his mother's laughter.

"Finish your breakfast, darling," she bade and added, less fondly, "And listen to me, Ashley Applegate: Right straight afterward, you go upstairs and study history. I've telephoned Martha Spofford and told her that Barbara can't come over till this afternoon. It's time you did a little work and besides, Cyril is painting the barn roof this morning and he's nervous enough up there without you children and Azrael cavorting all over the place. I don't want him to break his neck. Hired men are scarce."

"All men are in this part of the world," Muriel said and her candidly rueful tone heartened Lucy. She felt a reviving fondness for Dick Banning, no matter what disaster had overtaken him. He had irked Muriel, he had roused her curiosity and, for the moment at least, had turned her consideration away from Ward and made her forget her bitterness toward Larry Moncure.

Lucy was faintly alarmed by the sudden leap of her heart and tried to ignore it. A sense of unreality, a feeling that yesterday's glowing episode never actually could have happened, aided her, yet she flushed when she looked up into Muriel's watchful green eyes.

"You look very fit this morning, angel," the girl said. "Quite youthful in fact. Picnics seem to agree with you."

Her light speech banished Lucy's qualm lest Muriel should link, intuitively, Larry's disregard of her, the canoe ride, and the alleged rejuvenation. Lucy assured herself grimly that she need not worry. To girls her sister's age, women of thirty-four were improbable candidates for romance; empty if occasionally still attractive shells, drained alike of allurement and desire.

Muriel, in her youthful arrogance, could no more imagine a man like Moncure turning from her to Lucy than she could picture Lucy, herself, predatorily stalking Bailey Ward. It was hardly flattering, yet it was reassuring in a way. Nevertheless, for safety's sake, she picked up the conversation hastily.

"Is Dick coming to see you? I mean, did he say?"

"Not exactly," Muriel said with confidence, "but I imagine I'll be hearing from him this morning. And it would serve him right if I were too darned busy to see him. Really, Lucy! To come back —no matter what happened—without ever letting me know! A bit thick, I calls it."

Yet for all her profession of independence, the girl lingered about the house and, though the day was fair and the lake bright and the outdoor world alluringly free of Ashley's and Barbara's vociferous enterprises, never moved beyond earshot of the telephone. She ignored the plaintive, canary-like whimpering in which Azrael proposed that they go for a walk and refused with more asperity Lucy's suggestion that they delve together in the flower garden.

"Oh, please don't bother me this morning," she begged her sister.

"I've a million things to do, angel," and thereafter, with Lucy removed, did none of them but sat in the livingroom with a book open on her lap. Each time the Applegate number rang on the party line, Muriel pelted out to the instrument and paused beside it to get her breath and clear her throat and bolster her resolution before she picked up the instrument to treat Dick very, very coolly.

One call was from the express office in Walden, one from Bailey Ward who was desperately immersed in the records of the Volunteer Office, and two were wrong numbers. Banning was as silent as though he were still a thousand miles away.

"No word from Dick?" Lucy asked when she returned to the house for a spray gun. Her sister looked up from her ostensible reading with a puzzled frown, as though the name were only vaguely familiar.

"Dick Banning?" she replied. "Why, that's so; he hasn't called! I'd forgotten all about it."

Lucy went back to her gardening with a small smile stressing the dimple in her cheek. Dick's reticence might be sound strategy if he did not persist in it too long.

The breeze from the lake cooled Lucy's damp face; sunlight lay warmly upon her shoulders and freshly turned earth scented each breath she drew. She sprayed her roses vigorously while a small, contented singing went on in her heart. Life, for the minute, seemed bright and carefree as the day itself.

Drops of spray liquid, gathering in a scarlet Christopher Stone, were turned into opals by the sun. Lucy wondered whether the rose were conscious of its adornment. Surely in their still, slow way flowers must feel their own beauty, must be alive to admiration, must even thrill when a hand reached out to pluck them, or else they would not array themselves so gaily.

Left to itself, the Christopher Stone blossom would be impregnated—a clumsily unfair process it seemed to Lucy—by some absent-minded bee or fly and, having fulfilled its biological purpose, would lose its glory and become an inconspicuous knob of seed. Marriage and motherhood would destroy its beauty and glamor. A whole swarm of bees could buzz about it, thereafter, yet it would not bloom again. There were better fates than that—for flowers and for women.

Lucy picked up her shears, snipped off the rose, thrust it into the breastpin of her frock and smiled. She wondered whether the blossom were grateful. She herself was truly thankful to Larry

Moncure. He might not have meant, for more than that single instant, what he had told her; yet his voice, his eyes, the untrammeled desire on his face had done something for her.

She wondered, pumping her spray gun at neighboring roses, whether marital misbehavior were not so severely denounced by wedded women because their figures and faces, as well no doubt as their standards, disqualified most of them from even attempting it. Maybe the hoary decree imposing chastity on all her sex was a mistake, brought about by some ancient lawgiver's eccentric spelling. Women extolled chastity and men, in theory, encouraged them, but surely women would find life more sparklingly dear if they were chased just a little now and then, too. Moncure's narrowly intent eyes, his drawling voice that boded no good had brightened existence for Lucy. He might have marred her respectability; he had fortified her self-respect.

Muriel came down the uneven brick walk toward the garden, a lithe, an enviably young figure but Lucy knew from the stiff way she bore her head that all was not serene within her.

"Rena," the girl reported, "wants to know if it will be all right if we have lunch a little early."

"Why?" her sister asked vaguely. "Oh, of course; they want to go to the wedding. Goodness, I haven't heard Ashley's history, either. I'll do that now. Tell her yes, darling. In half an hour. That'll give us a long afternoon and we can do something pleasant, maybe."

"You can," Muriel replied, accenting the first word. "Bailey's in a mess with the Volunteer Office files and I'm going in to help him."

She turned toward the house, paused and flung back over her shoulder:

"And when Dick Banning does call, you can tell him where I am and that I'm too busy to see anyone."

The dimple in Lucy's cheek again was deep as she followed her sister. Cyril appeared by the dwelling's corner as she neared it. His ancient overalls, his weathered face were touched here and there with incongruously youthful green.

"Mis' Applegate," he reported. "I got 'bout half one side of the roof done. She soaks up stain like gosh a'mighty. I'm a-leavin' things, ladder'n stain'n all where they are so's I can start in early tomorra. 'T'won't rain, I mistrust, an' it tuck me a hull hour to get the rig together this mornin'. Mis' Applegate, I don't want them young ones to break their necks—not when I'd be sorta responsible, anyways. Will you bid them keep away from the barn while they're playin' today?"

"Yes," Lucy promised, "of course I will."

"Don't see," Cyril reflected, "how that dinged dog can bother, but I'll tie him up if you say so, Mis' Applegate. With a chain."

"No," Lucy told him. "I doubt myself if Azrael is able to climb ladders. I'll be home all afternoon, anyway, and I'll see to everything, Cyril. Don't worry."

CHAPTER XII

C YRIL AND RENA, IN THE GRIM FESTAL ARRAY OF THE REGION, AND Muriel, brusque with indignation at Banning's continued silence, left soon after luncheon; but it was impossible for Lucy to feel lonely. Barbara had appeared before the table had been cleared. Now she and Ashley sat in a pine's shade upon the lawn, engaged in the sedentary, contentious enterprise that was vaguely and inadequately labeled "play," while Azrael slumbered beside them.

No activity other than vocal attended the children's pastime. Ashley sat with his back against the tree trunk and hugged his knees. The fat little girl lay prone in the undulant posture of a couchant horse. Thus, they took their ease and reviewed the events of yesterday with the vehemence and vituperation which, at the ages of ten and twelve, are firm friendship's trademarks.

Inevitably, they were discussing Lydia Moncure and their conversation abounded in rancor. Chivalry's fell blight had not yet fallen upon Ashley. He recalled Lydia's boasted swimming powers with the indignation of the swindled. He remembered now his onetime enslaver only as a sodden and peevish spectacle, wrapped in a ridiculous white tablecloth, and atoned for his spent infatuation by hearty slander of her. It was only when Barbara outdid him in traduction that he opposed her, not from any wish to defend Lydia but because he felt that discipline should be enforced.

The little girl said, out of the deep, still well of her hatred:

"She made me sick, allatime twitching and squealing-like an' when Azrael pushed her overboard—"

"You pushed her," Ashley corrected. Barbara accepted the amendment with composure. No trace of guilt marred it; no hint of gratitude to Ashley whose glib mendacity had hid his associate's crime, was discernible. Though duty has nothing to do with it, the lines of untrammeled childhood's conduct are enviably straight.

"We both did maybe, sorta," Barbara conceded. "Anyways, she hollered like a—a old pig."

"So did you, when Azrael pushed you," Ashley reminded her. "Gosh, you squealed like anything. 'E-e-e-e!' "

She found his falsetto travesty affronting.

"Oh, I did not either," she protested in a louder voice. "I couldn't of hollered, on account of I was way under water."

She shuddered slightly. Her companion hesitated, impelled more by boredom than malice.

"Well, you came up, didn'tcha? You hollered plenty then. Worse'n Lydia."

"I did not," Barbara clamored.

"You did too," Ashley proclaimed even more vigorously. In all childish and most mature debates, the more proficient screecher is judged the victor. There was scant animosity in the argument but it sounded to Lucy, who sat on the porch and strove to read, like the prelude to a fight.

"Children," she called. "Ashley, Barbara; whatever is the matter?"

"Nothin'," Ashley said at length. "We were just talkin'."

"Could you possibly," Lucy asked, "go and talk somewhere else, then? Really, dears, I'd like to be quiet for a little. There are plenty of other places you can play."

The late disputants hauled themselves up with the dumb resignation to adult whim that children learn early.

"Go anywhere you please," Lucy directed, a trifle shamefacedly as she endured their mute disapproval, "just so long as it isn't quite so close. Only listen, Ashley, and pay attention: I don't want you to play around Cyril's ladder and paint down at the barn. Remember."

"Yes'm," he grunted and stalked away. Barbara followed and Azrael, scrambling to his feet, lurched along in the rear. Experience had taught him that this association sooner or later would furnish the excitement that he, also, felt the drowsy afternoon sorely lacked.

Lucy's eyes did not return immediately to her book. There were, she thought as she watched the brief procession trudge out of sight, innumerable unpleasantnesses to maternity that its rapturous and generally inexperienced celebrants conveniently overlook. So many things in life were vociferously overpraised because in unadorned reality, they were something less than agreeable.

It wasn't, she told herself quickly, that she objected to being Ashley's mother. Of all her possessions he probably was dearest to her, yet she wished that their association did not entail upon her the unpublicized roles of policeman, district attorney, and judge as well as mother.

She reopened her book with a sigh, but she stared for a long instant out across the lawn, where mellow sunlight dwelt and shadows were reaching eastward.

It might be that wives and mothers received so much praise in music, verse, and prose because life or morality or custom or something denied them what they really wanted more. It wasn't quite fair that Muriel, who had accomplished little beyond temporarily addling numerous masculine minds, should receive in abundance what Lucy, for fourteen years sustainer of a Home, so firmly was refused—admiration, flattery, more or less creditable pursuit by men. It was just possible that her need of these was greater than her sister's.

Just because you had borne a son who was now twelve years old, it didn't mean that you had reached the time when men would esteem you, if at all, for your wisdom, if any. Lucy could still regard her nakedness in the long bedroom mirror without dismay, though the strictures of brassière and girdle were needed to streamline her body's ripeness. Ripeness for what?

"Whoa," Lucy told herself. "You're in way over your head, Mrs. Applegate."

She bent to her book but she continued to think of men and their doubtful improvements upon existence—men in mass; not men like Larry Moncure. She questioned whether he had ever improved anything, except opportunities.

The car had come up the driveway so silently that the popping of gravel beneath its tires was her first warning of its approach. She had no time to rise before it halted directly in front of her— a glittering black coupé.

"God is good," Larry Moncure told her through the open window. "I was afraid you might be out."

"Everyone else is," Lucy stammered, "except Ashley and Barbara and me."

"God," he said, "is better."

His eyes went over her with unembarrassed appetite as she came to the porch steps. Lucy curbed her body's instinctive response. Once was enough. She had been warned by the ease with which he had stirred her yesterday. She would not let him slip through her guard again and strip away the calmly hospitable manner she had assumed as the best available armor. Her smile was cordial.

"Won't you get out?"

"Won't you get in?" he asked and did not stir. She widened her eyes. He grinned.

"Come on," he drawled, "let's you and me go ridin' an A Coupon's worth, anyway." His smile vanished and he said in a low voice:

"Please, Lucy."

His earnestness smote her and roused a pleasant sense of her own power. She had never seen him candidly beseeching, had never imagined him so nearly humble. Hope that he would flatter her by further pleading made her postpone instinctive refusal.

"We won't go far," Moncure promised, "and we won't be long. You'll be surprised to see how short a time it seems."

"Get out," she told him, "and I'll mix you a Scotch and soda."

"Get in," he imitated her manner, "and I'll show you my favorite view."

Raillery deserted him, leaving his face solemn; his voice so grave that it swayed her.

"Can't you see," he asked and his eyes were earnest, "that everything's been set for us—for a little while, Lucy? Opportunities like this don't just happen by accident. If you ignore them, they're likely not to happen again. The gods wish their arrangements to be appreciated. Listen to me, honey: On the honor of a southern gentleman, I'll bring you back here in an hour. Nothing really can happen in a single hour to people who need so very much of each other."

The devout sincerity fell away and he grinned at her with his head cocked a little sidewise. Lucy felt he was amused by her irresolution. She knew he would hide his flattering need if she refused, and substitute mockery. Familiar voices bade her decline; other, newer, more clamorous, urged her to accept.

While she wavered, Azrael ambled about a corner of the house, beamed at Moncure and stooped to sniff studiously at the coupé's tires. Ashley and Barbara followed him and stood impassively before the car.

"Hi, Ashley," the man said and the small boy grinned. "Lydia sent you her best, old son. She's still a bit water-logged. Mister, you can take care of this place while your mother drives in to town with me, can't you? That's what I thought."

He turned and smiled into Lucy's irresolute eyes.

"You see?" he asked. "Everything's fixed," and leaned over to open the car's further door. She found herself slowly descending the porch steps.

It was easier, she assured herself defensively, to surrender and to drive for a little while with the insistent man than to have the children witness the scene she was quite sure Moncure would stage if she refused. It was better to go, a less rational thought urged, than later to berate herself for silly prudence. This wasn't, after all, an illicit weekend before which she hesitated; it was a brief ride with a neighbor of distinguished family.

The smile she gave her son was apparently unforced. Her voice sounded wholly matter of fact.

"We won't be long, darling. You look out for things like a grown man—and don't play with the paint."

"Sure," Ashley told her.

Lucy climbed in beside Larry. She expected to see triumph on his face, but it was wholly expressionless. He reached across her to close the door. Its slam was like the shattering of innumerable standards and scruples. The sound startled her.

"Why on earth," Lucy thought in a spasm of alarm, "am I doing this, anyway?"

She stirred. The knowledge of how ridiculous she would appear, not only in Moncure's but in the children's eyes, kept her from leaping from the car. She forced herself to lean back, composedly. The starter churned. Ashley and Barbara stepped aside. Azrael uttered a dutiful bark as the coupé moved off, swung round the turning circle and sped up the driveway. Moncure said, looking straight ahead:

"A great many things would be quite simple for you and me if you didn't try to make them as complex as possible, honey."

"How's your wife?" she asked deliberately.

"Fine," he answered in a level voice. "And how's your husband?"

Azrael, having accorded the departing car a token pursuit, galloped back to Ashley and Barbara who stood together on the lawn, temporarily awed and muted by their suddenly enlarged domain. There was a strangeness about having an entire establishment left wholly in their charge. They said little while they strolled aimlessly through the backyard, surveying their responsibility, and the great black puppy padded expectantly behind them. The perverse and insistent voice that lures children, and their elders, toward a prohibited object guided the apparently aimless course of Ashley and Barbara and brought them at last to the barn and the foot of the ladder slanting up to its eaves.

They stood close together and stared in silence at the scene of Mr. Handrow's recent activity. Another and slighter ladder was attached to the ridgepole by an iron hook. To one side, the shingles were grayly weathered; to the other, they glistened verdantly with still damp stain and, braced against the barn's cupola on a platform of Cyril's own devising, sat a large can, streaked and spattered with green.

"I bet," Barbara said at last, "it's fun to paint a roof, kinda. I bet it's awful hard, though."

"Aw, phooey," Ashley scoffed. "All you have to do is climb a ladder and put on the paint. I could, easy as anything."

"You couldn't either," his companion told him.

"Nuts," he replied loudly, "I could, too; whaddaya bet?"

"You couldn't either," Barbara repeated calmly, "on account of your mother told you not to play around here."

This, for an instant, staggered him but he rallied quickly.

"Play?" he echoed. "Who's talkin' about play? If you think roof paintin's play, you oughta hear Cyril. It wouldn't be play, would it, to climb up there and put paint all over the roof?"

"No," she agreed, thoughtfully, "I guess it wouldn't."

Tranquillity, that now had degenerated into human argument, bored Azrael unbearably. Clearly, for the present at least, he must find his own amusement. His unreliable mind affected to see in an innocent-looking stick, peril to them all. Azrael pounced upon it with force that might have staggered a horse and snatched it up in his jaws. He uttered savage sounds as he shook it and, seeing that Ashley watched him with some interest, outdid himself. The puppy pranced about with a hackney gait, dropped the stick, stalked it elaborately, picked it up again, cavorted in a circle waving his burden like a drum major's baton.

"Hey," Ashley asked in mingled amusement and scorn. "You gone crazy?"

"Hi," a voice demanded. "Hi, Ashley, look at me."

He stared upward. Barbara had clambered, while he had watched the gamboling puppy, to the top of the eaves-supported ladder. In her present situation her globular form bore remote resemblance to a lollypop on a disproportionate and complicated stick.

"Hey," Ashley said, "you come down."

His indignation was inspired less by righteousness than by the fact that she had been the first to ascend.

"It's awful high," she said irrelevantly.

"You heard what my mother said," he warned.

"But I'm not playin', am I?" Barbara asked in her own version of his Jesuitry. "I'm just climbin'."

"Huh," he grunted, thwarted, and emulation overcame him. His grip upon the ladder wrung a squeal from her. He climbed as far as he might while she still blocked the way.

"Shucks," he told her, "this isn't high."

"You aren't," she pointed out, reasonably, "as high as I am. Ouch!"

He deliberately had shaken the ladder.

"Well, go on then," he bawled, galled by the thought that unless they clambered to the roof's peak she still would be above him.

"Ashley," Barbara quavered with a belated spasm of conscience, "your mother said—"

Preaching by her in her present exalted state was almost more than he could endure, yet he swallowed vituperation, which instinct told him would do no good, and tried to speak reasonably.

"Lookut, Barbs, all you gotta do is reach over and get on that other ladder; then it'll be easy as goin' upstairs. Lookut, I know what: We'll paint the roof, hey? That certainly won't be playin', Barbs."

She still hesitated. The ridgepole's sharp line across the sky seemed remote as an horizon. The ladder reaching toward it looked infinitely long and perilously steep. She told her associate dolefully:

"I guess maybe I don't want to."

Faltering like this by one whose example had lured him into his present, subordinate post swept away reason and drove him to force. Barbara squealed so sharply that Azrael, on whom unappreciated caracoling was beginning to pall, dropped his stick and stared upward. Ashley, climbing another step, had butted her forcefully in an unprotected area.

"Hey, quit," she shouted.

"Well, go on then," he bellowed. Breathing hard, Barbara reached for the roof-supported ladder, gripped a rung, squealed again as her hand slipped and, gathering herself, flopped solidly over. Thereafter, she ascended with a turtle gait, while Ashley's vituperative encouragement spurred her from behind. At the second ladder's end she halted, wheezing less from exertion than the stark terror of height.

The ridgepole was level with her chin and before her glazed eyes the further slope of the barn roof seemed to fall perpendicularly. On a level with her swimming head were the tops of trees. She craned her neck with difficulty and looked beyond the indignant face of her follower to the pleasant earth, lying maplike and so dwarfed by distance that Azrael seemed a dog of medium size.

"Ooo!" said Barbara, and palsy-smitten, clung to her perch.

"Look," begged Ashley, himself a little breathless, "get goin', willya?"

The question seemed peculiarly atrocious. The girl looked from her companion to the unsubstantial atmosphere above her.

"Go?" she echoed. "Where? I can't go further; there isn't any."

"Well, for gossakes, straddle the roof, can'tcha?" her associate asked with waxing irritation. "Like you wuz ridin' a horse or something. How'm I gonna get up if you don't?"

Demurral was on Barbara's lips. Transfer from ladder to ridgepole seemed a venture saturated with peril; but one look at Ashley's determined face stilled her protest. It was clear that if she did not move of her own volition, her associate would butt her again. With a sound suspiciously like a whimper, Barbara obeyed, so wholly stricken by dread that she did not notice her companion's startled objection. With eyes screwed tight, with knees frantically pressed to either side of the roof, she sat astride the ridgepole.

"Oh, for Pete's sake," Ashley exclaimed in a tone of hearty disgust. "Now, look at what you've done."

Gradually Barbara dared to look. One plane of the roof she straddled was glistening green. In her frenzy, she had dismounted from the ladder on the obviously wrong side and now half of her was parked on freshly applied shingle stain. At the moment, though creosote already was stinging her fat bare leg, it seemed to make small difference.

Breathing hard, Ashley ascended, flung a leg over the ridgepole and settled himself across it. In bifurcated attitudes, they faced the cupola, with the ladder between them.

"Hey there!" a voice suddenly hailed them from below. It was strange but it was neither denunciatory nor uncordial. Nevertheless, the spasm of guilt it evoked in Ashley well-nigh unseated him.

"What," the voice pursued, "are you kids doin' up there?"

With infinitely cautious movement, the boy leaned and looked down. The foreshortened figure that stood before the barn's open door lifted a sunburned angular face from which pale blue eyes peered with what seemed blighting denunciation to two guilty spirits. Azrael had bent before the stranger and was sniffing his legs with grave attention. The stately waving of his plumed tail expressed a growing delight. Ashley managed to force speech through dry throat.

"Nothin'," he gulped in reply. "That is, we're just gonna paint the barn some."

"Huh," the stranger said in ominous disapproval. "If you was mine—say, where's your folks?"

"They're out," Ashley reported. The other seemed to turn these tidings over in his mind and looked thoughtfully toward the house before he spoke again.

"Young fella," he confessed at length, "I'm lost. I was tryin' to hike around the lake and into Walden and I've got mixed up somehow. Maybe I'm trespassin', an' if so, I'm sorry."

"Oh, that's all right," Ashley said, exquisitely relieved by the other's humble manner. "If you go up our driveway and take the road uphill, that'll take you right into Walden."

"Well, thanks," the stranger said and his pallid eyes moved restlessly. "Say, how's chances of gettin' a drink of water before I hike along? I'm pretty dry."

"There's a pipe and faucet inside the barn," Ashley replied with a gesture half inviting, half balancing. "Help yourself."

"Thanks, kid; you're a pal," the stranger said and, followed by the cordial Newfoundland, strode out of view beneath the eave. His disappearance removed Ashley's alarm and all but a remnant of his guilt. The intruder's indifference also seemed to have revived Barbara who, now that her attention temporarily had been removed from her excessive height, bestrode the ridgepole with as much confidence as anyone with her high center of gravity could possess. Ashley whispered to her urgently:

"Hey, gimme that paint can."

It seemed to him vital for verisimilitude's sake that he actually be at work upon the shingles when the stranger reappeared. Barbara looked back at him as though her neck were stiff.

"It's right in front of you," he prompted with scant patience. "Reach out and get it, willya?"

He nodded to the container, perched on the platform at the cupola's base. Gradually, with infinite caution, Barbara extended herself. Her fingers scraped the can's side but failed to find a hold.

"Aw, for gossakes," Ashley encouraged.

The fat child hitched herself forward a trifle. Her stretching hand closed upon the bail and tugged. The can resisted and, not until she pulled still harder, relinquished its sticky site and swung outward. It was heavier than she had dreamed. Its weight, even while in air, jerked her sideways.

Frozen with horror, neither able to move nor cry out and equally powerless to look away from the developing catastrophe, Ashley saw his companion lose balance. He heard the compressed grunt of alarm as the can's momentum jerked Barbara off her perch. One fat leg flew over the ridgepole and rejoined its mate on the roof's newly stained slope.

A spout of green fluid leaped up as the little girl succeeded in grappling the can and clasping it tight. Stain, spattered on the roof, expedited her progress. With the stately, downhill movement of a launching, Barbara slid away.

Her departure, at first, was too deliberate for it to alarm her greatly. With the can clasped in both hands, the child pressed her feet against the roof and gave Ashley an apologetic smile. It vanished almost at once to be replaced by a look of intense personal concern. Despite her utmost effort to stop, Barbara was moving faster. Still clinging to the paint container in a cramped, votary attitude, she skittered downward.

Beneath her, as her pace increased, the shingles uttered a wetly fluttering sound. She was removing considerable stain in passage and was leaving behind her a paler streak on the roof. The horror that had throttled Ashley seemed to have enveloped his recent seatmate, for in her growing speed and peril Barbara uttered no sound.

Nor did she abandon her squatting posture until the roof edge was almost upon her and then her gesture was more the product of instinct than considered purpose. As she tobogganed toward the brink, Barbara cast the can of stain from her. It flew, bounced off the roof and, spouting vehemently, disappeared below the imminent eave. While it was still in air, the child flopped over and accomplished the last fragment of her visible journey upon her façade. Though her prone posture visibly diminished her pace, even the increased brake surface was unable to stop her.

Hindside before, Barbara vanished over the roof's edge with what seemed to the sole spectator a hideous deliberation. In the split second before it disappeared, a blank and chubby face, barely recognizable beneath a dappling of green, stared upward at Ashley. It seemed to him that its grisly look remained for a perceptible instant after its wearer had gone.

The boy clung with numbed knees and hands to a ridgepole that unaccountably had taken to swaying. It seemed to him an incredible time before he heard the dull clank of the castaway can. It smote, not the unprotestant earth, but something sentient that yelped earnestly—probably Azrael, Ashley's terror-clogged mind assured him. Multiple thudding compressed the outcry into a final loud grunt.

Ghastly stillness succeeded the brief tumult. Out of the silence that stretched eternally, a voice finally arose. It was Barbara's. There was complaint in its tone.

"Hey, Ashley," it demanded, "where are you?"

The relief that turned him hollow left him nothing with which to resent the query. He did not recognize his own voice. It croaked: "You hurt?"

"Kinda," the unseen Barbara replied. "Come here. Lookut."

His progress down the ladders was slow and shaky. Sight of the daubed ruin that had been his associate did not lift his spirit, though beneath a whimsically bestowed application of shingle stain, she was not visibly injured.

"I guess," Barbara said in a hideously calm voice, "he's dead or something."

She stood, soiled yet solid, beside a prostrate figure at which Azrael sniffed attentively. Whatever emotion her round face expressed was effectively concealed by streaks and spatterings of green. The man at her feet did not stir. He lay with the overturned can beside him and weltered in a pool of stain.

"I fell; right on top of him," Barbara reported and rubbed herself reminiscently. "I guess the can hit him, too, sorta."

In the silence, Azrael's tentative sniffings were shockingly loud. The sprawling body of the stranger, who apparently had issued from the barn at the instant Barbara had descended from it, did not even twitch. His hair was matted with stain, the portion of his face not hidden by a crooked arm was verdant and dripping.

Ashley said in a small voice:

"I'm sick."

He backed away from the drenched remains. Barbara retired with him.

"I guess," she ventured again, "he's dead."

"Let's," her companion said suddenly, "get outa here."

Azrael galloped gaily beside them as they fled toward the house.

His faith in his companions' entertainment value once more had been justified.

Guilt, exertion, and the horrid feeling that perhaps, after all, their victim had risen and was pursuing them with justifiable wrath, had robbed Ashley and Barbara of their last vestige of breath by the time they reached the dwelling. Spent, voiceless, they sat upon the porch's edge. It was Barbara who first recovered the power of speech. Her stout spirit resisted the horror in which Ashley still was wholly immersed.

"Lookut," she begged with pardonable concern. "What do they do to people who kill people but they didn't mean to?"

Ashley, still gasping, only shrugged and mumbled. The gray and green mask that recently had been his companion's pinkly innocent face, wrinkled.

"They wouldn't," Barbara asked in a resolute voice, "put them in an electric chair, would they?"

She twisted about as though the porch floor were actually that fell seat and flinched at the protest of a hitherto ignored bruise.

"Dunno," Ashley admitted in a thin tone. "I guess they wouldn't, maybe."

She found some comfort in his tepid reassurance.

"What was he doin' with an ax, Ashley?"

He stared at her.

"Ax? He didn't have any ax."

"He did, too. It lay there right beside him. It was all over paint."

He was too desolate to argue. The world had suddenly filled with menace. In some unwelcome fashion, his associate's guilt seemed to have included him also. He glared at her as though the deed had been her purposeful act and found her camouflaged visage more than he could stand.

"For gossake," he told her with weak irritability, "wipe your face."

Obediently Barbara searched for a handkerchief, found none and, taking the soiled fabric he held out, scrubbed. She succeeded only in spreading the paint and turning her face a more uniformly bilious hue. Ashley watched dully, weighed and muted by dread. If this ghastliness could be recalled, if in some miraculous fashion it could be made not to have happened, he was eager to pledge himself not to venture within hailing distance of ladders or paint for the rest of his life.

His associate's mind kept dwelling on her future with what Ashley deemed a morbid persistence.

"If they don't," she asked, "put them in electric chairs, what do they do with them?"

"Jail 'em, I guess," he told her.

"I feel awful," Barbara said suddenly. "I feel awful all over. I want my mother."

Azrael, who had sat and looked hopefully from one unaccountably wretched colleague to the other, suddenly flung up his head, sniffed loudly, and went helter-skelter around the corner of the house. The deserted pair heard a man's voice, joyously hailing the puppy by name.

"You old devil," it went on above scufflings and gusty panting. "Glad to see me, are you? Down, you black imbecile. Where's everybody?"

Neither aghast culprit spoke or moved.

"Hi! Anyone home?" the voice called again and the footsteps drew nearer. They crunched the driveway's gravel. Ashley rose rheumatically. He whispered:

"It's Dick Banning. Let's get outa here."

He turned to flee, but the man already had come into view.

"Ashley," he cried and, as though this were the voice of doom, the small boy quailed and stood still.

"What goes on?" Banning asked. "Aren't you glad to see me, old timer? Where's Muriel?"

His questing eyes fell upon Barbara, who clambered decrepitly to her feet.

"Saints and ministers of grace," the man asked in a dazed voice, "what's happened?"

"Nothin'," Ashley replied in an odd voice.

"That's what I thought," Banning said gravely. "You certainly got results, though."

He looked from one to the other with merry eyes; saw how the boy's white face twitched and marked, too, that Barbara's amazingly hued countenance was folding itself into an expression of imminent lamentation.

"Take it easy," Banning counseled. He sat down beside the fat child and patted her quaking shoulder with an incautious hand. While he found an unstained portion of her dress on which to rub it, he said to the irresolute Ashley:

"Come here, mister, and give. What goes on?"

Ashley mumbled and cleared his throat but confession burst from Barbara with a hiccupy sound.

"We—we killed somebody—I guess," she announced, impervious to her comrade's resentment of the inclusive pronoun. Both children watched Banning's thin face. It seemed hearteningly calm.

"Did, eh?" he asked politely. "How come?"

"I—I fell on him," Barbara blurted.

Banning considered her daubed portions for an instant and then nodded.

"Could be," he admitted.

He found a cigarette, lit it with a deliberation his companions thought encouraging, and grinned at the children.

"Now relax. Where is the late lamented? Down by the barn, eh? Ashley, suppose you show me."

He got up and squeezed the reluctant small boy's shoulder. Barbara joined them as they moved away.

"I'd ruther go too," she whimpered, "than stay here all by myself."

The paler streak, marking the course of her descent, still was clearly visible on the roof. Earth had not yet wholly absorbed the spilled shingle stain about the prostrate can. Banning glanced at this and subjected the dull faces of his companions to more searching regard.

"You're sure," he asked politely, "you two aren't taking me for a ride?"

Ashley could utter only a strangled sound but Barbara bent with a grimace of pain and pointed a green forefinger.

"He was right there," she insisted with relief in her voice. "I guess maybe he wasn't dead after all."

"It's a good guess," Banning told her, still a trifle grimly, and looked at them hard once more.

"He had an ax, too," she pursued. Relief swept over her and made her talkative. "Only that isn't here, either."

"An ax, eh?" Banning repeated with narrowed eyes and a thoughtfully puckered mouth. "Did he have it when you saw him first—when he said he was lost?"

"No, sir," Ashley insisted with a shake of his head. His voice quickened. "I bet it wasn't his ax at all. I bet it was ours and he found it in the barn."

He scuttled into the structure before the man could check him. Banning looked at Barbara as gravely as possible.

"Will you do me a favor?" he asked. "Will you think hard and not say yes unless you're sure? Was he a thick sort of man with pale eyes and yellow hair?"

She nodded, eagerly.

Ashley returned, headlong.

"It was our ax, too," he cried. "I bet he just came to steal it."

"Or picked it up in passing," Banning said half to himself. He considered the stained, substantial little girl. She did not understand his thoughtful look. Bruises, hitherto neglected in her woe, personal precincts that smarted from applications of creosote, so distracted her now that his comment made no sense.

"You know," Banning told her, "I'm sorry you aren't a hundred pounds heavier. Is the house unlocked? I want to use the telephone."

CHAPTER XIII

THE BLACK COUPE WENT UP THE HILL BEYOND THE APPLEGATE driveway with a gentle surge. The engine's effortless mutter beat softly on Lucy's ears. Conditioned to the clattering abruptness of the station wagon, she was uplifted now by such ease of motion. Wind blew through the open window beside her and troubled her hair. She welcomed its intrusion. She still felt scant of breath.

There was affinity between the car and the man beside her. They had a like smooth power. They moved as a single mechanism, too, for Larry drove with calm dexterity. He glanced at her and smiled. She knew she should resent the look in his eyes. For that matter, a reproving corner of her mind assured her, she should object to being here at all.

She hushed the unsought counselor, not caring what arid wisdom it still could utter. The breathlessness was gone and suddenly she felt intensely alive. The wind was mild, the sun was warm, and the roadside trees went by in a dervish dance. Her companion, she thought amusedly, was worth cherishing. By his mere presence he could make you feel as though you had had two dry Martinis.

The road forked. The car swung to the left. Lucy asked:

"We're not going to Walden?"

Moncure accorded her his gleeful, little-boy smile.

"Can do," he told her. "If you'll allow us two hours."

"No," said Lucy demurely, "never mind."

He gave a pleased chuckle.

"We'll concede we've already been to Walden, then. It's right heartenin' you don't think truth worth sixty minutes' time. All the while I'm discoverin' new things to like about you."

He had warmth that enveloped her and urged her to relax. She was silent for a little under its spell. When Larry spoke again, his voice was grave.

"What are we going to do, Lucy?"

His candor roused her vigilance. She asked "With what?" in an innocent voice that made him smile again. He went on, calmly:

156

"With my need of you; with your need of me. That's the more important. I'd like right well for you to have everything you want."

Hemlocks darkened the road. The car went easily over the uneven surface. Lucy asked at last, "Aren't you forgetting we're married?" and at once hated the question's canting sound. He deliberately misunderstood her.

"I frequently wish we were," he said in a thoughtful voice. "You wouldn't like it, though. I'm a better lover than a husband. Ask Hit sometime."

His candor startled her. She asked in light disparagement:

"Is this the 'My-wife-doesn't-understand-me' technique? I mean, that belongs to—to the Starkweather mansion period, doesn't it?"

"Or Eden," he agreed readily. "It's most likely what Adam said to Lilith. And it's still good."

"But shopworn, don't you think?" said Lucy. "I mean—it's not very original, is it?"

"What we have for each other isn't exactly original, either," he told her and dispelled his own solemnity with a wide grin.

"Honey, you aren't agoin' to waste our whole hour just dodgin' about, are you? I'm warnin' you, the gods disapprove perversity like that. If you really want a blueprint, Hit doesn't understand much of me, and what she does she disapproves of. Maybe you've noticed that."

She felt the amused condescension in his speech. It stung. Perhaps he thought he was irresistible and that she already had surrendered. Maybe he believed that getting into his car was as final as creeping into his bed. The coupé turned from the rough road it had followed and was now hauling itself up a narrow track where grass grew between parallel lines of packed earth.

"Where are we going?" Lucy asked so sharply that her companion laughed.

"To see a view I love," he reminded her. "You're quite safe, my dear. It's a virtuous road—straight and narrow."

"It would be nice," she told him, "if you would treat me less like a dull-witted child. I mean, I'm not—" She started to say "Muriel" and checked herself. "Not an infant," she substituted weakly.

"It would be nicer still," he answered and stared at her until her eyes fell, "if you'd stop pretending to be so many things you aren't and drop that look of wide-eyed, virginal innocence. You're quite adult, really."

"But over-proper?" she asked. "That's what you think. Maybe

I'm only trying to be fair—I mean, how would you feel if your wife were out driving with another man?"

Moncure shrugged and answered with deliberate stressing of his southern accent:

"Astounded, honey; I would indeed—and a little sorry for the gentleman. Hit arrived at the age of dissent long ago. Your mouth's too pretty, sugar—and sweet and bright for prunes and prisms."

"Oh, stop it," Lucy snapped in exasperation. Moncure chuckled again as he carefully lifted the car over bared rock ledge. She was exasperated by her inability to anger him. They were silent while the track twisted, uphill and down, and came at last out of the hemlocks' shade into sunlit, cutover land where brambles and brush grew rank and a few decrepit trees towered, misshapen and lonely, above the slash.

When Moncure spoke, his face and voice were thoughtful.

"I'm not a puritan, and neither are you. You just make puritanical sounds because your Sunday-school teacher taught you how. That's all that's left of puritanism, anyhow—just the noises. You know what's happening, don't you? The world is falling apart, Lucy —and we are damned, every last one of us, the sinners and the saints. I've lived on the threshold of this present hell, lady."

He gave her a crooked smile before he went on.

"I reckon that's the one thing I've done since our marriage—beside siring Lydia—of which Hit completely approved. She wanted me to go. She thought it would be The Making of Me. Well, it's on her own head—what I've learned."

He halted the car, as though his earnestness were an obstacle in their way, and looked directly at Lucy. The bitter smile had vanished. His mouth was gentler now; his eyes compelling.

"Everything is gone or going, Lucy; I've seen it. Honor and decency and kindliness and mercy. National treaties are a dime a dozen and overpriced. Individual pledges mean nothing. It's later than you think, sugar. The wise will get what joy they can right now."

The low voice, the gray eyes that, though Larry did not stir, seemed to be stalking her, sent small pricklings along Lucy's spine. She shied away from her emotion so hurriedly that she herself did not know if it were fear or delight and said as calmly as she could:

"The wise always have. I mean—well, what else is there? The pursuit of happiness and all that."

His eyes did not waver; his speech was unfaltering.

"Will you go away with me for a little while, my dear? In pursuit of happiness?"

He waited an instant, then leaned back and his laugh seemed to flout his own intensity.

"You see," he jeered softly. "The exact expression the well-brought-up woman should wear. Lucy, stop pretending you're surprised and shocked."

"I am not."

"Shocked or pretending? And over the goofiest pledge of them all: the marriage vow." He spoke the last words with an exaggerated nasal cadence and laughed again.

It was hard to follow him; it was difficult to meet his swiftly changing moods. Lucy said desperately:

"I don't think it's goofy. I mean—"

"Are you trying to make believe you don't think at all? How can anyone honestly swear to love anyone else forever? Would you promise seriously to like pink more than any other color or prefer lemon above all other pies for the rest of your days?"

"That isn't the same thing."

"Of course it isn't. Marriage is more idiotic. You pledge yourself to wear nothing but pink and dine exclusively on lemon pie as long as you both shall live. Darling, if you have to think, at least think straight."

"I think," said Lucy, faintly, "that we'd better go on to your favorite view," and wondered how her voice issued at all from chaos.

"It's here," Moncure answered. She stared in bewilderment at the surrounding desolation men had wrought before she looked at him. He was smiling tenderly.

"Opportunity to see you in seclusion, without competition: It's the loveliest view in the world, darling."

Inner turmoil was subsiding into a peace even more alarming—a soft sense of yielding, a slackening of body and will, a tranquil and mounting expectation.

"Honestly!" Lucy exclaimed with a shaky laugh. "And the road goes where?"

"Nowhere," her companion told her, adorning the impersonal words with a caressing sound. "This is the last place where we can turn around. Ahead, it crawls into the woods and dies."

He was watching her gravely, beseechingly, and there was something in his eyes from which she found herself unable to turn away.

She felt vigilance, rigid dogmas, weathered standards vanishing like frost from a sunlit window.

"I love you, Lucy," Moncure said and his low voice shook her. "We need each other—you and I."

It was hard to find words with his gently smiling face so close to hers. It was difficult to hold fast to any thought beyond the general impression that the whole world had been dumped upon a roller coaster and now swooped downhill with a daunting, delicious speed and a sound of small, insistently shrilling bells.

She felt his hands upon her shoulders. They turned her toward him and their pressure seemed to melt her bones. There was nothing she could do in her suddenly unsupported state, Lucy thought with dazed delight, but yield. There was nothing else, at the moment, that she wished. Prudence and propriety were faded labels with which she no longer was concerned. Her principles and her skeleton seemed to have vanished together. Moncure's face bent closer, obscuring the light, shutting out everything but the glowing sense of imminent rapture. To her dazzled sight, it seemed as though he had two faces.

Lucy blinked and drew breath. If he had two, why had he left one of them outside the car? It was staring in through the window. It wasn't Moncure's at all. It was an unearthly visage, yet it couldn't belong either to an outraged deity or an embodied conscience. Neither of these, Lucy thought solemnly, would wear a countenance splotched, dappled, and streaked with green.

Moncure, puzzled by her sudden rigidity, glanced over his shoulder. He too saw the apparition and, while he gaped, it vanished. Brush rustled and tapped against the car. Thereafter, they heard nothing but their own loud breathing.

"His face," Moncure announced at last as though each word were heavy, "was green."

"Green," Lucy confirmed in a thin voice. "Green like a goblin. I wish—I could get—enough breath together for a good hearty scream."

"Somebody," the man said, thrusting open the car door and standing on the running board to scan the shaggy landscape, "with an odd idea of humor was playing a joke."

He plainly took no comfort in this theory. All at once, the dreary prospect seemed eloquent with menace. Perhaps, Lucy thought while she struggled against the increasing sense of dread, this land of thick low brush, closely massed saplings, and lone deformed trees had an inhuman, green-visaged population of its own.

"I think," she told her companion, "I'd like to go home."

She was surprised and touched by his ready obedience; by the speed with which he wrenched the car about and drove it back along the ancient track.

The noise of their departure faded. Silence for a long instant held the dull wasteland. Then roadside brush fluttered, though there was no wind. Inch by inch, with an animal's hesitant movements, the shingle-stained unfortunate drew himself from hiding. In gesture, in attitude, even in hue, he seemed a proper part of surrounding desolation.

The man looked carefully about him, tenderly touched his skull, found that the lump beneath his paint-stiffened hair was increasing in size and sensitivity, and as he bent again to pick up an ax, also daubed with green, he began to swear. His blasphemy was liberal, including a number of persons and a deal of territory. It trailed behind him as he moved away.

When at last he had crossed the clearing and had entered the shack, he slammed the door behind him, cast the stain-dappled ax aside and spoke intemperately again. He was aware that his hands and raiment were a shocking sight. His face felt stiff and though the only sight he could gain of it was a sidewise glimpse of a verdant nose, he was certain it was an even more noteworthy spectacle. Recollection of the stricken state of the coupé's occupants when he had peered in assured him of that.

He shuddered and then groaned aloud as the full impact of his late misfortune and current plight smote him. He had been a fool to range so far by daylight, but long immunity had heartened him. He had been convinced that he had shaken off his hunters. Only that very morning, he had considered leaving this dreary hideout and, perhaps, even going back to the city.

Now he knew, and groaned again, that he dared appear nowhere. Whoever even glimpsed him would never forget him. He wondered how long it took shingle stain to wear off. It clung to roofs, he remembered with a sickening lurch of his stomach, for years on end.

Once more, he cursed the recklessness that had impelled him to inspect what had been an apparently empty car. Even if he had been able to steal it, it would have been useless to him in his highly colored state. Its occupants never would forget him, either. Sour mirth stirred within him at recollection of their stare.

If they had come so far to do their necking, they certainly were cheating. Probably they'd never mention to anyone that they had seen him, but he must not run such risks again.

Lucy Applegate, as she lurched about in the car that sped over the grass-grown way, was suffering that peculiarly intense repentance discovery inspires; and her companion was doing little to lighten her penitence. He drove rapidly and said nothing. There was a set look about his mouth. She thought he must be suffering chivalrous regret for the plight into which he had led her and the idea softened her. Men were not so often so considerate of women's qualms.

The coupé came down through the hemlock stand onto the more traveled road and Lucy had the hopeful feeling that she was emerging from a particularly bad dream. The site of her humiliation and the green apparition now were far behind. She sighed, leaned back against the seat and ventured a small uncertain laugh.

At the sound Moncure shook off his brooding with visible effort, glanced at her and smiled ruefully. It might be generous compassion that had muted him; it could be vexation at the ignominious ending of his carefully contrived hour with her. She found, to her astonishment, that she herself was beginning to regret the truncated outcome of the expedition.

Lucy was practically certain now that the painted intruder was a complete stranger. A sense of safety heartened her. The extreme rectitude to which, a moment earlier, she had dedicated the remainder of her life grew less alluring. Her shoulders still felt the warm, hard pressure of Moncure's hands.

The car took a curve in a smooth, careening swoop and she caught her breath so loudly that her companion smiled again. The abstracted look had dwindled. He pointed out:

"You said an hour. I'm trying to keep to schedule."

"I was only thinking," she said with feeble humor, "that we've had all the accidents we need for today."

He slackened speed and gave her a long look. She saw with an illogical lightening of her own heart how reviving admiration drove worry from his eyes.

"Maybe we've had our ration in one lump, honey, and hereafter the gods will be kind. Probably it was only Pan, pausing to give us his blessing. Are you worried?"

She shook her head, touched by his concern.

"Wait to worry," he bade, "until you have more cause. Maybe he was a leprechaun. They're green."

She was aware of new intimacy between them. They would be linked hereafter by this experience.

"I'm sure," she assured him, "that it was no one I've ever seen before. I don't see how he possibly could know us—even though our faces weren't painted."

"Are you sorry?" he asked abruptly.

"For what?" she evaded and was faintly alarmed by sudden recognition of her chief regret.

"For anything?"

His look was earnest, boyishly concerned. It warmed her.

"I think," she said, "that I'm sorry an hour has only sixty minutes."

"You're pretty damned sweet." His low voice shook her. "We've made a beginning, you and I—and I've still to bring back the tablecloth."

"I'd forgotten the tablecloth."

"Forget the leprechaun, too, darling. Or remember him only as our exclusive property. We'll never hear of him again."

The lake shone through the trees. Her driveway was just ahead. Moncure slipped one hand from the wheel and for an instant held fast to hers. He released it suddenly.

"Someone waiting for you?" he asked, nodding toward the figure just ahead. "Another suppliant?"

"Muriel's; not mine. It's Dick Banning. Whatever is he doing here?"

The man at the roadside raised a hailing hand. Moncure pressed down the brake and said from a mouth corner: "We went in to Walden."

"Hello," Lucy called over-cordially as the coupé halted. "Are you afraid to go in? This is our neighbor, Mr. Moncure—"

She hesitated for an instant over the title and compromised on "Mr. Banning."

"Hello," Banning said to them both and grinned at Lucy. "I've been in and I'm on my way out, waiting for a friend to pick me up. Isn't Muriel ever home?"

"All morning long, waiting for word from you and pretty mad by now about the whole thing."

"My luck. All you can say for it is that it's constant. I was too busy even to phone."

He hesitated, as though weighing his speech and then blurted: "You haven't by any chance run across a man plastered with green paint?"

CHAPTER XIV

For LUCY, THE WORLD TIPPED SUDDENLY. HER TONGUE SEEMED PER-manently stuck to the roof of her mouth. Banning misread her look and laughed.

"I'm not screwy, believe it or not."

Moncure's drawl rescued his companion.

"Are they beginning to paint us now? Clothes conservation or what?"

Banning shook his head.

"You can't blame this on the O.P.A. This lad went off with your ax, Lucy, and most of your shingle stain. If you talk tough to Ashley I think you'll squeeze out the details. He and his fat little friend certainly have had a field day. Glad I met you. Tell Muriel I'll catch her yet."

"She's in Walden." Lucy found voice at last. "Working on civilian defense with Bailey Ward."

"I don't like that," the young man objected solemnly. "I don't even like him. I wish he'd come around sometime when your progeny and his mate are roof painting. Be seeing you."

The car moved on. Moncure considered Lucy, sitting mute and numb beside him.

"I wish you wouldn't," he said gently.

"Wouldn't what?"

"Stampede so easily, darling. Why do you? We've just found out why leprechauns are green."

"Have we?" she asked with an uncertain laugh. "None of it makes sense to me."

Azrael, perversely mistaking them for hostile invaders, came roaring and bounding. Lucy was heartened by the sight of Ashley. He stood on the porch, apparently intact, though his response to her hail seemed automatic.

"Darling," she cried as the car halted beside the steps, "whatever has been going—"

She paused with the question half uttered. Her eyes had strayed from her son to his companion. Lurking with an undeniable air of guilt in the porch's deepest shadow, Barbara met Lucy's incredulous scrutiny with a face that had the impassivity and the curdled appearance of jade. . . .

At last things grew calm once more. At last, Lucy thought, standing at the washbowl and applying cleaning fluid to the stains transferred to her hands from Barbara's apparently permanently dyed visage, there was peace and time to reflect. No previous opportunity had been afforded her from the minute when Moncure had handed her gracefully from the car, until now.

Her eyes, as she had alighted, had been fixed upon the glowering, apprehensive figure of her son. The man had grinned at her resolute, maternal horror and had bent swiftly, close to her ear.

"Let me know when I can return the tablecloth," he had said in a low voice. She had been conscious of the bright promise but she could not deal with it then.

"Yes," she had told him and had filed his plea away for consideration in some more tranquil future.

"Green," Larry had assured her with gravity, "is the color of hope."

He had laughed as he had driven away. Until now, Lucy's thought of him had been a vague, sustaining presence in the back of a mind which had been intensely occupied with more immediate enterprises and problems.

She had cross-questioned Ashley, a toilsome task, yielding grains of fact only after patient winnowing of evasion's and irrelevance's chaff. She had sent her son, who still wore the look of one whom the world maltreated, upstairs to bed. There she had warned him, he was to remain all the morrow with only the doleful companionship of his history book. Lucy then had undertaken the partial rehabilitation of the ruin that was Barbara.

The plump child's raiment was beyond all aid but Lucy worked upon the bland, unprotesting and horridly stained face with cleaning fluid and public-spirited zeal. She was unwilling that anyone encountering Barbara on her walk home should start and quail at sight of that verdant visage. The little girl endured the ordeal without complaint, though she was aware that larger and sorer portions of her were more in need of attention. The ablutions accomplished little beyond staining Lucy's own hands.

Cyril and Rena returned just after Barbara had trudged away and Lucy was obliged to explain the violence done to Mr. Handrow's uncompleted project and to endure thereafter his profuse bereavement and his long-winded if not too sincere thanks that neither miscreant had been maimed for life.

The telephone was shrilling her number when she returned, somewhat deafened, to the house. Martha Spofford, having recovered from her first glimpse of her prodigal daughter, was filled with worry, traces of hysteria, and oblique denunciation of Ashley, all of which she insisted on expressing.

"I really think, Lucy," she said at last, "I really do think that it will be better if they don't play together so much."

"Much, much better for her—and Ashley, too," Lucy answered brightly and the conversation ended with the cloak-and-dagger heartiness mothers of erring children display toward each other. Lucy sighed as she turned toward the stair and gave a small moan when the telephone summoned her again.

It was Muriel, explaining that she would not be home to supper, thanks to the intricacies of the Volunteer Office records.

"And the Starkweather siren has come," the girl reported. "They're installing it on the roof of the Eagle House now. Bailey wants you to be his guest at the dedication tomorrow afternoon."

"On the hotel roof?" Lucy asked. "I don't think—"

"In the Control Center, silly," Muriel replied and added with faint malice, "All the Starkweathers will be there."

"Oh," her sister replied, "I'll see if I can. Thank him very much, darling. Incidentally," she added to requite her sister's spitefulness, "Dick called on you this afternoon."

"Did he?" Muriel's voice was grim. "If he comes again, you can tell him I shan't be home until late—too late to see him."

And now, Lucy was scrubbing vestiges of Barbara's new complexion from her hands and basking in the household's restored tranquillity. She had some difficulty in ridding herself of the cleaner but finally her palms smelled of nothing but toilet soap and she went to her bedroom to lie down before her solitary meal. It was not fatigue that sped her but an eagerness to be alone with her resolutely deferred thoughts.

Lucy lay, swathed in her dressing gown, and looked with half closed eyes at the gold that sunlight cast upon the westward branches of the pines. Her body, with the rest of the world, seemed steeped in the relaxed silence that precedes the sunset. Her mind delved into the stored memories of the past few hours with a miser's eagerness.

She would be alarmed and frightened if she believed that Muriel ever had cherished thoughts that she herself now was entertaining, quite calmly and with no perceptible iniquitous stain.

She had felt frightfully guilty when the green intruder had looked in upon them so short a time ago, but until that moment she had felt no consciousness of evil. Maybe if everyone minded his own business, exclusively, there wouldn't be any sense of wrongdoing in the world at all. She considered this gravely for a space, wondering whether that would be a good idea or not, gave up the mute debate at last and let her mind slide easily back to Larry Moncure.

He had said he and she had something for each other. Lucy was unwilling to argue this, either, but she wondered what in actuality it was. Were he and she like those chemicals—she could not remember their names now—that, brought into contact in her school laboratory, had immediately begun to glow and fume?

She didn't know. She was too entertained for the moment by her memories to question whither this strange thing one man and one woman had for each other might carry them both. The immediate past was still too fascinating for forward exploration to lure her. The future held only one certainty: Whether their association went on further; whether it led them far, Lucy was sure, with a recurrent thought of the face at the coupé window, that it must be conducted with more care. There must be no scandal, for Ashley's sake, for Harrison's—not to mention her own. Caution hereafter must be her watchword. Discretion was the better part of morals.

She was pleased with this and repeated it to herself. She thought with uncertain pride that perhaps she had made an epigram.

A robin began to gulp and squeal a premature vesper song. The sunlight lay like gold dust on the pines. Lucy stretched herself deliciously. She had thought she needed rest but she had only wanted ease. After all the afternoon's strenuous abnormalities, she felt warm and sleek and intensely alive. She found contentment merely in being, and wondered if she had not Moncure to thank wholly for this new, soft ecstasy.

There might be other equally accurate versions of the Snow White story. It could be that she married to live happily ever afterward and was awakened, fourteen years later, by the prince. Lucy wondered what Disney could do with that one and once more felt indignation at convention's unfairness.

Why should adventure for her sex be the province of only the very young? Why should the world smile at Muriel's efforts to twist every available man's head from his shoulders yet deplore if it knew where she herself had been this afternoon? Youth had more of excitement and variety than it needed or knew how to handle. What most women of Lucy's age called happiness was really nothing more than the absence of important unhappiness.

"Right on the nose, Mrs. Applegate," she said aloud and thought she would like to tell Harrison about it. The wish, popping unbidden into her mind, surprised and startled her. Yet she admitted, after trying to laugh it away, she could do with Harrison's counsel now. It wasn't that in her present situation she could Tell All to Harrison and ask his advice. He would certainly be prejudiced, yet there were principles and theories toward which her mind fumbled that she rather needed his help to capture whole.

She wondered whether Harrison could tell her why human rules bleached and thinned life at the time when it would be most triumphantly bright and full. Plays that had only a good first act didn't last long, but the girl babies who were being born every second had no better future—and most of them would run for fifty years or more. That seemed to Lucy a great waste. You never really understood existence until you had been married, and then what could you do with your enlightenment? You didn't learn to drive a car and then never take it out of a single short street.

Lucy heard movement and the clink of china in the dining room. Supper would be ready soon. She got up eagerly. She hummed as she dressed and found herself unusually hungry. She was happy and it would be silly to concern herself with the future while the present was so unusually pleasant.

She did her hair, considering herself in the glass. Perhaps she was really sin-stained. If so, she decided, the hue agreed with her. Moncure would be bringing the tablecloth back. Instinct told her that he would only wait until she indicated the best time. It was nice to know he was, for the moment anyway, at her beck and call. And he had been sweet about this afternoon's frustration. Memory of his concern for her was dear to Lucy and there would be grilled mushrooms, avocado pear salad, and lemon ice for supper.

She pulled her glowing face into an expression of rigid disapproval as she paused at Ashley's door on her way downstairs. Her son pretended not to see her. He was bent, in his bed, over the open history book in an intensely studious posture, rendered a little more singular by the fact, unsuspected by her, that he was seated temporarily on a less substantial volume entitled "Tom Swift and His Death Ray."

Lucy ran downstairs eagerly to her lonely meal and evening. Her mind, she felt, was too full of undeveloped entertainment for her to miss any other companionship.

She thrust back her chair at last with a sigh and said to Rena, who set a finger bowl before her:

"Everything was simply delicious. I've eaten like a pig."

Mrs. Handrow flushed like a peak at sunset and Lucy, filled with a sense of well-being, asked:

"Was it a nice wedding?"

"As sech things go," Rena answered judgmatically. "Always kinda sad, I call 'em. My niece Rena," she pursued with an archness puzzling to Lucy, "she's been workin' for the Starkweathers, you know."

"Has she?" her employer asked politely.

"Yes'm, but you wouldn't be likely to of seen her. She's been sort of cook's assistant, I guess. Could of had a better job with more money if she'd been willin' to wear a uniform an' do upstairs work, but she wouldn't."

Rena's downward glance at her own black and white raiment and the sigh she uttered stressed her large-mindedness in such matters. She assumed a roguish air and ogled her employer.

"Someone I know," she lisped, "was out riding with a gentleman this afternoon."

Lucy, partly conditioned to her hireling's occasional spells of elephantine playfulness, strove to hide surprise. How, in heaven's name, did tidings spread so rapidly in this half-empty land? It was a complete whispering gallery.

"Yes," she answered with blighting brevity. "There were some things I needed in Walden and Mr. Moncure drove me in."

"Did he bring back our tablecloth?" Rena inquired thriftily.

"No," Lucy told her and got up. "I imagine they're having it laundered before they return it."

The sun had set when she went out upon the porch. A band of flamingo-colored clouds stained the lake. Lucy watched the glow turn crimson and purple and faintly green below a lemon-hued star. Azrael, so filled with dinner that his body swung hammock-wise between his legs' supports, approached, puffed heartily in her face to indicate his readiness for any enterprise, and at her request cast himself down beside her and fell asleep. Light drained from a gray world. Moths, lured by the livingroom lamp, whirred and bumped against the screen door.

The stars hung high tonight. Lucy sat long in silence, watching them bloom in the darkening sky. She leaned over at last, patted the slumbering dog beside her and said aloud with a little laugh:

"Portrait of a Woman Considering Infidelity."

She might as well face it. That was the way her thoughts were traveling; that was what had made her feel so gay there in her room before suppertime. She had refused to look ahead then. Rena's kittenish raillery in some odd fashion had cleared her mind. Now, in the thickening dark, she wondered whether she actually were in love with Larry and, with a pang of uneasiness, if she were genuinely out of love with Harrison. She found no sure answer to either doubt.

Harrison was kind and forebearing and—and loyal, Lucy thought and flinched. She understood Harrison thoroughly. Maybe that was the trouble: maybe she understood him too well. You couldn't read with great interest a book you already knew by heart. You couldn't find excitement and adventure and perilous ecstasy in even the loveliest music if you played no other—ever.

Moncure was gay and ardent and wholly without compunction. When you said things to him, you were never sure what his response would be. Even his passes were youthfully charming and he hid their purpose under mockery, or mirth. He had a way of adorning whatever he said or did so that you kept wondering what actually lay beneath.

That was a good idea, Lucy thought. All human needs should be dressed up as much as possible. Until now, she sometimes had wondered if she ever again could need greatly. Maybe that was because surcease and Harrison always were at hand. Theirs had been necessarily undignified, unadorned, but courteously conducted enterprises.

You couldn't blame Harrison. Men woo and win and then, if honorable, they marry and, if prudent, hoard their gains. They don't fling them with gaiety to the four winds, or marriages would not last as long as hers had. Having won, respectable husbands put their winnings in their pockets to be used expediently at time of need. Probably that was the wise way. Lucy was sure it was not Moncure's.

Azrael snored loudly. She spoke to him and then wondered how much of their present situation was due to Larry Moncure, how much to her. She thought she never had felt so well, so calmly, intensely alive as she did now. And besides, curiosity drew her toward Larry. She forever wondered what he would do next, and how.

Yet all these were not the total ingredients of the spell. Lucy thrust her attempt at analysis aside and felt glee surge within her. She was having fun and for three more months she was, by Harrison's agreement, her own mistress.

She could drive herself as she pleased, where she pleased, with no carking gas rationing to check her. While she considered this vehicular metaphor with approval, she saw the lights of an approaching car.

Azrael, belatedly rousing, scrambled up and showed a befuddled willingness to defend the premises by assault and outcry. With a trace of frenzy, Lucy grappled with him and hauled him into the livingroom. This could not be Moncure, recklessly returning. If it were, neither she nor he wished the neighborhood to hear a canine proclamation of his arrival. Her hands bungled as she closed the screen door on her captive. There was a fluttering in her stomach.

She saw with an inner emptiness which might have been either relief or disappointment that the car, halting in the beam of light from the livingroom, was not the black coupé, but a far less patrician roadster, battered, mud-plastered. One of its occupants alighted. The other stayed in shadow behind the wheel.

"Hi," Banning said and grinned as he mounted the steps. He clasped her hand in a strong, bony grip.

"Dick," Lucy blurted, "I'm so sorry; she isn't home yet. It'll be late before she gets back, I'm afraid."

"H'm," he said equivocally. "It's you I sort of wanted to talk to anyway, Lucy. Can I come in? I won't be long."

"The green-faced man," she thought with a sudden heaviness about her heart. "He's come to ask me again about him."

Aloud, she told her visitor:

"Of course you can. Won't your friend come too?"

"No," he said, following her into the livingroom and fending off the Newfoundland's enraptured rush. "Get down, you blundering hippo. Yes—yes, I'm delighted to see you, too. Down, I tell you."

He laughed and pulled the wriggling puppy's ears.

"No," he told Lucy again. "He'll wait outside. He isn't exactly a friend. We're going into business together."

She did not ask the nature of the business, but she thought its demands must be great. Even in the livingroom's soft light, his face was haggard and there were dark smudges of fatigue beneath his eyes. His body had the slack lines of a weary horse.

"Sit down," Lucy bade. He obeyed but was not even then at ease. He perched on the edge of his chair and locked his hands together. There was trouble in his frank eyes. He drew a long breath and began explosively:

"This really isn't any of my business—or it wouldn't be," he amended, "if Muriel wasn't going to marry me."

"Really?" Lucy asked. He mistook her relief for irony and his sallow face grew red.

"She is," he insisted. "Maybe she doesn't know it yet, but I do."

"I'd be glad, Dick," Lucy said and his defiance collapsed.

"You're swell. I need you on my side. Plenty. She's an ornery wench."

Banning swallowed audibly and scowled.

"Lucy," he asked, "that guy this afternoon: He's Larry Moncure, isn't he? Old Beldame Starkweather's grandson-in-law? Does he hang around much? I mean, around Muriel?"

"Not at all," Lucy answered, crisply.

"Don't let him," Banning told her. "He's no damned good."

Lucy lifted her curved eyebrows higher. He marked her supercilious expression and grew redder still.

"Look," he begged. "I'm not warning you, Lucy. You're adult. You know your way around. Muriel just thinks she does. Moncure is bad medicine for young girls. That isn't hearsay. There was a guy in officer's training with me who knew him in Spain."

Lucy smiled. She wondered if he could see the dull, hard beating of pulses in her throat. She must go carefully now, not defending Larry too stoutly. Her voice was calm.

"He's just a neighbor. We've seen him and the Starkweathers perhaps half a dozen times, but isn't something someone told you about someone else really hearsay, after all, Dick?"

"Yes," he acknowledged, "it is, of course. What I meant is that Considine, who isn't given to speaking lightly, says he's the world's most eminent S.O.B."

He paused and looked at her hard, seeking encouragement in her still face, and cleared his throat before he went on.

"I just don't want Muriel to get hurt, that's all, and he's poison to girls who think they know more than they do. Or that's what hearsay alleges, anyway. He is—or is said to be—the sort of lug who stops at nothing, or maybe it's better to say he stops, extremely brutally, after something."

"I see," Lucy answered slowly. Banning got up. The look in his eyes reminded her of Azrael's in the throes of an apology and it softened her.

"That's all," the man said awkwardly. "I just thought you ought to know. I don't holler for help over my legitimate competitors. If I have to push Bailey Ward out of the window of his darned Control Center, I'll do it solo. It's only that, after I saw you and Moncure this afternoon, I got to worrying. Not about you; you're grown up. About Muriel. She needs a lot of looking after. You don't have to be on my side to do it; just on hers."

"Aren't you going to help at all?" Lucy asked. Even in the present confusion of her mind, she wondered why Banning, erstwhile lieutenant of marines, had returned to civilian existence and raiment and what the business enterprise was to which he referred so briefly.

"Me?" His surprise bewildered her and his immediate attempt to conceal it was more puzzling still.

"Yes. Oh, sure, I am. All the while—that I can. Only—I'm not on the deck right along. I don't seem able to get to see her."

"You haven't tried very much," Lucy said with a firmly fixed smile.

"All I could," he answered, hesitated an instant and then said: "Good night, Lucy. And thanks a million."

He turned, thrust back Azrael who strove to follow him and slipped out of the screen door. The waiting car moved away. It was odd business that made them in such haste at this time of night.

"I think," Lucy said to herself in a small voice, "I'll go to bed now."

CHAPTER XV

Lᴜᴄʏ ᴡᴏᴜʟᴅ ɴᴏᴛ ʜᴀᴠᴇ ʙᴇʟɪᴇᴠᴇᴅ ʜᴀʟғ ᴀɴ ʜᴏᴜʀ ᴇᴀʀʟɪᴇʀ ᴛʜᴀᴛ ꜱʜᴇ could now be so tired. Bed might be a refuge, too. Sometimes one could hide from things by going to bed, as she tried to dodge them now by moving about to set the chamber in order. She hated rooms that looked like the night before when you came down the next morning.

When the sofa pillows had been patted into plumpness, when the books on the table had been rearranged and Azrael had been induced to collapse upon his blanket before the porch steps, Lucy turned out the lamps and went into the hall. The dining room, beyond, was dark but light showed through the jamb of the further door. She found some comfort in delaying her retirement still further.

Cyril, seated at the kitchen table with the Walden newspaper spread before him, looked up owlishly over his spectacles as Lucy peered in. Rena paused with a freshly wiped platter in hand.

"I'm going upstairs now," Lucy told them. "Muriel isn't in yet but I shan't wait up for her. Good night."

"G'night, Mis' Applegate," Cyril replied mordantly. "Jes' sayin' seemed to me like I never was so wakeful. Sour stummick-like. Suthin' I et to the weddin' most likely. They had a pile o' vittles an—"

"Try bicarbonate," Lucy counseled hastily and withdrew.

At the foot of the stair, she lingered and a faint panic possessed her. Thoughts that she tried to avert by movement would be certain to follow her upstairs. They would sit about her bed in the dark—

"Oh, dear," Lucy said to herself, hesitated a moment and then stole shamefacedly back to the porch. It was cooler and more peaceful, somehow. She had the somnolent companionship of Azrael, too, and she could postpone what she feared might be a vain struggle for sleep.

But, now that she had resolved to deal with her thoughts, they

ceased to chase her and even became evasive. She heard the muffled sound of voices in the kitchen and a whip-poor-will, calling
breathlessly down by the lake. She wondered what agitation caused
his insistent outcry.

The cane porch chair creaked as she stirred. She told herself
bravely that she was ridiculous to be so upset by Banning's visit.
What had he revealed? Nothing that she did not know or suspect
already concerning Moncure's missing morals. Probably Dick had
exaggerated everything, too. No one could be more rigidly strict
than a nice boy in love. She would have thought, though, that the
marines might have melted some of his puritan principles.

It was really very silly to let his scandal make her so uncomfortable. She was perfectly well aware that Moncure wasn't without
reproach. He wasn't at all like that Sir Barnard, or whoever he was.
She might as well be honest with herself at least: The man's un-
reliability was part of his charm.

She didn't have to do anything, either, in response to Dick's
appeal. He was worried about Muriel. Well, Muriel was safe. Moncure had said so himself. And Dick had admitted that Lucy could
take care of herself. He hadn't advised her to watch her own step.

Could it be though—she felt her skin prickle at the thought—
that Banning actually had been warning her? It had been she he
had seen with Larry. Had he been trying with elaborate tact to
preach to her? That possibility stung. It abashed her, too. She
found herself growing angry with Dick for the sense of guilt he
had quickened. Sin was like nakedness—shameful only under an
intruder's eyes.

Lucy was startled by a harsh, pent sound close at hand. Until
it was repeated she could not identify it. Cyril, bicarbonate-laden,
had come silently out of doors and now sat with his misery on
the kitchen steps, out of her view but intimately within earshot.
He belched again and groaned.

"Thar," said Cyril and Rena's high voice inquired:
"Better?"
"Some," he conceded.

Lucy wished they would go away. She was about to stir and
make her presence known and immediately was glad she had not,
for there was incitation to eavesdropping in Cyril's further speech.

"Wal," he said, clearly resuming a suspended narration, "all I'm
a-sayin' is what the bridegroom tol' me an' he oughta know."

"Will Norton," Rena's voice disparaged. "He ain't never worked for Starkweathers, even."

"Gal he was marryin' did, didn't she? She'd tell him what the hired help said, wouldn't she?"

"Mebby."

"Mebby she would; sartin she did. Ten thousand dollars a year, free and clear, Mis' Starkweather gives him to behave himself."

"Ten thousand? Cyril, what for?"

"Jes' tol' ye, didn't I? Him'n Mehitabel don't get along too good. Old gal's a mite cracked, I mistrust, on fam'ly respect'bil'ty. Never no scandal, she says. Never goin' to be one. So she pensions him, like. For good behavior."

"Dear me suz; I don't believe it."

Lucy found that her body was stiff and that she breathed warily through open mouth. She did not relax or close her lips. Cyril's wry voice went on.

"Got it straight from Norton. Rena told him. Regular help told her. Upstairs gal's heard Mis' Starkweather combin' him out couple of times. High-flyer he is by nature, too, but ten thousand dollars is ten thousand dollars. Virtue comes high. Allus heerd so."

"Flies some still, what I hear," Rena tittered.

"Ehyah. Guess he does, but he has to be consarned careful. He'll never let on he was ridin' Mis' Applegate round this—"

"Cyril, hush."

"What fer? She's gone to bed, ain't she?"

"We better go, too. I'm tuckered out."

Lucy heard them rise. The kitchen door opened and closed.

Her hands ached from their grip on the chair's arms. She looked at them vaguely, then rubbed them together. She wished she might as simply bring competence back into her mind. It, too, seemed stiff and painful.

"Whew!" Lucy said, found her handkerchief and blew her nose.

Incredulity was her instinctive defense. She had been listening only to untrammeled, malicious gossip. But it was something more than that. It was the uncannily acquired, amazingly profuse neighbor-knowledge of New England's countryside and Cyril, she knew, was among its most authoritative exponents.

Besides, she thought—and squirmed—it had plausibility. She doubted whether Cyril or his informants would be able to create fiction that dovetailed so accurately with the few facts she knew, that did no violence whatever to the characters involved.

It would be like the strong-willed scandal-loathing matriarch to control by whatever means she found most effective a ne'er-do-well relative-in-law. Unbidden now and in Mrs. Starkweather's voice, recollection came to Lucy of a fragment of homily the old woman had delivered to Ben Spofford on the day of the now-more-than-ever abhorrent picnic.

"There has never been scandal in our family; there never will be, while I live."

There were other confirmations, too. They climbed over her flimsy barrier of disbelief. Mrs. Starkweather had lectured to Moncure on that ghastly day. He had said so, gleefully, himself. Thereafter, he had bewildered Muriel by leaving her almost rudely alone and had turned to Lucy—the most available second choice.

It could have been furtiveness and fear for his pension, not the consideration she had found so charming, which had made him so discreet in the preliminaries of liaison. She had believed that this afternoon he had been muted and worried by concern for her. He hadn't been at all. He had been scared lest he lose ten thousand dollars a year.

So the malign, insistent voices cried, giving belief no place or time to stand against them.

"Oh, damn," Lucy said aloud, matching her present confusion against the blithe excitement of an hour ago.

It simply couldn't be, she thought, remembering his ardor and then wondering wretchedly whether she were not confusing her own and his. She was shamed; she was angry, yet still not wholly convinced. Pride would not let her, even now, accept entire Banning's deliberate and Cyril's involuntary warning.

"I wish I knew," she whispered. "I wish I could be sure."

She might accuse him herself; she might spread her suspicions before him, but even as she considered this move, she knew it would do no good. He would jeer and laugh and twist her words about with a diabolical resourcefulness—and fascination. If she sternly sent him away, it was certain he would not go. Her sudden coolness would, she was sure, only increase his interest and his ardor. She was not at all sure she could withstand their full, thawing blast.

She discovered, and amazement smote her, that her heart was really less involved than her self-esteem; that she dreaded more the conviction that she had been fooled than the prospect of losing a lover. It was certainty she sought; not mere reassurance.

"What a mess," Lucy told herself. "What a dreggy mess. I can't just say to him, 'Do I mean less to you than your—allowance?'"

She gulped at the word. It couldn't be true. She resolutely declined to believe that this boyishly mocking, blandly unscrupulous creature was actually the Starkweathers' kept man, yet she did not find faith wholly easy.

There must be some way of reaching the truth, other than facing the redoubtable dowager and asking: "Would you stop paying your grandson-in-law to behave himself if you knew he was inviting me to sin?"

A resourceful person might lay hold of some more practical expedient. Lucy decided that she was not even remotely adroit. She wished now, earnestly, that she had gone to bed when first she had started thither. She then would have had only a tithe of her current distress to keep sleep away.

She knew, with a mingling of alarm and relief, that it was Muriel who approached in the rattling station wagon. Azrael, lifting his head, recognized her too. The girl drove directly to the barn and returned afoot.

"Goodness," she exclaimed when Lucy hailed her. "Sitting alone in the dark? I thought everyone was in bed."

"I'm not sleepy," the other said with entire truth.

Muriel withstood Azrael's greeting, found a chair and sat down beside her sister with a sigh of relief. The tidings that she related with gusto seemed to Lucy singularly flat. The Volunteer Office records at last were in order. Ward had praised her diligence and had taken her to dinner. He was immensely pleased with the siren. Walden was the first town in the valley to have such equipment. He was even more elated by the fact that Mrs. Starkweather had consented to dedicate the new alarm tomorrow. Muriel confided further that she was tired—but tired!—and that her feet hurt.

The girl listened apathetically to Lucy's account of the shingle-stain disaster. She seemed indifferent to her sister's light mention of Larry's call.

"He drove me into town," Lucy went on, adding what she felt would be distraction from these tidings. "And Dick called again this evening."

She was not disappointed. Muriel asked with untempered eagerness:

"Did he say when he'd be back?"

"No. He's going into some sort of business with someone. He didn't say who. He looks worn out."

"Probably," said Muriel in what she tried to make a dry, indifferent tone, "that fugitive from a chain gang who was with him in the Tavern. I wish—"

Her voice ran out. Lucy prompted:

"Wish what, darling?"

"I wish I knew," Muriel tried again with undisguised distress, "what's really happened to him. He must have done something; he must be out of the marines, or he wouldn't be here in civilian clothes. Nobody knows; almost nobody sees him and, even then, he doesn't say anything. Bailey thinks he's a Fifth Columnist or something."

"Bailey is an idiot."

"He's right oftener than you'd think and he's really sweet in some ways and very nice to me."

"Who wouldn't be, darling?" Lucy leaned over and squeezed her hand.

"Dick, among others, if you're going to take a census."

"I really think he's tried to see you."

"It's a two-way telephone." Muriel had rehidden her concern. "Good for incoming as well as outgoing calls."

They were silent for a moment. Then, the girl got up.

"I'm going to bed," she announced, "before I come all apart in my chair."

Lucy led the way, turning on a livingroom lamp for her sister's guidance. Muriel kissed her and went wearily upstairs. Lucy had put out the light and was about to follow when the telephone rang their call.

"Did I get you out of bed?" Moncure asked. She had trouble in answering him.

"I'm glad," he went on. "It's the exact reverse of my intentions. Are you alone?"

"Not entirely." Wonder whether Muriel were listening and the way her own heart misbehaved made level speech difficult.

"I am," the man pursued, gaily. "The Ancestress and all her household to the third and fourth generation are asleep. You can answer in impersonal monosyllables, can't you?"

"Oh, yes."

"Then make no plans for us tomorrow for I'll be out of circulation. We attend, it appears, some simple rural rite involving a whistle. Day after tomorrow?"

The warm voice swayed her. Lucy compromised by saying: "Perhaps; I can't tell yet."

"I'll come anyway; about mid-afternoon—and back out gracefully if you aren't alone. Please be, beloved. Good-night and have shameless dreams of me."

The telephone chattered briefly beneath her trembling hand as Lucy set it back upon its cradle. Her impulse to throw away suspicion, entire, while the man spoke alarmed her now. She stood irresolute for a moment, with a finger against her uncertain mouth.

She wasn't an unformed, easily molded nineteen. She was a grown woman. It was ridiculous that the voice of any male could make her, for the moment, so wholly eager to agree with what it said. It was outrageous that anyone, particularly any man, should be so sure of his irresistible charm. The worst of it was that he had it.

A vestige of his spell still worked upon her. Dick and Cyril might both be wholly wrong. It could be, after all—

"Whoa," Lucy said aloud. "Get hold of yourself, Mrs. Applegate."

It wasn't good enough. Whatever they had had was blurred and tarnished now by alien hands. Only the sure knowledge that what she had heard this evening was wholly false might burnish it again.

Moncure's furtive telephone call, after his grandmother-in-law, his wife and all other possible auditors were asleep was in step with what Dick and Cyril had said of him. Lucy switched off the hall light again. She wished, as she turned to the stair, that the man's Ancestress actually had been awake and eavesdropping. She wished Mrs. Starkweather were giving Moncure, right that very minute, the choice of ignoring Lucy thereafter or forfeiting his subsidy. Only, she thought unhappily as she climbed, in that event she herself could never be sure what had happened.

"You're a pulpy, string-spined, hot little piece," she informed herself. Invective did small good. She still wished she could be sure.

Muriel opened her bedroom door as Lucy passed it.

"It wasn't Dick who called, was it?" the girl asked.

"No, darling," Lucy assured her. "Just Martha Spofford. Sweet sleep."

She thought with relief as she entered her own bedroom that this was the last falsehood she need act or utter that day.

Sleep came to her no more swiftly than she had feared. She lay in the dark with eyes resolutely closed. She tried to relax completely but found her body mutinous. If she subdued her legs and forced them to be flaccid, her arms were taut. When she had disciplined these, she discovered her neck was tense. She was trying too hard to sweep out her mind and leave it wholly empty, when a bright unbidden thought blossomed there.

"How ridiculous!" Lucy told herself and then, with reluctance, "Maybe it isn't, at that. I never heard of such a thing, but that's nothing against it."

It was comfort, after so much aimless and wretched groping, to feel resolution form within her. At last, it made her rise, turn on the light beside her desk, sit down, select paper and pick up pen.

When she lay down again, she felt eased. The whole idea might seem fantastic on the morrow. It was a sedative now.

She found herself wishing, as her mind grew dim, that a twin to her own bed stood within arm's reach and that she could hear, as slumber rose about her, the gravely puffing exhalations that always informed her Harrison was asleep.

Muriel, coming down belatedly to breakfast next morning, stared in bewilderment at her sister who was alighting from the station wagon.

"I thought," the girl said, "that I heard someone drive out early. Angel, wherever have you been?"

"To Walden," Lucy answered, "to mail a letter."

"As important as that?" Muriel asked and slipped an arm about her. "You look very pretty this morning."

"I feel very pretty this morning," Lucy told her.

CHAPTER XVI

LUCY APPEARED PRETTY, TO HERSELF, AS SHE SAT BEFORE HER DRESSing table early that afternoon. Beneath the arched inquiring brows, her eyes were bright. Excitement, that the prospect of attending the dedication of a siren did not seem to warrant, had heightened her color beyond the need of rouge. She applied lipstick, dutifully, and the bright mouth of her reflection smiled back at her with the anticipatory glee of a small girl.

"You look like a kid off to the circus," Lucy thought, "and maybe you are at that."

Muriel, in uniform, drove the station wagon up to the door as Lucy, after final warning to the still bedridden Ashley, ran down the stair.

"If I didn't know better," the girl said as her sister climbed in beside her, "I'd say you'd just had a very stiff snort."

Others climbed the stairs to the Walden Control Center with Lucy and Muriel—middle-aged, intensely solemn men who wore white armbands with red and blue blazonry; unadorned citizens who successfully hid any trace of the importance that had made them worthy in Bailey Ward's eyes of invitation to the ceremony.

Most of the folding chairs that filled the chamber already were occupied and Lucy and her sister were forced to take places in the front row. Before them a low, narrow stage, bunting-trimmed, bore three chairs and a kitchen table, laden with gavel, water pitcher and glasses, and connected by a curlicue of black wire to an unhealed hole in the plaster wall. Empty seats on the left bore a clothesline across their shoulders, from which dangled a placard marked "Reserved."

"For the Starkweathers?" Lucy asked her sister and peered about. She leaned back at last with the satisfied feeling of one who had reached the theater before curtain time.

Bailey Ward, in flannels and with a notably resplendent brassard bound to the sleeve of his chocolate-brown sports jacket, entered, thrusting cordially along ahead of him a grimly glowering warrior in a well-filled olive drab uniform. Pride, importance, and a suppressed frenzy all were apparent, Lucy thought, on the defense director's seamed, brown face. He scanned the audience as he guided his companion toward the platform and saw Muriel and her sister with obvious relief.

"Duchess," he told Lucy, towing the olive drab personage toward her. "Delighted that you could come. Mrs. Applegate, Miss Ashley, I wish to introduce Major Moore, lent to the O.C.D. by the War Department as technical adviser, and an extremely valuable man, if he'll allow me to say so."

He clapped the major heartily on the shoulder.

"Pleased, I'm sure," said the warrior. He bowed, came erect again and stood, looking extremely valuable.

"The Starkweathers," Ward confided to Lucy and Muriel in an anxious mutter, "are five minutes late. You haven't heard why they are delayed?"

"They're coming now." Lucy nodded toward the door and felt her cheeks grow warm.

Moncure was holding the portal open for the entrance, diminuendo, of Mrs. Starkweather, Mehitabel, Mrs. Throckmorton, and Miss Pinch. Ward, with military support, opposed their progress and embarked upon complicated introductions. When the flurry was spent, he and Major Moore accompanied the matriarch to the platform. Moncure, amusement still discernible on his face, went with the others to reserved seats.

Mehitabel passed before Lucy and Muriel with a nod and a small smile; Mrs. Throckmorton bowed, momentarily adding two more chins to her supply; Miss Pinch looked at them with wan recognition. Moncure, following, gave his boyish grin.

"Hello," he hailed. "You got hooked, too?"

He moved on, to sit at the row's far end beside his wife. On the platform, Ward ended conference with his benefactress, rose, mopped his face and advanced to the table.

"Ladies, gentlemen and—" he began, then hesitated.

"He's going to say 'And Mrs. Starkweather,'" Lucy thought with a spasm of mingled panic and mirth. She held her breath, watching the grim, sexless figure upon the platform, but Ward had seen the pitfall. He gulped, cleared his throat and began again:

"Ladies, gentlemen and distinguished guests—"

Lucy did not follow his scrupulously recited address. Her eyes strayed down the row of chairs to the man who lounged at its end.

Perhaps she only imagined that beneath the polished surface there was today less than the normal ease; that in the instant when their eyes had met, she had marked sullen resentment in his.

Mehitabel turned her cropped head and Lucy looked hastily toward the platform where Ward's voice carefully ascended his concluding sentence. She applauded politely at its end, with only the dimmest idea of what she was approving. The defense director looked more than ordinarily satisfied, polished his glasses, reaffixed them, and presented Major Moore in well-memorized phrases.

"It can," the O.C.D.'s technical advisor announced so explosively that Lucy jumped, "happen here! You men and women of the civilian defense are the last line of protection against Hitler's airborne and desperate hordes."

For a person of his comfortable proportions—Lucy thought they might have been more comfortable in less restricting clothes—the Major seemed to have a disconcertingly unpleasant mind. He roared like the six-motor planes the Axis was holding in reserve to hamstring the Allied Nations by blowing up Walden. He boomed of calamity in a bomb-like voice, plunged oratorically through carnage, soared over smoldering rubble. Though the Major's face grew red and his voice became hoarse, he persevered. He predicted a long war and obviously considered he had plenty of time.

The opening vocal salvos really frightened Lucy. She got no comfort out of the spectacle of Mrs. Starkweather's composure—after all, there was no need for a person of her age to be very much frightened about anything. Ward, too, as he bent over to whisper in his distinguished guest's ear, seemed disconcertingly calm. Their fortitude abashed Lucy. She looked over her shoulder, hoping to find comforting, kindred alarm on some other face, but she could discover in the audience no companionship for her misery.

Ward's arm-banded subordinates were displaying impassivity that might be valor; that just possibly could be boredom. While the winged hosts of infamy evoked by Major Moore hovered above them, tanned bony faces portrayed no more violent reaction than uncomplaining patience. Several wore a long, watery-eyed look, as though they had recently swallowed yawns. Clearly, Lucy thought, they had been through similar Jeremiads before and if they weren't scared, she didn't see why she should be.

The Major shouted and pounded the table. She felt someone watching her and, turning, met Moncure's eyes. They roused responsive mirth in hers. Then, all at once, his face grew blank and

he turned his head away. Lucy glanced toward the platform. Mrs.
Starkweather was watching her grandson-in-law. In her vigilance,
in Moncure's sudden impassivity, Lucy sensed a disturbing quality
—something very like the crack of a whip in authority's hand and
quick, subservient compliance. She felt shocked, then humiliated
and, at last, indignant.

Major Moore ran down abruptly. He paused to mop his face.
Ward looked relieved, glanced at his watch and whispered urgently
to Mrs. Starkweather while the speaker reassembled himself, ran up
the springboard of his peroration and dived off into a spreading
pool of mild applause. The Major sat down, looking emptied but
content. Ward advanced to the table and cleared his throat.

This, Lucy recalled before the defense director had completed
his first awkward sentence, was no part of the carefully rehearsed
role Bailey had assigned himself in the ceremonies. He was hoping,
with more of resolution than enthusiasm, that the audience had
been as deeply moved as he by Major Moore's fine address. An
authority had told them what might happen. Ward dared anyone
to say, after what they had just heard, that the work and the devel-
opment and the discipline of the civilian defense movement were
not something to which anyone proudly could give of his best.

He paused, glanced at the grimly calm Mrs. Starkweather with
what Lucy thought was last-minute appeal and, unfortified, pursued:

"And now we come, since the hour grows late, to the final purpose of this gathering. I had hoped, I am sure we all had hoped,
that we could have been favored with an address from the distinguished donor of Walden's new air-raid alarm siren but since the
hour grows late, as I have said, and Mrs. Starkweather, even at her
advanced—I mean even today, is a person still too involved in important work to call her time her own, she has requested that she
be not asked to speak but simply press the button that will—well,
will set off the siren given through her generosity to her home town
for the first time. I take great pleasure in introducing now a woman
whose long and famous life has been intimately intertwined with
the history of our country, our neighbor and good friend, Mrs.
Eliphalet Starkweather."

Brisker applause rose as he turned and bowed to the somber, determined figure, helped her to rise and led her forward. He and
Major Moore together indicated to the redoubtable old woman a
spot on the table's surface. Mrs. Starkweather placed a black-gloved

finger upon it and confronted the audience with such authority that the handclapping died.

"It is," her virile voice announced, "with great pleasure that—"

The rest of her utterance was swept away by a tempest of sound. Mrs. Starkweather had rested too much weight on the siren's starting button and the instrument, once roused, clearly was designed to run its entire deafening course before it could be stilled.

The beginning of its utterance was a vast intestinal groan that shook the chamber. While the windows rattled, the tumult soared in a spiraling roar, a numbing blast of ever more strident noise that dazed the mind and set teeth on edge and spines to crawling with its high-pitched shriek.

While the uproar endured, Lucy sat with hands pressed tightly against her ears and watched the bleak, high-nosed face of Walden's benefactress. Mrs. Starkweather, though the tumult shook her, did not flinch. Her mouth still moved and Lucy thought the words she uttered in her indignation at this monstrous interruption had properly no place whatever in a dedication.

The siren's howl expired and was still. In the street below, voices shouted alarm and reassurance and above their conflict the dazed occupants of the chamber heard earnest yelling, the clatter and thump of a hurtling wagon and the hoof-beats of a runaway team. Someone in the rear of the room laughed hysterically.

Mrs. Starkweather stepped back from the table and dusted off her black-gloved hands. In the silence that followed the tempest's passage, her voice was startlingly loud.

"There it is. It is what your director wanted. I shall not say what I think of his choice."

She nodded and turned. The Major and Ward helped her down from the platform. Applause and laughter were followed by the scraping of back-thrust chairs and a shuffling of feet. Mrs. Starkweather's companions rose hurriedly and filed back, crescendo, past Lucy. Moncure stalked in the rear. He glanced sidewise and his mouth formed voicelessly the word "Tomorrow" as he passed. The silent, furtive promise did not soothe her.

The siren's blast had shaken Lucy. Jealousy also may have been part of her irritation—resentment that one who so lately had been her eager pursuer now seemed the subdued servitor of a domineering woman. She smarted at memory of the whipcrack it seemed now she actually had heard. While she struggled against this seizure of humiliation and anger, she found herself thrust forward by the outgoing crowd and pushed, before those behind her respectfully gave way, almost against Mrs. Starkweather who, in the doorway, was enduring Bailey Ward's effusive farewells.

"I'm so sorry," Lucy said involuntarily. The keen gray eyes met hers.

"Mrs. Applegate," the baritone voice announced. "How pleasant to see you."

Something clicked in Lucy's brain with a sharp sound and inflamed her mind.

"And you," she said sweetly. "We enjoyed Mr. Moncure's call so much yesterday. We do hope you'll come with him next time."

"You're very kind," Mrs. Starkweather said with no change of expression or voice. This might be, Lucy thought as she stood aside, the response of innocence; it might be the inviolable composure of the aristocrat. In time, she assured herself with unrepentant satisfaction, she would find out; she stepped back out of the moving crowd.

She found herself standing beside the platform with the olive drab bulk of Major Moore looming above her like a spent volcano.

"I enjoyed it so much," Lucy told the warrior and added with more candor, "Though you did frighten me a little."

"My intention," the Major answered with dark satisfaction. "I meant to. All of you. You can't build determination and preserve *esprit de corps*, my dear Madam, by sweetness and light. This is war."

"Yes," Lucy said apologetically. "I know."

Major Moore drew much of his abdomen into his chest.

"The best thing," he told her, "that could happen for civilian defense morale would be a good sound bombing of New York or Boston. It would, by Godfrey."

"Oh, goodness, I hope not," she said and stared at him with her most infantile expression.

The warrior squared his shoulders and looked ruthless.

"You can't," he instructed her, "make an omelet without breaking eggs, my dear Madam. The war must be brought home to this country's rank and file. Weed out the incompetents; put the fear of God into the hearts of the others, by Godfrey."

"I suppose so," Lucy said uneasily and scanned the dwindling crowd for Muriel. The girl talked with Ward and an earnest, armbanded stranger in the room's far corner.

"Ah, Duchess," the defense director beamed, as Lucy approached, "were you impressed by our little loud-speaker?"

" 'Stunned' is a better word," she answered. Ward chuckled.

"There'll be no question of your hearing the alarm hereafter, even where you live. This is Mr. Whipple, my chief warden, Mrs. Applegate. He and I and the Pulchritudinous Person were just agreeing that the siren will save us thirty, maybe forty, telephone calls."

Whipple nodded solemnly. Lucy said, to bridge a silence that grew awkward:

"I suppose it is a great advantage, but I should think telephone calls would be quieter. I mean, all that noise does seem a waste, doesn't it?"

Muriel looked at her with sisterly scorn. Ward's regard was more tolerant. Lucy endured its amused condescension and thought with a trace of spirit that he had the sort of mind which was best pleased by another's error.

"Speed," the defense director said with a professional air, "is what will count in the case of an air raid, Duchess. With the siren, we can alarm the whole town in thirty seconds after we get the signal from D.W.C."

"D.W.C.?" Lucy repeated, conscious that she was beyond her depth but caring little whether she sank or swam. "Driving while—?"

"Angel," Muriel begged sharply, flushing at Ward's broad smile, "pull yourself together. D.W.C. is District Warning Center at Birmingham."

"Oh, I see," Lucy said with no regard for verity. Ward interposed magnanimously:

"It's difficult for an amateur to understand these things. We would get our warning signal from Birmingham, Duchess, in case of a raid."

"By siren, too?"

"Not at all. By telephone. Let me explain to you the way it works," he pursued with gathering enthusiasm.

"Army sends its warning to Birmingham at the approach of hostile planes. Birmingham immediately telephones us. We have someone on duty here day and night. Suppose those planes were not detected until they were within five minutes' flight of Walden, to make the example as simple as possible. Birmingham would call us and say: 'District Warning Center; Army flash; Red.' Instantly, our man would press the siren switch and immediately, at its sound, the blackout would begin and the complex and efficient—if I do say so—organization of the local civilian defense corps would go to work. That's what the siren will do for us, Duchess. And all in less than a minute."

"Wonderful," said Lucy. It was clear he expected no milder acclaim. She saw the Major advancing with martial tread and told Muriel hastily:

"Darling, we must go."

They went together down the now empty stairway. The girl said abruptly:

"I wish you wouldn't make fun of Bailey."

"Fun?" Lucy repeated. "But I wasn't. I was really trying to learn. And I did, too. I mean, I know now that you can set off the siren by calling Bailey's office and saying 'Army Flash, Red.' "

Muriel's bright mouth was sullen.

"You were having a time at his expense, behaving like a wide-eyed innocent just to make him spread himself. He's rather pathetically fond of me, angel."

"That's a bond between us, anyway," Lucy said and squeezed her sister's arm. The girl observed with squinting, half-humorous suspicion her companion's high color and brilliant eyes.

"I don't know what's happened to you today," she said as they went out into the street, "but it's very becoming. You look practically infantile."

"Probably a second blooming," Lucy answered and laughed. She ventured as close to the truth as she wished her sister to come.

"It certainly was not the attention paid us by the Starkweathers. They kept themselves very thoroughly apart from the bourgeoisie."

"Bailey," the girl reported, "thinks she was angry because Major Moore talked so much. Wasn't she funny when the siren blew up right under her finger? I wish I could have heard what she said then."

"I could guess, just by watching her," Lucy said and climbed after Muriel into the station wagon.

She considered, as the car rolled sedately along Main Street, the substance of the elation that had buoyed her all day. Part of it must be reaction from her worries of last night; part of it was satisfaction over her brief interchange with Mrs. Starkweather. If there had been any verity whatever in Cyril's scandalous narrative, her serenely uttered words must even now be rankling in the matriarchal bosom. Lucy wondered about that, yet she could be patient. Larry had said "Tomorrow." It was easier to wait, now that she had arranged matters so that the morrow would make everything clear.

It might be that doubt was the worst of all possible ordeals. She thought, with a recurring seizure of the quiet glee that had accompanied her since waking, that she had invented a process which in a brief time would exorcise doubt. She had only to endure a little while now and then determine what manner of man her ardent pursuer actually was. She did not believe it had been wholly her imagination that had made her sense a distress hidden beneath his air of ease. She need not wonder over this, now. She had only to wait and see. Lucy hugged the knowledge closely as the station wagon trundled through shabbier Walden and was roused from her gloating by Muriel's exclamation.

"What did you say, darling?"

She glanced and then stared at the girl's too carefully composed face. Muriel gave her head a little, dismissing toss.

"Nothing of any consequence. Dick Banning just drove by with Lombroso's delight."

"Did he?" Lucy asked carefully.

"It gives me a very clear idea of whose company he prefers," Muriel said at last in a quiet voice. She was silent a long instant before she added:

"Remind me of that, if I ever seem to forget it."

Once, in the night, Lucy floated up from sleep's deep pool and felt the wind that runs before the dawn blow on her face and saw a white star burn above the hills. She sighed, closed her eyes and let the warm, dark flood immerse her.

When she awoke, it was day and robins in the pines were calling belated attention to the sunrise. She lay and felt with calm delight how slumber's apathy drained her cleansed body. At length she stirred and laughed.

She remembered Larry's furtive and voiceless promise of yesterday. She recalled Mrs. Starkweather's cryptic composure. They brightened the morning.

Beyond the pines' dark fronds, the sky was a blue that stirred her heart. Never had the world seemed fairer; never had she felt more gleefully contented. She thought her satisfaction must be due to the fact that she had not just sat and worried, woman fashion, after Banning's warning and Cyril's overheard gossip.

Emancipation of her sex had not been complete. Though feminine activity had been permitted in other less important fields, tradition still prescribed that women must accord amorous men either surrender or only passive defense. You let them in or you fought them off. You weren't supposed to take the initiative; you mustn't strive to manage things yourself. It wasn't customary; it wasn't nice.

"Phooey!" Lucy said aloud. She sat up and laughed again. She had attacked her problem yesterday. She felt now not only proud but more respectable, too. It was good to know you weren't just a pail, set out on the steps to wait a milkman's coming.

It would be nice, she thought with flagrant self-satisfaction, if all women not yet beyond the furthest reach of romance could share her discovery that they could dish it out; not just sit and take it. Women should be more like Boadicea, or—well, like Boadicea.

When she had had problems that troubled her, Boadicea's attitude had not been passive. She had hitched up her chariot and gone to war. There had been a picture of her at work in one of Lucy's childhood books.

There was, of course, Juliet—and Isolde and Dido and ever so many others. They might have spoiled a deal of poetry but they themselves would have been happier if they had stiffened their spines and used their heads. Romeo and Tristan and—Lucy wasn't quite sure whether it had been Anaeas or Ulysses—wouldn't have been too hard to handle.

She rose, slipped out of her nightgown and, before she picked up her bathrobe, let the cool air of morning flow deliciously over her. The lake glittered and the hills beyond were glowing. It was a beautiful day, Moncure or no Moncure.

She was startled to realize that ever since night before last she had been considering her would-be lover more and more as a problem, less and less as a provocation. She did not know whether he still had power to stir her. You couldn't very well be inflamed by anyone while you were trying to find out in your own fashion— Lucy wondered if she had actually invented it—whether he were a slandered hero or a heel. She had been thinking too much of his character to consider his charm.

She wondered as she picked up her bathrobe and wrapped it about her whether she could preserve this scientific detachment if his hands were on her shoulders again, drawing her toward him, and his voice spoke softly, close to her ear. This was a question the day would answer.

Lucy doubted, under the chilling blast of the shower, if her heart were really seriously involved. She wondered why so much was blamed upon an innocent organ which actually was the responsibility of its remote associates.

CHAPTER XVII

LUCY SANG AS SHE DRESSED. SHE RAN EAGERLY DOWNSTAIRS TO THE dining room. Muriel and Ashley, with his sentence expired, already were at breakfast.

"Good morning, darlings," she hailed. "Isn't it a perfectly lovely day?"

Neither of her tablemates looked as though he or she had given it any consideration. Her son bent over his cereal and bore, Lucy thought, some of the stigmata of the lately released convict. She saw weariness on her sister's face.

"I had a wonderful night's sleep," Lucy offered.

"I didn't," said Muriel.

The other woman forebore to ask why. This was one of the minutes when she would have liked to give Dick Banning a piece of her mind.

Lucy abandoned any further attempt to share her enthusiasm for the morning's fairness, but she told her son as brightly as possible:

"We'll get the history lesson over right after breakfast, Ashley. Then you can have the rest of the day to yourself. You've had plenty of time to study it. It ought to be very good."

Mother and child spent a postprandial hour together. It was not very good.

The clouds sailed high; the wind was cool and flowers in the garden nodded invitation. Muriel had gone to her room. Ashley had wandered resentfully away, followed by an unjustifiably expectant Azrael. There remained at least, Lucy thought as she put on gardening gloves and apron, companionship with earth, that reliable and tranquil comrade. She was digging witchgrass from among the iris roots when a dusty roadster came up the drive and halted abreast of her. Its driver called "Hi!," scrambled out and hurried toward her.

In the unscrupulous daylight Dick Banning looked wearier still. He grinned at her surprise and asked:

"If she isn't home now, can I sit down beside you and cry into your lap?"

"She is home," she admitted, "but she's very angry with you. Really, Dick, you might have—"

"What?" he asked less repentantly than Lucy had hoped. "There's been a squad of gremlins following me around. They're all waiting down the road right now. Tell Muriel I'm here, like a good egg, before they decide to come in. Oh, Lord!"

He sidestepped deftly as Azrael, who had approached unseen, cast himself at his erstwhile owner's bosom. Before the puppy could leap again, Banning had both hands on his collar, holding him down.

"Yes, yes," he soothed, "we're just too delighted for words to see each other, you and I, aren't we? Take it easy, though. Let's talk this over quietly."

"Darling," Lucy called from the stairs, "Dick is here."

Muriel did not answer immediately.

"He can wait if he cares to," she said at last. "I can't come down right now," and by the muffled quality of her voice Lucy knew she had been crying.

Sympathy and loyalty put her thoroughly out of patience with Banning again, but when she returned to the porch where man and dog sat side by side, she found a pathos in the slack lines of Dick's body that took edge from her speech.

"She'll be down in a few minutes," was all she said. There really was no need for Lucy to reproach Banning. Muriel, she was sure, would attend to that adequately.

Ashley came wandering around the corner of the house, lost his expression of disconsolate boredom and hailed the visitor. Lucy said to her son, with the haste of one who suddenly has recalled an importance:

"Dear, come in with me. There's something I want you to do at once."

Ashley trailed unwillingly after her into the house, through the livingroom and to the hall, where his mother faced him.

"You and I," she told him solemnly, "are going for a walk. I can't help whether you want to or not, Ashley. Muriel and Dick haven't seen each other for a long, long while and I'm not going to have them disturbed."

She took the boy firmly by the arm and marched him away. Their haste was needless. Twice, Banning looked at his wrist watch and the second time cursed beneath his breath before, at last, Muriel appeared.

Impatience left him then. There was scarcely room in his spirit for the awe that anything so truly lovely could belong to him. She was bright and cool as the young morning and for a breath's passage he watched her, unable to speak. He held out both his hands. She let him take hers. They were cold.

"Hi," said Banning. "It's been a long time."

When he kissed her, she averted her face. His lips touched only the smooth skin of her temple and the hair above it. For an instant he simply held her. He did not try to break her passive resistance or by his warmth to quicken response in her. He thrust her away at last and held her at arm's length to look carefully at her composed face; to meet the steady regard of her ice-green eyes.

"So," he asked gravely, "that's the way it is, is it?" and, after a pause:

"Let's sit down, gal, and talk it over."

Azrael, who had stood close beside them, observing each movement with an umpire's attention, betrayed disappointment as they sat, silently facing each other. He had hoped for more; a walk perhaps, or some mild gaiety. Muriel asked with false brightness:

"There isn't really much to discuss, is there?"

Joy ebbed from Banning's face and a careful yet faintly amused look replaced it. The girl saw the wrinkles deepen at his eye corners. She knew the sign. Even now, he was going to confront her just indignation with that irksome, humorous composure that he knew, darn him, always confused her. Banning asked:

"Must you celebrate our reunion by talking to me over your tonsils?"

"What do you mean?"

"The same old system," he told her with a grin. "Whenever you don't want to answer a question, you ask another."

Azrael gave the couple a final look in which hope was almost spent, sighed, and ambled away. His pace grew brisker as he marked the parked car. Next to his twin, dishearteningly inert deities, and possibly food, automobiles were to the Newfoundland the most fascinating things of earth.

Anger was kindling in Muriel. Its glow shone on her face. She would not be treated with indulgence like a spoiled child. Her glare did nothing to subdue the amusement in Banning's eyes. He offered, more seriously:

"I've tried to see you. Remember?"

"Now and then," the girl amended, grimly.

"Repeatedly; whenever I had an hour to spare." He looked at his wrist watch as he spoke.

"What you mean is: When you weren't busy about more important things?"

"Precisely." His agreement was so prompt that it took her breath. He enjoyed her indignation.

"You'll have to take my word for that," he added.

"Oh, gladly." Muriel tried to make her acceptance as nasty as possible.

Azrael slowly was circling Banning's car, sniffing each tire in turn. The scents he inhaled were standard equipment for motor vehicles but they filled his simple spirit with joy. There was only one thing pleasanter than smelling an automobile; that was to be in one.

Banning rubbed a fist into its opposing palm thoughtfully.

"Could you possibly believe," he asked at length, "that practically everything unpleasant you've been thinking of me—with some encouragement from Bailey Ward—isn't so? I love you at your most poisonous better than any seven things in the world. You haven't been much help to me so far, and I'm in a jam."

Muriel stirred. Her voice was warmer.

"A jam? How?"

"That's the hell of it, darling. I can't tell you."

The girl drew breath sharply. She felt as though, deliberately, he had slammed a door in her face. She begged with polysyllabic hauteur:

"You'll pardon the unwarranted intrusion upon your private affairs, won't you?"

Azrael was circling the car for the second time. His head was up; his thoughts were illegal but aspiring. The doors were closed and the top was raised. It would take a leap of more grace and accuracy than even he believed he could accomplish to gain the seat. He sighed and padded further.

"I wish," Banning informed the girl mildly, "that you'd use the brains God gave you. It shouldn't overtax them to imagine some creditable reason—for a change—why I can't confide even in you at present."

The immense puppy stood still now by the car's right rear mudguard. Dick and Muriel were hidden from view. More important still, the rumble was open. To Azrael, the padded back, indicating that there was an actual seat below it, offered an irresistible invitation. He looked about him. There would be no witnesses to the invasion.

Azrael stood on wabbling hind legs and peered into the rumble. If either of the couple upon the porch had been less absorbed in increasingly unpleasant dispute, they must have heard the scuffling, the scraping of claws, squeaking of springs and slither of a heavily haired body that proclaimed the stowaway's progress. Once aboard, Azrael prostrated himself on the seat, which fitted him rather snugly, and waited. Experience had taught him that the quieter and smaller he made himself, the better were his prospects of an eventual ride.

"Are you," Banning was asking with his determinedly amused air, "going to waste what little time we have in being rigidly frigid, or frigidly rigid—or whatever?"

He looked down at his watch again. She let her anger speak.

"I'm afraid I'm keeping you from more important things."

"Not much longer," he informed her with a grin. "It's almost time for me to go."

"To see your friend, the so-called lumber man?"

"Among other things. Are you being as disagreeable as you possibly can?"

"Don't you find the lumber business"—she delicately tinted her words with scorn—"rather a let-down after the marines?"

He was still for an instant. Then he asked in a thoughtful voice: "Oh-ho! So that's what's the trouble, eh?"

"Who's answered one question with another, now?"

Banning looked down ruefully at his disreputable tweeds, his briar-scored and muddy shoes. His voice was less tolerant.

"Why not? You know all the answers, don't you, my sweet? And what your nasty little mind hasn't thought up for itself, Ward, the Warlord of Walden, has supplied. He's had the local police sneaking around after me. One of these days, when I'm not too busy, I'm going to pop him right on his snoopy nose."

It comforted Muriel to see his good humor flake away. She tried to anger him further.

"Bailey is director of civilian defense and—"

Banning had recovered quickly. Now he laughed.

"Defense of what? This vital sector of the front?"

He got up quickly and she caught her breath, thinking for the moment that she saw stark anger in his eyes, yet his voice when he spoke was quiet.

"I'm going before I lose my temper with you. Your foul mood is beginning to infect me."

He stood directly above her.

"You're spoiled," he told her calmly, "you're selfish and vain and stupid. You've got a ten-cent brain in a ten-thousand-dollar body job. You're a pretty distasteful wench to inspire the fine way I feel about you. You belong to me; oh, yes, you do, and if I can stand it, you certainly can."

He bent too swiftly for her to resist and pulled her up out of her chair. He kissed her and she slapped him. Instantly, he slapped her, not too lightly, and kissed her again. Pain and shock turned her body limp. Before she could recover, he had half lowered, half dropped her into her chair and had turned away. She sat with her hands before her eyes where tears were gathering and heard his feet go across the porch, down the steps and over the driveway gravel. His car door slammed.

Muriel looked up as the battered roadster shot past the porch but Banning, with his face set grimly, stared straight ahead. Dazed and wretchedly penitent, the girl drew breath to call and stood in silence, open-mouthed, while regret and contrition drained away.

Behind her angry lover, barred from him by the fabric of the car top, an enormous black creature now sat upright in the rumble, ears flapping in the wind, an inane grin almost splitting his Stygian head in twain.

"Oh," Muriel gasped and again, "Oh!"

She stared while the car rushed past the birches, swung round the distant curve and vanished.

Anger, stirring briefly, surrendered to dismay. This had been Dick's reprisal. Muriel's own eyes had seen it too clearly for disbelief or even doubt. She had enraged him so that he had rushed away, taking with him his cherished gift. Twice he had struck her —once in the face, once again where the hurt was far deeper—and it had been her own fault.

Muriel held her hand against her still smarting cheek. She had been abominable to her lover—cold, repellent, derisive. All the same, her reeling self-esteem tried to reassure her, Dick had had no right to abduct Azrael. She got small comfort from the thought. A tear ran down beneath her fingers. She wiped her eyes hastily at the sound of voices. Lucy came blithely up the porch steps.

"Ashley and I," she announced, "have had a perfectly lovely walk."

She beamed upon her dreary son whose aspect supplied scant endorsement and looked more carefully at her sister.

"Why, where's Dick?"

"Gone," said Muriel.

"Ashley," Lucy bade in a determinedly light voice, "run away somewhere now. Muriel and I want to talk."

"—so," said Muriel ten minutes later, "he went storming away and he took Azrael with him. I've ruined everything, Lucy. Whatever shall I do?"

She held her sister's hand in both of hers.

"Darling," Lucy asked slowly, "what do you want to do?"

"I want," the younger woman said in candid misery, "to have him bring Azrael back."

"Then the best way, it seems to me, is to ask him to," Lucy offered brightly.

"Angel, I can't; how can I?"

"There's the telephone, dearest. Mrs. Banning will know where Dick is, if he isn't home. Or that lumber man he's taking around— whatever his name is—might be able to tell you."

"I'll see," Muriel said uncertainly. Her sister sighed, got up and went into the livingroom. The world would really be a pleasanter place—less exciting probably but more serene—if its inhabitants were all of one sex. There were disadvantages to the idea, of course, but at moments like this it had a certain appeal.

Ashley sat in the livingroom. He was engaged in no further enterprise. He had slumped in a chair, to stare gloomily at nothing.

"Darling," Lucy suggested, "why don't you get a book and read?"

"I read all of yesterday," Ashley reminded her. "I'm sick of reading."

"Then go out and play, Ashley. It's such a lovely day."

Her son twisted himself into a still more melancholy posture.

"You can't play all by yourself," he reminded her in a patient voice. He writhed. Lucy, surveying him with some alarm, did not know that his agitation was the outward sign of an inner war between need and pride.

"Couldn't," Ashley blurted at last, "couldn't Barbs come over?"

"Why, I don't know, dear; I really don't. I suppose so, if you'll keep out of trouble."

"We will, Mom; honest we will."

Lucy smiled down at her suddenly revived son.

"Then phone her, darling, and see if she can."

"I'd ruther you did," Ashley told her warily. He had an idea that Mrs. Spofford might not greet him cordially and masculine pride would be sustained if his mother, not he, proclaimed his loneliness.

"Good morning, Martha dear," Lucy said to her neighbor with resolute gaiety. "Isn't it one of God's own days?"

"Simply swell, darling. It makes you glad just to be alive. How are you all?"

"We're well. I wondered, my dear, how Barbara was, poor child."

"Surviving," Mrs. Spofford reported, a shade grimly.

"Do you suppose, darling, that she could come over? We'd be delighted to have her stay to lunch."

"Lucy-love," the other inquired, "have you any idea what my poor little Barbara looks like? I've scrubbed and I've bleached and I've done everything but actually boil her. She's still—well, 'camouflaged' is the politest word I have for it. I couldn't possibly let her go anywhere until she fades. Thank you all the same. It was sweet of you to ask her."

"I'm so dreadfully sorry, Martha dear. I wish there were something I could do. I feel so terribly guilty about the whole thing."

"You mustn't, darling. It certainly wasn't your fault and Barbara insists it wasn't Ashley's, either. She's a fantastically loyal little thing."

"She always seemed to me the most completely honest person I know," Lucy replied sweetly. "Well, good-by, dear. Be seeing you soon, I hope."

She turned from the telephone.

"Vindictive woman!" she said to herself.

Muriel was standing in the livingroom when Lucy reappeared.

"I guess I'll telephone," the girl said with a shamefaced abruptness. "If you really think I should."

"I never said you should, darling," Lucy answered cautiously. "I only said I would."

Never during his brief yet ardent acquaintance with cars had Azrael so thoroughly enjoyed a ride. The wind had blown away the last remnant of worry. When the roadster moved off, he still had feared that the fate of the discovered stowaway might fall upon him. Now, it was clear that he was not to be molested. Contentment was fermenting into a heretofore unwonted elation.

The roadster's top, intervening between him and the fuming driver who was wholly unconscious that he carried a passenger, gave Azrael a heady sense of privacy and importance. He had the

dim feeling that he actually was driving the car himself. It is doubtful whether he could have pushed it along more recklessly. It is
certain that he never would have called Muriel Ashley any of the
things Dick Banning muttered to himself.

Azrael was growing intoxicated by the ruthless speed of their
progress. The wind blast was so enlivening that he stood up, the
better to savor it. The sway and the lurch of the rumble seat beneath his paws entertained him. Nothing in his life had ever thrilled
the puppy so completely; nothing in an existence marred by cause-
less thwartings and many things snatched unreasonably away ever
had left Azrael so suddenly.

Banning drove the car full tilt down a steep pitch. The roadster
leaped over the bump at the decline's foot and roared up the further slope. Azrael did not tumble. He was cast a considerable distance into air by the give and consequent violent upthrust of the
rear springs. For an instant he believed that the power of flight had
been added to life's sudden benisons. When he descended to his
former altitude, neither seat nor car was there any longer.

The road exploded into dust as the puppy hit. It seemed to rip
apart for several yards as he slid. Had he been a compact, tightly
jointed animal with any considerable rigidity of body, Azrael might
have burst into fragments. Even in his gelatinous state, breath was
thoroughly banged out of him. Consciousness deserted him for an
instant while he made several complete revolutions. Failing momentum cast him into the tall roadside weeds.

Banning, startled by the roadster's odd bounce and a queer sound,
tramped on the brake and glanced through the rear window. There
seemed to be inordinate haze in the road behind him, but otherwise
it was clear.

"What the hell could that have been?" the man muttered and
made haste once more. The dust of his passage had sifted back to
earth before Azrael, reviving, rose unsteadily and hauled himself
out of the ditch. He was still breathless and suffered from sense of
ill usage, betrayal and heartless abandonment, as well as sundry con-
tusions, but the hopeful philosophy that Newfoundland pups have
to learn early if they are to exist at all, sustained him.

Azrael looked about him. The surroundings were unfamiliar and
the treatment he just had endured seemed equally strange. He had
been ousted in an inexplicable, emphatic fashion but he cherished
no grievance and was certain that it all had been a mistake.

The puppy attempted to launch a wabbling pursuit of the now

vanished car but even to so optimistic a spirit it soon grew plain that the attempt was no good. Azrael hurt all over; his legs proved to be less than ordinarily co-operative. In his third awkward bound, they tripped him and he fell severely on his chin.

Bit by bit, he reassembled himself and sat in the road to consider the problem. He felt abused, then lonely. He was thirsty, too, for he had inhaled so much dust that his throat seemed lined with sandpaper. One demanding emotion overcame all other distresses. It was noon; it was dinnertime and Azrael was hungry.

His need for food grew while he considered it. If he lingered here longer, he might be guilty of the, to him, cardinal sin of being late to meals. He decided he must hasten and therefore abandoned the road and set off with a high heart and a clamorous digestive tract cross country toward where, he serenely believed, home lay.

Azrael climbed a stone wall and hurried through brushy pasture beyond. Thereafter, he went for a long way through woodland.

He loped along hurriedly, trotted when his breath failed and, recovering it, loped again. He had no gift for topography. The eerie directional sense which dogs are supposed to have—and few possess—was wholly missing from the puppy's cosmos.

Up hill and down, through forest and glade, with anticipatory eye and watering mouth, Azrael hurried home. If the puppy had held to the direction in which he so confidently progressed, he would have circled the globe before he attained his goal.

Banning parked his car before the Eagle House and went into the hotel. His face was dreary; beneath failure's waxing burden, his shoulders sagged. He had botched his first independent detail; he had lost his girl. Memory of the confidence with which he had returned to Walden made him seem a particularly tragic figure. Ahead lay nothing more enlivening than a telephoned confession of error to his superior and consequent, humiliating recall.

He thought, with a spark of interest, that he might interview Bailey Ward before he left but enthusiasm lived briefly. If he belted Bailey, he probably would break his own arm. That was the way his luck ran.

The big, red man jumped up to stand stiffly as Banning entered his room.

"Oh, skip it," the intruder said wearily. "Relax, Sergeant. And you might as well pack up, too. We're through."

"The Lieutenant," Sergant Dade, assigned to Intelligence, asked, "ain't found anything?"

"Plenty." Banning's voice was grim. "But none of it gets us anywhere. We're whopped. I'm going to phone Captain Whitney and tell him so."

"Yes, sir." Dade scowled and ran a hand through cropped hair. "Seems though, even out here in the boondocks, we ought to be able to find him if he's all over green paint."

"We haven't and you saw the letter I got from Captain Whitney this morning. We don't even know that this Easter egg is Wise. All his people have moved away. It may be just a tramp or sneak-thief, living off the country."

"I got a sort of hunch, Lieutenant."

"I had, myself," Banning said bitterly, "and look what it got us."

He strode about the room as though movement might ease his misery. The call he soon must make would, at least, put an end to this bungling. There had been, he thought sourly, nothing but bungling from the beginning.

They had bungled in the navy yard where they should have arrested August Wise, civilian employee, as soon as they detected him at treason, instead of waiting to entrap other, more important quarries. Bungling had alarmed the man and had marred the belated raid upon his lodgings. Wise had vanished before they had broken in, leaving behind nothing more evidential than a smell of smoke and, in a grate, charred paper that red spark worms ate to ashes.

Sole clue had been an unconsumed envelope corner with the Walden postmark. Banning's hunch had been born from this, from the fact that Walden was his own home, from dim memory that a Wise family had lived there. The lieutenant had been sure the fugitive would scurry north, and had wrung from his superior permission to drive with Dade in pursuit.

Bungling had continued to afflict the pair since the morning when they had parted briefly at Walden's edge. The lieutenant had walked into town and informed his mother, to whom any military irrationality seemed normal, that he was home for a holiday. Dade had registered at the Eagle House, posing as a purchaser of timber land, and Banning, encountering him by apparent accident, had volunteered to guide him.

Nothing, the lieutenant now thought wryly, had gone right. They had found no trace of Wise, unless the shingle-stained marauder possibly were he. Their own cryptic comings and goings had challenged local curiosity, had even subjected them to clumsy police surveillance, inspired, Banning was certain, by Ward.

The unhappy man ceased his pacing and turned with resolution to the telephone. It rang as he moved and Dade, answering, turned and said:

"Lady to speak to you, Lieutenant."

"Dick?" It was Muriel's warm voice and Banning felt his heart turn over. "Dick, I was a beast. I'm—I'm so wretchedly ashamed."

Her profession seemed to echo through the room. Banning glanced desperately at Dade and pressed the receiver hard against his own ear.

"Look," he begged. "I'll call you later."

"I don't want you to call me. I want you to come back—darling."

"As soon as I can," he promised, sweating.

"And you'll bring my precious infant, too?"

Dade's face, peering attentively at the ceiling, was a mahogany mask.

"Who?" Banning gulped. His ear hurt. Muriel's voice seemed increasingly loud.

"Don't pretend, Dick. I deserved it, but it wasn't very generous of you."

"What are you talking about?" he begged desperately.

"Really, Dick! Haven't I humbled myself enough? Azrael, my own dear puppy."

"What has Azrael got to do with—"

"Oh!" He winced at the sudden change in her voice. "If you are going to be nastily vindictive, I'm sorry I called."

"Will you," he asked with what sanity remained to him, "skip it, for now? I'll try to see you later."

"With Azrael?"

"Why do you keep talking about Azrael? I haven't—"

"I tell you I saw the whole thing. Don't lie to me."

"Thanks for the compliment. Do you care to tell me what you think you're talking about?"

"Oh," she cried, "how can you ask me that you—you despicable dog stealer?"

He heard the connection break, sighed, and set down the telephone. This was of a piece with preceding confusion and woe. He said to Dade, who still stared at the ceiling:

"You can unrig your ears now, Sergeant. I'll phone the Captain and then we might as well eat before we pack."

CHAPTER XVIII

AZRAEL HAD ACCOMPLISHED ONLY FOUR OF THE TWENTY-FOUR thousand miles that, by the route he followed, lay between him and home but hunger, too intense for dalliance, and growing loneliness urged him on. This latter, in time, surpassed his never inconsiderable appetite. He was an extremely social member of a humanity-loving race. Mankind's companionship was essential to his happiness, and here in this increasingly dreary wilderness there was none. A new sound associated itself with the castaway's loud puffing. As he hurried along, Azrael wept softly.

The dwarfing trees, the unpleasant forest's gloomy shade gave way at last. Sunshine lay on open land and Azrael's lamentations ceased. He at least could see now where he was going, though the landscape was wholly unfamiliar. He moved more briskly past blackened brushpiles and rotting stumps.

Suddenly, he checked and stood with lowered head to indulge in rapturous inhalations. Azrael had encountered a path that recently, so protracted snuffings informed him, human feet had trod. The man scent was familiar and with it was blended a faint yet infinitely heartening flavor of food. Azrael launched into lumbering pursuit.

It was a long chase. The encouraging scent led him across the open land, along a rutted road and sharply off again into woods. The quarry, Azrael's nose informed him, was closer now. Each gusty breath seemed more fragrant than the last. The immense puppy burst at last into a brushy clearing and saw, midway between him and the moldering cabin in its center, the object of his search. Joy burst from Azrael in a bellow.

August Wise, returning belatedly from a foray with a sack containing a slab of bacon and two early cabbages, leaped high, looked back and fled. Stouter fiber and a purer spirit might have been upset by sight of the bounding black monster and Wise's conscience was definitely bad. He had dreaded pursuit for so long that, now, he could imagine nothing following him for other than the direst purposes. He ran for the shack and Azrael ran also.

It was a brief yet vigorous race and the puppy, despite his handicap, almost won it. A glance over his shoulder nearly undid Wise. He saw the black enormity that gained upon him. He marked with pardonable dread the whitely rolling eyes, the gleaming teeth. He did not see, in his panic, the stump before him.

Wise fell and the sack flew far. He rolled over, leaped blindly up and, with the sound of pursuit hideously close behind, plunged into the cabin, hurled the door shut in Azrael's disconcerted face and collapsed, spent and half-senseless, on the floor.

While the man's mind whirled, he heard beyond the barrier wheezings and a whine that, though it only expressed disappointment, sounded definitely carnivorous.

Azrael, having asked politely if breathlessly for admittance, sat down to wait. In time, his simple mentality assured him, his friend would open the barred portal and make him welcome. Meanwhile, after the vast and oppressive loneliness, even remote proximity to mankind was appeasing.

As the puppy's panting ebbed, his nose informed him of further benisons. Azrael heaved himself up, backtracked briefly and came upon the jettisoned sack. It took him time to claw its contents free, but when he succeeded, he divided them scrupulously.

He reserved the cabbages for his friend and was finishing the bacon when the cabin door cried on rusted hinges and Wise's stained face peered out haggardly. The portal slammed as the Newfoundland cordially rushed forward, but an instant later reopened. Wise at last had recognized his late pursuer. Anger and shame sharpened his voice.

"You git. Go home."

Azrael looked bewildered. He did not understand the animus in his associate's speech. Furthermore, even if willing to obey the order, he had not the faintest idea in which direction home lay. He sat down, panted heartily and beat upon earth with his tail.

"Scram, you," the man bade, closing the door for an instant and reappearing with a stick, which he waved menacingly. Azrael rose and lunged forward, eager to co-operate in a sport he knew, but immediately thereafter yelped, wheeled, and fled for a space. The stick thrown by Wise had smitten him in the ribs.

From a distance, the puppy stared reproachfully at his assailant, who now gathered a handful of stones and hurled them with vindictive energy but poor marksmanship. Grazed twice, hit once, the

Newfoundland lurched out of range. Midway between the cabin and the encircling woods, he sat down once more.

It was better to tarry in a currently hostile atmosphere than to wander again through the wilderness. If he waited, things would be better. Whatever offense he had committed would be forgiven or forgotten. Already, the puppy had learned that this was what happened, if you waited.

Wherefore he sat, deaf to repellent shouts; retreating still further when, once, Wise emerged and, ax in hand, advanced balefully; drawing near again when the man, thwarted and cursing, retired to the shack. Patient, loyal, hopeful yet increasingly depressed, the puppy kept vigil. Earlier elation was evaporating and gradually the woe that replaced it no longer could be borne in silence.

Azrael lifted his blunt muzzle skyward, filled his shaggy chest and uttered misery in a long, resonant howl. It made him feel a little better, so he repeated it. It was having its effect also on Wise, who came to the door of the cabin and yelled. The puppy drew a deep breath and tried again. The organ-like keening rolled echoing through the hills.

Luncheon in the Applegate household was not the most satisfactory repast over which Lucy ever had presided. She sat with her dismal son, her glowering sister, and wondered whether her own resolute cheer served any better purpose than, by contrast, to intensify the gloom. Muriel's telephone conversation with Banning had neither lightened her spirit nor quickened her appetite. Most of the time she merely sat, saying and looking at nothing. Anger's hard color gave her face smoldering loveliness. She ate little and what fragments of speech she did release reminded her sister of sparks cast up by an inner fire. Lucy could not tell from the disjointed utterances whether bereavement for Azrael or rage at Banning were uppermost in Muriel's mind.

"If ever he does come back—" the girl began with heat, gulped and was still again, leaving Lucy to doubt the pronoun's antecedent. Later, she burst out, darkly and still indefinitely:

"Don't think he won't regret this."

Ashley was no foil for his aunt's smoldering state. He ate sadly though heartily and boredom was an actually perceptible load upon him. It drew his freckled countenance down into dolorously sagging lines and stunted his power of speech, compressing it into grunts of

varying length and pitch. Lucy was glad when the meal abruptly
ended.

Muriel thrust her helping of lemon jelly away and pushed back
her chair in a single determined movement.

"I'm going to see Bailey," she announced. "I'm going to find out
from him if Azrael isn't my dog and if I can't have Dick arrested."

"Oh, dear!" Lucy began and added, weakly, "Oh, I wouldn't."

"Why not?" her sister asked with violence. "It's theft, nothing
else."

"But Dick said he didn't do it. Isn't that so?"

"I don't know what he said. He—he practically blithered. Whatever it was, it probably was a lie. I've got eyes, haven't I?"

"Of course," the older woman ventured, speaking for safety's
sake more to herself than her sister, "it could be that Azrael got
into the rumble himself and hid—he loves so to ride. Dick doesn't
generally lie, does he?"

She was astonished to find that Muriel seemed more cheered than
affronted by her intervention.

"Could be," the girl said at last with a more moderate voice and
look. "Do you really think—?"

Her face hardened again. She asked indignantly:

"If that is so, where is Azrael now? If Dick really hasn't seen him,
what's happened to him?"

"Couldn't he have jumped out?" Lucy asked carefully. "I mean,
Dick may have stopped somewhere and—"

She followed the suggestion no further. It sounded really ridiculous, even to her, yet the girl seized upon it eagerly.

"He might," she agreed. "If he did, then the poor lamb is lost.
He'd never miss a meal purposely. I'm going to take the car, anyway, and drive in to Walden. I'll stop at every house and ask each
person I meet. Someone certainly must have seen him."

She strode toward the door. Lucy rose.

"Finish your dessert, dear," she bade Ashley as she left the room.
She found pathos in the eagerness with which Muriel had grasped
the proffered straw. Only a woman truly in love could believe so
willingly in the improbable.

Muriel had paused halfway to the barn to speak to Cyril. Lucy
joined her while the one-sided conversation still endured.

"Yes'm," Mr. Handrow was saying in his own version of cheer,
"he'll be shot sure as hell's afire if he's lost. Lot of folks out, game
laws or no game laws, every day now, what with meat bein' so

scarce. They'll take one look at that big black critter and be sure-certain he's a bear."

"Oh, nonsense, Cyril," Lucy intervened and went on with her sister to the barn.

"I'd go with you, darling," she pursued as Muriel climbed into the station wagon, "but I have a lot to do this afternoon."

"I'd rather be alone," the girl replied ungraciously and drove away. Lucy watched her out of sight, then went back toward the house.

Concern for Muriel, worry over Azrael's continued absence retired to the back of her mind while she considered with awe how circumstance was clearing the way, by no effort of hers, for her tryst with Larry that afternoon. She supposed she should feel guilt instead of this solemn satisfaction yet, somehow, she couldn't. This was Fate's doing. So many things—most things—really worked out better if you just left them alone to solve themselves.

Ashley had finished his lunch and now sat on the porch edge, swinging his legs and observing his mother's approach with something less than his maximum glumness. His speech, when Lucy paused beside him, thrilled her, not by its content but because she recognized still another evidence of Fate's purpose.

"Mom," said Ashley with a surly reluctance, "maybe I'd better go over to Barbs' this afternoon, just to see how she's gettin' along and all like that, huh?"

Lucy knew that his gruffness hid the young male's fear lest he be accused of kindliness or sentiment. He was lonesome for Barbara and terrified lest anyone suspect it.

"Why, darling," Ashley's mother said, "I think that would be a very kind thing to do. Barbara must be having a rather wretched time, poor little thing."

"Well," her son granted, clouding intention with words, "I could just as well as not, I guess."

"It's sweet of you to be so thoughtful, Ashley."

"Aw," he said, reddening. "Aw, nuts!"

"I'm sure Mrs. Spofford won't mind. Remember one thing, dear; be sure to tell her as soon as you get there how sorry you are you got Barbara into trouble."

"Me?" her son said and gaped in honest indignation. "I didn't do anything. She fell off the barn and onto that burglar. How's that my fault, I'd like to know?"

Lucy sighed.

"Just do as I tell you," she bade. "Don't ask why."

Yet the bewilderment on Ashley's face hurt her. Children had so much to learn! Impulsively, she reached out and smoothed his rough hair.

"Darling," she told him, "you won't understand for ever so many years but I wish I could make you believe this one thing; when a woman is angry about something she thinks you've done, it's much better just to tell her you're sorry, no matter whether you did do it or not. And brush your hair before you go, Ashley. It looks like a fish hawk's nest."

She sat on the porch and watched the boy trudge down the driveway. A quickening excitement possessed her and with it a reverent gratitude. The stage had been cleared for Moncure's entrance. The two most difficult witnesses to his call obligingly had withdrawn themselves, and this had been accomplished without her own least effort. Fortune, Lucy reflected, really could be much kinder than most people believed these days.

If now, they only would stay away until her interview with Moncure had ended! It might be brief; it might endure. There were times, she thought, when uncertainty was really dreadfully exciting.

Lucy rose. She would go upstairs and dress now. She hoped Muriel would recover Azrael, but she hoped, too, that her sister would be a long while finding him.

CHAPTER XIX

Banning thrust himself into the disreputable roadster along-side Dade, waved to his mother, who stood on her porch, and tramped on the starter. They moved away in a series of plunges as he savagely shifted gears. Presently, as Walden's ranked houses dropped behind and the highway unrolled, broad and fair ahead, the taut young man relaxed and granted his seatmate a crooked grin.

"Good-by," he proclaimed, "to a lot of things and if I never get back, it'll be soon enough."

"Yes, sir," the sergeant replied, flinching as they hurtled around a curve. "Well, we done our best."

"Which was something less than good enough," Banning reminded him. "Captain Whitney called that to my attention."

His ears still smarted from the brusque recall he had received from his superior who had a nautical breadth and saltiness of language. He was faintly abashed by memory of the implausible lies he had told his mother to account for his sudden departure. Thought of Muriel was a hard, angry feeling in his stomach's pit.

As Banning drove along, he assembled a collection of caustic phrases he intended to embody in a letter to his erstwhile love. He would not mail it. They would find it on his body where carnage had been the thickest and send it back to her. By then, though, he considered wretchedly, she probably would be married, with three children, all looking like Bailey Ward.

Muriel Ashley was a trifling, two-timing, gold-digging little wench and the hell with her! She had been pleased to consider him a possible deserter, she had slapped his face—he released one hand from the wheel to rub a cheekbone reminiscently—and because she apparently had lost her dog (how one could mislay anything of Azrael's size was beyond him) she had accused him of thievery. All right, he assured himself ominously. Wait!

They roared through the bridge over the lake's narrows and ahead of them the highway split. The left fork crawled up over the hills and down into Chester. It was the shorter and rougher route. The right road, Banning knew, curved past the Applegate driveway. A small wheedling voice urged him to turn right and, perhaps, even pause for the smallest instant at the old brick house. He found a grim satisfaction in quelling the idea and swung to the left.

"Short cut," he told the sergeant. "It'll save us time."

They jolted and lurched uphill into the shade of towering hemlocks. Banning was not sure why time should be saved. He wished there were some dignified way of letting Muriel know he had foregone deliberately his last opportunity to see her. Perhaps she was waiting for him, penitent once more and anxious. Let her!

The road was more uneven than he had remembered, the grades steeper. He rushed them without compunction until Dade, clinging to his seat, ventured:

"Heating up a bit, ain't she, Lieutenant?"

Vapor was squirting from about the radiator cap, and when Banning cut the switch, they heard the engine's loud, intestinal rumblings.

"Damn!" he said, pulling up the emergency brake. He peered uncertainly through the gloom cast by arching trees.

"A brook runs through here somewhere."

He scrambled out and scuffled in the rumble for a possible water container, jerked head and shoulders free and stood, open-mouthed, listening. Dade ventured:

"Fire somewheres, maybe. It ain't that air-raid sireen loose again?"

Full-bodied, august, the sound rolled over them and died away. Dade grunted. Banning said in an awed voice:

"That's not a siren; it's Azrael. I'd know that whoop of his in Timbuctoo."

After a pause, he added as one unwillingly admitting a miracle:

"By all that's holy, he was lost then; he still is."

Wavering impulse moved him toward the forest-obscured source of that haunting bellow; thrust him backward a step. Anger was fading and pity now abolished it.

"The black imbecile," Banning told his companion defensively, "probably broke his tether and has caught it around something out there. I'll have to find him. Stay here. He can't be far."

Again the desolate howl arose. Banning thrust his way through brittle lower branches of the roadside hemlocks . . .

Shade reached out across the brush-dappled clearing when Azrael's rescuer entered it, after a quarter hour's scramble, but the

decaying shack still stood in sunlight and from its doorway someone gesticulated and shouted at a black creature who sat by the
edge of the encircling woods. Azrael reuttered his woe.

So vast was the soaring sound, so disorganized was the cabin's
occupant that the advancing Banning was close at hand before the
other man was aware of his presence.

The Lieutenant heard breath whistle through the greenish nose;
saw the stained face contort.

"August Wise?" he said and, as the other quailed, moved his
own hand toward his hip. Wise shuddered and asked with weak
defiance:

"So what?"

"So I'm Naval Intelligence," Banning replied cheerfully. "We've
been looking for you quite a while."

Across the clearing, Azrael stood up. His ears were raised, his
head high. He still was uncertain, yet his plumed tail moved, slowly,
then faster.

"You'd still be looking," the prisoner began with bravado that
dwindled into whimpering, "spite of all they done to me, if it
wasn't for that dam bellowin' whatever-it-is."

"Right," Banning agreed promptly. "He ought to have all the
credit I'm going to take for myself."

Across the clearing toward them a monstrous black creature,
with rolling eyes, with ears that flapped like inadequate wings,
came bounding. Banning drew Wise into the shack and closed
the door.

"We'll wait," he said, "for a moment, until he quiets down a
little."

Lucy's feet, as she ran downstairs, made disproportionately loud
noise in the quiet house. She paused in the livingroom to consider
herself at the mirror there. It reiterated the assurance of the long
glass in her bed chamber. She was looking extremely well in her
best yellow afternoon frock.

She supposed, as she settled herself on the porch to wait, that
soldiers felt like this when they put on their best uniforms and
went into battle. Only, soldiers didn't dress well these days. The
greater the danger, the worse they looked. Plumes and braid and
valiant deeds that got into poetry, all were things of the past. Or
maybe it was Romance that had been discarded.

So much that used to be romantic wasn't any longer. It was too bad that this should be so. Many things were much pleasanter if you could pretend successfully that they were something else. People prided themselves on facing facts today, on being honest; but Lucy's mother would have said they were just being common.

She listened for a moment to the sound of a distant car but it went, unseen, past the driveway's end.

After all—she picked up her thought again—disguise, which was just another name for Romance, made decent existence possible. You tried not to think of the poor steer or lamb when you bought a piece of him at the butcher's and when you got it home you disguised it still more by cooking and garnishes and sauces. You didn't serve food raw, even if you had been married fourteen years. She didn't see why you couldn't be as romantic, or fanciful, or whatever you wanted to call it about other appetites.

Such preparations took time, she knew, and people were dreadfully busy, but she wondered whether, really, they weren't busiest about the wrong matters.

Didn't most of them ever grow hungry, not directly for the essential substance itself, but more for the ceremonies and rites and decorations that could be made to grace it?

She looked at her wrist watch. Ashley must have reached the Spoffords' before now. Perhaps Muriel had found Azrael and was on her way home. She wished Larry would come.

He was part of the very thing she had just been thinking of. He was exciting because he was romantic. He did things so attractively you forgot until someone conscientious, like Dick Banning, or scandal-loving, like Cyril, pointed out what lay beneath the adornment—or what might lurk there.

She was really, Lucy thought, grateful both to Cyril and Dick, especially to Cyril. He had, without knowing it, slammed on the brakes when she needed them most. She might otherwise have gone off the deep end where Muriel had tottered. If Lucy hadn't eavesdropped on Cyril, dreadful things might have happened. Things might happen still, she told herself stoutly, but she was going to be certain first that they wouldn't be dreadful. That was why she was waiting here, in her best yellow frock, for Moncure.

Even Romance itself wasn't too good, if a man offered it to you just because you happened to be at the moment the most available woman. It was dreadfully irritating, too—having overheard Cyril—to keep wondering how far cash actually influenced her lover's conduct. Money might have made him drop Muriel. Would fear for his alleged subsidy impel him to abandon Lucy, too? It was a horrid question. It made her feel disreputable—a little like a harlot in reverse.

Suppose, she thought with a sudden qualm, that after all this contriving and preparation he did not come at all? Suppose that Cyril's third- or fourth-hand scandal was the truth? Might not Lucy already have frightened Moncure off by mentioning to Mrs. Starkweather the fact that he had called? If he didn't come, she would never know what had happened. She would have the wretched feeling always that he had discarded her. Like an old glove. Why, she wondered, were women always jilted like an old glove and never like an old necktie or a pair of worn-out socks?

She could, of course, have dismissed Moncure, but then she never could have been sure. She would always have felt, miserably, that she had been frightened away from enchantment by mere gossip. She wanted to be certain; she had taken pains that she should be. And now, suppose her late pursuer simply didn't come?

"Oh, dear!" Lucy said unhappily.

"Oh, dear!" another voice repeated with a wholly different intonation. She jumped up, whirled about.

Larry stood at the foot of the porch steps and smiled up at her. He had approached with extreme stealth. Not even a stir of gravel beneath his feet had betrayed him.

He was amused, composed, and there was possessiveness in his eyes as they moved slowly over her from head to foot. It alarmed Lucy to feel how quickly she responded. She faltered:

"Good heavens! Did you drop from the sky?"

"Or pop out of the earth, like Mephisto?" he jeered and came up the steps with grace that his limp could not mar. Lucy gave way before him and sat down again. He dropped a proprietary kiss upon the top of her head and drew a chair about to face hers.

"I came by canoe," he told her. "It seemed—more discreet."

She wondered whether it were imagination that made her think distraction, concern, outright worry lay beneath his surface confidence.

"A drink?" she asked. He shook his head.

"No, strangely enough. It would waste time. We've got a lot to talk about and I can't stay long. You're alone? Nice going, darling."

He paused. It was the first time, Lucy realized, that she ever had seen him at a loss.

"Sugar," he said at last, "you certainly put your pretty foot into it clear up to your doubtless even lovelier hip, yesterday."

"I?"

"Yes; you, honey. You told the Ancestress I'd been here the day before."

"But—but I don't understand," Lucy told him and admired the innocence in her voice. "Why shouldn't I? Others knew you were here—Rena, Cyril, the children. It certainly wasn't a secret."

"I know," he acknowledged, "but—" And again the singular irresolution checked him.

Lucy tried to look unconcerned and succeeded only in appearing confused, which apparently did just as well.

"I said nothing at all about—our ride together."

"You didn't have to." His smile was less youthful now. "That had been attended to already."

Her lips were dry, her heart had begun a violent pounding. Moncure's voice was rueful.

"We're right unfortunate, you and I. The gods still are houndin' us. You see, yesterday noon someone favored the Ancestress with an anonymous letter."

"Mentioning me?" Lucy sat up straighter. He shook his head in humorous woe.

"Mentioning me. You mentioned you later, and very thoroughly put yourself outside the sanctified pale. You're a Shameless Woman, sweetness, and A Threat in the Ancestress's eyes. You're taboo."

"You mean," Lucy asked slowly, "that—that she really feels that way?"

"Why not?" he returned and shrugged. "She's elected herself the family's moral guardian and she works at the job—never think she doesn't."

"But I still don't understand. You're adult, aren't you? You can call on whomever you please. Does your wife disapprove? Is that it?"

"My wife," he told her with the little sharp edge to his speech that usually accompanied his mention of her, "doesn't even know. It was the Ancestress who got the letter."

"And just what business," Lucy asked, "is it of hers?"

"Honey," he kept his voice light with perceptible effort, "you just don't know her."

"But even if I did, I don't see why she has the power to—to tell you you mustn't have women friends."

He drew a long breath. His distress was plain now. For a fleeting instant Lucy was sorry for him.

"Listen, darling: Must I be explicit? The poison pen wielder—a woman I should judge from her handwriting—has no inhibitions and a gift for exaggeration. According to her, I went out with a lady—whose name you obligingly gave the Ancestress—and very thoroughly seduced her."

"Oh," said Lucy.

"Precisely," he agreed. "It's a mess, sugar."

"What," she asked, "do you think I should do?"

Tenderness came into his voice and drove worry from his face. "Not 'I'; we. It's you I'm thinkin' of most, honey. We'll have to go underground together. You cut me if we meet again; I'll ignore you. It won't be long, darling. We're leaving soon—sooner than anyone thought till yesterday. Then the gods will be kinder. We'll meet in New York—anywhere you please—whenever you can manage."

His eyes with their unabashed desire half-fascinated her again. He took her hands, lifted them to his face, kissed each cold palm.

"It'll be perfectly safe, soon," he told her, "and lovelier for waitin'."

"Safe for you?"

He stared at her from beneath raised brows. He said with reproachful indignation:

"For you, Lucy. It's you I'm thinkin' about."

His pose of concern set off a silent explosion in Lucy's head, blowing away compunction and uncertainty, wholly clearing her mind. She pulled her hands back and gave a sharp little laugh.

"What an accomplished liar you are!"

He said at last:

"Pardon?"

"All this touching thought for me." Her voice was lightly indulgent. "Do you really expect me to believe it?"

"Would you like me," he asked gravely, "to send you a copy of the letter?"

She drew a long breath and answered, deliberately:

"It's not really necessary, my dear man. I mean, all the letter says is: 'Are you aware that Lawrence Moncure took an attractive neighbor for a long automobile ride yesterday afternoon?'"

She stared at him. He did not stir. She pursued, more lamely:

"I put the 'attractive' in just out of vanity. I mean, you see, I wrote the letter myself."

"You what?" He dragged the words from bewilderment's swamp.

"I did," Lucy insisted and her laugh was faintly apologetic. "You see, a woman of my age ought to be very particular, I think, if she's taking a lover. I mean, she ought to want something more than—well, than just a good physical specimen."

She looked at his blank face and gave him no time to rally.

"With young girls it's different, isn't it? I mean, they're really your specialty—if Mrs. Starkweather doesn't hear about it. If she does, she stops your allowance, doesn't she?"

Larry cleared his throat with a thick sound and leaned forward in his chair.

"That's what I've been told," Lucy went on, dimly wondering whether she was feeling enjoyment or terror. "I've also been told that you are the complete S.O.B. So I thought I'd better find out."

He rose and stood above her. His eyes, looking down into hers, seemed less boyish now and his smile was crooked.

"Lady-bird," Moncure said, "there are certain words that, in the presence of women, are never used by southern gentlemen."

He paused. Lucy asked:

"Why do men from the South always speak of themselves as 'southern gentlemen'? I mean, are they afraid that, otherwise, people will make a perfectly natural mistake?"

"You're a common little thing, aren't you?" he asked.

Lucy drew a long breath. She bade, quietly:

"Go now, please."

For a long instant, he did not seem to have heard. The intensity of his look candidly frightened her now. He shrugged, turned, and limped away.

She watched him move deliberately through the flower garden, over the meadow, and down its slope toward the lake.

"There goes my youth," Lucy told herself softly. "The very last of my youth."

She considered the sentimental elegance of her thought with satisfaction. It really did sound like something out of Maeterlinck or one of those unreadable Russians. She didn't quite understand how she could be pleased by it at a time like this, yet she was.

"That's really a very nice thing to say, Mrs. Applegate," she said aloud, "and rather pitiful, too, I think."

She was dismayed by the tide of relief that rose about her,

soothing her, in some queer fashion making her feel light and freshly bathed. It was an odd sensation—rather, she supposed, like repentance and absolution; rather like hitting a slot machine's jackpot, too.

"Well," Lucy told herself, "that certainly is that."

If all women who rejected their suppliants felt so pleasantly virtuous, Lucy wondered why they didn't do it oftener. Sometime, she admitted thoughtfully, she might regret this afternoon. There might be moments when she would think, maybe a little wistfully, of Moncure. She was too proud of herself—righteously, not sinfully proud, now—to worry about that.

All by herself, she had driven the wolf from her doorstep; had outwitted and overwhelmed a notorious character by a simple system of her very own. She had tried Larry in a balance of her invention and had confirmed Dick's and Cyril's testimony. She would be less intolerant hereafter, when her hired man gossiped. As a matter of fact, it might be valuable to encourage Cyril's scandalous anecdotes concerning his neighbors. They were apparently more factual, and therefore entertaining, than she ever had suspected.

Lucy found herself wishing that Cyril would come shambling into view, now, not for reminiscence but for the sake of mere companionship. The house was uncomfortably still; the bright hush of the afternoon made her feel rather terribly alone. Not even further contemplation of her achievement could cheer her completely. It was one of the things that you needed to share with an intimate.

If Harrison were only here! She was startled and shocked, too, by the unbidden thought. This was one of the very few subjects that she never could discuss with Harrison. Or with Ashley, or with Muriel, even.

Lucy sighed. An excitement or a triumph wasn't very much of either if you couldn't reveal it. You needed a confidant to keep elation bright. She felt that already, without this necessary burnishing, her self-satisfaction was growing dull. She was restless and increasingly uncomfortable and wished that her sister would come home—with Azrael or without him.

CHAPTER XX

ASHLEY HAD BEEN HOME A LONG TIME BEFORE MURIEL RETURNED. He had come back from the Spofford home obviously cheered but firmly reticent and Lucy had not questioned him. She had learned long since that the mildest query merely seals the lips of even the youngest male who is generous with information only if it appears that nobody wants it.

Mother and son sat upon the porch. Lucy was knitting—it seemed to her an appropriate pastime for one who had foresworn all life's vanities; for one who had discarded the remnants of youth to assume the bleak trappings of age. In no time at all, now, she reflected somewhat drearily, people would begin to refer to her as "Mrs. Applegate, that nice old lady." She hoped they would say "nice." Her future conduct certainly would merit at least that mild tribute.

Ashley stared out over the lawn where shadows were stretching in a bath of late sunlight. He sniffed with relish odors from the kitchen.

"Mom, old keed," he offered, as though this were the middle of a lively conversation, "I guess Mrs. Spofford doesn't like the Stark-weathers; I guess she's mad at you on account of you do like them."

"Indeed?" Lucy sniffed with grim amusement. "Well, you can't please everybody. You'll find that out, darling. Sometimes you can't even please anybody."

"She keeps," Ashley persisted, "sayin' things about 'Your mother's friends.' You know; sort of as if she wished they weren't."

"You probably just imagined that," Lucy assured her son, yet she considered with distressed resignation an additional discord in a once harmonious world. This, too, she thought ruefully, had probably been her own fault. She wondered whether Martha Spofford were jealous or angry or righteously disapproving. If she knew what had happened in the last forty-eight hours, she could not possibly be any of these. But you couldn't safely confide in Martha,

Lucy admitted regretfully. She was the sort of wife who told her husband everything.

She dropped a stitch, muttered impatiently and wished with a small flare of resentment, that, instead of signing the Declaration of Independence, the Founders had outlawed picnics. The trouble sown at that outwardly simple Fourth of July festivity already had yielded a bumper crop. The sun had gone down. Muriel was flagrantly late and Rena, no doubt, was becoming momentarily more indignant.

"She wanted to know," Ashley pursued, stimulated by apparent maternal indifference, "if I wouldn't rather play with old Lydia than Barbs. She makes me sick."

"Mrs. Spofford? Barbara?"

"Aw, not them; Lydia. Alla time creepin' up on you, sorta, and tryin' to get you to hold hands or kiss her or somethin'. I think she's wacky."

Impulsively, Lucy patted her son's grubby hand. The small movement spanned more than two decades. At either end woman and small boy stood in utter harmony.

"I know, dear," she said.

"Barbs is swell," Ashley went on. "She doesn't make you keep remembering she's a girl. She's awful green, still, though," he added dutifully.

"It'll wear off," his mother told him. "Most things wear off, little son, if you just are patient."

Ashley stirred and drew a wistful, snuffing breath.

"Hey," he demanded, "when do we eat, Mom, my little chickadee?"

"It's time now. Muriel must have had trouble finding Azrael."

"I bet I could find him, Mom. I bet I could find him easier'n Muriel on account of I know him better. He's awful goofy—but he's nice, though. Maybe I better go look—"

"Maybe," Lucy interrupted, considering his soiled state, "you better go right upstairs and wash. Then you'll be all ready when Muriel does come."

"There," Ashley cried, jumping up and pointing, "she is now. She hasn't got Azrael, either."

Muriel was the approaching station wagon's sole occupant. Even at a distance, her white face shone in the twilight and she bore her head so erectly that Lucy found omen in her pose.

"Go up and wash right away," she bade her son hastily. "Muriel's bound to be tired and famished."

The car stopped with a jolt before the steps. If hunger and weariness affected Muriel, some starker emotion hid them.

She leaped from the station wagon, slammed the door, sprang up to the porch as though steel were tightly coiled within her. Her eyes shone greenly in her grim face.

"I got the mail," she said, and tossed it on the porch table.

"You poor dear," Lucy soothed. "No sign of him at all?"

"Azrael?" Muriel asked with a small, blighting laugh. "Oh, yes, I found him all right, but I didn't get him."

"Didn't get him?"

"Precisely, angel. Dick has him. Isn't that enchanting?"

"Dick? Has Azrael? Oh, darling, no."

Muriel strode to the porch's far end and back, as though movement were necessary to ease her rage. She said in a low, savage voice:

"I've had an enchanting afternoon, hunting from hell to high water. I stopped at every house on the way into Walden. I asked the people in a dozen cars. No sign of Azrael. Then Bailey—bless him—dropped everything and helped me. We drove over all the back roads he knew, looking for that puppy, but we couldn't find him. I was worried practically sick. But sick."

Her voice jumped higher; for an instant her bitter mouth twisted.

"Darling," Lucy begged, "sit down. You're all apart."

"Am I?" Muriel asked tautly. "I don't think so. I'm angrier than I've ever been in my life, that's all. Of all the mean, contemptible, snide tricks I ever heard of anyone being low enough to play—"

Rage choked her. She lit a cigarette with jerky movement, drew once upon it, threw it down and ground it vindictively beneath her shoe. The childish violence soothed and shamed her. She grinned down crookedly into Lucy's concerned face.

"I suppose," she challenged, "I'm very, very funny. No doubt he's laughing his head off right now. And to think that I—I wanted so much to believe he hadn't stolen my dog that I swallowed his damn barefaced lies. I'm really a born comic."

She laughed again. Lucy said:

"If you'll just tell me why you're so sure Dick—"

Muriel nodded.

"I don't wonder you don't understand. Want to hear what sort of a heel your—candidate's turned out to be? All right, angel. Listen and I won't boil over again:

"I'd left Bailey in Walden and started back home, calling at every house to ask again if they'd seen Azrael. I'd stopped at Merica's—you know; the house just the other side of the bridge—and was standing in the barn talking to Mr. Merica who was milking, when I saw a car go by. Well, angel, Azrael was in it."

"And Dick?" Lucy faltered.

"Are you ready for the sixty-four-dollar question? Dick and Azrael were sitting together in the rumble, with the wind blowing my dear infant's ears and the idiotic smile he always wears when he's riding."

"Darling, there must be some mistake. Did Dick see you?"

Muriel gave her sister a hard little grin.

"Obstinate female, aren't you? No, he didn't see me, but he certainly wasn't bringing Azrael home. The car was going toward Walden. Dick's sub-human friend was driving it, and a man was in the front seat with him. I didn't see him plainly. I just stared at Dick and Azrael. I didn't believe it myself, for a moment."

"It's incredible," Lucy said at last. Her sister shook her head sharply.

"No. Just enlightening. We quarreled. He's taken his gift back and the hell with me and my worry and distress and—yes, my penitence too. That's the man I once thought I loved more than anything. My mistake, angel. It won't happen again."

"You can eat now," Rena announced from the doorway. Lucy rose and called Ashley.

"I'll skip dinner, I think," Muriel said in a tight voice. "My stomach seems to have shrunk."

"Soup and a glass of milk, anyway. It'll make you feel ever so much better."

Muriel consulted her wrist watch.

"Oh, don't worry about me," she said. "I'm not the pining type. I'll probably have time to change afterward, though. Bailey is coming out tonight. You might as well be the first to know—even ahead of him. I'm going to marry Bailey, Lucy."

"Oh," Lucy began and said no more.

"Thanks," her sister told her wryly, "for the hearty felicitations."

Banning set the telephone back on the Walden police chief's desk and grinned at Dade who stood behind it.

"The Captain is pleased, Sergeant. He seems to think well of us."

"Which is," he added, intoxicated by his superior's recent praise, "a lot more than most people in this town have thought for the past few days."

He stood and beamed upon the local chief, whose jowls were a bright flamingo hue.

"Jeeze, Dick," he begged, "what could we do? You come back; you don't say nothin' and Ward says plenty. If he'd had his way, we'd have locked you both up. No hard feelings, Dick?"

"None, Jerry. The way I feel now I might buy even Hitler a beer. Sergeant, you better go eat. I've still a job to do."

He nodded at Azrael who had occupied in slumber a large part of the office floor and who now raised his head at the mention of food.

Dade stood by the door to the cell block. He peered in at the prisoner who sat dejectedly, as though it were rain instead of dim radiance that poured down upon him from the ceiling light.

"I'll send out for a sandwich," he offered, "and stay right here. I'd just as soon not take my eyes off him. That gook has been hard to get, Lieutenant."

"Good here," Banning told him. "I'll be back before train time."

For a moment he hesitated, looking at the telephone. His hand went up to his cheek, where Muriel had struck him. Let her worry a little longer, he thought vindictively and bade:

"Come along, Azrael."

The great dog heaved himself up and followed the Lieutenant out into gathering darkness.

If meals in her household were to be steadily increasing ordeals, Lucy reflected when dinner was half over, it would be pleasanter hereafter to have her own served by tray in her bed chamber. She wondered why distress always seemed doubly abhorrent if you took it into the dining room with you. She doubted, though, whether she now could flee anywhere without her current anxiety's company.

Muriel, at the table's far end, seemed to be suffering less than her sister. That was youth. It stamped and walked the floor and conducted itself with unlimited vehemence—and then recovered its appetite. Elders, particularly women like herself who had turned away from youth's last vestige toward the refuge of age, had to

preserve their dignity but all that did was to dam things up inside
you.

Ashley, sitting between the sisters, was not an enlivening spectacle, either. He had come bursting into the dining room, demanding
details of the search for Azrael, and Lucy had quelled him.

"Dick has found him," she told her eager son, "and is going to
keep him for a while."

"Where did he find him? Why is he keeping—?"

"Oh, eat your soup and don't ask so many senseless questions,"
his mother had interrupted with the candor of strained nerves and
Ashley had retired forthwith behind haughty indignation, difficult
to bear.

Nevertheless, Lucy thought wretchedly while the meal progressed
in conversational torpor, both her son and her sister were enjoying
themselves more than she. They could eat, at least.

Muriel was determined—you could tell it by the very way she
sat, by her look that seemed to challenge her sister to argue the
matter with her—to throw herself at Bailey Ward. It was not passion that impelled her; it was not even anything so creditable as a
desire to make a prudential marriage. She was going to engage
herself to Bailey to get even with Dick. The insane child was going
to decapitate herself in the hope that Banning would bleed.

Lucy found herself wholly out of patience with her sister. Each
time someone offended her she threatened to marry Bailey Ward.
Muriel was an imperious, reckless, arrogant, spoiled youngster and
what she needed most was a thorough spanking by an expert. It
did not cheer Lucy to recognize that she herself could do nothing
about it.

And there seemed, she admitted drearily while she vaguely pushed
her salad about her plate, scant ground for defending Dick. No
mere quarrel with Muriel could justify his taking her dog and
callously letting her search and suffer. It was thoroughly beastly,
completely unlike the boy. She still couldn't quite believe, in the
face of eye-witness testimony, that he had done it. She wondered
why women of Muriel's age were always so intolerant of men,
while women of Lucy's forever were trying to find excuses for
them.

"I'll skip the dessert," the girl said, rising. Her manner was composed; her voice, determined. "Bailey will be here any moment,
now. Take care of him till I come down, angel."

She left the room with a cool smile. Lucy sat and stared at the vacated chair. "Any minute now!" It paralyzed her. She had no idea whatever how she might have swerved her sister's intention, even with hours to spend, but the lack of time filled her with numb dismay.

"More pudding, dear?" she asked her son absently.

"It was pie," Ashley replied with a woeful dignity. "May I be excused, please?"

He rose and stalked out. Practically all Lucy's associates, she thought despondently, cherished grievances and with each of these she seemed intimately involved.

Any minute now, Bailey would arrive and all she seemed able to do was cherish a dim, unlikely hope that he might wreck his car in passage. She was ashamed of so ruthless a wish and besides, the chance of its fulfillment was discouragingly slight, for Ward drove always with scrupulous care.

Her mind ran numbly and futilely about, picking up preposterous schemes and discarding them. If only there could be an air-raid alarm tonight! That would keep Ward away—but then, it would summon Muriel, head of the Women's Auxiliary Corps, to her chieftain's side. That wouldn't help.

Lucy sighed as she left the table. The sound was admission of defeat. Instead of wishing that Bailey might break his neck, or at least smash his car, she might better compose herself to greet him pleasantly. You shouldn't be deliberately rude to your future brother-in-law. She gagged at the thought and jumped as the telephone rang.

"Duchess?" Ward's voice asked, and while she answered an incredible hope set Lucy's spirit soaring. "Is the Pulchritudinous Person within reach of your dulcet voice? Well, never mind, then. Just tell her I've been delayed."

Ice formed on the wings of Lucy's hope. It lost altitude as the genial voice pursued:

"We had a rumor there might be a surprise blackout early this evening but it evidently was false. I'll be leaving for your palatial abode in a few minutes now."

She climbed the stair with new resentment glowing dully within her. She had additional grievances against Bailey who, it seemed, had sent her spirits high for the pleasure of bringing them down.

"Toad!" Lucy said with hushed violence, knocked at Muriel's door and delivered the message.

"And, darling—" she added impulsively. Standing there in her ivory slip, with her coppery hair tumbling about her shoulders, her sister looked so young, so like an angry little girl, that Lucy's eyes smarted.

"Well, what?" Muriel prompted, quite calmly.

"Nothing," the other answered, withdrew and closed the door. She heard a car pass the house. It couldn't be Bailey as soon as this. It probably was Cyril, driving the station wagon to the barn. But she thought she remembered hearing him take it away while they were all at dinner. Then it must be some friend of the Handrows'. Lucy herself certainly wasn't expecting callers. She no longer, she reflected desolately, had any available friend who would take the trouble.

She looked out through the livingroom's screen door and a vastness, dimly outlined against the night, stirred and panted at her.

"Azrael!" Lucy said in a dazed voice. She heard claws rattle as the monster moved. His tail beat against a porch pillar with a rhythmic sound. Feet crunched the driveway gravel and Banning, hastening from the turning circle where he had left his car, came up out of the gloom and grinned at her through the door's wire mesh.

"Hi," he said, "I've brought back the prodigal."

"Dick," Lucy said, and knew there should be more disapproval and less relief in her voice. "Oh, Dick."

"Is anything wrong?" he asked quickly. "Where's Muriel?"

"Upstairs. Dick, you—"

"Tell her I've got to see her right away. It's urgent."

"I—I'll," Lucy faltered, "I'll tell her," and fled.

Muriel sat with arms upraised before her dressing table. The hands that worked upon her hair lay still an instant while Lucy blurted her tidings, then deftly resumed their task. She did not turn her head. It was the calm face in the mirror that regarded the intruder.

"Tell him," it bade, "that he can take that dog—and himself—away."

"Azrael? Take him away? Why, darling, he's your own dear puppy."

"He was. He isn't any more. I don't want him."

"Well, I do then," Lucy told her with a flare of spirit. "I'll take him if you won't. And I think," she pursued more feebly, knowing the vanity of her plea, "that you might at least give Dick a chance to explain."

The mirror's reflection did not stir. Its eyes watched the swiftly moving hands.

"I've a date this evening," Muriel said. "You can tell him I'm engaged."

Her double-edged speech cut deep.

"Muriel, please."

The girl twisted about on the bench. Twin spots of rouge were sharply outlined on her face.

"I refuse to see him. He stole Azrael and deliberately let me suffer. I won't see him, I tell you—now or ever."

Lucy saw in the dining room as she came down the stair a black enormity waiting patiently before the door to the kitchen. Azrael was hungry.

She let him out, heard Rena's voice raised in surprised greeting and then hurried to the livingroom. Banning stood there. His face grew grave, his eyes narrowed at Lucy's gesture of despair.

"Dick," she reported, "she says she—doesn't want to see you ever again."

Banning's voice, Lucy thought, was disconcertingly vigorous to be a rebuffed lover's.

"I've got to see her, Lucy. I'm leaving tonight. You'll have to help me. Please, Lucy."

His appeal completely relaxed her failing hold upon disapproval.

"You haven't," she told him with a wan smile, "done very much to help yourself today. Taking her dog, Dick, and—"

"Listen," he broke in and told her in abrupt little bursts of speech of his mission and its outcome, of Azrael's recovery and why his return had been delayed.

"That's what I want to explain, Lucy. Don't you understand why I have to see her? I'm going upstairs, myself."

"No, Dick; don't. If she hears you coming she'll lock the door. I'll try again."

The door, Lucy found with dismay that turned quickly into anger, already was locked. From beyond it, Muriel's tight voice asked: "Has he gone?"

"You're acting like a five-year-old brat," Lucy told her incautiously. "If you don't see Dick Banning now, you'll regret it as long as you live, Muriel. He's leaving on the midnight train."

There was a moment's silence. Then the girl bade:

"Tell him that if he drives to Chester, he can get an earlier."

"Muriel!"

"And tell him if he hasn't gone by the time Bailey comes, I'll have Bailey make him leave."

"She will, too," Lucy thought, appalled and feeling a little sick.

All the ingredients for a thumping scandal were assembling. If this kept on, after Ward's arrival, almost anything could happen—violence, uproar, police intervention, arrest. The possibilities seemed innumerable and increasingly ghastly. And viewing it all from a ringside seat, Cyril, the unfathomed repository of regional calumny, would file away an eye-witness narrative for later relishful broadcasting.

"It's no use," she told the grim young man at the foot of the stair. "You might just as well go. Really, Dick. Bailey Ward is on the way here now."

"Bailey? What for?" His face grew red.

"I—I think she's going to marry him, Dick."

"Marry him? Here?"

"Oh, not now, but he's coming to propose and she is going to accept him, I think to punish you."

"By God," he said through his teeth and strove to push past her. She caught his arm.

"Where are you going?"

"To make that idiot listen to me, if I have to break down the door."

"Dick," Lucy wailed, "you can't; you mustn't. Bailey's coming."

"I know," he said in what seemed to her a peculiarly nasty voice. "That'll be some satisfaction."

"And Rena and Cyril are in the kitchen. Don't speak so loud. All you'll do is make matters worse. Please, Dick; let me think."

He paused. Her mind was mutinous—and sticky, adhering perversely to the infinite prospects of disaster that lay ahead, offering her nothing more enlivening than the ghastly realization that Bailey soon would appear. If only he didn't come; if only the rumored alarm that had delayed him would sound now! He was on his way here, yet if they set off the siren, the sound certainly would stop him and turn him back. It might even bring Muriel out of her room.

"Well?" Banning asked ominously.

"If," she said, trying to hide her mental poverty behind speech, "if only Bailey weren't coming, I think— Ouch!"

The thought was so daring, its impact so sharp, that for an instant she believed something actually had hit her. She stared at the glowering man while her mind swung, pendulum-like, toward acceptance, toward rejection, back to acceptance again.

"Lucy," Banning prompted.

"Oh, do wait," she begged. "I don't know if I remember, quite. Yes, I'm sure I do. Dick, do you suppose I dare?"

"Dare what?" he asked in pardonable bewilderment, but she did not heed. She was staring in stark fascination at the telephone on the hall table. She advanced, reached out a hand, withdrew it and then snatched the instrument from its cradle.

"One nine four," she said in an odd voice. It was the number of the Walden Control Center. Muriel called it daily.

Banning watched her with blank amazement.

"Walden Control. Haskell speaking."

"District Warning Center," Lucy said in a strained voice. "Army flash; Red."

"Hey?" The voice was startled.

"District Warning Center," she repeated more sharply. "Army flash; Red."

"Gaw! Army flash; Red. Okay."

"For God's sake—" Banning began in awe. Lucy reseated the telephone and turned upon him.

"Go away," she bade in a low voice. "Hurry. Drive your car down the road and park it somewhere and then come back on foot as fast as you can. Oh, don't stop to ask questions, Dick. Do as I say."

Far down the valley, Walden's new siren said "Ooo!" in a bovine voice, clung to the utterance, whirled it higher and tore the night's calm to tatters with hollow screeching. It died to rise again and again in whooping, anguished spasms that reminded Lucy, listening with creative pride, of an actively nauseated giant.

CHAPTER XXI

BANNING WAS REGARDING HER WITH A STRICKEN LOOK. SHE POINTED toward the door. His dazed movements as he departed were, to Lucy, a sincere and affecting tribute. She felt for the instant immensely competent and daring—a little, she supposed, like Napoleon in his more masterful moments. If Bonaparte in crises felt scared, as well as directive, the resemblance really was startling.

The siren uttered an expiring gulp and was still, leaving a silence that daunted Lucy. She heard Banning drive off. She heard also thumps and scufflings that betrayed frantic movement in Muriel's room. Her door unlocked with a small, curt sound. The girl called:

"Lucy, did you hear that?"

"Hear it?" Lucy almost added, indignantly, "I did it," but substituted "Am I deaf, darling?"

"Where's Dick?"

"He just drove away." There was something wholesome, now and then, in the truth.

"Mom," Ashley crowed from the stair's head where he was jerked about by excitement's invisible wires, "it's a blackout. You can see from my window, way down the valley. Mom, is it a real air raid? Is it, Mom?"

"Be quiet," Lucy bade, "and put all the lights out upstairs— Muriel's too, the instant she leaves. Darling," she called to her sister, "is there anything I can do?"

By the gasps and rustlings that oddly punctuated Muriel's reply, it was plain that she furiously crammed herself into her uniform.

"You can," she called, "if you will—angel. I've got to report—as soon as I can. Poor Bailey—he wondered if this—wouldn't happen. If you'd get the station wagon—and bring it to the door, it would save me time."

Lucy hurried out, switching off lights as she passed. The kitchen was dark and the Handrows stood on its steps, scanning the skies from which, Lucy gathered as she hurried by, Cyril expected momentarily a storm of demolition bombs.

She drove the station wagon back to the house in such haste that Banning, returning, was dazed by the glare the headlights swung upon him and leaped to safety just in time. Lucy glanced up, then switched off the lamps. Muriel's window was still a single bright oblong in the house's dark bulk.

"Dick?"

He came to her side. She wondered whether his breathlessness were due to emotion or his recent bare escape.

"You—you set that damn thing off down the valley," he said and she could not tell whether his voice was denunciatory or reverent. She giggled and was shocked. It was a frivolous utterance for Bonaparte's avatar.

"Lucy," the man went on, "one of us is a stark, staring lunatic. Maybe both of us."

"Oh, hush," she begged in a low voice and got down from her seat. "I don't know how I ever thought of it but it's worked, so far. Bailey must be on the way back to Walden now. I fancy he's breaking the speed limit, too, for once in his life. Muriel's driving in the instant she's dressed. So there you are, Dick."

"I still don't see," he whispered, "what—"

"Goodness," Lucy told him in a violent murmur, "I can't do everything. Get into the car you—you zombie. Scrunch yourself down in the rear seat. Do you expect me to go along and—dictate to you? All you wanted was to be alone with her, wasn't it?"

For a breath's passage, the man's dim face was turned toward hers. Lucy could not see, yet somehow she felt its awed admiration.

"Marvelous woman," Banning said and clambered into the car. Lucy checked another giggle. There was faint scuffling, the thin squeaking of a spring, as her companion settled himself out of view.

Muriel's light went out. They heard the quick rattle of her feet on the stair.

"Dick Banning," Lucy murmured solemnly, "don't you ever tell a single living soul. Because somehow I think there's going to be a lot of trouble about what I've done and—"

"Well, darling," she exclaimed heartily and switched on the headlights, "that was a quick change. Drive carefully, won't you?"

Muriel settled in the driver's seat.

"Don't wait up," she called above the motor's tumult, "I'll be late."

Lucy stood in the driveway. Twin tail lamps leered at her, shrank into red sparks, vanished. Not until then did she release her breath.

The affair was out of her hands now. Muriel and the stowaway were safely off the premises. What would happen was Dick's problem, not hers. The marines were supposed to be able to handle any situation.

The livingroom windows were suddenly bright. Rena's bulk darkened the screen door.

"You mustn't," Lucy called. "It's a blackout."

"No'm," Mrs. Handrow reported, "they just called from Walden. It was an accident-like and Bailey Ward wants to speak to Muriel."

"She's just left," Lucy said nervously and felt a chill run along her spine. It was dark out here. The silence was turning her recent elation into something like dread.

"Of all the crazy things you ever did—" she told herself and dared not complete the indictment. She feared what Bailey might do if he knew; she wondered still more desperately what, under the law, he could do.

Rena was coming back to the screen door with the ominous deliberation of a storm cloud.

"He wants to speak to you, Mis' Applegate."

"Tell him—" Lucy began in utter fright. "No, never mind. I'll come."

The condemned must feel like this when they mounted the scaffold. It was knowledge that she didn't really need. If the porch had had one more step, Lucy was sure her knees would have failed her.

"Hello," she croaked into the phone.

"Duchess?" Bailey asked abruptly.

"Yes."

"It doesn't sound like you. What's the matter?"

"I've a frightful cold; I can hardly speak." She had no time to be farsighted or ingenious in duplicity and besides her utterance was practically half verity.

"You heard the siren?"

"Oh, yes, indeed," Lucy babbled, and was alarmed to hear how naturally she spoke and hastily reassumed a strangled squeaking.

"We blacked out as quickly as we could, Bailey, but Muriel had to get into uniform and she couldn't very well in the dark."

"It," Ward said ominously, "was a false alarm."

"How exciting!" She wished belatedly that she could have thought of a better word.

"Preliminary investigation," the defense director told her in a detestable voice, "already has shown that the call, which purported to come from D.W.C., actually was sent over your party line."

"Good gracious!" Lucy's free hand found a handkerchief at last and stealthily mopped her face.

"It was a woman who phoned, Duchess. You haven't an idea who she could be?"

He was creeping up on her like a—a fat old serpent. In another instant, he'd have her. Napoleon in such a dire moment wouldn't have cringed and gasped and prepared to yield.

"Bailey Ward," Lucy inquired with hauteur and hastily made her voice catarrhal once more, "have you any idea what you're asking? Honestly!"

"Now, Duchess, don't take that tone. I only—"

The foe's line wavered. "Charge," cried Bonaparte.

"That is certainly the most peculiar thing anyone ever said to me, Bailey. I mean, have you taken entire leave of your senses?"

Her question seemed to Lucy to have a genuine First Empire flavor. Ward gave ground.

"There's no need for you to be offended, Duchess. We're asking the same question of every subscriber on your party line. It was probably somebody's idea of a joke."

"Well, it certainly wouldn't be mine," Lucy told him in complete sincerity.

"It won't be the—ah, culprit's when we find her, I assure you. Malicious mischief, sabotage, maybe treason itself. The state's attorney is looking the question up now.

"We're going to get whoever did it," Ward promised in a disagreeable Northwest Mounted tone, "and we intend to prosecute to the fullest extent of the law. Muriel isn't there?"

"She went streaking off for Walden just as soon as she could, poor child. I suppose you suspect her, too."

"Oh, no," Bailey began with fervor, corrected himself and said more resolutely:

"At this stage of the inquiry, we suspect everyone."

"Of course," Lucy agreed. The floor seemed to tip beneath her; she felt faintly seasick as she relinquished the telephone. She had repelled, if she had not routed, Ward's suspicions, but it would have required someone with a far more cheery outlook to have called the engagement even a drawn battle. She was certain, at this moment, that she felt much worse than Bailey.

"Malicious mischief, sabotage, maybe treason." The words stuck in her mind like burs. A horrid inner voice kept repeating them.

"I think," Lucy told herself, "I'll go upstairs and see that Ashley gets to bed."

She felt a desperate need for human companionship.

The station wagon labored on the hill beyond the Applegate driveway. Muriel dropped it into second with an impatient exclamation that was stopped in mid-utterance.

"It's Dick," a voice murmured in her ear. "Quiet, please."

No request could have been less necessary. His hand had clasped over her mouth and the angle of his elbow, in a queer fashion, was clamped to her head, holding it rigid. Banning's free arm, with serpentine swiftness, reached past her and twisted the ignition key from its lock.

Instinctively, Muriel trod on the brake. The car halted. The man pulled back the emergency lever, then pinned the girl's arms to her body with a dextrous embrace, not ardent but purposeful.

"Howya, wench?" he inquired with amusement. "Will you be a good quiet girl if I let you go? No?"

The shriek she had intended to utter was pressed into a nasal whimper as he replaced the stoppering palm. She tried to twist free and hurt herself.

"Much better not," he counseled. "This is one of Major d'Eliscu's holds—he teaches us to fight dirty—modified somewhat for feminine use. If you'll promise to listen, I'll let you go. Nod your head if you will. No, no! Bite me, and I'll hurt you."

His skillful, gently administered strength stirred her against her will. He had made her wholly helpless.

"I'll talk then, solo," he told her, "and you'll listen. There isn't too much time. This is what has been happening, darling; this is what I've had to do without any encouragement or sympathy or trust from you, you little lug. Three weeks ago, we lost a spy, one August Wise—"

Muriel tried not to hear. She strove to replace ebbing fright by righteous anger. It was difficult to be furious with one so powerful and yet so tender. He really was not hurting her at all and his low voice, speaking so close to her ear, warmed her.

She was following what he said with a waxing excitement. She felt tidal relief flow in upon her, sweeping away distrust and bitterness.

Muriel did not even know that Banning had removed the precautionary hand until he turned her head toward his and kissed her mouth.

In the dark, ringing silence, in the warmth and the slaking need and the dear fragments of speech, irrelevant thought came to the girl. She said with a broken laugh:

"Darling, the air raid; I forgot."

"Keep on forgetting," he bade softly. After a little, he added: "Your sister, beloved, is a highly improbable person."

Ashley had been stowed away in bed and Lucy had come down to sit alone upon the porch.

On the lake shore, in the mist's faint shining, a frog thumped fitfully upon his flat-toned drum. A bird woke in a door-yard pine, sang sleepily and slumbered again. Darkness and quiet and the cool fragrance of night enveloped Lucy. They could not soothe a variety of distresses to which Ward had added a lively fear of the police. Neither Benedict Arnold, she was sure, nor even Vidkun Quisling had shared in full her accumulation of miseries. Some of theirs may have been worse but hers was the larger assortment.

The house was uncomfortably still. She wished Muriel would come back, with Dick or without him. She would have welcomed, with reservations, a call from Bailey Ward in his most pompous and suspicious mood. The vindictive officers of the law who probably were enclosing her in their dragnet—whatever that was— would be pleasanter associates than herself.

Heaven, Lucy thought with a dreary feeling that she never had been further away from that precinct, didn't really need to be elaborate. It could be just a place where, if you'd done something wrong, you could rub it out and start over again. "My mistake," you would say and then, behold, you wouldn't have done it. A future life like that would be something to work for.

She heard Rena carrying on what seemed to be wholly one-sided dispute. A door slammed. Feet shuffled along the driveway and Azrael, evicted from the kitchen where he had obstinately lain in hope of still further provender, hauled himself up on the porch and lay down at Lucy's feet with the sound and shock of a collapsing building. His presence was comfort, but he slept immediately and even in his most active state, the puppy would not have been able to inform her what were the penalties for malicious msichief, sabotage, and treason.

"Why did you ever do it?" Lucy asked herself. "What on earth made you?"

The judge, before sentence, would ask her these very questions. The crowd that filled the courtroom would stir and in the front row Ward and Larry, Mrs. Starkweather, Martha Spofford, and maybe Muriel herself would glare implacably.

Why did you do so many other senseless things, prisoner at the bar? You haven't a friend in the house and it's all your own fault. Why did you get tight at the Starkweathers' and ask them all to the picnic? Why did you pay them so much attention that Martha was hurt? Why did you get yourself into a jam with Larry Moncure and crawl out of it by alarming Mrs. Starkweather? And why, for God's sake, why, did you set off the siren tonight, enraging Bailey, rousing the law's minions, probably alienating your sister as well?

"Because you were so very, very clever," Lucy told herself without mercy. "You knew all the answers. You were on a Sabbatical and could do as you pleased. Gay and glad and free again! Martha thinks you're a snob; Mrs. Starkweather is sure you're a menace; Larry Moncure knows you're a bitch and Bailey Ward has set the cops on you. Phooey to you, Mrs. Applegate!"

She thought of that bright morning, only a few weeks ago, when she had stood in the doorway and had been shaken by beauty about her, by the dear uplifting sense of freedom. If she only could have known then the general unpopularity into which her liberty was to plunge her; if she only could go back to that joyous moment and start over once more! She would settle, as far as that went, for the right to recommence this single day.

The frog continued his drumming, though apparently ignored by all his race. He and she, Lucy thought, had much in common—an identical hopefulness, a like neglect. He and she, furthermore, both were in it up to their necks. That was a usual attitude for frogs. It was becoming a customary posture for her.

She still had friends, she told herself optimistically, but none who now were her neighbors. It was possible, too, she considered with increasing self-pity, that her very household might turn against her. Muriel was quite likely to come back in a fine fury over Lucy's interference. Ashley had seemed to regard his mother today as a barely endurable affliction.

As for Harrison—he had lived without her for weeks now. Probably it had become a habit and he would be content to jog along, permanently wifeless.

That wasn't quite fair to Harrison, though. This whole idea had been Lucy's, not his. She had urged it, he had acquiesced, and a fine, dreggy ruin she had made of the whole thing! It had all been her fault—even Harrison's unbroken sojourn in Washington. Practically everything except the weather that had happened lately seemed to have been Lucy's responsibility.

Loneliness was becoming a more and more relentless pressure. Dread of arrest, by comparison, was a minor misery. Lucy might as well confess to Bailey and go to jail. Prison might really be a haven for a woman of her years and in her predicament. She had forfeited the esteem of her associates. Youth and the gaiety, romance and the sparkling sense of male pursuit that were youth's chief treasure were gone, too. She had cast them away, all of them, and now—her throat ached at the thought—they would never come again; not to an incipient convict, thirty-four years old.

"Oh, dear," she whimpered. "Oh, damn!" and laying her arms upon the porch table beside her and her head upon her arms, cried so softly that Azrael did not rouse. Her fingers touched paper's cool smoothness. Envelopes? Of course; Muriel had tossed the mail there this afternoon. It made no difference now. Age and wretchedness had so firm a hold upon her that she no longer could expect the miracle that once she had believed each mail delivery might bring.

Lucy sat up and blew her nose.

"Weepy old fool," she said to herself. "Senility's tears, no doubt."

She shivered. Bed did not attract her. It would be better if she were to be arrested, to appear properly—even attractively clothed. Yet it would be warm in bed and it was chilly here on the porch. She gathered up the letters, bore them into the livingroom and sorted them there. There were two for Muriel, three bills, four advertisements and Harrison's weekly missive to Lucy. It was bulkier than usual. She opened it and glanced over the first of its several pages.

"How ridiculous!" she said, smiling at her mistake, and reread the page more carefully. She stopped an instant again to stare at the careful handwriting. Why, it simply couldn't be—yet it was. Why, Harrison never had sent her anything like this, even when they had been engaged. Of course things were different and—well, less enlightened then. And—

She turned the page. Her running accompaniment of mental exclamations was checked for an instant by sheer astonishment. Fancy anyone—particularly fancy Harrison—writing so beautifully! How could he possibly set such things down in so steady a script when her own hands were shaking and warmth was melting her interior where unidentified organs wabbled as though their hinges were loose. Harrison, of all people!

"Oh, darling," Lucy said aloud, and hurriedly turned a page.

Could it be that Washington's summer had done something tropical to Harrison? Could it be that always he had loved her like this but had never felt the need to tell her so till now? Why, he was writing poetry—practically: Not the sort that got printed, maybe, but its dear and beautiful essence. Why hadn't he, she wondered with flushed face and eyes that shone, said all this long ago? Never, never, never would she let him hide it again.

He wanted to come home. He missed her too sorely to stay away. He listed his needs so exquisitely that it overwhelmed her. Lucy sat down, suddenly, for the inner warmth seemed to have melted her knees. She looked at the letter for a long moment after she had finished it. It couldn't be Harrison, yet it couldn't possibly be anyone else. There were tears in Lucy's eyes.

"Oh, my dear, oh, my darling," she whispered. "Thank goodness it couldn't be anyone else."

It was some time before she dared trust her legs to bear her to the telephone. . . .

She was in bed and had reread the letter twice when Muriel returned. Lucy waited apprehensively in the dark while the girl came upstairs and advanced with singular hesitation to her sister's door.

"Angel?" Muriel whispered and, as the other answered, begged: "Don't turn on the light."

She came in with a rush, knelt beside and embraced her sister. Lucy felt tears upon the girl's cheeks.

"Why, darling," she said in immense relief, "why, my dear, what's the trouble?"

"There isn't any trouble," Muriel said in an unsteady voice. "Everything's all right. He's coming back soon, he says, and then we'll be married."

She gave a happy little sound and hugged her sister tighter.

"You should have been the first to be told, but I drove Dick to Walden—he didn't have time to come back for his car and he's leaving it here—and I saw Bailey and I told him."

"What—?" Lucy began with a pang of distress, but Muriel's eager voice ran over her question.

"He was quite nice, for him. I've really been a genuine louse, haven't I? But genuine! And anyway, Bailey has his defense organization and his siren. It went off by accident tonight, but you wouldn't know anything about that, would you, angel?"

She laughed. Lucy kissed her and said with attempted unconcern: "He called after you left, to ask if I did."

"He called everyone on the party line. He certainly doesn't suspect you. I told him we were all sitting together on the porch for half an hour before it blew."

"Oh," Lucy said, and her sister laughed again.

"That," she whispered, "is just a token payment on what I owe you."

Later, when she rose to go, Lucy told her lightly:

"Harrison's coming tomorrow for the weekend."

"Oh, swell!" Muriel said and went on to her room. Lucy smiled to herself. Youngsters believed with such sublime error that so many things were their exclusive property!

The morning wind came swinging up from the lake to shake the tall pines' branches and sway the delphiniums' spikes; the young sun laid intricacies of light and shadow on the lawn. Lucy stood on the porch watching Cyril push the lawnmower.

A feeling of intimacy, a sense of unity with the day's unspent strength, with the climbing sun and the youthful wind, possessed her. Her breath came quickly and the flutter within her must be, she thought, unuttered laughter. There was great lightness in her heart.

Once, she had believed such undeterred rapture never would lift her again. She knew its present source; Harrison was coming on the afternoon train.

Azrael, at Cyril's earnest bidding, moved deliberately out of the mower's path and lay down again where he would block its return journey. Muriel sang softly in her bedroom. In his own, Ashley pored over the history of his country, spurred to industry by his father's imminent arrival. All the world seemed better for Harrison's coming. Moments like these, Lucy thought, were almost too beautiful to bear.

Life was bright and fresh, cleansed of old worries and ancient problems. Life was clear and brilliant as a new silver coin. All that

Lucy would need of life, hereafter, would be harbored here in her own dear home. With this small universe she would be content, serene, happy, seeking no adventure, avoiding all entanglements, yearning for no perilous freedom. Harrison would be here soon and then her brimming cup would overflow.

The cheerfully whirring blades struck a pebble and jammed. Cyril grunted and bent to clear them. Lucy watched while the blue-jeaned reservoir of regional calumny straightened up and wiped his forehead on his sleeve.

"Sightly day, ain't it?" Mr. Handrow asked.

"Simply lovely," Lucy replied. "Cyril, have you learned anything about the Debevoises, those new people who have taken the old Taylor farm?"

"Wal, now," said Cyril, "from what I hear—"

THE END